Foggy Mountain Breakdown

'McCrumb draws you close, makes you care, leaves you with the sense, sought for in most fiction, that what has gone on has not been invention but experience recaptured.'
Los Angeles Times

'Mystery and history, action and abstraction, suspense and sociology, all bound together in an enthralling narrative. McCrumb has a deep, sometimes disturbing sense of the past, yet hers is a thoroughly modern mind.'
Reginald Hill

'A fresh new voice . . . Sharyn McCrumb is a born storyteller.'
Mary Higgins Clark

Also by Sharyn McCrumb in New English Library Paperbacks
The Rosewood Casket
She Walks These Hills
The Hangman's Beautiful Daughter
If Ever I Return

About the author

Sharyn McCrumb, a native of North Carolina, lives with her husband David, an environmental engineer, and their three children in the Virginia Blue Ridge, less than a hundred miles from where her family settled in 1790 in the Smoky Mountains that divide North Carolina and Tennessee.

She is the author of sixteen novels. She has twice won the Appalachian Novel Award as well as the Macavity, Edgar and the Agatha for her crime fiction. *She Walks These Hills* was awarded the Anthony, Macavity, Agatha and Nero Awards for the best crime novel in 1995. Mostly recently, she received the prestigious 1997 Award for Outstanding Contribution to Appalachian Literature.

Foggy Mountain Breakdown

Sharyn McCrumb

NEW ENGLISH LIBRARY
Hodder and Stoughton

First published in 1997 by Ballantine Books
First published in paperback in Great Britain in 1998 by
Hodder and Stoughton
A division of Hodder Headline PLC
A New English Library Paperback

10 9 8 7 6 5 4 3 2 1

ISBN 0 340 71716 5

A CIP catalogue record for this title is available
from the British Library

Printed and bound in Great Britain by
Mackays of Chatham PLC, Chatham, Kent

Hodder and Stoughton
A division of Hodder Headline PLC
338 Euston Road
London NW1 3BH

To Mary Frances Amick Hinte,
wherever she is.

Contents

Foggy Mountain Breakdown

Introduction

~

I come from a race of storytellers.

My father's family—the Arrowoods and the McCourys—
settled in the Smoky Mountains of western North Carolina in
1790, when the wilderness was still Indian country. They came
from the north of England and from Scotland, and they seemed to
want mountains, land, and as few neighbors as possible.

The first of the McCourys to settle in America was my great-
great-great-grandfather Malcolm McCoury, a Scot who was kidnapped as a child from the island of Islay in the Hebrides in 1750,
and made to serve as a cabin boy on a sailing ship. He later became
an attorney in Morristown, New Jersey; fought with the Morris
Militia in the American Revolution; and finally settled in what
is now Mitchell County, western North Carolina, in 1794. Yet
another "connection" (a distant cousin) is the convicted murderess
Frankie Silver (1813–1833), who was the first woman hanged for
murder in the state of North Carolina.

I grew up listening to my father's tales of World War II in the
Pacific, and to older family stories of duels and of escapades in
Model T Fords. With such adventurers in my background, I grew
up seeing the world as a wild and exciting place; the quiet tales of
suburban angst so popular in modern fiction are Martian to me.

Storytelling is an art form that I learned early on. When I was a
little girl, my father would come in to tell me a bedtime story,

which usually began with a phrase like "Once there was a prince named Paris, whose father was Priam, the king of Troy. . . ." Thus I got *The Iliad* in nightly installments, geared to the level of a four-year-old's understanding. I grew up in a swirl of tales: the classics retold; ballads or country songs, each having a melody, but above all a *plot*; and family stories about Civil War soldiers, train wrecks, and lost silver mines.

My mother contributed stories of her grandfather, John Burdette Taylor, who had been a sixteen-year-old private in the 68th North Carolina Rangers (CSA). His regiment had walked in ragbound boots, following the railroad tracks, from Virginia to Fort Fisher, site of a decisive North Carolina battle. All his life he would remember leaving footprints of blood in the snow as he marched. When John Taylor returned home to Carteret County, southeastern North Carolina, at the end of the war, his mother, who was recovering from typhoid, got up out of her sickbed to attend the welcome home party for her son. She died that night.

My father's family fund of Civil War stories involved greatgreat-uncles in western North Carolina who had discovered a silver mine or a valley of ginseng while roaming the hills, trying to escape conscription into one marauding army or the other. There were the two sides of the South embodied in my parents' oral histories: Mother's family represented the flatland South, steeped in its magnolia myths, replete with Gorham sterling silver and Wedgwood china. My father's kinfolks spoke for the Appalachian South, where the pioneer spirit took root. In their War between the States, the Cause was somebody else's business, and the war was a deadly struggle between neighbors. I could not belong completely to either of these Souths because I am inextricably a part of both.

This duality of my childhood, a sense of having a foot in two cultures, gave me that sense of *otherness* that one often finds in writers: the feeling of being an outsider, observing one's surroundings, and looking even at personal events at one remove.

So much conflict; so much drama; and two sides to everything. Stories, I learned, involved character, and drama, and they always centered around irrevocable events that mattered.

This book is a collection of almost all the short stories I have ever written. Some of them are serious character studies ("A Predatory Woman," "Among My Souvenirs," "The Matchmaker"); some are sad stories set in the Southern mountains ("Precious Jewel," "Telling the Bees," "Old Rattler"); and some are whimsical tales of fantasy and humor ("An Autumn Migration," "Remains to Be Seen," "Nine Lives to Live"). The difference in styles reflects the duality in my nature: Mountain versus Southern, Daddy's side versus Mother's side. I like to think that both of them win.

The earliest story in the collection, "Love on First Bounce," is a semidocumentary of my adolescence in a small Southern town, and the first draft was written when I was in high school. It marks the first appearance of Elizabeth MacPherson, the heroine of many of my novels. I hear her voice, too, in the narrator of "Southern Comfort." Compare the sunny life of that suburban child to the dark, spartan boyhood described in "Foggy Mountain Breakdown," which is a portrait of my father's youth in the Tennessee mountains.

Sometimes when I write short stories I set myself a task. "Precious Jewel," based on my father's family, was an attempt to see if I could write a short story in which the most vivid character does not appear: Addie McCrory is dead when the narrative begins. "John Knox in Paradise" is the old Scots Border tale of Thomas the Rhymer, retold in modern terms, with True Thomas and his captor the Queen of Elfland recast as a modern Scot and a young American woman.

The ideas came from many different places: from correspondence with a reader I've never met ("Gentle Reader"); from something I saw that triggered an idea ("Remains to Be Seen"—the mummy described in the story really was on display in an army

surplus store in North Carolina years ago); from a newspaper
article ("Not All Brides Are Beautiful," my cynical reaction to the
wedding of an inmate on Virginia's death row).

No matter where the ideas originate, though, they are all
filtered through my own split perception, to be sorted into
"Southern" or "Mountain." If I had to pick out one common
thread present in each of these vastly different stories, I would say
that it is this: in every single story, there is someone who feels like
a stranger.

Precious Jewel

↳

Dying cost nothing and could be done alone—otherwise, Addie Hemrick might have lived forever. As it was, she grudgingly loosed her spirit from its wizened body, saying no goodbyes to the kinfolk duty-bound to her bedside, and leaving nothing to anyone except the obligation to bury her in sufficient style to satisfy the neighbors that the family had "done right by her." Gone, but not forgotten. Legends of her temper and anti-sociability might outlast the marble slabs in the little mountain graveyard.

She was a McCrory from up around Cade's Cove; one of the Solitary McCrorys, as opposed to the Tinker McCrorys or the Preaching McCrorys. Her clan was known for living in little cabins as far up the mountain as they could get and staying put. They didn't hold with churchgoing, and folks in the cove said that if a bee-tracker or a drummer headed for their cabin, they hid in the woods until he went away again. Not scared, the McCrorys weren't. It was just in their blood to keep to themselves. A Solitary McCrory could no more make small talk than he could lay an egg.

So it was one notch short of a miracle when Wesley Hemrick, the circuit preacher's sixth boy, let it be known that he was marrying Miss Addie McCrory, of the Solitary McCrorys.

She had spent a few months in the one-room school learning her letters. Probably the meeting took place there, and Wesley

Hemrick may have hunted squirrel in her neck of the woods on purpose thereafter. However it came about, she accepted the proposal and became a sullen, gawky bride one Sunday after meeting. Strangers clabbered around her, and she blinked at them. No telling what they meant for her to do, so she stood patiently until they went away.

A few days later they went down the mountain to catch the logging train, and no one saw them off. Wesley had got a job in the machine shop of the Clinchfield Railroad in town. They clattered down from the hills, standing in the engineer's cabin, holding everything they owned in two paper sacks. That logging train would someday become Tweetsie, a children's ride in a tourist park. Addie Hemrick's grandchildren would ride squealing through tunnels on Tweetsie; she never went with them.

They rented a little frame house close to the railroad, and set up housekeeping. Addie was a town-dweller now, but she kept to her old ways. Neighbors were nodded at across a privet hedge; she rarely spoke and never visited.

Company did come to call, however, in the form of Wesley's five brothers: M. L., Lewis, Francis, and the twins Tom and Harvey. In the evenings after work they'd appear in the backyard and slip into the smokehouse for their guitars and fiddles. They couldn't keep them up home, because the Reverend John B. Hemrick claimed that stringed instruments were of the devil, and he wouldn't have them on the place. He always contended that the upright piano in the parlor was a percussion instrument. So Wesley's house became the gathering place for the pickers. They'd sit in kitchen chairs beside the smokehouse and sing "Barbry Ellen" and "A Fair Young Maid All in the Garden," while the Mason jar was passed from one free hand to another.

Addie never set foot in the yard when that was going on, but she watched from the kitchen window, feeling as trapped as if she were tied to a chair. One of them might come in for a glass of water or some such excuse, and he'd glance over her kitchen and the little parlor, and, whatever he saw, he'd be talking about it to those people back up the mountain. The house was always clean and neat, with just the two of them, but if they came in, they'd find something to say, and she couldn't bear to be talked about. She imagined their voices in her mind, and it felt like being in a cage poked with sticks.

She stood it for months—until that first baby was on its way, due in the winter—and then one August evening she charged out of the house with a broom, screaming for them to get off the place. "And take your liquor!" she'd shouted between sobs, "and don't you'uns ever come back!"

They hadn't.

In fifty years, they hadn't. Other factors were in play, of course. Lewis, Tom, and M. L. all went north to Detroit to work in the factories; Francis got a farm near Spruce Pine, and influenza took Harvey in 1920, the year Sam was born.

Sam was followed a year later by Frances Lee, and then came two stillborn babies—both boys—and then no more. The babies were always clean and seen-to, fed amply of whatever there was, but they stayed strangers. Addie peered into their wobbly infant eyes and decided no, she didn't know them at all.

Frances Lee married at sixteen and ran off to Chicago, away from her mother's cold stare. Sam took a little longer, long enough to work his way through a semester of Teachers College, and then he let the army take him out of east Tennessee and into Normandy. That war and two others had come and gone, and the family was coming home.

The old frame house was bulging with kinfolk, mostly Wesley's side of the family. The women and their young'uns sat together in the tidy parlor, having put their bowls of beans and potato salad on the dining room table.

"A-lord, I wish Addie could be here," sighed Sally Hemrick, M. L.'s wife.

The others nodded in mournful agreement.

If she was, thought Frances Lee, *you'd all be going out the window.*

Nobody had been allowed in that parlor. Even the sofa, of stiff green fabric laced with metallic threads, was deliberately uncomfortable. If anyone came to call, they sat on the back porch, if they got in at all.

Frances Lee and her second husband, Wayne, had driven down from Brookfield after Aunt Sally phoned them the news. They had delayed just long enough to drop the boys off at his mother's house, and for Frances Lee to get a Kitty Wells permanent at the Maison de Beaute. In a way, she felt good about going home. Wayne's brassy Chrysler was the biggest car in the driveway, and thanks to the union, he was doing all right at the factory. They had a four-bedroom ranch house and a camper. Frances Lee thought she must be about the most successful person the family ever had.

"Has anybody heard from Sam?" she asked.

Aunt Sally nodded. "He's flying down from Washington. Tom's oldest boy went to pick him up."

"Well, I guess I'll go see what the menfolk are doing," said Frances Lee.

She found them in lawn chairs in the backyard: Daddy Wesley, Uncle M. L., and Wayne. Lewis had his old Stella guitar, and he was picking out "Precious Jewel."

"May the angels have peace, God rest her in heaven; they've broken my heart and they've left me to roam."

Addie was lying alone in DeHart's Funeral Home, as she would have wished.

Major Sam Hemrick settled back in the front seat of Tommy Ray Hemrick's pickup truck, and closed his mind to the blare of the local country station. Things hadn't changed much in the county since he was a kid: same rambling farmhouses gently decaying into green hillsides. The road was better, of course. He remembered when Model A's skirted the ruts in the deep, red clay, and the fifteen miles to the city had been an all-day excursion. He glanced at his watch, the silver Omega he'd picked up in Germany. His plane had landed at three, and they'd probably be at the house by four-fifteen.

"Who was there when you left?" he asked his cousin.

"A passel," said Tommy Ray. "Dad, Uncle Lewis, M. L. and Aunt Sally and their young'uns. Frances Lee and Wayne got in last night. They're staying at Mrs. Lane's Boarding House, though. They figured it was easier than driving in from one of the farms every day. Don't know how long they'll be staying, though."

Not long, thought Sam. Frances Lee could get bored with the homeplace mighty quick. She always did. But she still came back, from time to time: maybe the dutiful daughter, maybe just to show off.

Not like him . . .

It had been more than twenty years since he'd left home, and even after the anger had burned itself out, he hadn't gone back. Not even to see Dad.

Sam missed him sometimes, though. In the autumn he'd get to thinking about hunting with Wesley and Uncle Francis in the hills above Cade's Cove. He'd sit in camp surrounded by leaves that always stayed green, and remember the bands of red and gold ridges against a cloudless blue sky back home. And he'd be cleaning an M-16 instead of the Winchester 30-06 he used to have.

He still remembered the smooth feel of the walnut stock of that rifle, and the carving above the trigger that he kept shining with alcohol. It had been a custom job, and the seventy-two dollars it had cost might as well have been seven hundred in 1940. It took him nearly a year of working every job he could talk anybody into giving him, but he finally saved up enough to buy it. With a jarful of change from picking blueberries at ten cents an hour, the five-dollar gold piece he'd got for winning the spelling bee, and a stack of dollar bills from a month of Saturdays at the sawmill, he paid the seventy-two dollars plus tax (donated by Wesley), and bought the gun. Oh, but it was worth it! He used to brag that he could take the wings off a fly on top of the smokehouse, and he almost believed it.

Parting with that rifle was like leaving behind a chunk of himself, but he had decided to go to college, and firearms were not allowed in dormitory rooms. He had tucked it away carefully in the back of his closet, telling himself it was just as well he was leaving it home. After all, somebody might steal it. In a way, somebody did.

He had come home for the first time on the weekend of Thanksgiving. Teachers College was only twenty miles away, but he worked nights and weekends to pay his way, so he missed most of the hunting season. He'd make up for it, he told himself, by spending as much time up in the hills as the folks would allow. When he opened his closet to clean the Winchester his first night home, it was nowhere to be found.

"Mom!" he called. "Where'd you put my gun?"

She had appeared in the doorway, as cold and impassive as ever, and said simply that she had sold it. It was cluttering up her house.

Sam was half Solitary McCrory, and they never were much on arguing. He just put his clothes back in the canvas valise and walked out. The army sent them a form letter when he graduated from boot camp, and a telegram when he was wounded in Normandy. Years later he took to writing a few lines telling them where he was, and about his brief marriage to Mildred, who couldn't understand that the army came first with him. He sent them a cuckoo clock from Germany one Christmas (Mildred's idea), and Wesley had gotten a watch from Japan, but they never wrote him back. Neither one of them was much on writing letters. He wondered if Wesley had aged much. Funny, he always pictured him as he had been all those years ago—just a little over forty.

"Well, we're here!" called Tommy Ray, pumping the horn. "And there's everybody in the yard, a-waiting on us."

"Which one . . . which one is Dad?" asked Sam.

Frances Lee gave her brother time to adjust his memories to the real thing before she tackled him for the talk they had to have. He'd kept calling Lewis's teenage granddaughter "Frances Lee," and he'd had to make war talk with the menfolk in the backyard, and tell the women what things were like overseas. Then they'd all gone off to the funeral home to view the body for the last time before tomorrow's service. But now—finally—the house was quiet. The kinfolk and their covered dishes had disappeared around ten o'clock, leaving them in peace. Wesley was in his room.

She'd settled Wayne in front of the TV and gone out to the porch where Sam was reading this week's copy of the *Clinchfield Scout* with a bemused smile.

"Anything interesting?" she asked, curling up on the glider.

He shook his head. "Fred Lanier became a lawyer."

"On his daddy's money," snorted Frances Lee. "If Dad had been a shop foreman making good money, there's no telling what you coulda done."

"I did all right," he said. "Washington is good duty to pull."

"I guess I did all right, too," said Frances Lee. "We got two cars and a camper. Leastways, we both got out of these hills."

Sam smiled. "Like M. L. and Lewis and Tom. The trick is not to come back. But everybody does sooner or later."

"You thinking about coming back?"

"I don't know, Fran. Why?"

"Because we've got to figure out what to do about Dad."

She told him how, after fifty years of marriage, he couldn't even fry an egg, and might be too old to learn. The question was: should they try to hire him a housekeeper, look into retirement communities, or arrange for him to come and live with one of them?

"Washington or Chicago," said Sam. "That's a pretty big change for a man his age."

"Well, he might like it," snapped Frances Lee. "Lord knows, anything would have to be an improvement after living with Mama all these years. He can finally start to enjoy himself."

"Okay," said Sam. "Go get him and we'll talk about it."

The straight-backed kitchen chair on the porch was always Wesley's chair. He sat down in it now, feeling a little like a man asking for a bank loan, in front of these two stern-faced adults who were—and weren't—his children. Frances Lee was doing most of the talking, but he couldn't quite make out what they wanted. It was too soon after . . . the other . . . for him to think about anything else. It had to do with his future, though.

"Of course, we want you to do whatever will make you happy, Dad," his daughter was saying. Her voice used to be like her mother's, but she had a Yankee accent now, and the resemblance was gone.

"Happy . . ." he echoed, catching her phrase.

"We don't want to force you into anything." She smiled, patting his sleeve. "You had enough of being bossed around from Mama. So we want you to feel free as a bluejay. You can finally be happy and do as you please."

Do as he pleased . . . Her voice faded in his mind and became Addie's voice. They had been courting for a few weeks that fall—mostly just walking in the woods while he called himself hunting. He had done most of the talking—about his knack for machinery, and his plans to make something of himself. She had walked along beside him in silence, sometimes nodding at what he said. She was small, with a broad bony face under a cloud of black hair, and though she never said anything about how she felt, her blue eyes shone when she looked at him. When they were alone. Never at any other time.

"I've got to get down outta these hills," he told her that day.

"Makin' a livin's easier in town. I can get a job with the railroad, workin' in the machine shop. But I got to live in town to do it."

"You do as you please," said Addie McCrory.

"But . . ." he hesitated with the weight of the asking. "I want you to come with me."

He didn't say any more, and she didn't either. No Solitary McCrory had ever been fool enough to leave the hills. They weren't used to town ways, and they couldn't change any more than a chicken hawk could. Kept to themselves and didn't make friends. "Ain't nothing we want bad enough to go to town for," the McCrorys used to say. He had almost realized even back then what it would be like for her to be set down among people who never would understand. A house in town and all those strangers: it was like asking anybody else to live in a cage, but he had asked because he wanted her with him. He would have gone anyway, but he wanted her with him.

She looked at him for a long time before she finally said: "I'll come."

He reckoned she liked him then, but he hadn't really understood until after she was his, and he learned that McCrory feelings were like a fire in a woodstove: the flames were hid behind iron walls, but inside they burned brighter and longer than any open fire. She had gone with him, and never once in all those years that followed had she mentioned it, or asked to go back. If she had, he would have gone with her.

"Dad?" said Frances Lee a little louder. "What would you like to do?"

"I don't reckon it matters," said Wesley.

Telling the Bees

~

The road was even narrower than he remembered. It lurched and bucked through the granite spines of the Unaka Mountains, cutting through tilting pastures and scrub forest like the dusty tongue of a coon dog lapping the Nolichucky River a few miles farther on. They weren't going that far, though. The trail to the old homeplace should lie past a few more bends in the road. There would be a mark on an outcrop of limestone, his cousin Whilden had told him, and a little turnoff where he could park the four-wheel drive. They would have to walk the rest of the way.

"Course you can't drive up there," Whilden had warned him. "It's purt near straight up. We couldn't hardly get a mule up there to clear timber."

That was fine with Carl. He would welcome the isolation, but he'd had a hard time convincing Whilden of that. "A-lord, Carl-Stuart," his cousin kept saying. "You don't want to spend your honeymoon in that old place. Why, there ain't no lights nor running water." He had even offered the newlyweds his own room, reckoning he could bunk on the sofa if they were so dead set on coming for their honeymoon. Carl smiled a little, remembering their phone conversation. Whilden didn't come right out and say it, but it was plain enough that he thought that if he were a big-time engineer in San Francisco, he'd find a better place to take

16

his bride than Cabe's Hollow, Tennessee. Carl wondered what Whilden would consider a suitable location for a honeymoon: Bermuda, Atlanta . . . or Myrtle Beach, South Carolina? Elissa had talked about going to Mexico, but he told her that he wanted her to see where he'd grown up. The folks were dead, of course— except for a passel of cousins—but the land had hardly changed at all. He smiled at a couple of white-faced calves poking their noses through a fence: except for a score of years, they might be Bushes and Curly, the pair he had lovingly raised as a 4-H project.

Why had he been so insistent on coming back here? He hadn't been back to Tennessee in years. Perhaps it was some sort of familial instinct—this urge to bring his bride back to the family seat, as if the ghosts would look on her and approve. Anyway, he had wanted Elissa to see the hills. Maybe then she would understand why California's mountains just weren't the same. His homesickness for the mountains was unassuaged by jaunts to Lake Tahoe. The silver-capped Rockies stretching out like a Sierra Club calendar left him unmoved, while these stubby weathered hills, silver with winter birches, made his heart tighten. Damn near twenty years, and he still thought of it as home.

"So these are your precious Appalachians." Elissa smiled, nodding at a not-too-distant skyline. "They don't seem like mountains."

"I know." He had thought about that when he realized that the Rockies were different from his mountains. The Appalachians don't stand back and pose for you, he finally decided. They come up close and hold you, so they don't seem so big and imposing. Cabe's Hollow must be about three thousand feet above sea level, but you didn't feel it, because you were in the mountains. Among them.

"This is Cabe's Mill Road," he told her. He remembered the gristmill at the end of it, down by the river. It was probably abandoned now. He'd heard that Old Man Cabe had died, and he didn't suppose that Garrett would have stayed around to run it. Garrett always was a hell-raiser. Used to chase girls through the fields waving a black snake like a bullwhip. Maybe they'd go down and take a look at the mill sometime. Past a steep bend in the road, he saw the flash of an X mark in yellow rock. "Here's the turnoff to the cabin."

Elissa straightened up and looked out the window. "Good. I'm stiff from riding. First the airplane, and then all these archaic little roads. What cabin? I don't see any cabin."

Carl grinned. "Now, Mrs. Spurlock, you're talking like a city girl."

She made a face at him. "Give me time. I've only been married to a hillbilly for six hours. But where is the cabin? I don't see it! Is it behind those trees?" She pulled out her compact and began arranging her hair and dabbing at her nose.

"You see that mountain there?" he said. "Well, the cabin is at the end of a little path that goes straight up it."

Elissa lowered her compact slowly. "Is this the surprise you promised me, Carl?"

He flushed a little. "Elissa, I just had to get you to see it. This land has been in my family for a hundred and fifty years. My great-grandfather built this old cabin. It's important to me. Please?"

She straightened her alpaca ski hat and smoothed her bangs. "You want me to walk all the way to the top of a mountain to look at a cabin?"

"No. That's where we're going to stay. Remember? I told you I'd called my cousin Whilden, who owns this land now, and he—"

She smiled carefully. "Is that what you meant by a cabin? It's not a ski lodge or anything like that?"

"Just a cabin. Remember how you said you'd go camping with me sometime?"

"But, Carl, it's December!" said Elissa, still smiling.

"There's a fireplace." He looked up at the mountain, darkening against a red sky. The trees were no longer distinct. "We'd better get started. The light's going."

He pulled down the back tailgate and hauled out his canvas valise, while Elissa stood at his elbow, making little clouds with her breath. "It's getting late, so I'm only going to make one trip tonight. Which one of these do you need?" He pointed to the three pieces of matching pink luggage.

"All of them, I guess," said Elissa in a puzzled voice. "I don't remember what I packed where."

Carl rubbed his chin and considered the problem as if he were at work, plotting out the weight distribution in a B-1B. Finally he said: "I'll carry my bag and that big suitcase of yours. If you need anything else, you'll have to carry it."

He hoisted her suitcase out of the truck. After a moment's hesitation, she picked up the makeup case and nodded for him to close the hatch.

"Don't forget to lock it, Carl!"

He smiled. "This isn't Aspen, Elissa. The only people on this road are the Pattons and the Shulls—and they wouldn't take sugar packets from a diner, much less rob a truck!"

"Things might have changed in fifteen years, Carl!"

He looked around him. Things might have changed—but that hadn't. Cabe's Mountain stood just as bare and wild on this December evening as it had years ago when he'd hunted squirrel with Garrett up this very path. Only he had changed: the engineer with a Ph.D. from Stanford and an aerie of chrome and glass overlooking the Bay. He had come a long way from Cabe's Hollow. "Come on, Elissa! We're burning daylight!"

They were following an old logging trail which led to the foot of the mountain. She clumped along beside him in her slim leather boots, crackling leaves with every step. Just as well they weren't hunting squirrels; she was making enough noise to wake up the bears.

"Are we almost there, Carl?" panted Elissa, after a few moments' silence.

Carl turned to look at her. He could still see the truck parked by the road. "We haven't started yet." He smiled reassuringly. Elissa was so beautiful in her embroidered white ski parka, her cheeks pink with cold. She looked expensive and—his mind fumbled for the word—classy. Like one of those evening gown models in the old Sears Wishbook. She did him proud.

He came to the edge of a branch of swift-running spring water. It was clear, about ankle-deep, and four feet across.

"Where's the bridge?" asked Elissa at his elbow.

"See that cinder block in the middle? You step on to that and then over to the other side."

"But the cinder block is under water, Carl!"

"About an inch."

In the end he had to take the suitcase across, and then come back and carry her over the stream. She was afraid she would fall, and she kept saying that she couldn't get her new boots wet. She held out one small foot, pointing to the shining leather boot with its dainty two-inch heel. Carl frowned. "I told you to wear walking shoes, Elissa. How are you going to climb in those things?"

Her face fell. "Don't you like them? They cost a hundred and eighty-five dollars."

He sighed. "Just watch where you're walking. It's rained here in the last day or two, and the ground is apt to be slippery."

"I'll be fine, darling. I jog, don't I?"

The path up the mountain to the cabin was not so much a trail as an absence of underbrush in a wavy line weaving its way upward. Fallen trees obstructed the way, and outgrowths from nearby bramble bushes slowed them down. Carl went first, stopping to untangle Elissa from the briars or to lift her over a tree trunk. She had not spoken since they began the climb; he could hear her breath coming in labored gasps. Every twenty feet or so they stopped to rest, until her breathing was normal again, before resuming their climb.

"Jogging on flat land is a lot different from mountain climbing," he said gently. "You just tell me when you want to rest again."

"No. No. I'm fine, but this boot heel is coming loose." She took a deep breath. "You don't think I'm going to let a man twelve years older than I am beat me up a mountain, do you?"

Carl smiled. "You're doing fine." He slowed his step a little and began to talk, to take her mind off the climbing. "You know, that branch back there put me in mind of my uncle Mose. He used to come here bee-tracking in the summertime. Of course, bees need water in the hot summer to make honey and to cool the hive, so they fly to the nearest stream to get it. Well, my old uncle Mose would locate a bee watering place, and he'd sit down nearby, and just watch those bees leave with a stomachful of water. He'd follow their flight with just his eyes for as far as he could see them. Past that sumac bush or that service tree. After a while he'd move to that tree and sit and watch several more bees go by, and note the next place he lost sight of them. After a couple of short hops like that, he'd finally get to the hollow tree they were headed for. He'd mark the tree so he could find it again, and go on home."

He glanced back at Elissa. She seemed to be concentrating on the path. Her face glowed from exertion, and she pushed at her wet bangs with the wrist of one glove. Impulsively, he took the makeup case from her and tucked it under his arm. She did not look up.

"Course now, the reason Uncle Mose would mark that tree would be so that he could find it again come fall," Carl went on. "Long about late October, he'd come back down the mountain with a zinc washtub, ax, rope, and a little box, and he'd set to work. He'd split that hollow tree open, catch the queen in a box, scoop all the honey out into the washtub, and carry it home. The bees would usually swarm on a branch, so he'd cut down the branch and take it home, where he'd built some hives in the back garden. Then he'd let the queen bee out of the box, and put the branch down beside the homemade hive, which had some of the honey put in it for the bees to winter on. The rest of the honey went into pint jars for the family. It took patience, but the results were worth it." He turned to look at her.

Elissa regarded him steadily. "I loathe bees."

They stood on the mountaintop, a narrow ridge of sturdy pines, and looked down at the little meadow cupped in a hollow below the summit. The land had been cleared and cultivated years before, and the little cabin, which sat in a puddle of sunlight at the edge of the garden furrows, seemed sturdy for its age. Brown winter grass stretched away to the forest which encircled it, and aluminum pie tins, strung from branches to keep the birds from the garden, twirled soundlessly in the wind. The stillness was so absolute that it might have been a sepia photograph from Carl's family album, or a dream in which time elapses in slow motion. Carl tried to remember times he had been at the cabin, when the old folks still lived there, as though calling them to memory might make them come alive in the barren landscape. The rotting wooden boxes near the woods would be painted white and set upright. Uncle Mose would be moving among them in his cover-alls and veil, bees hovering at his side. Grandfather would be sitting on the porch steps, soaping the sidesaddle Grandmother used when they rode to church. Without wanting to, Carl turned and looked at the gray headstones beneath the cedar trees.

"Carl! I'm freezing! Are you going to stand up here all day?"

He looked at her for a moment before he realized what she had said. Then he nodded and helped her down the embankment toward the meadow.

Elissa wrinkled her nose at the sight of the cabin. "I don't suppose there's any heat," she said flatly.

"Just a fireplace. Whilden left us some wood." He had known where to look for it—stacked in a pile by the kindling stump.

As they walked through the garden plot, Elissa stopped to look at a child's plastic rocking horse, set up as a yard ornament under a leafless dogwood.

"How tacky!" she sighed.

He helped her up the flat rock steps to the porch, and set the suitcases down by Granddad's whittling bench. "Do you want me to carry you over the threshold?" he asked Elissa as he pushed open the door.

She peered into the darkness and shuddered. "Are there snakes in there?"

"No. If you'll wait out here, I'll light the oil lamp so you can see."

"Oh, all right. Just hurry up!"

He could hear her pacing outside as he fumbled with the chimney of the oil lamp Whilden had left on the table. Finally he succeeded in putting the match to the lamp wick, and the small room glowed in lamplight. He saw that it had been freshly swept—although the window was still streaked with dirt—and a brace of logs had been carefully arranged in the fireplace. A clean quilt in a churn-dasher pattern covered the few shreds of up-holstery left on the old sofa. On the table near the woodstove, Whilden had left a jar of coffee, a box of cornflakes, some evaporated milk, and—for decoration—red-berried pyracantha branches in a Mason jar.

"You'd think somebody would have cleaned this place up," snapped Elissa in the doorway. She turned her head slowly to study the room, her eyebrows raised.

Carl brought in the suitcases from the front porch. "The bed-room is in there," he said, leading the way. "I can heat you some well water on the stove if you'd like to wash. First, though, I'm going to get this fire going in the fireplace."

Elissa sat down on the couch to watch. Carl knelt on the stone hearth, rearranging some of the smaller sticks. "See if you can find some newspapers," he told her.

"Newspapers?"

"Yes. Or leaves. Anything I can use to get this fire started."

Elissa began to wander around looking behind the couch and

poking in drawers in the kitchen part of the room. "How about this old calendar on the wall?" she called.

Carl turned to look at the wall decoration: a 1945 calendar with a drawing of a Flying Fortress against an unfurled flag. "No," he said. "Not that."

With a sigh of exasperation, Elissa continued to search. "Well, it certainly wasn't one of your ancestors who discovered fire, Carl! Why don't you just strike a match and let the logs burn?"

He put a match to one of the smaller sticks, holding it there until it burned his finger, but although the stick glowed tentatively for a few moments, it faded to darkness again. He reached in his pocket for another box of matches.

"Carl, I found some little pieces of cloth. Will they do?" Elissa held up four short strips of black crêpe. "Are these from a quilt?" she asked.

"Bring them here." He took them from her outstretched hand. "I haven't seen these since Grandma died. They're crêpe for the beehives."

"The beehives?"

"Yes. For mourning. You have to tell the bees when there has been a death in the family, or else they'll leave the hive and start one somewhere else. When Grandma died, Uncle Mose hung these black streamers on each beehive when he told the bees."

"You're teasing me!" Elissa protested.

"No. When somebody's gone, you have to tell the bees they're not coming back."

Elissa shook her head. "There are some strange goings-on in your mountains," she said.

Carl tucked one of the streamers away in the pocket of his jeans. He looked at her for a moment. "Well," he said at last, "I guess I'd better start this fire."

She answered the tone, rather than the words. "Carl! Are you angry with me?"

"Guess I'll go out and gather up some leaves for kindling." He started to get up.

"Carl! Please don't go yet!" There was a catch in her voice, and she began to pace, not looking at him as she spoke. "I understand about your wanting me to see where you grew up and all, but I'm not used to this! I just didn't know what to expect! I mean, you said *cabin*, but this isn't like the cabins I've stayed in on ski trips! Carl, this is our honeymoon! I had to tell people we were going to Aspen, because how could I possibly explain that you wanted to come and stay in—this?"

He held another match to the sticks, concentrating on the feeble light in his hand.

"You dragged me up here and ruined my new boots—and for what? A shack with no water, no lights, and no heat!" She sat down on the arm of the sofa and sobbed. "I married an engineer, not a— a hillbilly!"

Carl watched the spark in the fireplace until it flickered out. "It's all right, Elissa. We'll leave in the morning. We'll go wherever you want."

She managed a moist smile. "Aspen?" she quavered.

"Sure. Aspen. Fine."

"Oh, thank you, Carl! Things will be all right when we get back where we belong. You'll see!"

He brushed off the legs of his pants. "I'll go out and get those leaves now."

"Do you want me to come along?"

"No. I won't be long."

He stood on the porch and looked at the quarter moon webbed in branches on the ridge until his eyes became accustomed to the dark. When the black shapes in the yard had rearranged themselves into familiar objects—a tree, a wagon wheel—he began to walk toward the back garden at the edge of the woods.

Tomorrow he would stop at the farm and tell Whilden they were going. Maybe he'd send him something from California. Elissa would be all right when they got back. He pictured her at their glass-topped table pouring wine into Waterford goblets. She would be blond and tanned from a day of sailing, and she would tease him when he alternated Vivaldi and Ernest Tubb on the stereo. Elissa didn't belong here, but ... He tried to picture Roseanne Shull entertaining his engineer friends in the glass room over the Bay. It was time to go back.

He had reached the end of the garden. Glancing back at the cabin, Carl tried to remember how long he had been walking. Elissa would be impatient. It was time to gather the leaves and go back to her. He looked down at the abandoned beehive at his feet, the last of Uncle Mose's collection. He had to go back. Pulling the black streamer from his pocket, he laid it gently on the box, and hurried away.

Love on
First Bounce

~

I squinted back at the glass double door of Taylor High. Despite the glare of the afternoon sun and the glares of departing seniors, who kept jostling me back and forth as they passed, I saw Carol Lee's grinning face in the doorway. She was twitching with excitement. I could tell by the way she was hugging her notebook as if it were a teddy bear and the way the ponytails over her ears bobbed up and down. She kept looking all around, obviously for me, so I prepared to be bored. By the time she fought her way through the crowd and reached the bottom step, I had an expression of utter disdain.

"Guess what, Elizabeth!" she said in tones of breathless excitement.

"I cannot imagine," I said wearily. Trying to guess what Carol Lee Jenkins was excited about was always an exercise in futility. It could be anything from a B on a biology lab quiz to Neil Sedaka's using her name in a song. (I kept telling her that she was not entitled to take "Oh! Carol" personally. Fat lot of good that did; she mooned over it for weeks.)

"There's the cutest boy whose locker is right across from mine! I just noticed him."

"Oh? Who is he?" I was only slightly curious.

"I don't know. I think he's a senior, though. He has the same lunch period as mine. I bumped into him after second period."

27

I started to say "Accidentally?" and then thought better of it. Actually, I didn't want to know. Encouraging Carol Lee only increases her intensity. Instead I said, "What does he look like?"

"Well, he's kind of hard to describe, but he's very cute. He has feathery brown hair and wire-rimmed glasses."

"Incredible," I said. She was too wound up to hear my sarcasm, but mentally I applauded my efforts.

"There he is. Coming out over there! Look! No—over *there*, stupid!"

I sniffed loudly and purposely stared in the opposite direction. "Good grief!" I hissed. "Do you *have* to point?"

"Look!" she pleaded.

I dutifully turned, expecting to see the president of the school or the star football player. Carol Lee was just idiotic enough to flip over somebody like that, but the object of her affections was not one of the school's superstars. "You mean the one who's bouncing?"

"Hey, yeah," Carol Lee took only a moment to consider my description before she cheerfully agreed. "That's exactly what it is: he's bouncing."

I'd never seen the boy with the weird gait before. I would have remembered that walk. He sort of loped along, bobbing up at every other step, like a rubber duck caught in the current of a bathtub drain. He was nice-looking in an ordinary kind of way: not too tall, not muscle-bound, definitely not a jock. He walked by himself, instead of surrounded by a clump of laughing madras-and-Weejun-clad companions, so he wasn't one of the popular kids, into school politics and serious partying. All the candid shots in the yearbook seemed to be of the same eight people, laughing and posing prettily, with every hair in place, and he wasn't one of them. He wore a plaid sport shirt and tan chinos, instead of a black turtleneck and black jeans, which meant that he wasn't one of the "posturing poets for peace" crowd, either. I couldn't place him in the rigid social hierarchy of Taylor High. He was just a guy who happened to be in school here.

I wondered what had made Carol Lee notice him in the first place. Of course, there is no telling what will attract Carol Lee to a guy; her affections are as random as tornadoes, and of similar duration. She likes to build souls for mysterious strangers; I suppose getting to know someone would spoil the effect. For one entire bewildering week in eighth grade, though, she actually had a crush on my brother Bill. Even she recognized the absurdity in that, and after a couple of chances to observe him closely, while she was visiting me, she gave it up. Bill would not notice someone flirting with him unless she used a flamethrower, and having lived a few doors down from him for most of her life, Carol Lee found it hard to fantasize about Bill as Mr. Wonderful. As I kept reminding her: she knew better.

I looked at her latest victim with clinical interest. Being a freshman, I knew by some sixth sense that the bouncer was definitely a senior, but despite that aura of upperclassman grandeur, he looked like a big kid. Except for the oversized glasses, he had a round cherub face and a pleasant, if absentminded, expression.

Just before he reached the square of sidewalk where we were standing, I dropped my eyes and gazed intently at a wad of chewing gum fossilized in the pavement. As soon as he was out of earshot, Carol Lee breathed rapturously into my ear, "He smiled at me, Elizabeth! He actually smiled at *me*."

"What did you expect him to do? You were staring at him like he was Baldur the Beautiful. He probably thought you were a dangerous lunatic, and he was trying to pacify you by not making any sudden moves."

Carol Lee wasn't listening. "His eyes are the most beautiful shade of brown," she sighed.

"Like horse manure," I said briskly. "Can we go home now?"

It is a half-mile walk from the high school to Sycamore Street, where Carol Lee lives—around the corner and two houses away from me. I yawned all the way home, listening to Carol Lee's endless babbling about the mysterious senior. There was no point in trying to work up any enthusiasm for her latest obsession, because Carol Lee fell in love about every three weeks, always with some good-looking total stranger, and after she wore herself out scheming over ways to meet the object of her affections, and speculated endlessly on what he was "really" like, she would lose interest and direct her attention to another victim.

Honestly, I thought, *she might as well develop a crush on Paul McCartney; he is no less unattainable than any of her other crushes.* Carol Lee disdained movie poster romances, though; she dwells in possibility, which in her case is a very long commute from real life. She never actually dated any of her idols; in fact, I think she barely spoke to any of them. The chief victim of her delusions was me: I had to hear about Mr. Wonder-of-the-Week in our nightly phone conversations. The only thing that made it bearable was the short duration of each crush. About the time I got bored with hearing about the Piggly Wiggly bag boy or the minister's son, her fantasies had a cast change, and the whole process began again. I predicted that this crush would last exactly one week: the time it would take Carol Lee to notice that the bouncing Mr. X wasn't wearing his class ring.

A week later, though, Carol Lee's ravings showed no sign of tapering off, and I was beginning to worry.

Friday night the phone rang.

"Elizabeth! I found out what his name is. You know—*the* boy."

Of course I knew. She had scarcely talked about anything else in days. "Hello, Carol Lee," I said. That was encouragement enough.

"His name is Cholly Barnes, and he's—"

"Charlie?"

"No. Cholly. C-h-o-l-l-y. It's a family nickname. Short for Collins or something. My informant wasn't sure. Anyhow, he goes to the Grace Methodist Church, and he drives a green Chevy. He's a photographer for the yearbook staff, and he plays the guitar. He likes apples—"

"And he's going with somebody else."

"What?" gasped Carol Lee. "Oh. You noticed that he's not wearing his class ring, didn't you? He lost it on a fishing trip. Actually, he doesn't date much."

"According to the FBI wiretap, I suppose?"

She laughed. "I just talked to a couple of girls who know him, that's all."

"Like his mother and sisters?"

"He doesn't have any sisters," Carol Lee replied promptly. "But Daddy knows his grandfather."

"Oh, Carol," I said (and I was *not* quoting Neil Sedaka), "have you no sense of decency? What will you do next? Start peeking in his windows?"

"Hey, that gives me an idea!"

"Oh, no . . ."

"Tomorrow is Saturday. We can go for a bike ride."

"And?" Actually I didn't want to know.

"We can ride by his house. I found out where he lives, too. Maybe he'll be outside, mowing the lawn or something."

"Absolutely not. I refuse. I am not going. You can't make me."

I said that the whole mile over to his house. "This is ridiculous!" I said that about fifty times, too. I don't know why I kept muttering. Carol Lee wasn't listening, and I didn't need any convincing.

We kept going around and around the block. I began to feel like a vulture. To relieve the monotony and take my mind off how stupid I felt, I started counting the bricks on the left side of his house. The only reason I kept going was loyalty. Carol was my friend, and it was my duty to stand by her in her madness. *Sancho Panza on a Schwinn—that's me,* I thought.

He's never going to come out. I pictured him lurking behind the living room curtains, watching two giggling freshmen in orbit around his block. *There's no way he's coming out of that house,* I thought. *He'll stay barricaded in there until doomsday. He won't check the mail; he won't retrieve the newspaper; he won't go to school on Monday. He'll never come out. He'll probably leave instructions that when he dies, they are to cremate him in the toaster oven and flush his remains down the toilet. Meanwhile we'll just keep circling. And Carol will never leave. We'll be doomed to an eternal bike path around this block.* I could hear Rod Serling solemnly describing our trajectory: "Elizabeth MacPherson and Carol Lee Jenkins, two typical teenage girls with ordinary hopes and dreams, who started out on a Saturday morning bike ride, and ended up perpetually circling, forever straining for a glimpse of Cholly Barnes as they hurtle past the brick ranch house on Maple Street, trapped in an orbital obsession known only in *The Twilight Zone.*"

Finally, I had enough. I was tired, sweaty, hungry, and, above all, I felt utterly foolish. "Look, Carol Lee," I said, edging my bike to within earshot. "I'm going home now. I've got motion sickness."

"Oh, just a few more minutes," said Carol Lee. "He's bound to come out sometime."

"Sorry," I told her. "I'm all pedaled out." As we turned the corner onto Fourth Street, I steered my bike away from Carol Lee's and headed straight for Elm Avenue. I was going home. I glanced back to see her pumping furiously along, determined not to abandon the vigil.

I had been home about two hours—long enough to take a half-hour bubble bath, fix myself a sandwich, and immerse myself in *The Collected Stories of Dorothy Parker*—when the phone rang.

It was Carol Lee, wailing.

I almost dropped the phone. "What's the matter with you?"

"Oh, Elizabeth! The most *awful* thing happened."

She's been hit by a truck, I thought. *She's in the hospital, and they've allowed her one last phone call before they cut off her—oh, wait.* I suddenly remembered who I was dealing with. This was Carol Lee Jenkins, the Star-Spangled Queen of Melodrama, to whom every hangnail was a tragedy, and she was no doubt calling on her pink Princess phone from her white lace French Provincial bedroom in perfect health.

"What happened?" I sighed.

"He saw me!"

"What?"

"He saw me. Cholly Barnes *saw* me. He came out to get the newspaper, and he was just straightening up as I came around the block, and he looked right at me."

Maybe something did happen, I thought. *Maybe he smiled and waved for her to stop, and then he went over to the curb to chat with her, and they hit it off beautifully, and now she's calling to tell me that they're going to the movies later tonight. Oh, wait, this is Carol Lee's theoretical love life. Motto: "Not on* This *Planet." Okay. Maybe he went out into his yard, picked up the biggest rock he could find, and waited for her next revolution. . . .*

"Okay," I said. "He came out into the yard, picked up the news-paper, and saw you. Then what?"

"That's it," said Carol Lee. "Then I came home."

"So he saw you. Why are you hysterical? Oh, wait. Did he catch you rooting through his garbage cans?"

"No, of course not!"

I didn't think there was any *of course* about it, but I was relieved that she had restrained herself. "Okay, he saw you on your bike. Isn't that what you wanted?"

"No!" She was wailing again. "I just wanted to see him. I didn't want him to see me."

I told Carol Lee that if that was her idea of a romantic

encounter, she would be much better off falling in love with a Paul McCartney poster, but she was not amused. Well, I thought, at least I've heard the last of Cholly Barnes.

I hadn't, though.

Carol Lee continued to stake out a lunch table so that she could keep Cholly under surveillance while we ate, and her obsession with him showed no sign of letting up. She managed to discover his birthday, his dog's name, his food preferences, and about a zillion other completely useless biographical details, all of which she regaled me with as we watched him eat. If Taylor High had offered a course in Cholly Barnes, we would have passed it with honors.

Phase Two of Carol Lee's Doomed Romance began early in May. One afternoon she set down her lunch tray with an expression of tragic suffering on her face. I thought it was the meat loaf that had prompted this air of gloom, but as she sat down, she said, "Oh, Elizabeth, it's *May*."

I looked doubtfully at the meat loaf. "Yes," I said. "I don't mind May, myself."

"But school will be over in a few weeks."

"Yes. That prospect doesn't distress me, either. I'll be out of Mrs. Baxter's geometry class forever."

"But he's *graduating*!"

"Oh."

"I can't live without him."

It was useless to point out that she wasn't even remotely living *with* him. "You'll get over it," I said, as consolingly as I could manage.

"I've lost him. We had so little time together."

None, actually, I thought.

"I'll never forget him, though," said Carol Lee. "I'll probably go off and tend lepers in the African veldt, or run a small lending library somewhere, and I'll grow old and gray, with only my memories of *him* to sustain me. But I shall suffer in silence. I shall never speak his name again."

I began counting the hours until graduation.

A week later the euphoric phase of the obsession returned. Carol Lee came down the steps after school, squealing in ecstasy. "Guess what I've got!" she said, in tones suggesting possession of the Hope diamond or an Irish sweepstakes ticket.

"Offhand I'd say schizophrenia," I replied.

"No. Look!" She reached in her pocket and took out a small white square of cardboard. "His calling card!" she said, handing it over for inspection.

I took the slightly creased and grubby *Jeremy Collins Barnes* card, studying the engraved italic script with polite disinterest. "Very nice," I said. "Where did you get it?" I pictured Carol Lee throwing him down on the floor of the hall and searching his pockets.

"One of the senior girls got it for me," said Carol Lee. "Look on the back! He *wrote* on it."

I turned the card over. There in tiny, script letters, Cholly Barnes had written: *I shall pass through this world but once. If there be any good that I can do, or any kindness I can show, let me do it. Let me not defer it or neglect it, for I shall not pass this way again.*

I didn't think he would pass at all.

But he did. He passed, and he passed us in his white cap and gown as the seniors marched in two rows down the concrete steps of the stadium on graduation night. It is hard to bounce to the beat of "Pomp and Circumstance," but Cholly Barnes managed to do it. I watched the white tassel bob its way down the steps of the bleachers and onto the field with the rest of the senior class, waiting for commencement exercises to begin. Carol Lee sat beside me in the bleachers, shredding a damp tissue and murmuring, "He's leaving. He's actually leaving."

"We all have to go sometime," I muttered.

"But he's going away, and I'll never see him again."

"You never see him now," I pointed out. "Except when you have him under surveillance, I mean. Maybe you could take some snapshots of him, and have them made into a poster. It would be about the same, you know."

"He's really leaving," her voice trembled with misery. "He is going out of my life."

"You look like a basset hound!" I hissed at her. "People are staring at you. Snap out of it!"

"I'll never forget him," said Carol Lee in her most mournful tones. "I'll treasure the memory of him forever."

Ah! I thought, *the Nobility Phase of the Grand Passion has kicked in.*

"I'll treasure these memories of him, and someday when I am old and gray . . . when I'm thirty-five . . . I'll tell my children about my first real love."

"If your memory isn't gone by then. Advanced senility."

Carol Lee gave me a reproachful look through her tears, and I decided to save my breath. We watched the rest of the graduation ceremony in silence, punctuated by an occasional sniffle from the Bereaved One.

At last it was over. The diplomas were handed out, the mortarboards were thrown into the air, as the seniors had been carefully instructed *not* to do, and the spectators filed onto the field to mingle with the newly certified high school graduates. As we left the bleachers, Carol Lee trailed behind me in silent misery.

After a few moments' reconnaissance, I spotted Cholly Barnes, diploma in hand, chatting with three of his classmates.

"Why don't you go over and congratulate him?" I said. "He's standing right over there with some of the other seniors."

"Oh, I couldn't!" whispered Carol Lee.

"Sure you could. It's a public celebration. Just go over and say, 'Congratulations. Best of luck in the future.' "

She looked stricken. "No, I couldn't," she said. "I don't *know* him!"

We stood there for a few more minutes watching flashbulbs pop in the twilight, and then we turned and watched the white figure, gown flapping, bounce off into the warm June night.

John Knox
in Paradise

~

I loaned her eight guidebooks of Scotland, and all the maps that I had, but she only looked at the castles, and the pictures of mountains against the sky. "Not like my mountains," she said. "There aren't any trees, but it's close enough. I guess they must have felt at home."

Her people, she meant: the McCourys. Sometime a few centuries back, to hear her tell it, they left Scotland for the New World, and walked the mountain passes from Pennsylvania to settle in the hollows of east Tennessee. She knows more history than I do, but she takes it all personally. Her eyes flash when she talks about the Jacobite cause, but she mispronounces most of the battles—Cul-*low*-den, she says. I tell her how to say them correctly, but I can't tell her much about them. It was a long time ago, and nobody minds anymore.

She tells me I don't look Scottish, whatever that means. Lots of people have brown eyes and brown hair. What would she know about it? She had never been in Scotland. "I'm a Celt," she says, the way someone else might say, "I'm a duchess," though I think it's nothing much to be proud of, the way they're carrying on in Belfast. She has the look of them, though, with that mass of black hair and the clear blue eyes of a bomb-throwing Irish saint. She looks at me sometimes, and she knows things I'd never dream of telling her.

38

She seems to expect me to know some kind of secret, but she'll never say what it is. *Fash't*, she'll say. "Do you have that word?" Or *clabbered*, or *red the room*. Sometimes I've heard them, from my grandmother, perhaps, and she'll smile as if I'd given her something, and say, "From mine, too."

I wasn't much help with the songs, not being musically inclined. I told her the ones I'd learned in Scouts, but she said they weren't the right ones, and she sang a lot of snatches of songs—all sounding pretty much the same to me. She seemed hurt when I didn't know them as well: "Barbry Ellen" . . . "A Fair Young Maid All in the Garden." I collected Beatles cards in senior school.

The song that interested me was "True Thomas," about a fellow from the Borders who gets carried off by the Queen of Elfland. He was minding his own business in the forest one day, and up she comes in a silken gown of fairy green and carries him off to the fairy kingdom. "I can see why he went," I told her. "Even if it's a bit dangerous, it's a chance to escape from the dullness of ordinary life. But what did the Queen of Faerie want with an ordinary Scot?"

She smiled. "Perhaps Scots aren't ordinary at all to a fairy queen. Or maybe she saw something in him that no one else could."

"Wasn't he supposed to be a prophet of some sort?" I asked, half remembering.

She shook her head. "That was later. She gave him that." She sang the rest of the verses for me—about the queen showing Thomas the thorny path to heaven, the broad high road to hell, and the winding road to her kingdom. And how they traveled through the mists, past a stream where all the blood shed on the earth passed into the waters of Faerie. And finally she gives him an apple that will give him the gift of prophecy. "And 'til seven years were gane and past / True Thomas on earth was never seen."

"He got back then."

"Yes. And became quite famous as a prophet. But the legend says that one day when Thomas was attending a village feast, a messenger came running in and said that two white deer had appeared at the edge of the forest, and Thomas said, 'They've come for me,' and off he went forever."

"She made him go back again?"

She thought for a moment. "Perhaps she allowed him to go back again. Maybe they're still together. Where is his village, Ercildoune? Does it still exist?"

"Earlston," I corrected her. "Oh, yes. The A68 goes right past it."

I don't remember telling her that she could go along when I went back to Scotland. It's as if one moment I was advising her on things she might like to see someday, and the next I was writing my parents for schedules of festivals that we might want to visit.

She fell asleep on my shoulder in the airplane, which was a bit strange, since she always seemed so worried about me whenever I took a flight anywhere. I held her, a little awkwardly, and it was hard to turn the pages of *U.S. News & World Report* with one hand; besides, I knew what people must be thinking, and I was right. As we were coming in to the airport, the stewardess told me to wake up my wife so that she could fasten her seat belt. "She's not my wife!" I said. "Her passport is blue."

I'd made a sort of schedule, starting with Edinburgh, because a number of tourist attractions are close together, but after we'd landed at Prestwick, she said she wanted to go and see the Roman wall, which is miles to the south. "I want to make sure it's still standing," she said. I assured her it was, because we drove past it every time we went to visit my uncle in Yorkshire. "It hasn't kept them out, though," she said sadly. I've no idea what she was talking about. I told her that we were going to do Edinburgh first, and that her border patrol could bloody well wait.

I took her to the Palace of Holyroodhouse, and the Royal Mile, and St. Giles, and tried to tell her about them. She always listens very carefully, but then she'll laugh and say, "You don't pronounce short *e*'s; you make them sound like *a*'s," and I know she hasn't understood a word. Except when she gets me to talk about myself, and then she hears things whether I say them or not.

I showed her the skyscrapers in Glasgow, and the Forth Road Bridge, and the new IBM plant, but I don't think she was paying attention, because straight after that, she asks me which side I would have taken in the '45. I told her that independence would have been an economic disaster—look at Eire and the mess they're in. "Now then," I said, "would you rather see the botanical gardens or the university?"

"Culloden," she said softly.

That's miles to the north, near Inverness. I told her we might get there eventually—too bloody soon for my taste, whenever we got there. It's only an old field, I said. The battle's been over for centuries. And it'll probably be raining.

I wonder what Thomas would have shown the Queen of Elfland if they had stayed in this world? I suppose they'd have skipped John Knox's house. We should have done. I don't know what I expected of her there—a story about her great-grandfather the clergyman, perhaps. She looked around a bit at the exhibits, but she was most interested in whether Arthur's Seat was visible from the upstairs window. That was her favorite place in Edinburgh. She wanted to know if that was the hill of the sleeping warriors, and I'd no idea what she meant. It's folklore, apparently. A legend that King Arthur and his knights are sleeping under some hill in Britain (not that one, I'm sure!), and that if the country ever needed them, they would awaken and do battle. When she told me that, I thought of her Tennessee kinfolks, who seemed to be sleeping under every hill in Strathclyde, as often as they haunted our travels.

Anything was likely to conjure them up from the hollows of their own hills—her father and uncles, from some outlandish place called Pigeon Roost, Tennessee—and she'd tell me this story about their mining days or that tale about a bee-tracker. Sometimes I had to look at the mountains, bare against the sky, to remember whose country we were in.

She finds history in the strangest places, and misses it entirely when it's really there. I could barely get her to look at the armor and French swords in the museum at Edinburgh Castle, but she spent nearly an hour in a nasty wind looking at a herd of shaggy cows on a hillside. She wanted to climb over the fence to go and pet one, but I was firm. I could hardly get her to look at the steam engine exhibits in the Royal Museum of Scotland, but a jumble shop on Drummond Street fascinated her. She found an old wooden Marconi radio, the sort people must have listened to Churchill on during the war. "At home, it would have been an Atwater Kent," she told me. "When my daddy was a little boy, nobody in town could afford one. It was the Depression, and people had been laid off by the railroad. So when the Dempsey-Tunney fight was to be broadcast on the radio—why, of course everyone wanted to hear it. It was the first live broadcast of a thing like that. The furniture store downtown opened up that evening and invited the whole town in to listen to the fight on their display model Atwater Kent. My dad still talks about it." She and the proprietor went on about Churchill (him) and the Grand Ole Opry (her), until I had leafed through every copy of *Punch* in the shop.

She's never forgiven me for not speaking Gaelic. What good is it? My schoolboy French is useless enough. But she picks up every word she can, and mangles the pronouncing of it. She learned how to say "I love you," and she says it to me often, though of course it doesn't count, being a language neither of us speaks. *"Tha gaol agam ort,"* she'll say, with a teasing smile, when I've corrected her about the silly way she holds her knife and fork to cut. Even if it's in Gaelic, I know what it means, and it makes me uneasy. What would people think?

We wouldn't have time to go to the Highlands, I told her. The conference I had to attend would keep me busy for most of the week, though I could take some time off in the afternoons to show her around. There were lots of things to see in Strathclyde, after all. Edinburgh alone could take weeks if you did it properly. She hardly looked at the exhibits in Knox's house, though, just kept looking out the window toward the hill as if she were waiting to be rescued. I gathered she didn't care for John Knox, but I'm Church of Scotland, of course, so I felt that I ought to say something on his behalf.

She stamped her foot. "You could have done without John Knox," she told me, coming between me and the display of Bibles I was trying to look at. "He has turned your Celtic blood to holy water, and locked your spirit into the soul of a chartered accountant." She looked up at me with a taunting half smile. "Are you going to kiss me or not?"

If she had known how nervous I was, it would have proved her point, but before I had time to consider the blasphemous implications of doing it under Dominie's very roof, I took her by the shoulders and kissed her. It wasn't supposed to be much of a kiss—I pursed my lips the way people do when they're miming a kiss from the window of a train—but she flattened her mouth against mine and moved her head a little. I nearly backed into the case of Bibles.

"You need practice," she said briskly.

"So do you!" I shot back. I had to help her pick up the map of Scotland and twenty postcards that were scattered all over the floor, but we went to lunch right after that, and laughed and talked as if nothing had happened.

We rented a white Morgan roadster for our tour of the Highlands. An old one, of course, but it was in pretty good shape. When she wasn't driving (flying would be a more accurate way of describing it), she'd lean back against the door and sing tuneless Gaelic songs that she must have learned off an Alan Stivell tape. Scottish music, she called it.

It was no good taking the map along when she wouldn't follow it. She'd navigate by instinct, or sheer folly, I sometimes thought. I'd complain about it, but she'd never let me hear the end of it when it worked. Once she took us up a dirt track into some farmer's cow pasture, and I despaired for the car's suspension system, but there in the middle of a stone-studded croft was a fairy ring in the grass and a marker saying that Thomas the Rhymer was believed to have lived near here. I don't know why she chose that path, when there was a perfectly good trunk road and a paved side road to choose from as well, but she said the other roads were too well-traveled for her.

"I wonder why the fairies left Scotland," I mused, trying to humor her.

She answered me in Gaelic. I've no idea what she said.

We nearly got lost trying to navigate around Inverness. The haar swirled around the Morgan like a white shroud, so that we seemed to be entirely alone on the road. I tried to help her by consulting the city map of Inverness, and by looking for road signs, but she told me to be quiet or we'd be lost on that godforsaken road forever. I gave up and went to sleep. Had nightmares about people's faces appearing in patches of fog, but I couldn't make out what they were saying. I woke up when the car stopped; she'd found what she was looking for: Culloden.

I knew I shouldn't have let her go there. She looked out at the flat field buried under the low-lying mists just as if there were something there to watch. "This was so stupid," she said softly, the mist in her eyes. "Where's the glory in it? They brought the wrong size ammunition for the cannon; they left the food in Inverness; they hadn't slept for days; and they charged an army of muskets and bayonets with unwieldy swords."

"It was a long time ago," I said.

"A year for every day I've known you." She smiled. "Well, you'll be safe. I can't see you out there with kilt and claymore, missing a meal."

I nearly said, "Of course I'm safe from a war that's finished," but something about the dark meadow in the fog made me uneasy.

I half expected her to conjure up some family ghosts from the Highland dead, but she just walked around a bit, looked at the cairn of stones commemorating the soldiers, and read the inscriptions on the historical markers.

"It was all so pointless," she said, as we walked back to the car. "Why couldn't they see what was going to happen?"

I was thinking out my answer, involving previous confrontations, discrepancies in weaponry, and inept leadership, when she stepped ankle-deep into a puddle and began to cry. I surrendered my handkerchief, which she proceeded to use to wipe the muddy water from her foot, still crying.

"You're not hurt, for heaven's sake!" I told her. "You're carrying on as if it were blood!"

I thought she was all right by the time we reached Queen's Garden, an old-fashioned bed-and-breakfast place she'd found in some guidebook to Scotland. I couldn't get her to stay in anything that was less than a century old. I sent her in to book the rooms, while I was seeing to the tire pressures on the Morgan. She was waiting for me downstairs when I came in, looking quite at home in a chintz-covered chair. She looked up at me, smiling. "You can bring the bags in later. I want to go to dinner now."

She may have been rather quiet through dinner. I don't know. I was telling her about the Loch Ness Centre, thinking that the monster would be an entertaining distraction from this afternoon's bleakness, but she didn't seem interested. She pushed her dish of apple crumble and custard toward my side of the table, and continued to toy with her napkin. I had just tasted the first forkful of apple, when she said, "I'm not sleeping alone."

I gulped a mouthful of hot dessert, and managed to say, "Well, if you find you can't sleep, tap on my door, and we can come downstairs and talk until you get sleepy."

She smiled. "I booked a double room." She looked like a cat lapping cream, knowing that the disabled bird will not be able to get away.

I didn't quite see what I could do about it. Telling the proprietor that we weren't married and that I wanted a room of my own would make me look foolish, but suppose we ran into someone from Edinburgh? It had to be just a matter of time before friends of my parents ran into us somewhere, and then what? She'd been married at least once (she won't say much about her past), she'd got too much education for her own good, and she equated housework with indentured servitude. This was not the "nice girl" Mum was always on about my bringing home. *Well, perhaps she's just frightened of having nightmares about Culloden,* I thought. There wouldn't be any harm in my sleeping in the other bed, in that case. Except that there wasn't one.

I went through seven copies of *The Scottish Field* after dinner, paying scrupulous attention to window treatments and garden layouts. "Imagine the care they take in planning a fox hunt," I remarked, trying to strike up a conversation with the silent creature watching me from the counterpane. "They have to stop up the earths so that the fox will have no place to retreat to, make sure of the terrain. Such a lot of planning."

"I know," she said.

I read the magazines silently after that, hunched in the tiny chair beside the radiator, in a narrowing circle of yellow light from the rose-china table lamp. She looked asleep, curled up in the middle of the bed, her dark hair spilling onto my pillow. I supposed it *was* going to be my pillow, sooner or later. I undressed as quietly as possible and slid into the bed a good distance away from her. A few moments later I felt her hand like a warm cat's paw along my back, and her lips brushed my shoulder blade.

I rolled over on my stomach and rested my head on my wrists. "Do you have permission to touch me?" I asked, as gently as one might remove a new kitten from velvet curtains.

"May I have permission to touch you?" She sounded amused.

"No."

I heard a little intake of breath—she hadn't expected that—and

I was working out what to say about sin, and propriety, and all the rest of it, but she only said, "He whose love is thin and wise may view John Knox in paradise."

I asked if she'd still read the map for me the next day, and she laughed.

We talked for a long time in the dark after that, about castles and mountains and train wrecks in Tennessee. She lay propped on one elbow, and talked to me as unselfconsciously as ever. After a while, I became so involved in talking that I forgot to be afraid, and I rolled over beside her, lying on my back and talking as if we were tent-mates in Scouts. The spell didn't break when she kissed me, and I found that I knew what came next without thinking about it.

We stayed seven days past our scheduled time to return to Edinburgh, but then she had to leave for America, and I stayed on. I gave her the eight guidebooks to Scotland and all the maps that I had, but I still don't know what she was looking for in the phrases and the mountains and the faces of children in the villages.

At Christmas—surely the bleakest time of year in Scotland, foggy and dark and cold—I had a card from her. On the front was a snow scene of two deer standing in the shadows of a pine forest, and inside she wrote of her work, and people we'd known, and about how a possum had taken to stealing cat food from a dish she left on the porch. Nothing more. But I knew even before I opened it that I was going back.

Southern Comfort

↶

L ove," Vicki used to say, "is like flushing yourself down the toilet: a nice cool ride, and a lot of crap at the end." I was standing in the dorm mail room, rereading Anthony's letter for the fifth time, but it still said the same thing: "Surely, by now you realize there can never be anything more between us. . . ." I would definitely have to talk to Vicki.

I plunged up the stairs toward 308, still clutching the antiseptic green notepaper, and not even crying. I just felt numb all over. Vaguely I wondered what miracle Vicki Baird would accomplish to get Anthony back for me. She was bound to produce one. After all, she was a senior, pinned to a ΔKE, and she had actually invited Joan Baez to her high school commencement exercises. (Joan didn't go, of course, but Vicki had received a nice letter from her secretary explaining that Joan was on a peace march with Dr. King, and wished her well. Vicki had the letter framed and hanging above her Donovan poster.)

Vicki's door was the one with the poster of LBJ and Lady Bird dressed as Bonnie and Clyde. When I got there, a sign tacked to Lyndon's nose said that Vicki had gone to the post office and would be back before dinner. I slumped down beside the door to wait.

How could Anthony do this to me? I was an English major, for God's sake! Didn't I stay in on Friday nights and write to him instead of going out? And no matter how many times people said it was uncool to still be tied to your high school honey, I'd always smile and say that we had been lucky to find each other so young. And now this. It was a judgment, I decided. A curse. I'd laughed when Sophy thought she was pregnant. Back in September, I'd gone to Rosh Hashanah services with her (and became—from force of habit—the first person to genuflect in the UNC Hillel), and she met a med student named Bundschaft. I tried to tell her not to go off and spend the weekend with him, but no! Sophy wanted to experience Life. She came back Sunday night with a green lab coat and a blow-by-blow account of the weekend. Told me I ought to try it with Anthony, and I'd sniffed and said that Southern men didn't expect that kind of thing from their fiancées. I sniffled a little, remembering it. How did I know what Anthony expected? Some Yankee bitch at Duke might be screwing him on the fifty-yard line for all I knew. And then when Sophy thought she was pregnant—well, she had been rather melodramatic about it. Alternately planning to drop out of school and raise it alone or tell no one and brazen out the year. Finally one evening after dinner, when we were all walking back through the parlor where the guys wait on little loveseats for their dates, Sophy announced her latest plan: "We won't tell anybody. And then in May when the time comes for the delivery, you can all come in and help me. We'll boil water in the hot pots—"

At that point the absurdity of the whole situation overcame me—her period was only nine days late—and I dropped to my knees in the parlor, crying: "Oh laws a mussy, Miz Scarlett! I don't know nothin' 'bout birthin' babies!" It was wicked and I deserved to be punished—but it did put a stop to the planning. And then a few days later, Sophy had timidly taken the matter to Vicki, who glanced up from her chemistry book, studied the supplicant for a few seconds and flatly declared: "You aren't pregnant. Go study." At breakfast the next morning, Sophy had announced in hushed tones that Vicki had been proved right. The crisis was over.

I began to relax a little. Anthony ought to be easy after that miracle.

"Hey! McCrory! What are you doing sitting out in the hall?"

I looked up to find Sophy's roommate P. J. Purdue hovering over me, dressed as usual in a black turtleneck and black slacks. She looked like a drill sergeant's impersonation of Mia Farrow. I didn't want to tell her about Anthony. P. J. Purdue was not what you'd call a sympathetic listener. In fact she was a Vietcong of the sexual revolution; her exploits had passed into campus mythology. P. J. Purdue had once humiliated a flasher in the campus arboretum. She'd been walking back from class when the guy jumped out of the bushes and exposed himself. He'd picked the wrong victim. Purdue said: "Are you bragging or complaining? Listen, buddy, I've seen Vienna sausages that were more impressive than that! Wait! Before you jerk off, I'll lend you my tweezers!" The guy slunk off into the shrubbery and never worked that park again. I could imagine Purdue's reaction to my broken heart. Purdue had lost her virginity in high school in the backseat of a '63 Corvair, and she claims her reaction was: "That's it? You mean, that was *it*?" I sometimes wondered if there was a Trappist monastery in Charlotte filling up with victims of Purdue's sexual contempt.

Before I could think up an excuse for camping outside Vicki's door, Purdue said: "Anyway, you're just who I wanted to see. I want your wastebasket."

"My *wastebasket*?"

"Yeah. My parents are coming down for the weekend, and ours is filled with cigarette ashes and God-knows-what. So we want to borrow yours." She walked away. "Bring it down to our room!" she yelled back.

I was too dazed with personal sorrow to argue. I gave up my vigil outside 308, and went to deliver my chaste and virginal wastebasket to their den of iniquity. Sophy was sprawled out on her bed under the poster of the statue of David—with a fig leaf taped in a strategic area. She waved a languid hand at me as I came in.

"Hi, kid! Still subscribing to *Modern Bride*?"

"Not for long," I said. "I just got a kiss-off letter from Anthony." There's something about Sophy and Purdue that makes people blasé about anything.

Purdue looked up from *The Village Voice*. "So that's why you were camped outside Baird's door! Trauma case. Tough luck about the boyfriend, though!"

"What should I do?" I quavered.

Purdue shook her head. "Nah. All that emotional counseling crap is strictly Baird's department. Now if you had a sexual problem, I'd be the one to go to!"

Sophy snickered. "*Not* Baird!"

Purdue shrugged. "Oh, you mean the phone call? That was a stitch. But we were freshmen then."

"What phone call?"

"Freshman year for us. Vicki Baird was always a missionary, even back then. Everybody's aunt. But she was pretty naive herself, having just got here from Middle Earth, North Carolina, or someplace. So one day the hall phone rings and she answers it, and this guy says he's going to jack off." Purdue made the appropriate hand motion to illustrate the procedure. "Got it? Yeah, your basic obscene phone call. Well, Baird was such a twit with her shrink complex that she thought he was going to commit suicide. So she stays on the phone with him trying to talk him out of it, for chrissakes! 'Oh, don't do that. Life is beautiful. I'm sure there are people who care about you.' Finally, the guy says he feels much better, and she says she's glad. Guy says: 'Can I call you back?' And the idiot says: 'Oh, yes! Any time you feel like this, you can call and talk to me!' So Baird hangs up the phone feeling like a minister of grace. That glow lasted until dinner that night. We're sitting at the table—"

Sophy stopped laughing long enough to interrupt. "Yeah, Baird says to P. J.: 'Oh, Purdue, some poor guy called our hall this afternoon and he was so depressed he was going to jack off!' And Purdue *freaked*. Coffee went everywhere."

"Did you tell her—"

"Yeah, she took it pretty well. Baird's okay. She's a big help to sensitive types." She looked meaningfully at Sophy.

"I've aged a lot since September!" snapped Sophy.

She had, too. Since the Bundschaft incident, Sophy had taken up the pill, and a succession of rugged primates who may have been football players. She called this her zaftig period, which we took to mean something like *hunks*. No one was ever exactly sure what Sophy was talking about, because she had arrived at our Waspish Southern school from Queens, New York, speaking something which was decidedly *not* English. "Listen!" she'd say to us in the laundry room. "Don't let me nosh, anymore, okay? I hate to kvetch about my weight all the time, but I have such tsuris with my metabolism—" And we'd say: "You wanna run that one around the barn one more time, honey chile?" Mutual comprehension arrived in a few weeks' time. Now I knew what tsuris was. Boy, did I know!

"Listen, thanks for the trash can," Purdue was saying. "And you know, if you wanna write that shit Anthony a nasty letter, I'll be glad to help, but—" She shrugged. "Advice to the lovelorn—that's Baird's department."

I nodded solemnly and trudged back to 308. The sign was off Lyndon's nose, so I knocked.

"Come in!"

Vicki was sitting on her bed, frowning at a chemistry book. She looked up when I came in and her eyes widened. After leaving Purdue's room—where crying is *not* permitted—I had let all my misery wash back over me until I had reached a climax of self-pity. I looked wretched enough to command her full attention.

"Mary Frances McCrory! What is the matter?"

I tossed her the letter with a terrible smile that indicated that I was incapable of speech. She began to read Anthony's inhibited scrawl, her eyes getting wider and wider at every word. "Damn!" she said, jumping up from the bed.

She began rummaging around in the medicine chest, muttering something about Duke students, which Anthony was, and bastards, which Anthony had certainly proven to be. Finally she turned around holding a prescription bottle, from which she extracted two white pills. "Valium," she said, filling a glass. "Take two. I'll be right back." She hurried out of the room in the direction of the phone, while I sat there sniffling with a mental image of Anthony superimposed over scenes of my becoming a nun or perhaps opening a small lending library. I was just administering Chaulmoogra oil to a leper in the African veldt when Vicki reappeared and announced: "You are dating a brother at the Phi Kapp House tonight. He is probably a lizard, and you're going to enjoy yourself if it kills you."

This was my wisdom from the oracle of Addison Hall? "Vicki, I can't!" I wailed. "I just want to slink off into my room and never come out again. If I even look at a boy today, I'll probably throw up!"

Vicki nodded. "I see. And what do you want?"

I could practically see her looking around for the mice and pumpkins. "I want Anthony back," I blubbered. "I haven't dated anybody else since I was sixteen! I'll never love anybody else! I want Anthony to hold me like he used to—"

Vicki was brisk. "That's enough of that! Hysteria makes you puffy. And you have to be presentable by seven o'clock. Go take a shower."

I looked at her piteously, through brimming eyes. "I *have* to go?"

"You have to." Then she relented a little. "Well . . . if it's too much of an ordeal, then at ten o'clock you can tell him you're a diabetic and you have to come back to the dorm to take an insulin shot." Vicki believed in lying.

I said I'd go.

A few minutes later I stood in the shower contemplating my own misery. My own true love had just proved to be a creep and

no one understood. Maybe I should have stood on the ledge of
the new library building until a whole crowd gathered and the
Channel Five news department sent a camera crew over. How
would you like your letter read on the six o'clock news, Anthony?
Meanwhile, I was stuck going to a fraternity party with a total
stranger. I was not the frat party type. Anthony and I were strictly
free flicks and duplicate bridge people. It was going to be awful.

"Flush!" came a scream from the other room.

Automatically I stepped out of the path of the shower, as I
heard the whoosh of a toilet flushing. Strictly a reflex action; if I'd
thought about it, I would have stayed under the shower and gotten
scalded. It would have gotten me out of the blind date anyway—
and who knows, if my frail form were swathed in bandages in
Memorial Hospital, maybe Anthony . . . After that I waited for
somebody else to flush, but nobody did.

Addison Hall has neurotic toilets, so one important feature of
freshman orientation is toilet training. If you flush while somebody is taking a shower, all the cold water to the shower is cut off,
and you have an irate burn victim to confront. So we devised a
system whereby if someone is taking a shower, you yell "Flush!"
before you do it, so they'll have time to crawl in the soap rack until
the crisis is past. The older girls spent a lot of time in orientation
programming us to yell flush. I internalized this command so well
that when I went home for Thanksgiving, I got up at seven A.M.
and yelled "Flush," forgetting I was at home. My father yelled
back: "It won't obey spoken commands!"

When I got back to my room, everyone had already gone down
to dinner, but there was a note on my door from Vicki: *Don't
wear black!* How did she know? I skipped dinner, as I thought suitable for a person in my state of bereavement. After finishing off
a third of a package of Oreos to pass the time, I halfheartedly put
on my navy blue church dress and went down to Vicki's room for
inspection and final instructions.

"Navy blue." She nodded. "I approve. You've made your statement without being obvious. Now just be relaxed and try to enjoy yourself. And for heaven's sake, don't talk about Anthony!"

"I have no small talk," I said mournfully. "What can I say to this person?"

Vicki thought for a moment. "Well," she said. "I used to pretend to be an exchange student from Denmark. That was always good for a tour of the campus, but that won't work for you, Mary Frances. It takes practice. You're just going to have to play it by ear."

"Are you sure this is what I should do? Go out with this guy?"

"I'm positive. It's exactly what you should do."

"What's he like, anyway?"

"I have no idea. I have never met him. Was that the house phone?" She jumped up and ran out into the hall, and I heard her say: "By the grace of God and the genius of Alexander Graham Bell, you have reached the third floor of Addison Hall. . . ." It was too late to invent a migraine. He was here.

She walked me down the stairs for moral support. "It's going to be just fine, Mary Frances. Let go of the banister." We peeped out the doorway into the parlor and saw him standing nervously in front of the gilt-frame mirror.

Fortunately, he looked nothing like Anthony. He was tall and angular, with hair, eyes, and skin all the same neutral shade of tan. His face was impassive. He looked as if he had never had a thought in his life.

"I couldn't warm up to him if we were cremated together!" I hissed to Vicki.

"He looks like a moron. Now go out there and be charming!" she hissed back, giving me a push.

I walked over to the Brown Thing and gave myself up. He acknowledged my existence with a grunt, and we put on our coats and walked out into the rain. In the seven minutes it took to walk from Addison to his fraternity house, we managed to cover a great deal of trivia. Such as: where are you from? what's your major? what year are you? and do you know Bernie Roundtree from your hometown? In seven minutes we had exhausted every possible conversational gambit I could come up with for the entire evening. And I couldn't become a diabetic until ten o'clock.

I learned that the lizard's name was Hampton Branch III, that he was a history major, planning to go into law or politics, and several other bits of information that passed through my mind leaving no impression whatsoever. *Perhaps I should have written myself a script,* I thought. Hampton and I didn't talk much for the rest of the walk. There weren't many subjects that he was qualified to discuss, and I wanted to commune with my sorrow. I didn't feel like telling him the history of nursery rhymes ("Ring around the Roses" is a recitation of plague symptoms), which is what I usually do to entertain strangers. His fraternity house was a blur in the mist. I wouldn't be able to recognize it if I saw it again. When I try to picture it, I get *House of Usher* with Vincent Price standing on the porch.

I followed Hampton downstairs to the party room, where two hundred identical people were herded together shouting at each other over the music. The room was dimly lit, tiled, and furnished entirely in contemporary American bodies, arranged in small circular groups, holding drinks, laughing. Unfortunately they were alive, and might have to be conversed with.

Hampton, I noticed, had lurched over to the jukebox and was seeing to it that "My Girl" would play thirty-six times in succession. Dutifully, I followed.

I was standing there studying the checkerboard pattern on the floor, when I suddenly realized with horror that I had not spoken for nearly twenty minutes.

"Hamp, I'm sorry I'm so quiet!" I blurted. "But today I just broke up with the guy I've been going with for three years."

"Gee," said Hamp.

An electronic scream shook the room, and the lights on the juke-box faded out. A combo, with the name THE FABULOUS PROPHETS OF ECU painted on their drums, had just set up in a corner of the room, and they were either warming up or playing their opening number. It was hard to tell which. The couples surged toward the dance floor, pressing us up against the bandstand with approximately two feet of space in which to move. Hampton was spinning around like a wound-up toy mouse to the blare of the band. I moved mechanically to the rhythm, but really the noise was wrapped around me like a cushion, too loud to scream through, holding my thoughts inside. I thought about all the trivial things I'd been saying to Hampton, and all the real conversations I used to have with Anthony. It was an odd wake to bury three years. Hampton disappeared briefly between dances and came back with two plastic cups of warm beer, one of which he pressed into my hand. I smiled and nodded, indicating that I understood I was to drink it. I sipped enough of it to get the level down so it wouldn't slosh while I was dancing, I had only managed to drink two-thirds of it. Hampton, by then, was several beers away.

I wondered what time it was. Nine-thirty by now, surely. But on reflection, I decided that I could think about Anthony here as well as anywhere. The music prevented conversation, and the company was certainly no distraction.

The last time I'd seen Anthony, we went to dinner at the Pines, and then sat down under a tree in the arboretum and talked about life. It had been dark and quiet there, with stars shining between the leaves, and Anthony had held me while we talked. I had felt that I really belonged there. Now I didn't belong anywhere, and I didn't know what to do or say when smiling cardboard people came up and screamed imitation questions. I wished I could ex-plain all this to Anthony, because he would understand. But he didn't care now. He didn't care at all.

There was a sudden silence in the room, and I was there again. The Fabulous Prophets of ECU began to play a slow, sad melody, "I'll Be There," and people began to surge together. Hampton returned from orbit and looked at me with a curiously human expression. Without a word, he held me. I clung to him, occasionally remembering to move my feet, thinking how good it felt to be close to somebody. It felt warm and safe . . . and . . . just the way it always did with Anthony.

Suddenly I knew why Vicki had sent me. She wanted to put an emotional Band-Aid on my suppurated ego. And I nearly fell for it. But she was missing the point: I didn't want to feel better, I wanted to get back at Anthony! By the end of the slow dance, Hampton and I were looking at each other with new interest: I was seeing an instrument for revenge, and he was seeing a five-foot-three-inch mound of fresh meat. When he suggested that we go for a walk in the arboretum, I didn't even pretend to think it over.

We left the party hand in hand and headed for the arboretum in silence; we still couldn't think of anything to say to each other. Hampton led me to a spot between two large azalea bushes that he apparently knew quite well, and we sat down on the wet ground. Fortunately it had stopped raining. At this point I considered mentioning my inexperience, but I decided to rely on dance etiquette: let him lead and do your best to keep up. What followed could best be compared to having a pelvic exam while someone blew beer and Lavoris fumes in your face. After a discreet interval—the time it took for Hampton to smoke one Benson & Hedges cigarette—he walked me back to my dorm. As we reached the front door, Hampton shuffled his feet awkwardly and mumbled: "I'll call you."

"Yeah, sure," I said. "Good night." I didn't offer to tell him my real name; I was inside and running up the stairs before he got to the edge of the porch.

When I reached the third floor, the hall was dark and quiet—most everybody was in Vicki's room and the door was half open. Confessions would be heard until one A.M. I hesitated outside her door for a moment, staring down the barrel of LBJ's machine gun, and then I turned and walked off toward the lair of P. J. Purdue.

There comes a time when you outgrow Vicki Baird.

A Snare as Old as Solomon

~

Franchette belted her car coat over her swollen belly and eased her way down the icy back steps. Ramer was still in the shed. Her breath made little puffs of smoke in the chill morning air as she stumbled down the path toward the road. She hurried as if she could still hear the cries coming from the crate out front, or the sound of the hatchet on the hen's neck.

She didn't look back as she made for the dirt road beyond the trees. The crocuses she'd planted were beginning to put up green shoots. It was going to be an early spring, and that was good. Soon she wouldn't have to worry about the pipes freezing, or about having to carry firewood in her condition, when Ramer went out drinking and left her alone. She couldn't stop to look at the plants just now, or to check for deer tracks in the yard. She wished she could do something about the prisoner in the crate, but she couldn't. She had left the kettle boiling on the stove, and the butcher knife laid out on the newspapers, just like Ramer had asked her to, but she had to get out of there.

If she ignored the catch in her side, she could be around the bend to Della's trailer in five minutes. Della worked the lunch shift at her uncle's diner in town, so she'd be leaving soon. If Franchette said she had a doctor's appointment on account of the baby, Della would let her ride in to town with her for nothing. She couldn't tell Della the real reason she wanted to go. Della's man was living over across the river with a bleached blond dental assistant, and he never sent Della a cent for the kids or the payments on the Pontiac. Della would laugh and say that pregnant women always got fanciful, that Ramer was being protective like a man ought to be, and he was a heap better than some. Maybe he was being protective, but Franchette didn't think so. She thought he was saving his own pride at the cost of hers. And the worst part was the way he'd done it. It was like the Bible story turned inside out, but she hadn't seen that until today. Della couldn't be made to understand. She'd say: "Ramer killed that old stray hen. So what?"

It had been no use trying to talk about it to Ramer either. They had been married a year now, and already the talk had run out. Used to be, Ramer would listen to her way of looking at things, her dreaming out loud, but now when she tried to talk to him, he'd look at her for a minute and then go back to what he was doing. It wasn't all his fault, though. Being out of work was hard on a man's pride. When he took her high school diploma down off the wall, she hadn't said anything, because she knew it was reminding him that he'd quit in tenth grade, and maybe if he hadn't he'd be working. Things had been different when he had the job in the sawmill. He'd wanted her to finish high school before the wedding and at graduation he'd showed up in his white tie and suit coat and had taken her out to dinner at the Beef Barn to celebrate. Those were happy times. They talked about her getting a typing job in town so that they could buy a new truck and maybe a dish-shaped antenna for the television. He had let her go and get the birth control pills at the clinic, so they could save up and have a few things before the babies started to arrive. But that was before. Now if she even brought home a book from the bookmobile, he accused her of showing off her education. So Franchette had given up reading and started a quilt. Sometimes she thought something had died inside Ramer, and that he'd be damned if he'd let it live anywhere else.

That morning Ramer had been staring out the kitchen window,

same as always. The want ads page of the *Scout* lay crumpled beside his coffee mug, ready to be thrown out with the coffee grounds. First thing after breakfast (oatmeal mostly; eggs at the first of the month), Franchette would clear up the dishes and Ramer would run his finger down the want ads. It never took him very long to go through them. Since the mine shut down and the sawmill laid off, there weren't any jobs; and if there was one—say, painting a barn—there were twenty people trying to get it, and the one closest related to the barn owner got hired on. So far that hadn't been Ramer. He was staring out at the pasture and the hills beyond as if he were looking for deer to come down the ridge, but he wasn't seeing. Franchette cleared up the breakfast dishes in silence.

No use trying to talk to him. No use, either, asking for the want ads. She'd tried that when he first got laid off, and he'd given her a cold, dead look and said: "What's the matter, Miss High and Mighty? You want to be the boss of this family now?" She'd snapped back that it would be better than the welfare, and Ramer had left the house and hadn't come back for three hours. After that, she'd try to sneak and read them before she put them in the garbage, but it hadn't been any use. Ramer had seen to that.

"I'm going to kill that damned chicken!" Ramer had shouted, bringing his fist down hard on the kitchen table.

Franchette wanted to tell him to leave it be. It wasn't doing any harm this early in the spring. But she knew that taking up for it would only make him madder. Anyway, she didn't think he could catch it; that old hen knew about people, at least enough to stay out of range. She was a scraggly old Red, gone wild from somebody's farm, and living on whatever she could forage. Wasn't enough meat on her to make a mouthful; anybody could see that. All winter she'd clucked and rambled across their yard, a friendly sight to Franchette, and to Ramer a sign of one more thing he couldn't control. Sometimes he would go out and shy rocks at her, but he never came close to a hit, and the next day, she'd be back like nothing had happened.

A couple of days after the first thaw, the hen had showed up with one puny chick following behind her—probably the only survivor of an early nest. They'd pecked and cackled at each other in the patches of late snow, while Ramer sat at the window and watched them, day after day.

He never made any move to catch the pair of them, and never said anything about their presence in the yard. He just watched them with eyes like slits. Franchette thought Ramer might be easing up toward the old hen, seeing as how he was going to be a father himself in a few months' time, but that hope had ended today. He must have been planning it for a couple of days, since he put the wooden crate on the front porch and the gun by the front door.

He hadn't said anything else after the first outburst. He just grabbed the half-eaten toast from Franchette's plate and walked out into the yard. Franchette watched him from the window. He stood there stock still in his work clothes, no coat or gloves, and waited for the hen to come closer. Then he threw down a piece of bread. The hen cocked her head at him, like she didn't like what she saw. She bustled away toward the trees, but her chick hadn't learned better. It came up to see what had fallen. Ramer tossed a smaller piece of bread and backed up toward the porch. The chick followed him at a careful distance, gulping down bread crumbs, until Ramer was on the porch, tossing crumbs into the flower bed by the steps. The hen came a few yards out of the trees and shrieked at her baby, but it was too dumb or too hungry to hear her. Finally, Ramer dumped the rest of the bread crumbs into the flower bed and eased the wooden crate toward the edge of the porch. When the chick bent down to peck the bread, he leaned out and slammed the crate down on top of it. Franchette put her fist in her mouth to keep from yelling at him to let it loose. She thought he would wring its neck then and there, but instead he got up and slammed into the house.

"What did you want to do that for?" she asked when he got inside.

"You'll find out," he said without looking at her. He was watching the crate.

The chick had found it couldn't get out, and was flapping around inside, screaming in terror. You could see it through the wooden slats, thrashing against the top and sides. The hen could see it, too. She answered its cries with distressed sounds of her own and edged nearer the box. Every step or so, she'd cock her head and look up at the house where Ramer waited, and she'd back up a few feet, but the chick's cries always pulled her closer. It took a good five minutes for her to get to the crate. The chick's cries were coming louder than ever, and she circled the crate, peering in at it and screeching.

Ramer picked up the gun and eased open the door.

"Oh, Ramer, don't!" Franchette whispered, grabbing his sleeve.

"I guess that settled it," he said, grinning at her, and he was gone.

She wished she had gone back to the kitchen and not watched Ramer level the gun at the frantic hen. The hen had looked away from the crate when he came out; she had to have seen the gun, but she stayed there by the crate as if it didn't matter. He got her with one shot. The chick was still shrieking inside the crate when Ramer picked up its mother's body and carried it off to the shed to dress it out. He would scald off the feathers and gut it, and then he'd bring it to the house for Franchette to cook. Franchette knew that if she ever tried to eat that hen, she'd never be done with vomiting, but that wasn't why she had run.

It was the way Ramer had grinned when he said "I guess that settled it." It had puzzled her for a while, trying to think what it reminded her of. She had been setting the kettle on to boil when it came to her. After she'd asked for the want ads that time, and then gotten Della to ask her uncle if he could use another waitress, Ramer had told her to wait till after Christmas to start to work, and she'd been happy that he'd taken it so well. It had almost been like old times again for a couple of weeks. Ramer had been so loving again. He'd thrown away her birth control pills, because they cause cancer, he said. And he told her he'd use something to make it safe. He never had, though. And when around Christmastime, she'd known she was pregnant, he smiled just that same funny way, and said that settled it. She was going to be a mother. She couldn't work. No wife of his was going to leave her kid and go to work. He didn't seem very happy about the baby, though; he never wanted to talk about what to name it, or anything. He'd just say that she had to stay home and look after it.

It wasn't until she saw him shoot the hen today that she understood what he'd done and why. It was like the story about Solomon: when the king offered to cut the disputed baby in two, and the real mother was willing to give it up rather than see it killed. That poor old hen had been willing to do anything to save her baby. And Ramer had tried to make her give up her life, the chance to make something of herself, using their baby as a weapon. But Ramer was no Solomon; he would have cut the baby in two, just to make sure that everyone was equally unhappy.

Ramer hadn't even noticed her when she came in the shed. She had been crying, but they were silent tears. By the time she had walked from the kitchen out to the shed, she wasn't angry anymore, just sorrowful that everything had turned out so wrong, and that Ramer had turned into somebody she had to escape from. The gun had been propped up against the wheelbarrow; he didn't even turn around when she picked it up. He was intent on his butchering, and his hands were red to the wrists. Franchette walked around in front of him, balancing the gun around her swollen belly. He did look up then, just as she fired. She put the gun in his hands, and went back to the house to wash away the blood. The hen's blood and Ramer's were all mixed together on her hands.

She spent the walk to Della's house taking deep breaths, trying to feel calm again, and thinking how she should react when she got home that afternoon and discovered that Ramer had shot himself in the shed while cleaning his gun. Maybe she should be real upset, and then say that she couldn't sit around the house all day dwelling on the tragedy, and that a job would take her mind off things.

She stopped at Della's mailbox to catch her breath. In the white tube labeled *Scout* was a rolled-up newspaper like the one she'd left behind on the breakfast table. Franchette eased it out and carried it up the walk to Della's front door. On the way to town she was going to read the want ads.

The Witness

It happened on no particular day—not close enough to Christmas or his birthday for Sam to mark the time. It was warm, though, because he was playing outside, and there were white flowers on the tree in Aunt Till's yard. Her cat Old Painter lay tucked in the hedge, keeping one yellow eye on the birds wobbling on the clothesline. He scarcely moved when Sam crept close to his hiding place and snapped a twig from the hedge. Sam was thinking about elephants.

Dad ought to be home soon. Maybe he could get him to tell the story again. Sam walked to the ditch at the edge of the yard and looked down the gravel pike toward town. No one in sight; it was too early yet for Dad to have walked the three miles home from the machine shop. The ghost train had just rattled past on the tracks behind the house.

When the family first rented the white frame house, the year Sam was three, it was supposed to be haunted. Pictures fell off the wall for no reason; dishes rattled on the shelf and sometimes fell. Something white had been seen at night moving behind the house. A few weeks after they moved in, their neighbor "Aunt" Till had been hanging out her washing and had called across the hedge to pass the time of day with Sam's mother. The two women met at the privet hedge, and Aunt Till talked a mile a minute. Addie, who like all Solitary McCrorys lived in mortal fear of being talked at, stood twisting her apron until she came up with something to say.

"What about them ghosts?"

She started to recite the peculiar goings-on, but by the time she finished Aunt Till was smiling and shaking her head.

"Shoot far," she said. "When them heavy coal drags come south or the time freight goes by headin' north, that whole little house of yourn purt near shakes itself to pieces. No wonder yer pictures fall. You'll fall out of bed if you ain't keerful."

But the white phantom out back?

Aunt Till studied about it. "Well," she allowed, "sometimes of an evening I go out back there in my nightgown, looking for that no-good rascal Old Painter."

They weren't bothered by haints after that, though Old Painter continued to roam and squall. They took to calling that northbound freight the Ghost Train, first as a family joke, and then from force of habit.

Sam was twisting the hedge twig into the damp ground, trying to make it stand up by itself. He pulled the leaves off the lower part of the stem to give himself a better grip. After a few more turns the stick found a wobbly purchase in the wet earth. Sam scooped up a handful of dirt and patted it around the base of the twig. He wondered if it would take root if he left it long enough, like Grammaw Hemrick's switch. Every time they went up home to Preachin' Grampaw's, Sam would stare at the mulberry tree in the front yard, and try to picture Grammaw as a young bride from Sinking Creek riding sidesaddle over the mountains with a young black-haired Preachin' Grampaw.

He must have heard tell a dozen times how she got off her horse at her husband's homeplace and stuck that riding switch in the ground in the front yard, where it grew into a mulberry tree with limbs strong enough to support him and Jamie both for berry-picking. Sam liked going up-home even if he was a little scared of his stern old grandfather. The house was always full of grown-up uncles, and there was Jamie, the youngest, who was only two years older than Sam, even if he was an uncle. That mulberry tree was the least of the wonders up in Pigeon Roost. The uncles had rigged up a generator in the barn and made their own electricity with creek water, so that the old homeplace had real electric lights, while Sam's parents' house like the rest of those in town was still using oil lamps. Sam liked to hear the uncles tell how they rigged up the old waterwheel on the gristmill with the materials Lewis brought back from up north, and how they wired up the house, the barn, the outhouse, the chicken shed, and even the backyard and put in electric lights. Then Francis would tell one of his stories about coon-hunting or bee-tracking. He always had a couple of hives in white boxes down near the creek. Last, and best, was Sam's daddy's turn. Wesley, the town-dweller now, would allow as how it was all right to track coons or play with your mechanical toys, but he was a man of experience: he'd been there when they hanged the elephant. Sometimes he'd even get Grammaw to take down the family album and he'd turn to a picture of himself and announce: "That was the day they done it." The photograph showed a solemn young man with the Hemrick cheekbones staring into the camera. It was a close shot of his head and shoulders against a gray sky; there was no sign of the elephant or its railroad gallows, but Sam never forgot which picture was the crucial one, proving that his daddy had actually been there.

Sam tested the twig with his forefinger. It gave a little to the pressure, but remained firmly in position. The gallows was ready. Now he'd go and get the tiny wooden elephant that Dad had carved for him. It took Sam a while to get back out of the house, once he got in. He found the elephant right off, but when he went to ask his mother for twine, she'd put him to work setting the jars of home-canned pickles and beans on the table. She was busy in the kitchen frying up side-meat and potatoes for supper. By the time he got back out, Dad was already home, chopping firewood for the kitchen range.

"Don't get too close here," he warned when Sam stopped to watch. "Wood chip might catch you in the eye."

Sam nodded and took a step back, but kept watching. Dad wouldn't be doing any storytelling now—too busy. Once he got the stove wood chopped, they'd have to go in and eat, and by then it might be too late for him to be allowed outside. Sam thought about this stay of execution for his wooden elephant. He almost had the story down by heart, anyway. He decided to go back to the twig and do it from memory. He could always ask Dad later if he forgot any of the parts to the story.

Sam walked over to the hedge and took the string and the carving out of his pocket, and lay down in the grass beside the gallows-twig. He wrapped the twine once around the tiny elephant's neck, and began to experiment with different ways of wrapping the end to make a knot. As he worked, he thought the story to himself in the words Dad always used.

"Her name was Murderous Mary—leastways that's what they called her after Kingsport. She was a performing elephant with one of them little traveling circuses, and they were doing a show in Kingsport. Some figure she had a new trainer; boy didn't seem to know much about the beasts, seems like. He was a-setting on her head and parading all them circus elephants to a water hole, when Mary spied a watermelon rind by the side of the road and she went for it. Well, when she veered out of line, that feller on her head, he jerked at her hard with a spear-tipped stick that they have, but he musta done it too hard because Mary threw back her head and let out a bellow. Then before he knowed what was a-happening, she reached around with her trunk and snatched him off her back and threw him at a lemonade stand.

"He probably coulda lived through that, but Mary wasn't about to let him. She went over to him and stepped on his head, and that was all she wrote. That was one dead trainer. The blacksmith run out of his shop right then with a 32-20 pistol and put a couple of shots into her, but it didn't do no good. They say she didn't even act like she felt it. I wasn't there when it happened. That was in Kingsport. They got her on back to the circus with the rest of 'em and she was in the show that same evening.

"By morning, though, people had been a-studying about it and decided that if she'd gone and killed a man, she'd best be made to pay the price. They couldn't do the job in Kingsport, though. Warn't no gun around that could put her down. I've heerd they tried to electrocute her, but that didn't do no good. Said she just danced a little, that's all.

"Then somebody took a notion they ought to hang her, and the circus came on over to Erwin. It mighta been a-coming here anyway. Mary was still a-working. Wasn't no place to lock her up. They used her to push the wagons off'n the freight cars and set the tent poles up, and that afternoon, when the show was over, they took her down to the railroad yards, where they kept the big derrick—"

"Get in the house!" The voice in Sam's head was drowned out by the same voice from behind him, the quiet kind of yelling that really meant business.

Sam looked up at his father. For a moment he thought that Dad was angry about his elephant game, but then he saw that he wasn't even looking at Sam. He kept glancing toward the back-yard. Before Sam could get to his feet, Dad jerked him up by the scruff of his trousers, and gave him a swat on the bottom.

"I said: *git!*"

Sam got.

He ran for the house without a word, because he could tell from Dad's voice and the look on his face that something was up. Dad was still standing there in the yard. Sam glanced over at the wood-pile beside the car shed. The ax was stuck in a log, just where Dad had left it. He took the steps two at a time and slammed the front door behind him.

In the small parlor, Sam looked around. Mom was still in the kitchen, seeing to the biscuits, or maybe she was in their room feeding Frances Lee. Anyhow, she hadn't seen him come in. He hoped she hadn't heard the door. Walking as quiet as he could to make up for the door-slamming, Sam slipped off to his room at the back of the house. The window beside his bed looked out on the backyard and the railroad tracks. It was a little, bitty square of a window set high up the wall just to let light in, but Sam knew that if he stood tiptoe on the top of his mattress he could just see out of it. He used to count the cars on the night train that way when the folks thought he was already asleep.

Sam scrambled up on his bed, and braced his hands against the wall to steady himself. When he stood up on tiptoe, his eyes and nose just cleared the sill of the window.

Dad was standing a foot or two away from the side of the out-house, his hands in his pockets, like he was waiting, but Sam couldn't see for what. No train was coming. The track in front of him was empty, and past it was Old Man Larson's pasture, then the woods, then Buffalo Mountain, like the back of a big green elephant against the red sky. Sam turned his head again to see what Dad was doing, and a movement down the tracks caught his eye.

Down the tracks walked a young black-haired man in a gray suit coat and bib overalls. He was a good long way away, but he kept walking slowly down the tracks, between the rails, not on the rails like Sam did when he was playing tightrope walker. Sam looked to see where he was headed, and by then he had got it fig-ured out. Up the tracks came a tall, sandy-haired man in white painter's overalls.

And Sam had a ringside seat!

The two of them kept walking toward each other, not saying a word. When one of them got level with Aunt Till's house and the other got level with Sam's, Sam saw Dad duck behind the out-house, and he heard the crash and whine of revolvers. He just had time to see the gun in Black Hair's hand before the man fell on his back. Sandy Hair stood still for a minute watching him, and then he turned and walked into Sam's yard, where Dad met him. They talked to each other for a moment and Sam could see Sandy Hair pointing to the blue-steel revolver he still carried. Dad nodded, and Sandy walked past him into the car shed. Dad made no move to follow him. He came out almost at once and left. Sam noticed that he wasn't carrying the gun anymore.

He turned to look at Black Hair on the railroad tracks. An older man in a black coat had reached him, and was getting him to his feet. Sam could see the red splotch on the bib of Black Hair's overalls. The older man had put his shoulder under Black Hair's arm and was half carrying him down the railroad embankment and into Sam's yard. Dad spoke to the older man for a few moments— the hurt man had his eyes closed and didn't say anything.

Then Dad went into the car shed and backed out the Model T Ford. He helped lay the hurt man in the backseat of the car, and then he got behind the wheel, nodding for the older man to get in. The man motioned for Dad to wait and disappeared into the car shed. In less than a minute he came hurrying out and got in the car. Dad backed down the driveway, and Sam ran to the front window to see which way they were headed. He got there in time to see a flash of black turning up dust in the direction of Johnson City.

"Reckon we'll eat," said Mom, coming up beside him.

It still wasn't dark. Dad had come back home and parked the Ford in the driveway, but he didn't come in the house to eat. Sam waited until Mom got busy in the kitchen with the washing up and then he slipped out the front door. Dad had a bucket of water and a rag, and he was cleaning off the backseat. Sam watched him scrub the leather seat covers with the rag and then wring it out red into the water bucket.

"Is he gonna be all right?"

"Like as not," said Dad, without looking up. He didn't turn around or leave off scrubbing until he heard the other car pull up

into the driveway. The second black Ford stopped a few feet be-
hind Dad's car, and the driver got out and came toward them.
He was a big man with a white coat and a Wyatt Earp mustache.
On his finger was a big ring in the shape of a snake, with two red
stones for eyes. Sam knew him from church: he was the High
Sheriff of the County.

"Go on off and play," said Dad.

Sam trudged off as slow as he could safely go, to the spot by
Aunt Till's hedge where the elephant was still hanging. He took it
down from the hedge twig and stuffed it in his pocket. If he took
it back to the house now, he could walk past the cars and hear
what was being said. Sam took the elephant back out of his pocket
so that his errand would be conspicuous, and, dangling it on a
string in front of him, he started back for the house. The High
Sheriff was standing there with his hands on his hips, looking at
Dad with his head cocked sideways like a rooster.

"I wish I could help you, Sheriff," Dad was saying as Sam drew
close. "But I didn't see a thing."

"You sure now?"

"Well, I was in the car shed here, arranging some tools when it
happened, so I—"

Sam saw that Dad had stopped talking because he'd noticed
him listening. Dad hadn't seen the fight? But Sam had seen! He
was just opening his mouth to tell the wonderful tale to the High
Sheriff when Dad grabbed his arm and swatted him on the bottom
again. He chased him into the house and told him in no uncertain
terms to stay there, so Sam had to watch the rest of the conversation through the parlor window, hiding in the curtains.

After a few more minutes of conversation, the High Sheriff got
back in his car and drove off. Dad came in the house then.

"Is there gonna be a trial?" asked Sam's mother from the kitchen
doorway.

Dad shook his head. "No witnesses. And the wounded man
don't know who shot him." He turned to Sam who wanted to ask

questions, but thought better of it. "Don't play in the car shed for a couple of days."

Sam nodded, and went off to his room. That question didn't need asking.

The next day while Dad was at work and Mom was making bread, Sam pilfered the car shed. The sides of the shed were lined with shelves filled with fruit jars, tools, and odd scraps of wood and metal. Sam picked his way past the two-by-fours and the brass-bound trunk and began to investigate the bottom shelf where the tools were kept. When he noticed three red-and-white fishing floats on the shelf, he opened Dad's tackle box and found the first revolver, a .32 special, nickel-plated. It was a shiny thing with red rubber grips on the handle, and it used to hang by the trigger guard on a nail over the bed. One of the family stories that they told up-home was how Sam had been a fretful baby the summer he was teething, and he used to cry for the shiny toy hanging on the wall above him. Finally Mom unloaded it and gave it to him to play with, and the rubber handle grips felt so good to his itching gums that it did keep him quiet. When Dad finally traded it for that Atwater Kent table radio, it still had Sam's tooth marks on the grips. Sam held the Smith & Wesson up to the light, using both hands to steady it. One of the cylinders was empty. Sandy Hair's weapon. He found Black Hair's stuck in a fruit jar at the back of the jar shelf. Sam couldn't reach it, but he could tell by the shape that it was a .38 Colt revolver, nickel-plated from the shine of it. Sam was careful to put things back the way he found them before he left the shed.

A couple of days later Sam was helping Dad untangle fishing line, when the older man in the black coat came up the driveway. Sam excused himself to go out back to the outhouse, and he went around the corner of the house toward the backyard. When he thought it was safe to peek around the corner, he saw the man go into the car shed and then drift back out and stroll back down the driveway. When Sam got back to the front steps, Black Coat was gone. So was the nickel-plated Colt when he checked the car shed the next day.

On Saturday Sandy Hair himself came up about supper-time. Dad was chopping stove wood, and Sandy Hair even took a turn or two with the ax while they were talking. Sam stayed still at his marble circle near the privet hedge, hoping nobody would notice him and chase him inside. He kept shooting aggies, pretending not to notice the visitor at all. He was too far away to hear what was said, but he kept watching for Sandy Hair to head for the car shed, and sure enough in a couple of minutes he did. He stayed around for a few more minutes, talking to Dad, and Sam thought he could see a bulge in his brown suit coat. When Mom came out on the steps to call them in for supper, Sandy nodded to her and strolled away. It was Sunday morning before Sam had a chance to check out the shed again. The family was getting ready to go to church, so Sam got himself ready in a hurry and said he'd wait for everybody outside. He slipped into the shed and went straight to the tackle box. The floats were back in place, and the Smith & Wesson was gone.

That afternoon the family piled into the Ford and took the dirt road across the mountains to Pigeon Roost. After Grammaw Hemrick's Sunday dinner of fried chicken, mashed potatoes, and new peas, Sam got to sit out on the porch with Dad and all the uncles, and Dad told the story about the day they hanged the elephant. Sam waited for him to tell the new story, the one about the duel and the hidden gun, but he never did. Dad never did tell that story, and finally Sam came to understand why.

More than twenty years later, Sam would come home from the Pacific with captain's bars and medals for what he did in the Philippines. He'd talk about the war anytime his children asked about it, but always just the one story: about a little monkey he'd found orphaned in the jungle, and made a pet of. Just the one story, over and over.

Not All Brides Are Beautiful

~

They say that all brides are beautiful, but I didn't like the look of this one. She came into the prison reception area wearing a lavender suit and a little black hat with a veil. Her figure was okay, but when she went up to Tracer and that other photographer from the wire service, there was a hard look about her, despite that spun-sugar smile. I knew it would be easy to get an interview—she'd *insist* on it—but that didn't mean I was going to enjoy talking to her.

"Is it true you're going to marry Kenny Budrell?" I called out.

She redirected her smile at me, and her dark eyes lit up like miners' lamps.

"You're here for the wedding, honey?" she purred. "Have you got something I could borrow? I already have something old, and new, and blue."

Just a regular old folksy wedding. I was about to tell her what I'd like to lend her when I felt a nudge in my side. Tracer—reminding me that good reporters get stories any way they can. I managed a faint smile. "Sure, I'll see what I can find. Why don't we go into the ladies' room and get acquainted?"

She smiled back. "This is my day to get acquainted."

"That's right," said Tracer. "You've never met the groom, have you?"

Kenny Budrell had been a newsroom byword since before I joined the paper. By the time he was eighteen, his clip-file in the newspaper morgue was an inch thick: car theft, assault and battery, attempted murder. He did some time in the state penitentiary about the same time I was at the university, and it seems we both graduated with honors. The next news of Kenny was that he'd robbed a local convenience store and taken the female clerk hostage. Tracer was the photographer on assignment when they found her body; he says it's one of the few times he's been sick on duty. It took three more robberies, each followed by the brutal murder of a hostage, before the police finally caught up with Kenny. He didn't make it through the roadblock and took a bullet in the shoulder trying to shoot his way past.

The trial took a couple of weeks. The paper sent Rudy Carr, a much more seasoned reporter than I, to cover it, but I followed the coverage and listened to the office gossip. The defense had rounded up a psychologist who said Kenny must have been temporarily insane, and he never did confess to the killings, but the jury had been looking at that cold, dead face of Kenny's for two weeks and they didn't buy it. They found him guilty in record time, and the judge obliged with a death sentence.

After that, the only clippings added to Kenny's file were routine one-column stories about his appeal to the State Supreme Court, and then to Washington. That route having failed, it was official: in six weeks Kenny Budrell would go to the electric chair.

That's when *she* turned up.

Varnee Sumner—sometime journalist and activist, full-time opportunist. In between her ecological-feminist poetry readings and her grant proposals, Varnee had found time to strike up a correspondence with Kenny. The first we heard of it was when the warden sent out a press release saying that Kenny Budrell had been granted permission to get married two weeks before his execution.

It shouldn't have come as a surprise to me that Varnee Sumner wanted to be pals—that's probably what my city editor was counting on when he assigned me to cover the story.

"What's your name?" she asked me as she applied fuchsia lipstick to her small, tight mouth.

"Lillian Robillard. Tell me—are you nervous?" I decided against taking notes. That might make her more careful about what she said.

She smoothed her hair. "Nervous? Why should I be nervous? It's true I've never met Kenny, but we've become real close through our letters—I've come to know his soul."

I winced. Kenny Budrell's soul should come with a Surgeon General's warning. Maybe *she* wasn't nervous about marrying a mass murderer, but I would have been.

My thoughts must have been obvious, because she said, "Besides, they're not going to let him come near me, you know. Even during the wedding ceremony he'll be on one side of a wire screen and we'll be on the other."

"Will they let you spend time alone with him?"

That question did faze her. "Lord, I hope—" I'd swear she was going to say *not*, but she caught herself and said, "Perhaps we'll have a quiet talk through the screen— Honey, would you like to be my maid of honor?"

"I'd love to," I said. "And would you like to give me an exclusive pre-wedding interview?"

"I wish I could," she said, "but I've promised the story to *Personal World* for ten thousand dollars." She straightened her skirt and edged past me and out the door.

I didn't think it was possible, but I was beginning to feel sorry for Kenny Budrell.

"You looked real good out there as maid of honor," Tracer told me as we left the prison. "I got a good shot of you and the warden congratulating the bride."

"Well, if I looked happy for them, pictures *do* lie." The television crews had arrived just as we were leaving and Varnee was granting interviews right and left, talking about Kenny's beautiful soul and how she was going to write to the President about his case. "You know why she's doing this, don't you?"

Tracer gave me a sad smile. "Well, I ruled out love early on."

"It's a con game. She stays married to him for two weeks, after which the state conveniently executes him, and she's a widow who stands to make a fortune on movie rights and book contracts. *I Was a Killer's Bride!*"

"Maybe they deserve each other," said Tracer mildly. "Kenny Budrell is no choirboy."

I pulled open the outside door fiercely. "He grew up poor and tough, and for all I know he *may* not be in his right mind. But there's nothing circumstantial about what she's doing!"

Tracer grinned at me. "I can see you're going to have a tough time trying to write up this wedding announcement."

He was right. It took me two hours to get the acid out of my copy. But I managed. I wanted to stay assigned to the story.

I didn't see the new Mrs. Budrell for the next two weeks, but I kept track of her. She went to Washington and gave a couple of speeches about the injustices of the American penal system. She tried to get in to see the Vice President and a couple of Supreme Court justices, but that didn't pan out. She managed to get plenty of newspaper space, though, and even made the cover of a supermarket newspaper. They ran a picture of her with the caption COURAGEOUS BRIDE FIGHTS FOR HUSBAND'S LIFE.

Because of the tearjerker angle, her efforts on Kenny's behalf received far more publicity than those of the court-appointed attorney assigned to his case. Allen Linden, a quiet, plodding type just out of law school, had been filing stacks of appeals and doing everything he could do, but nobody paid any attention. He wasn't newsworthy, and he shied away from the media blitz. He hadn't attended Budrell's wedding and he declined all interviews to discuss the newlyweds. I know, because I tried to talk with him three times—the last time he'd brushed past me in the hall outside his office, murmuring, "I'm doing the best I can for him, which is more than I can say for—"

He swallowed the rest but I knew what he had been about to say. Varnee wasn't doing a thing to really help her husband's case, although she'd been on two national talk shows and a campus lecture tour, and there was talk of a major book contract. Varnee was doing just fine—for herself.

The whole sideshow was due to end on April third, the date of Kenny's execution. The editor was sending Rudy Carr to cover that and I was going along to do a sidebar on the widow-to-be. I wondered how she was going to play her part: grieving bride or impassioned activist?

"I'm glad to see it's raining," said Tracer, hunched down in the backseat with his camera equipment. "That ought to keep the demonstrators away."

Rudy, at the wheel, glanced at him in the rearview mirror and scowled. He had hardly spoken since we started.

I watched the windshield wipers slapping the rain. "It won't keep *her* away," I said, feeling the chill, glad I'd worn my sheepskin coat.

"You've got to give the woman credit, though," Tracer said. "She's been using this case to say a lot of things that need saying about capital punishment."

I sighed. If you gave Tracer a sack of manure, he'd spend two hours looking for the pony.

"She's getting rich off this," I pointed out. "Did you know that Kenny Budrell has a mother and sisters?"

"And so did two of the victims," added Rudy with such quiet intensity that it shut both Tracer and me up for the rest of the trip.

The prison reception room was far more crowded for the execution than it had been for the wedding. By now Varnee had received so much publicity she was a national news item, and when we arrived she was three-deep in reporters. She was wearing a black designer suit and the same hat she'd worn for the wedding. I knew she wouldn't give me the time of day with all the bigger fish waving microphones and cameras in her face, but I did get a photocopy of her speech on capital punishment from a stack of copies she'd brought with her.

"You'd better talk to her now," Tracer said. "In a few minutes they're taking the witnesses in to view the execution and you're not cleared for that."

I stared at him. "You mean she's going to watch?"

"Oh, yeah. They agreed on that from the start."

I might have gone over and talked with her then, but I noticed Allen Linden, Kenny's attorney, sitting on a bench by himself, sipping coffee. He looked tired, and his gray suit might have been slept in for all its wrinkles.

He looked up warily as I approached.

"You don't have to talk to me if you don't want," I said.

He managed a wan smile. "Have I seen you somewhere before?"

I introduced myself. "You've dodged me in the hall outside your office a few times," I admitted. "But I didn't come over here to give you a hard time. Honest."

He let out a long sigh. "This is my first capital murder case," he said in a weary voice. "It's hard to know what to do."

"I'm sure you did your best." He was very young and I wasn't sure how good his best was, but he seemed badly in need of solace.

"Kenny Budrell isn't a very nice person," he mused.

I was puzzled. I thought lawyers always spoke up for their clients. "You don't think he's innocent?"

"He never claimed to be," said Linden. "At one point he expressed surprise at all the fuss being made over a couple of broads, as he put it. No, he's not a very nice person. But he was entitled to the best defense he could get. To every effort I could make."

I guess it's inevitable for a lawyer to feel guilty if his client is about to die. He must wonder if there is something else he could have done. "I'm sure you did everything you could," I said. "And if Varnee couldn't get him a stay of execution, it must have been hopeless."

He grimaced at the sound of her name. "She's not a very nice person, either, is she?"

I hesitated. "How does Kenny Budrell feel about her?"

"Very flattered." Linden smiled. "Here is a minor celebrity making his case a prime-time issue. He has a huge scrapbook of her—he keeps her letters under his pillow. He said to me once: 'She loves me, so I must be a hero. I've worried a lot about that.' "

There was a stir in the crowd and the warden, flanked by two guards, came into the room. I stiffened, dreading the next deliberate hour.

"It will be over soon," I whispered.

"I know. I hope I've done the right thing."

"Are you going to watch the execution?"

Linden shut his eyes. "There isn't going to be one. I found an irregularity in the police procedure and got the case overturned. I've just made Kenny Budrell a free man."

"But he's guilty!" I protested.

"But he's still entitled to due process, same as anyone else, and it's my job to take advantage of anything that will benefit my client." He shook his head. "I can't even take credit for it. It just fell into my lap."

"What happened?"

"Remember when they captured Kenny at the roadblock?"

"Yes. He was wounded in the shoot-out."

"Right. Well, in all the excitement nobody remembered to read him his rights. Later, in the hospital, when he was questioned, the police assumed it had already been done. One of the state troopers got to thinking about the case and came forward to tell me he thought there had been a slipup. I checked, and he was right: Kenny wasn't Mirandized, so the law says there's no case. The trooper told me he came forward because of all this business with Varnee. He said maybe the guy deserved a break, after all."

Tracer got a first-class series of pictures of the warden telling Varnee that her new husband was now a free man until death do them part, and of Varnee eventually starting to scream right there in front of the TV cameras. As far as I'm concerned, they deserve a Pulitzer.

A Shade of
Difference

↷

Milton Palmerston tapped his pencil against his mono-
grammed coffee mug as if he were calling himself to order.
Tacked to the wall in front of him was a sign he'd printed with his
laundry marker: EXAM TOMORROW! The fact that his floor was
buried beneath piles of scribbled notes and political reference
books should have been sufficient reminder of this, but Milton
couldn't be sure. Last February he had left his overcoat on the bus
to Petersborough, and hadn't noticed the loss until his advisor
drew him aside a week later and offered to lend him the money for
one. That had been during finals week, too.

After that he had taken to jotting reminders on his hand. His
left hand at the moment read: GLOVES! BREAKFAST! DIEFENBAKER/
RECIPROCITY! He stared at the message. Did he somehow owe a
breakfast to John G. Diefenbaker? Surely not. He hazarded another
guess. *Gloves*—in his coat pocket. *Breakfast*—a French roll to be
eaten on the way to the university. And *Deifenbaker/Reciprocity*
must refer to the article he had just spent an hour reading, of which
he remembered nothing. He reluctantly admitted to himself that he
knew the rest of the course material like the back of his hand—
which was to say, that it made very little sense to him at the
moment. He was blanking out again from the pressure.

Obtaining a master's in history was more difficult than his
family cared to believe, although they were grudgingly impressed

that someone who had to keep a copy of his own address—*twenty-four Wessex Drive,* he thought hastily (just checking)—could memorize so many less familiar names and dates. Usually such facts and figures danced about in his head—*what was the importance of a fly swatter in the diplomatic history of the French Third Republic?* (he never forgot that)—but during exam week, his mine of information became a barren tunnel salted with surface trivia.

Milton sighed. Trying to figure out what caused his anxiety was a bit like trying to figure out what caused the German inflation of 1923. Eventually you sit down, and sigh, and admit that *everything* caused the German inflation of 1923.

Perhaps a study break would help to clear his mind. He considered dropping in for a chat with what's-his-name, the New Yorker across the hall—but that might turn into an all-night debate, which it often did. The New Yorker, Gerald—what *was* his last name? Ford? Probably; it sounded familiar. Anyway, Gerald was specializing in international diplomacy. "You're studying Canadian *domestic* politics?" he had demanded when they first met. Milton had acknowledged that this was so, and the Yank had grinned facetiously. "Isn't that a bit like raising dairy cows for foxhunting? I mean, the potential seems hardly worth the effort. All you guys do diplomatically is referee. Now my country . . ." Milton shook his head. He wasn't up to debating tonight. Better reread that piece on the Liberal Party of Canada. He groped for the book.

"I am here to demand that you change your vote on the Western Grain Stabilization Act," said a stern voice from behind him.

For a stricken moment, Milton thought that he had warped out in the middle of Professor Paulsen's exam, only to find himself unprepared, but no, this was definitely his room. Cautiously, he turned around and saw that it was only Mackenzie King, who had been dead since 1950 and could hardly be appearing as a guest lecturer at York. He smiled with relief. It was only a hallucination. He'd been expecting them, anyway.

"Don't sit there smirking at me!" snapped the apparition. "I tell you, the Western Grain Stabilization Act simply will *not* do!"

"Oughtn't you to be weighted down with a chain forged of old ballot boxes or something?" asked Milton mildly.

"Nonsense! You're confusing me with a U.S. president! Several, in fact."

"Very possibly. At any rate, you're confusing me with someone else as well. I can't vote in parliament. I'm a graduate student."

The late prime minister pointed to Milton's coffee mug. "M.P.— there it is, sir, plain as day!"

"My initials," said Milton diffidently.

There was a short silence. "Oh." Another pause. "Isn't this twenty-four Sussex Drive?"

Milton consulted his wrist. "Twenty-four *Wessex* Drive," he announced.

"Oh. I haven't got the hang of this yet. It was easier when I was on your side. Just sit at the table and stay alert: one rap for yes, two for no. Now I'm expected to navigate. Higher plane indeed! Oh well, sorry to have disturbed you. Carry on!"

The figure walked into the wall and began to fade from sight, its features mingling with the roses on the wallpaper. Milton cleared his throat. "Actually, though, there isn't anything *wrong* with voting for the Western Grain Stabilization Act . . ."

The figure ceased to blend. It seemed to seep outward from the wall again, taking on a distinct, even portly form, which began to walk back toward him. "I *beg* your pardon?"

"I said: 'There's nothing wrong with voting for the Western Grain Stabilization Act.' It will stabilize the whole economy of the region without costing the taxpayers anything. Because, you see, you have to consider the multiplier effect, which in the case of a farmer is a factor of three; therefore—"

"No! No! Don't give me twaddle about multiplier effects. Have you talked to the farmers? Have you asked them what *they* want?

You have to approach this in a spirit of compromise, to—I thought you said you weren't in politics."

Milton drew himself up. "I'm a graduate student in Canadian history. Naturally I follow politics," he said, warming to the topic.

The apparition smiled complacently. "Quite an opportunity for you—talking to me!"

"Uh . . . well . . ." Milton hedged.

"Politics. I can certainly set you straight about that."

"Er—the fact is—"

"Have you read my book? *Industry and Humanity*?"

"I find it most helpful at times," said Milton carefully.

"Should think you would." The late prime minister nodded.

Milton forbore to mention that he found *Industry and Humanity* most helpful when his worries about course work had reached such a pitch that he was unable to sleep, and found himself speculating on whether there was an alternate universe in which he *had* returned a copy of Ursula Le Guin's *Malafrena* to the university library. About the time his musings turned dark and he began to wonder whether one could be digested by one's bed, he would flip on the light with shaking hands and lose himself in the soothing monotony of William Lyon Mackenzie King's prose style. This treatment never failed to work: soon he would awake to the clanging of his alarm clock, the book still in his hands. As an alternative to sleeping tablets, Mackenzie King was without equal. As a political mentor—Milton Palmerston, contemporary Liberal, questioned his value.

". . . probably know more about politics than anyone else alive," the apparition was saying.

Milton blinked at this. "But you're not alive," he pointed out.

"Do you think the voters would hold it against me?"

Milton considered the members of parliament presently in office. "Probably not," he conceded. "Er—you weren't thinking of standing for North Waterloo again, were you?"

"What? After I got the Industrial Disputes Investigation Act passed and the ingrates voted me out in 1911? I should hope not! I was thinking of my other old job—prime minister, you know."

Milton nodded, wondering if perhaps reading Mackenzie King had not, after all, been safer than tranquilizers. It seemed to produce its own hallucinations.

"I suppose they still need me," mused the late prime minister. "How are things going with labor? And the French—are we getting along better internally now? I suppose I'm sorely missed among the Liberals?"

Milton's instincts toward courtesy to deceased heads of state battled with his pedantic desire to make political pronouncements. God knows he didn't have much of a chance to do either, but the urge to make political pronouncements proved stronger. With the dim suspicion that he might be following in Cassandra's dainty footsteps, Milton spoke.

"The fact is, sir, you're not considered sound. The modern Liberal consensus is that while we respect your—er—place in history and all that—well—as my professor put it last term: 'You can follow Mackenzie King just so far.' "

Having delivered this pronouncement, he looked up to see the apparition rapidly fading in and out—the spectral equivalent, he supposed, of taking deep breaths. After a few moments, the oscillation subsided, and a very substantial-looking statesman fixed him with a most uncompromising glare. "Indeed!" The apparition began to pace about the room, in the exact spot where Milton's mound of notes and reference books had been erected; he did not trip on them however, but merely walked through them, as if they, not he, were ethereal. Milton's eyes strayed to the note posted on his wall: EXAM TOMORROW! He really must study, and since the exam did not cover the Mackenzie King era at all, this interruption could do him no good whatsoever. He wondered at the propriety of evicting a deceased prime minister from one's room. It wasn't covered in *Robert's Rules of Order*, he was sure of that.

The unwelcome visitor continued to pace.

He glanced at the clock. Two A.M. Exam in six hours. Milton considered exorcism. What would one use to banish the ghost of a Liberal prime minister? He dived for his Diefenbaker text.

Before he could locate a sufficiently inflammatory passage, the ghost discovered a newspaper that Milton had been saving to line his leaky boots. He bent down and studied the front page carefully: unemployment statistics, a picture of an overcrowded nursing home, an article on inflation.

"I see you're having another Depression," he remarked.

"Actually, it's my nerves," Milton confided. "I can't sleep, but I'm taking sedatives and considering lightening my class load."

"I was referring to the country!"

"Oh."

"There was a Depression during my term as well," said the ghost. "I got the country out of it, of course!"

Milton nodded. He decided not to mention that Mackenzie King's solution to the Great Depression was called World War II. There was always the chance that even an oblique reference to the Führer might bring him goose-stepping into the room to join the debate. There were the neighbors to consider.

Mackenzie King plodded to the laundry-laden armchair and sank down on—or rather, through—the pile of clothes. He put his head in his translucent hands. "What a disaster!" he moaned. "I am the only one who can possibly save Canada—and I'm dead!"

Milton considered the problem; perhaps he could profit from providing assistance. If there were such a thing as ghosts, then perhaps spirit-writing was also possible, and he could persuade a grateful Mackenzie King to get his impending exam ghost-written, as it were, by Diefenbaker. Unless, of course, the Liberals' imprecations had been correct, in which case Dief was now residing in a much more tropical region than Ontario.

"Do you see much of Diefenbaker?" he asked casually.

"What? Old fellow? Rides a unicorn? That's not important! Pay attention. I am trying to save the country!"

"Well," said Milton doubtfully, "perhaps you could do it in an advisory capacity. Are any of your favorite mediums still alive?"

"I've tried that. I've spelled out messages on the Ouija board until my head spun, but my contacts couldn't even get an appointment with—" He waved his hand. "You know—what's-his-name." The apparition shook his head dolefully. "Once I even appeared at a government reception. They mistook me for Larry Reynolds."

Milton sighed. He supposed that he would have to help: saving the country took precedence over passing History 604, but he didn't expect any gratitude for it. Nothing ever went right for him; he'd known that at the age of six, when he bit into his chocolate Easter Bunny and broke out in hives. How could the Dominion of Canada possibly be saved by a shortsighted, mild-mannered, pedantic, mediocre— He looked again at Mackenzie King. Then again . . .

"Could I suggest a compromise?" he ventured.

The ghost brightened visibly upon hearing the magic word. "Compromise?" he said eagerly.

"Yes. I was thinking that instead of meddling—er—intervening directly in domestic policy, you might tell your ideas to me, and I could see to it that someone in Parliament hears them."

"You have influence?"

"A certain amount." Milton smiled, wisely deciding not to mention that his parliamentary contacts consisted of his presence on the mailing list of the M.P. from Moosejaw.

The late prime minister tapped his fingers together. "Well . . . I suppose you'll have to do," he said grudgingly.

"I'm better than nothing," Milton reminded him.

"Humph! Well, I always did have a fondness for ruins. All right, then. Pay attention. Get a pencil. I shall begin."

Milton ferreted out a pencil from the debris on his desk, turned to a clean page in his course notebook, and looked expectantly at the speaker. This would be easy. Graduate students in history are able to take down lecture notes in their sleep. Unfortunately, this is what Milton did. The sonorous cadence of the William Lyon Mackenzie King political address was even more soothing than his literary efforts. Milton's hand diligently jotted down the words, but his mind had warped out to blissful oblivion. Occasionally a phrase like "social credit" or "contra-cyclical financing" would penetrate his stupor and reverberate through his own reveries, producing nightmares of political farce. The Western Grain Stabilization Act became a circus performer from Manitoba who juggled loaves of French bread. . . . The Western Grain Stabilization . . .

Milton returned to consciousness to see that the late prime minister had indeed worked his way round to that topic. Suppressing a yawn, he forced himself to listen. After much rambling and personal digression, Mackenzie King began to outline his political plan. A few minutes later Milton was wide awake. This fellow's ideas weren't so ridiculous after all. Quite sensible, really. But what was this bit in his notes about prostitutes? He must have dreamed that part. . . . What was he saying now? Soon Milton found himself leaning forward, saying excitedly: "Yes! Yes! That would work! What else?"

"Well, it's quite simple really. . . ."

Milton suddenly noticed that the clock, whose alarm he had forgotten to set, said 7:30. He was due in class in half an hour! It seemed a pity to interrupt such brilliance, but he had his academic career to think of.

Milton ventured to interrupt. "Excuse me, sir," he said timidly, raising his hand. "I have to be getting to the university now."

"In a moment," said the ghost, and went on talking.

Five minutes later, Milton decided that he would have to be firm. "I have a test at eight. I must be going now."

The great man frowned. "I haven't finished yet," he said peevishly.

"Really, I have to leave."

"Well . . . I suppose I'll come along. We can talk on the way."

Milton got ready to leave, idly wondering whether the rest of the class would be able to see the visitor. Would he be invited to address the class? Perhaps the test could be postponed in his honor. Milton grabbed for his coat, scarf, and briefcase while the ghost continued to lecture steadily; in his present spectral state, it was no longer necessary for him to pause for breath. They left the room together, nodding and gesturing about various political details.

"... Registered Retirement Savings Plan ..."

"Yes! Yes! I'll make a note of it!" Milton scribbled furiously.

"... Temporary Wheat Reserves Act ..."

"Of course!"

They continued down the hall, the ghost orating happily, while Milton nodded and noted, until they arrived at the end of the corridor, where a left turn would take them to the stairs. The deceased prime minister, deep in a monologue about taxable income, continued to walk straight ahead, passing gracefully through the brick wall. Milton, attempting to follow, slammed face-first into cold, solid reality. As the last strains of the voice reached him from some great beyond, Milton dabbed at his profusely bleeding nose, and reflected that Professor Paulsen had been right after all: you could follow Mackenzie King just so far. . . .

A Wee Doch
and Doris

~

He stood for a long while staring up at the house, but all was quiet. There was one light on in an upstairs window, but he saw no shadows flickering on the shades. *Not a creature was stirring, not even a mouse,* Louis smirked to himself. Christmas wasn't so hot if you were in his line of work. People tended to stay home with the family: the one night a year when everybody wishes they were the Waltons. But all that togetherness wore off in a week. By now everybody had cabin fever, and they were dying to get away from the in-laws and the rug rats. That's how it was in his family, anyway. By New Year's Eve his ma had recovered from the thrill of receiving candy from Anthony, bubble bath from Michael, and a bottle of perfume from Louis, and she had started nagging again. Louis always gave her a bottle of perfume. He preferred small, lightweight gifts that could be slipped easily and unobtrusively into one's pocket.

He also preferred not to have endless discussions with his nearest and dearest over whether he was going to get a job or enroll in the auto mechanics program at the community college. Neither idea appealed to Louis. He liked his schedule: sleeping until eleven, a quick burger for brunch, and a few hours of volunteer work at the animal shelter.

Nobody at the shelter thought Louis was lazy or unmotivated. He was their star helper. He didn't mind hosing down the pens and cleaning the food dishes, but what he really enjoyed was playing with the dogs, and brushing down the shaggy ones. They didn't have a lot of money at the shelter, so they couldn't afford to pay him. It took all their funds to keep the animals fed and healthy; the shelter refused to put a healthy animal to sleep. Louis heartily approved of this policy, and thus he didn't mind working for free; in fact, sometimes when the shelter's funds were low, he gave them a donation from the proceeds of his night's work. Louis thought that rich people should support local charities; he saw himself as the middleman, except that his share of the take was ninety percent. Louis also believed that charity begins at home.

Christmas was good for the shelter. Lots of people high on the Christmas spirit adopted kittens and puppies, or gave them as gifts, and the shelter saw to it that they got a donation for each adoptee. So their budget was doing okay, but Louis's personal funds were running short. Christmas is not a good time of year for a burglar. Sometimes he'd find an empty house whose occupants were spending Christmas out of town, but usually the neighborhood was packed with nosy people, eyeballing every car that went by. You'd think they were looking for Santa Claus.

If Christmas was bad for business, New Year's Eve made up for it. Lots of people went out to parties that night, and did not plan on coming home until well after midnight. Being out for just the evening made them less security conscious than the Christmas people who went out of town: New Year's party-goers were less likely to hide valuables, activate alarms, or ask the police to keep an eye on the premises. Louis had had a busy evening. He'd started around nine o'clock, when even the tardiest guests would have left for the party, and he had hit four houses, passing on one because of a Doberman pinscher in the backyard. Louis had nothing against the breed, but he found them very unreasonable, and not inclined to give strangers the benefit of the doubt.

The other four houses had been satisfactory, though. The first one was "guarded" by a haughty white Persian whose owners had forgotten to feed it. Louis put down some canned mackerel for the cat, and charged its owners one portable television, one 35mm. camera, three pairs of earrings, a CD player, and a collection of compact discs. The other houses had been equally rewarding. After a day's visit to various flea markets and pawnshops, his financial standing should be greatly improved. This was much better than auto mechanics. Louis realized that larceny and auto mechanics are almost never mutually exclusive, but he felt that the hours were better in freelance burglary.

He glanced at his watch. A little after midnight. This would be his last job of the evening. Louis wanted to be home before the drunks got out on the highway. His New Year's resolution was to campaign for gun control and for tougher drunk driving laws. He turned his attention back to the small white house with the boxwood hedge and the garden gnome next to the birdbath. No danger of Louis stealing *that*. He thought people ought to have to pay to have garden gnomes stolen. A promising sideline—he would have to consider it. But now to the business at hand.

The hedge seemed high enough to prevent the neighbors from seeing into the yard. The house across the street was vacant, with a big yellow FOR SALE sign stuck in the yard. The brick split-level next door was dark, but they had a chain-link fence, and their front yard was floodlit like the exercise yard of a penitentiary. Louis shook his head: paranoia *and* bad taste.

There was no car in the driveway—a promising sign that no one was home. He liked the look of the rectangular kitchen window. It was partly hidden by a big azalea bush, and it looked like the kind of window that opened out at the bottom, with a catch to keep it from opening too far. It was about six feet off the ground. Louis was tempted to look under the garden gnome for a spare house key, but he decided to have a look at the window instead. Using a key was unsporting; besides, the exercise would be good for him. If you are a burglar, your physique is your fortune.

He walked a lot, too. Tonight Louis had parked his old Volkswagen a couple of streets away, not so much for the exercise as for the fact that later no one would remember seeing a strange car in the vicinity. The long walk back to the car limited Louis's take to the contents of a pillowcase or two, also from the burgled home, but he felt that most worthwhile burglary items were small and lightweight, anyway. The pillowcases he gave as baby gifts to new parents of his acquaintance, explaining that they were the perfect size to use as a cover for a bassinet mattress. Even better than a fitted crib sheet, he insisted, because after the kid grows up, you can use the pillowcases yourself. Louis was nothing if not resourceful.

He stayed close to the boxwood hedge as he edged closer to the house. With a final glance to see that no one was driving past, he darted for the azalea bush, and ended up crouched behind it, just under the rectangular window. Perfect. Fortunately it wasn't too cold tonight—temperature in the mid-thirties, about average for the Virginia Christmas season. When it got colder than that, his dexterity was impaired, making it hard to jimmy locks and tamper with windows. It was an occupational hazard. Tonight would be no problem, though, unless the window had some kind of inside lock.

It didn't. He was able to chin himself on the windowsill and pull the window outward enough to get a hand inside and slip the catch. With that accomplished, another twenty seconds of wriggling got him through the window and onto the Formica countertop next to the sink. There had been a plant on the windowsill, but he managed to ease that onto the counter before sliding himself all the way through. The only sound he made was a slight thump as he went from countertop to floor; no problem if the house was unoccupied.

Taking out his pen-sized flashlight, Louis checked out the kitchen. It was squeaky clean. He could even smell the lemon floor cleaner. He shined the light on the gleaming white refrigerator.

Some people actually put their valuables in the freezer compartment. He always checked that last, though. In the corner next to the back door was a small washing machine and an electric dryer, with clean clothes stacked neatly on the top. Louis eased his way across the room and inspected the laundry. Women's clothes— small sizes—towels, dishcloths . . . ah, there they were! Pillowcases. He helped himself to the two linen cases, sniffing them appreciatively. Fabric softener. *Very* nice. Now he was all set. Time to shop around.

He slipped into the dining room and flashed the light on the round oak table and the ladder-back chairs. Two places laid for breakfast. Weren't they the early birds, though? The salt and pepper shakers looked silver. They were in the shape of pheasants. Louis slid them into his pillowcase and examined the rest of the room. The glass of the china cabinet flashed his light back at him. Bunch of flowery plates. No chance that he'd be taking those. He looked around for a silver chest, but didn't see one. He'd check on it later. He wanted to examine the living room first.

Louis flashed an exploratory light at the fireplace, the chintz couch covered with throw pillows, and the glass-fronted bookcase. There were some candlesticks on the mantelpiece that looked promising. As he crept forward to inspect them, the room was flooded with light.

Squinting at the sudden brightness, Louis turned toward the stairs and saw that he wasn't alone. The overhead lights had been switched on by a sweet-faced old woman in a green velvet bathrobe. Louis braced himself for the scream, but the old lady was smiling. She kept coming daintily down the stairs. Smiling. Louis stared, trying to think up a plausible story. She couldn't have been more than five feet tall, and her blue eyes sparkled from a wrinkled but pleasant face. She patted her white permed hair into place. She looked delighted. Probably senile, Louis thought.

"Well, I'm glad to see you!" the woman said brightly. "I was afraid it was going to be my daughter Doris."

Definitely senile, thought Louis. "No, it's just me," he said, deciding to play along. He held the pillowcase behind his back.

"Just after midnight, too, isn't it? That's grand, that is. Otherwise I'd have to ask you to go out and come in again, you know."

Louis noticed her accent now. It was sort of English, he thought. But she wasn't making any sense. "Come in again?"

"Ah, well, being an American you wouldn't know the custom, would you? Well, you're welcome all the same. Now, what can I get for you?"

Louis realized just in time that she meant food or drink, rather than jewelry and savings bonds. "Nothing for me, thanks," he said, giving her a little wave, and trying to edge for the front door.

Her face fell. "Oh, no. Please! You must let me fix you something. Otherwise, you'll be taking the luck away with you. How about a piece of cake? I made it today. And a bit of strong drink? It's New Year's, after all."

She still didn't look in the least perturbed. And she wasn't trying to get to the telephone or to trip an alarm. Louis decided that he could definitely use a drink.

The old lady beamed happily up at him, and motioned for him to follow her into the kitchen. "I've been baking for two days," she confided. "Now, let's see, what will you have?"

She rummaged around in a cupboard, bringing out an assortment of baked goods on glass plates, which she proceeded to spread out on the kitchen table. She handed Louis a blue-flowered plate, and motioned for him to sit down. When she went in to the dining room to get some cloth napkins, Louis stuffed the pillowcase under his coat, making sure that the salt and pepper shakers didn't clink together. Finally, he decided that the least suspicious thing to do would be to play along. He sat.

"Now," she announced, "we have Dundee cake with dried fruit, black bun with almonds, shortbread, petticoat tails . . ."

Louis picked up a flat yellow cookie, and nibbled at it, as his hostess babbled on.

"When I was a girl in Dundee—"

"Where?"

"Dundee. Scotland. My mother used to bake an oat bannock—
you know, a wee cake—for each one of us children. The bannocks
had a hole in the middle, and they were nipped in about the edges
for decoration. She flavored them with carvey—caraway seed. And
we ate them on New Year's morning. They used to say that if your
bannock broke while it was baking, you'd be taken ill or die in the
New Year. So I never baked one for my daughter Doris. Oh, but
they were good!"

Louis blinked. "You're from Scotland?"

She was at the stove now, putting a large open pot on the
burner, and stirring it with a wooden spoon. "Yes, that's right,"
she said. "We've been in this country since Doris was five, though.
My husband wanted to come over, and so we did. I've often
thought of going home, now that he's passed on, but Doris won't
hear of it."

"Doris is your daughter," said Louis. He wondered if he ought
to bolt before she showed up, in case she turned out to be sane.

"Yes. She's all grown up now. She works very hard, does Doris.
Can you imagine having to work on Hogmanay?"

"On what?"

"*Hogmanay.* New Year's Eve. She's out right now, poor dear,
finishing up her shift. That's why I was so glad to see you tonight.
We could use a bit of luck this year, starting with a promotion for
Doris. Try a bit of the Dundee cake. It's awfully rich, but you can
stand the calories, from the look of you."

Louis reached for another pastry, still trying to grasp a thread of
sense in the conversation. He wanted to know why he was so welcome. Apparently she hadn't mistaken him for anyone else. And
she didn't seem to wonder what he was doing in her house in the
middle of the night. He kept trying to think of a way to frame
the question without incriminating himself.

Steam was rising in white spirals from the pot on the stove. The old lady took a deep breath over the fumes, and nodded briskly. "Right. That should be done now. Tell me, lad, are you old enough to take spirits?"

After a moment's hesitation, Louis realized that he was being offered a drink and not a séance. "I'm twenty-two," he mumbled.

"Right enough, then." She ladled the steaming liquid into two cups, and set one in front of him.

Louis sniffed it and frowned.

"It's called a het pint," said the old lady, without waiting for him to ask. "It's an old drink given to first footers. Spirits, sugar, beer, and eggs. When I was a girl, they used to carry it round door to door in a kettle. Back in Dundee. Not that I drink much myself, of course. Doris is always on about my blood pressure. But tonight *is* Hogmanay, and I said to myself: Flora, why don't you stir up the het pint. You never know who may drop in. And, you see, I was right. Here you are!"

"Here I am," Louis agreed, taking a swig of his drink. It tasted a little like eggnog. Not bad. At least it was alcoholic. He wouldn't have more than a cup, though. He still had to drive home.

The old lady—Flora—sat down beside Louis and lifted her cup. "Well, here's to us, then. What's your name, lad?"

"Louis," he said, before he thought better of it.

"Well, Louis, here's to us! And not forgetting a promotion for Doris!" They clinked their cups together, and drank to the New Year.

Flora dabbed at the corners of her mouth with a linen napkin, and reached for a piece of shortbread. "I must resolve to eat fewer of these during the coming year," she remarked. "Else Doris will have me out jogging."

Louis took another piece to keep her company. It tasted pretty good. Sort of like a sugar cookie with delusions of grandeur. "Did you have a nice Christmas?" he asked politely.

Flora smiled. "Perhaps not by American standards. Doris had the day off, and we went to church in the morning, and then had our roast beef for dinner. She gave me bath powder, and I gave her a new umbrella. She's always losing umbrellas. I suppose that's a rather subdued holiday by your lights, but when I was a girl, Christmas wasn't such a big festival in Scotland. The shops didn't even close for it. We considered it a religious occasion for most folk, and a lark for the children. The holiday for grown people was New Year's."

"Good idea," grunted Louis. "Over here, we get used to high expectations when we're kids, and then as adults, we get depressed every year because Christmas is just neckties and boredom."

Flora nodded. "Oh, but you should have seen Hogmanay when I was a girl! No matter what the weather, people in Dundee would gather in the City Square to wait out the old year's end. And there'd be a great time of singing all the old songs. . . ."

"Auld Lang Syne?" asked Louis.

"That's a Scottish song, of course." Flora nodded. "But we sang a lot of the other old tunes as well. And there was country dancing. And then just when the new year was minutes away, everyone would lapse into silence. Waiting. There you'd be in the dark square, with your breath frosting the air, and the stars shining down on the world like snowflakes on velvet. And it was so quiet you could hear the ticking of the gentlemen's pocket watches."

"Sounds like Times Square," said Louis, inspecting the bottom of his cup.

Flora took the cup, and ladled another het pint for each of them. "After the carrying on to welcome in the new year, everyone would go about visiting and first-footing their neighbors. My father was always in great demand for that, being tall and dark as he was. And he used to carry lumps of coal in his overcoat to be sure of his welcome."

"What," said Louis, "is *first-footing*?"

"Well, it's an old superstition," said Flora thoughtfully. "Quite pagan, I expect, if the truth were told, but then, you never can be sure, can you? You don't have a lump of coal about you, by any chance?"

Louis shook his head.

"Ah, well. First-footing, you asked." She took a deep breath, as if to warn him that there was a long explanation to follow. "In Scotland the tradition is that the first person to cross your threshold after midnight on Hogmanay symbolizes your luck in the year to come. The *first foot* to enter your house, you see."

Louis nodded. *It's lucky to be burgled?* he was thinking.

"The best luck of all comes if you're first-footed by a tall, dark stranger carrying a lump of coal. Sometimes family friends would send round a tall, dark houseguest that our family had not met, so that we could be first-footed by a stranger. The rest of the party would catch up with him a few minutes later."

"I guess I fit the bill, all right," Louis remarked. He was just over six feet, and looked more Italian than Tony Bennett. His uncles called him Luigi.

"So you do." Flora smiled. "Now the worst luck for the new year is to be first-footed by a short, blond woman who comes in empty-handed."

Louis remembered the first thing the old woman had said to him. "So Doris is a short blonde?"

"She is that. Gets her height from me. Or the lack of it. And she can never remember to hunt up a lump of coal, or bring some wee gift home with her to help the luck. Ever since Colin passed away, Doris has been first foot in this house, and where has it got us? Her with long hours, and precious little time off, and me with rheumatism and a fixed income—while prices go up every year. We could use a change of luck. Maybe a sweepstakes win."

Louis leaned back in his chair, struggling between courtesy and common sense. "You really believe in all this stuff?" he asked her.

A sad smile. "Where's the harm? When you get older, it's hard to let go of the customs you knew when you were young. You'll see."

Louis couldn't think of any family customs, except eating in front of the TV set and never taking the last ice cube—so you wouldn't have to refill the tray. Other than that, he didn't think he had much in common with the people he lived with. He thought about telling Flora about his work at the animal shelter, but he decided that it would be a dangerous thing to do. She already knew his name. Any further information would enable her and the police to locate him in a matter of hours. If she ever cottoned on to the fact that she had been robbed, that is.

"Do you have any pets?" he asked.

Flora shook her head. "We used to have a wee dog, but he got old and died a few years back. I haven't wanted to get another one, and Doris is too busy with her work to help in taking care of one."

"I could get you a nice puppy, from—" He stopped himself just in time. "Well, never mind. You're right. Dogs are more work than most people think. Or they *ought* to be."

Flora beamed. "What a nice young man you are!"

He smiled back nervously.

Louis nibbled another piece of shortbread while he considered his dilemma. He had been caught breaking in to a house, and the evidence from the rest of the evening's burglaries was in the trunk of his Volkswagen. The logical thing to do would be to kill the old dear, so that he wouldn't have to worry about getting caught. Logical, yes, but distasteful. Louis was not a killer. The old lady reminded him of one of the sad-eyed cocker spaniels down at the shelter. Sometimes people brought in pets because they didn't want them anymore, or were moving. Or because the kid was allergic to them. Often these people asked that the animal be destroyed, which annoyed Louis no end. Did they think that if they didn't want the pet, no one else should have it? Suppose divorce worked like that? Louis could see putting an old dog to sleep if it was feeble and suffering, but not just because the owners found it inconvenient to have it around. He supposed that his philosophy would have to apply to his hostess as well, even if she were a danger to his career. After all, Flora was old, but she was not weak or in pain. She seemed quite spry and happy, in fact, and Louis couldn't see doing away with her just for expedience. After all, people had rights, too, just like animals.

He wondered what he ought to do about her. It seemed to boil down to two choices: he could tie her up, finish robbing the house, and make his getaway, or he could finish his tea and leave, just as if he had been an ordinary—what was it?—*first footer*.

He leaned back in his chair, considering the situation, and felt a sharp jab in his side. A moment's reflection told him what it had been: the tail of the pheasant salt shaker. He had stashed the pair in the pillowcase, now concealed under his coat. He couldn't think of any way to get rid of his loot without attracting suspicion. *Then* she might realize that he was a burglar; *then* she might panic, and try to call the police; *then* he would have to hit her to keep himself from being captured. It was not an appealing scenario. Louis decided that the kindest thing to do would be to tie her up, finish his job, and leave.

Flora was prattling on about Scottish cakes and homemade icing, but he hadn't been listening. He thought it would be rather rude to begin threatening his hostess while he still had a mouthful of cake, but he told himself that she had been rather rude, too. After all, she hadn't asked him anything about himself. That was thoughtless of her. A good hostess ought to express a polite interest in her guests.

Flora's interminable story seemed to have wound down at last. She looked up at the kitchen clock. It was after one. "Well," she said, beaming happily at Louis. "It's getting late. Can I get you a wee doch and dorris?"

Louis blinked. "A what?"

"A drink, lad. *Wee doch and dorris* is a Scottish expression for the last drink of the evening. One for the road, as you say over here. Scotch, perhaps?"

He shook his head. "I'm afraid not," he said. "I do have to be going, but I'm afraid I will have to tie you up now."

He braced himself for tears, or, even worse, a scream, but the old lady simply took another sip of her drink, and waited. She wasn't smiling anymore, but she didn't look terrified, either. Louis felt his cheeks grow hot, wishing he could just get out of there. Burglars weren't supposed to have to interact with people; it wasn't part of the job description. If you liked emotional scenes, you became an armed robber. Louis hated confrontations.

"I hope this won't change your luck for the new year or anything," he mumbled, "but the reason I came in here tonight was to rob the house. You see, I'm a burglar."

Flora nodded, still watching him closely. Not a flicker of surprise had registered on her face.

"I really enjoyed the cakes and all, but after all, business is business."

"In Scotland, it's considered unlucky to do evil after you've accepted the hospitality of the house," the old lady said calmly.

Louis shrugged. "In America it's unlucky to miss car payments."

She made no reply to this remark, but continued to gaze up at him impassively. At least she wasn't being hysterical. He almost wished that he had given up the whole idea.

Louis cleared his throat and continued. "The reason I have to tie you up is that I have to finish getting the stuff, and I have to make sure you can't call for help until I'm long gone. But I won't beat you up or anything."

"Kind of you," she said dryly. "There is some spare clothesline in the bottom drawer of the left-hand cabinet."

He looked at her suspiciously. "Don't *try* anything, okay? I don't want to have to do anything rough." He didn't carry a gun (nobody was *supposed* to be home), but they both knew that a strong young man like Louis could do considerable damage to a frail old lady like Flora with his fists . . . a candlestick . . . almost anything could be a weapon.

Keeping his eyes on her, he edged toward the cabinet, squatting down to pull out the drawer. She watched him steadily, making no move to leave her seat. As he eased the drawer open, he saw the white rope clothesline neatly bundled above a stack of paper bags. With considerable relief at the ease of it all, he picked up the rope and turned back to the old lady.

"Okay," he said, a little nervously. "I'm going to tie you up. Just relax. I don't want to make it so tight it cuts off circulation, but I'm not, like, experienced, you know? Just sit in the chair with your feet flat on the floor in front of you."

She did as she was told, and he knelt and began winding the clothesline around her feet, anchoring it to the legs of the chair. He hoped it wasn't going to be too painful, but he couldn't risk her being able to escape. To cover his uneasiness at the silent reproach from his hostess, Louis began to whistle nervously as he worked. That was probably why he didn't hear anything suspicious.

His first inkling that anything was wrong was that Flora suddenly relaxed in her chair. He looked up quickly, thinking, *"Oh God! The old girl's had a heart attack!"* But her eyes were open, and she was smiling. She seemed to be gazing at something just behind him.

Slowly Louis turned his head in the direction of the back door. There was a short, blond woman of about thirty standing just inside the door. She was wearing a dark blue uniform and a positively menacing expression. But what bothered Louis the most about the intruder was the fact that her knees were bent, and she was holding a service revolver in both hands, its barrel aimed precisely at his head.

Louis looked from the blond woman to Flora and back again, just beginning to make the connection. A jerk of the gun barrel made him move slowly away from the chair and put his hands up.

"This is my daughter Doris," said Flora calmly. "She's a policewoman. You see, you were lucky for us, Louis. I'm sure she'll get her promotion after this!"

Remains to
Be Seen

~

When the two elderly ladies from the Craig Springs Community for Seniors saw the mummy on the top shelf of the army surplus store, one of them gasped, "Where did it come from?" The other one opened her purse and said, "How much?"

George Carr, the owner of the Craig Springs Army Surplus Store, decided to answer the first question before he worried about the second.

Every Thursday the van from Craig Springs brought a group of its sprier residents on a shopping trip downtown. There wasn't much that anyone actually needed to buy—toothpaste, maybe, or the new *Cosmopolitan*—but they enjoyed the outing, and the chance to exercise and window-shop at the same time. George Carr was used to seeing some of the old gentlemen in his establishment. The World War II veterans loved to come in and reminisce about the old days, using his merchandise as visual aids for their war yarns. This was the first time, though, that any of the Craig Springs ladies had paid him a visit. George thought it was strange that they had.

"We were tired of the usual round of drugstores and dress shops," said the dumpy one in the black dress.

Since he had just been wondering that very thing, George laughed and said, "You read my mind!"

She turned triumphantly to her friend. "There, Lucille! I told you I'd been working on it. A dab of chicken blood behind each earlobe, and that Latin phrase I learned."

Lucille Beaumont, whose silver hair did not seem to go with her sharp black eyes and her hawk-bill nose, patted her friend's arm. "Yes, Clutie. You've told me," she said in patient but repressive tones. "Wouldn't you like to look around?"

Clutie Campbell shook her head. She looked up at the mummy. "You were going to tell us about him."

"Oh, Herman. Don't know that that's his real name, of course. But that's what we call him. We've had him for the last twenty years."

The ladies turned and stared at the glass-sided wooden coffin resting on the top shelf of the far wall. Below it was a tangled assortment of knapsacks and canteens, and a hand-lettered sign that said: YOUR CHOICE—$5. Just visible through the dusty glass was the body of a man: a wrinkled, leathery face poking out from the folds of a tatty-looking black suit that seemed rather large for its owner.

"Is it real?" asked Lucille Beaumont, sounding as if she rather hoped *not*.

George Carr nodded. He was accustomed to the questions. Every time a stranger visited the store, the same conversation took place: *He real? How'd you get him?*

"How'd you get him?" asked Clutie Campbell.

George started his well-rehearsed tale at the beginning. "In the early Twenties, a traveling carnival came here to Greene County. You know how it was: they'd pitch a tent in the old fairgrounds, set up the booths and the rides and the girlie shows, and three days later they'd be gone, with the pocket money of every kid in town."

Clutie nodded impatiently. "So—what was *he*? A sideshow exhibit?"

"No. Herman up there was a working member of the carnival. I think he was one of the construction crew, setting up the booths and all."

"A roustabout," murmured Lucille, but she was shushed into silence by Clutie, who clearly did not want the conversation to be derailed into a discussion of vocabulary. In her youth Lucille had been in show business, and she was entirely too fond of showing off her expertise by correcting people's speech and by critiquing the performances on *Days of Our Lives*. Clutie, for one, was sick of it.

George Carr, well into his story by now, paid no attention to their bickering. "The way I heard it, Herman here died on the second night in town. I think maybe a beam knocked him in the head, or something. An accident, anyway." He looked a little nervously at the stiff, leathery figure on the high shelf. "I never checked. Anyhow, his body was sent to Culbertson's, the local funeral parlor. They got right to work embalming him, and they had him all ready for the funeral."

"I expect they provided the suit," said Clutie with an appraising glance upward.

"Culbertson's had him all ready for the funeral and drew up their bill for services—and they come to find out that the carnival had pulled up stakes and left town. Nobody claimed Herman, and nobody paid the mortuary."

Lucille Beaumont frowned. "Couldn't they have notified his next of kin?"

George Carr shrugged. "Didn't know who in Sam Hill he was. But Old Man Culbertson was firm on one point: no money, no funeral. So they kept him. As a floor model, you know. Showing what a good job they did at embalming. He was a curiosity around here when I was a kid. My pals and I used to love to go into Culbertson's to look at Herman."

"How did you get him?" Clutie wanted to know.

"Old Man Culbertson died back in '68, and the funeral home went out of business. So Herman here was auctioned off with the rest of the fixtures. I've had him here ever since."

Clutie pushed her gray bangs away from her glasses and peered up at the exhibit. "How much did you say he was?"

Her friend touched her arm. "Oh, Clutie, you know you don't—"

Clutie Campbell slid a credit card out of her pigskin wallet. "Can I put him on VISA?"

The Craig Springs minivan had the usual fourteen passengers for the return trip to the retirement community. George Carr had agreed—after some negotiation—to deliver the purchase and to leave Herman in the toolshed behind Craig Springs one hour after sunset. When he asked what the ladies wanted him for, Clutie had replied, "Religious reasons," in a tone that did not invite further discussion. In a way, it was true.

Lucille Beaumont had steered her friend to the back of the van, in hopes that Mr. Waldrop's snoring would drown out their ongoing discussion.

"You *cannot* purchase a corpse as a conversation piece!" Lucille whispered as the bus pulled away from the curb.

Clutie Campbell sniffed and directed her gaze out the window. "It is not a conversation piece. This is just what the organization needs. The book lists all kinds of spells that you can work with a deader."

"It's probably *illegal*!"

Clutie smiled vaguely. *"Do what thou wilt shalt be the whole of the law."*

Lucille shook her head. "I do wish you'd give this up, Clutie."

Her friend patted her broom-straw hair. "I think you ought to join us, Lucille. Emmie Walkenshaw thinks we're the oldest coven in the country."

"I am a Presbyterian!" hissed Lucille Beaumont between clenched teeth. "I *refuse* to join a group of satanists!"

"Weren't Presbyterians once called *covenanters*?" asked Clutie in mock innocence. "I'd look into it if I were you, Lucille. There may be no conflict of interest after all." She smiled through a frosty silence for the duration of the ride.

Lucille Beaumont was so out of sorts that evening that she sat with the ancient Mrs. Hartnell at dinner, which was as close as you could come to eating alone at Craig Springs. Annie Hartnell was fond of asking people, "Did you have a nice life?" And after that she pretty much ignored you until you went away. Usually people took pains to avoid her, but tonight Lucille decided that Mrs. Hartnell was the only company she was fit for.

Really, she thought, Clutie Campbell's satanist business was getting out of hand. Clutie was a widowed schoolteacher who claimed that the routine of Craig Springs bored her, and that the intellectual climate was nil. Her earlier attempts at culture—a poetry society and a debating team—had failed miserably, but the drama and secrecy of witchcraft had attracted a following. At first a group of folks had gone along with her because it made a nice change from square dancing and canasta, but now it was more than a game. The thirteen recruits had progressed from Ouija boards to table tapping to pentagrams and incantations. So far the staff was unaware of this diversion, and Lucille was determined not to be a snitch, but the coven was getting bolder (*sillier!* thought Lucille), and discovery seemed inevitable.

As she carried her dinner tray to the service hutch, Lucille could not resist a warning to the head witch. "Clutie," she said dramatically, not even bothering to lower her voice, "there is great danger in tampering with the forces of darkness!"

Just then Mrs. Hartnell was wheeled by in her chair, beaming and nodding at the table of satanists. "Did you have a nice life?" she asked sweetly.

Tinker's Meadow was a quarter of a mile from the retirement community. It was bordered on three sides by piney woods and was fronted on the east by a little-used dirt road. High Priestess

Clutie chose it for the ceremony for privacy—and because it was as far from the home as they could carry a mummy in a glass-fronted box.

A pale dime-sized moon shone on the long grass, and an autumn wind made the coven shiver. It was just after eight o'clock. Midnight would have been a better time for spells to work, but several folks had to be back by eleven to take medication, so they had to make do with the darkness, the full moon, and a real corpse.

Clutie wore a homemade Egyptian collar over her black evening gown, clumps of rings and bracelets, and a black pageboy wig reminiscent of Cher. But she was very dignified. She clutched her copy of *Ancient Spells & Rituals* with an air of solemn authority. At her direction, Mrs. Walkenshaw drew a pentagram on the ground (with chalk borrowed from the Craig Springs billiard table). Mr. Waldrop and Mr. Junger took the mummy out of its shabby coffin and placed it faceup within the circle. There was a smell of moth-balls from the vintage suit.

"He feels like the cover of a Bible," Mr. Junger whispered to Miss Fowler.

Clutie motioned for her followers to join hands and form a ring around the pentagram. She closed her eyes and threw back her head. "We are invoking the black angels with this once-living mortal—with this terrible sacrifice from *A gulf profound as that Serbonian bog Betwixt Damiata and Mount Casius old, Where armies whole have sunk; the parching Air Burns frore, and cold performs th' effect of Fire.*" (The Craig Springs library copy of *Paradise Lost* had been missing for several months.)

"In exchange for our demonic offering, we ask for power—" Clutie clanked her bracelets and made her voice rise to a howl as she chanted a few Latin phrases from the magic book.

"Power!" murmured the coven members, swaying rhythmically as she chanted.

"I drop fresh blood upon this offering and command you, Demon, to reveal yourself unto your priestess!"

The circle began to writhe as the members turned and threaded their way to the left through the group, clasping each other's hand as they passed. This completed, they rejoined hands and paced solemnly to the right in one full rotation. *(Allemande left and circle right.)*

That was when the *thing* appeared at the edge of the woods. The coven members with better hearing had claimed to hear a snarl or a roar a few seconds before the apparition, but all eyes turned almost simultaneously to the dark clearing where a white shape had materialized. It was no more than a flash in the blackness, but suddenly—where its mouth ought to be—a long tongue of flames billowed forth like a fiery banner. Slowly, deliberately it began to move forward.

The thirteen members of the Craig Springs coven thought they were screaming, "The Demon!" but in fact the sound came out more like "Aarggh!" Everybody got the message, though. In less time than you could say *amen*, the senior-citizen satanists had dropped hands and were sprinting toward the road. Clutie Campbell, her black drapery hitched up around her knees, was leading the pack. As they headed off in the direction of the retirement community, several members paused for breath and announced their intention of disbanding the coven. Mrs. Walkenshaw recited the Lord's Prayer as one long word, refusing to look back. Clutie Campbell wondered if she ought to wait a week before she suggested a synchronized swimming team.

The book of magic and the tatty roustabout mummy lay forgotten in the dirt of Tinker's Meadow.

When the shouts of the departing coven had faded into the autumn night, a solitary figure stepped out of the woods and walked toward the abandoned pentagram. Its white robe rustled in the long grass as it stopped to retrieve a long wooden-handled implement from the ground. The mummy's leathery face remained impassive in the moonlight.

"Well, that's that," said Lucille Beaumont softly as she looked down at the erstwhile sacrifice. "Of course, you probably didn't know what was happening to you, but it was downright disrespectful, and I had to put a stop to it. Whoever you are, you deserve a proper funeral. All I can manage is a prayer and a few old hymns, though. I hope that will do."

Lucille rolled up the sleeves of her white Presbyterian choir robe and picked up the Craig Springs gardener's shovel. "You deserve to get buried, too," she told the mummy. "I was in a carnival when I was young, just like you, and us carnies have to stick together." Lucille Beaumont's second husband had been the fire-eater, and he'd taught her the tricks of his trade. Although she had much preferred being the fortune-teller, she never forgot her lessons in pyrotechnics. She had had to improvise the fire-eating materials for the Tinker's Meadow performance, but she had apparently been a most convincing demon. She smiled to herself, remembering the satanists' screaming retreat. Good thing there weren't any heart patients in the coven.

"I reckon a lifetime in show business is long enough," she remarked. "A person ought to be allowed to retire. And you sure don't want to keep on in show business when you're dead, do you, mister?"

Gently, but matter-of-factly, she placed the mummy back in his glass-fronted box, and she said a simple prayer for the repose of both body and soul. When that was done, she sank the shovel deep into the clay of Tinker's Meadow to begin the makeshift grave. As the spadefuls of earth plopped softly on the grass, Lucille Beaumont sang her second husband's favorite hymn—"Give Me Oil in My Lamp, Keep Me Burning"—in a voice like a rusting calliope.

The Luncheon

~

She must be careful not to let her anxiety show. Even if something were said during the lunch hour, she must take it calmly or, even better, pretend not to understand at all. Above all she must seem just as usual, no more or less quiet, attentive to the eddies in their lives.

Usually this was not difficult. Kathryn and Jayne required no more than token contributions from her, since it was tacitly understood that her life was less interesting than theirs. Occasionally Thursday lunch turned into an inquisition, when she let something negative slip—such as a quarrel with Andrew that morning. Jayne had pounced, demanding that her problem be "shared," and they had dissected it over chicken breast in wine sauce. By the time the dessert crêpes had arrived, Andrew's forgetting to put mustard instead of mayonnaise on her sandwich had become an act of chauvinism.

Miriam had said that she would rather handle matters with Andrew in her own way, but they had laughed and asked her if she were trying to be *The Total Woman*. Kathryn told her that if Andrew refused to respect her personhood, she should take a lover, but Jayne contended that self-awareness was a healthier approach. She insisted that Miriam attend assertiveness training class with her, so Miriam went twice, because she didn't want to say no. Usually when other people insisted on a thing, and Miriam didn't care much either way, she let them have their own way. She had noticed, though, that some people nearly always cared a great deal about everything—such as where they had lunch and when they went—so that Miriam seldom got the default of getting to choose. But each thing was too trivial in Miriam's view to be assertive about. Somehow, though, they added up.

The jeweler's clock said 12:20, and she only had another block to go. Miriam slowed her walk to a trudge, but she still arrived for 12:30 lunch at 12:23. She decided, against her own inclinations, to go into the Post and Lentils and wait. It had been Kathryn's choice today, so lunch would be one of the Post's thirty-seven salad combinations, with commentary from Kathryn on the nutritional value of each ingredient. Miriam wished she'd bought a newspaper. She hated waiting with nothing to do. Jayne would not come for another fifteen minutes—to show that, as an executive, she was not tied to the clock hands. Miriam had nearly memorized the menu by the time Kathryn arrived.

"Well, hello, there, Miriam. How are *you*?"

Miriam wondered why Kathryn always seemed surprised to see her when they met for lunch every week. In fact, the Vietcong streak in Miriam's mind bristled at the inevitable greeting, but the meek and courteous part that was usually in control of her actions mumbled: "Fine. And you?"

She let Meek and Courteous continue the conversation on automatic pilot while the rest of her considered the question of why Kathryn made her uncomfortable. She was friendly, even effusive, but . . . but it was that *gushing* kindness—the way the Homecoming Queen treats the fat girl, as if to say: "You know you're not worth it, and I know you're not worth it, but I'll be kind to you to show everyone what a swell person I am." Miriam thought that putting up with Kathryn might be good practice for when she was eighty and was treated that way by everybody.

"Am I late?" cooed Kathryn. "I hope you didn't mind waiting."

Miriam said no, she never minded waiting. Sometimes, of

course, she did mind, and she made great violent scenes in her head, scenes that were always scrapped when the other person arrived. Usually, though, she enjoyed a short wait. It was like a little breather offstage while you waited for your next scene. She would study the trees and the sky, and perhaps run over a bit of forthcoming dialogue, making sure to stay in character, and by then whoever she was waiting for turned up, and her self-awareness dissolved in a flurry of civilities.

"God, I'm tired," Kathryn was saying. "It can't be my blood sugar. I just had it checked." She pulled a bottle of pills from her purse and studied it thoughtfully. "More iron? Maybe I should have kelp today."

Miriam didn't smile. She was studying the abstract painting hanging above the booth and wondering how anybody could pay to have such ugliness about them, regardless of its technical merit. She had wanted to be an artist herself once, until it was impressed upon her that being able to draw well had nothing to do with it. She still liked to look at paintings, but she wondered why no one ever did pleasant or harmonious things. *Suppose I had to hang that in my bedroom for a year,* she would say to herself. She once ventured this opinion to Kathryn and Jayne, and they had smiled at her together and gently explained that paintings were not supposed to be pretty; they were supposed to reflect life. Miriam had wanted to answer that an artist of all people ought to be able to see the beauty in life, but the conversation had gone on by then to other topics.

"Having lunch with the Gorgons today?" Andrew had asked her. It was his oft-stated opinion that the *y*'s in Kathryn and Jayne's names were their compensation for a missing, but coveted, male chromosome. He said he got along perfectly well with Jayne when he needed library material put on reserve, and since Kathryn was a secretary for the department next door to Geology, he often said hello to her in the halls, but their friendship with his wife did not extend to him. Perhaps, in fact, it excluded him automatically. (But she didn't want to think about Andrew.)

Miriam sometimes wondered why she kept up the lunch dates. The staff computer class where she had met them was long since over, but their habit of a weekly luncheon persisted. Still, you had to eat *somewhere*, and Miriam could not face the paper-bag lunch five days a week. It made it too easy to spend your hour running errands instead of eating, and then you were more tired than when you started. She supposed that she had nothing better to do: many, if not most, university friendships amounted to no more than that.

"I can't eat too much today," Kathryn was saying. "I'm playing racquetball this afternoon with Kit. I didn't get to see him last weekend because his daughter was down visiting. I think we have our relationship more clearly defined now. . . ."

Miriam wondered what she was going to think about until Kathryn finished her monologue. She always thought of it as the *Cosmo* Speech. Whenever you go out to lunch with an unattached woman over thirty, her conversation always comes around to a speech that sounds like a feature article from the magazine: His Career/My Career; His Kids/My Kids; or, most often, He Says He Loves Me, But He'll Screw Anything That Moves.

Miriam had heard variations on all these themes enough to know that it was never wise to offer any advice, particularly common sense, which almost always amounted to *Dump the Creep*. So she tried to look earnest while they talked, and behind the glazed look in her eyes she thought about her other regular outing "with the girls," as Andrew facetiously put it, although surely everybody in the Chataqua County Garden Club was over fifty. Except herself, of course. They were meeting tonight. Since refreshments were served at the meeting, she had told Andrew that she would be leaving him a salad to eat with the leftover lasagna.

She had expected Kathryn and Jayne to approve of the Chataqua

County Garden Club (a "sisterhood," of sorts), but oddly enough they hadn't. They had not come right out and said so, but their attitude implied: *Of course it is chic for professors (and their wives) to move out into the country, but not so far out as Miriam and Andrew have moved . . . and not to socialize with the . . . locals.* Once, Miriam had made the mistake of mentioning that one of their neighbors had offered them some deer meat. Jayne had been unable to eat another forkful of lentil loaf, and for the rest of the lunch hour they had said dark things about the "carnivores" who were native to the North Carolina hills.

Miriam understood that the proper country place for university people to live was south of the campus town, in Williamson County, a lovely, unspoiled rural haven, with an herb shop, a "free press" (the word *Nicaragua* was always contained on page one, while on the back pages were vegetarian recipes and ads for goat's milk and meditation classes), and evening yoga classes at the Alternative Children's Academy. If Miriam and Andrew should wish to pursue rural living, according to Kathryn and Jayne, they should do so in Williamson County with the civilized people. Miriam had mentioned this to Andrew, and he'd laughed about it and said that he didn't see why all those Earth Shoe People didn't just move to California, but that maybe they wouldn't have to. Maybe, he said, California would just suck them right across the country like a giant vacuum cleaner. After that, Miriam told people that she didn't want to live in Williamson County because of a fear of tornadoes.

Andrew had agreed to move there only because it was so much cheaper than closer places, but Miriam liked Chataqua County. Conversations with the neighboring farmers made a nice change from all the university talk that she got during the rest of the week. (Most of the farmers had been to college, too, but they weren't Academic—which is not the same thing as being educated.) Sometimes Barbara down the road would tell her about an auction at the old schoolhouse in Sinking Creek, and they'd go for the evening, packed tighter than baled hay in the little auditorium, eating hot dogs from the 4-H concession stand, and watching somebody else's life pass before them as a string of possessions. Sometimes they'd bid on an applewood rocking chair or a collection of old kitchen utensils, but never on the really nice pieces of furniture or the silverware. Dealers always jacked the price up on those. Or the university people. "You got to watch out for the skinny women with no makeup, wearing jeans and an *old* cashmere sweater," Barbara warned her. "They got all kinds of money."

Chataqua County was lambs in the spring, and Ruritan apple butter, and the garden club. One Tuesday a month in the Sunday-school room of the Mt. Olive Baptist Church, two dozen ladies would meet to compare flower arrangements, discuss civic projects (like taking baked goods to the senior-citizen home), and catch up on all the news. It had taken Miriam a good while to follow it all, being the only one "not from around here," but she was beginning to get it sorted out now.

Miriam's favorite part of the garden club meetings, though, was the plant lore. The older women, especially, were full of tales about healing plants, and herbal teas, and old traditions. "You know why they's a mountain ash planted beside most every door in Scotch Creek?" they'd ask her. "Why, because the mountain ash is the American kin of the rowan tree back in Scotland. My grandmother used to say that in the old days, folk thought a rowan would protect you from the evil spirits, so them Scots that came over here went on a-planting 'em by the doorway."

Miriam was always afraid that someone from Sociology with a tape recorder, or one of the Earth Shoe People, would find out about the garden club and horn in, but so far they hadn't. Last November, when Kathryn was dating the latest divorce-casualty in Appalachian Studies, she had suggested that they drive out for the meeting, but Miriam had put her off by reminding her that it was hunting season, and perhaps not entirely safe. The matter had rested there.

"Sorry I'm late," said Jayne, not sounding sorry in the least. "Some guy needed a reference, and I could *not* get him off the phone." Jayne was the humanities reference librarian, a job she described as "having to suffer fools gladly." She was in her not-to-be-mistaken-for-a-secretary outfit: navy blue straight skirt and blazer, blue tailored blouse, red foulard tie. Sleek, short haircut; no mascara. Sometimes, Southern-born professors over sixty absent-mindedly called her "dear," but everyone else got the message.

She sat down and looked meaningfully at Kathryn before picking up the menu. *Uh-oh,* thought Miriam.

"So," said Jayne, glancing through the salad list. "What have you been talking about?"

"Nothing much," said Kathryn. She meant, *I haven't said anything yet.*

Miriam said, "I think we'd better order. I need to get back."

Kathryn glanced at her watch. "It *is* getting late."

The waitress appeared then, and the next few minutes were occupied with detailed instructions—"Iced tea. Very light ice." "Is that low sodium?"—and so on. Miriam toyed with a pink packet of saccharin while these proceedings were taking place. She was trying to think about something else.

"How is Andrew?" asked Jayne, trying to make it sound perfunctory.

"He's fine," said Miriam. *He doesn't know that I know. I wondered if he suspected that you did.* Andrew had forgotten that she had taken the university computer course for staff. As a professor, he had an electronic mailbox, and one day (just for fun?) she had accessed his "mail" on her terminal. The password was easy to figure out. True to his specialization, Andrew alternated between *aquifer* and *mineral.* Miriam did not know what she had expected to find on the university computer system. Love letters, perhaps, since Andrew had been preoccupied lately. She supposed, after all, that electronic mail was just as private as the other kind. Or just as un-private.

So she had found out about Andrew's project weeks ago, and now that it was nearly to the press-release stage, Kathryn must have learned about it from gossip in the department of ... Andrew's co-conspirator. He had not discussed it with her, of course. He was going to present her with a fait accompli. He would make a lot of money from the sale, and as the letters from the other professor had stated, "There weren't many people to be considered." Chataqua County was not populous. She knew that sooner or later the weekly luncheon would be devoted to a discussion of Andrew and his project, but Miriam did not want to "articulate her feelings" with Kathryn and Jayne. They'd be on the same side for once, but she preferred to handle matters in her own way.

She had already talked the matter over with the garden club. A couple of the older ones had to have things like "toxic chemicals" and "groundwater" explained to them, but finally they understood why she was so upset about Andrew's offer to sell the farm to the university for a landfill. She told them about some of the chemicals that certain departments couldn't dump down the sink anymore, and what had happened to the pond on campus when they used it for dumping.

After that there had been complete silence for a good three minutes. And then the talk returned to gardening. At first Miriam thought that the issue had been too complex for them to understand. She wondered if she ought to explain about cancer and crop contamination, and all the other dangers. Listening to their calm discussion of plants, she thought that they had just given up considering the problem altogether, but looking back on it later, she understood.

"Cohosh sure does look nice in a flower arrangement, doesn't it?" said Mrs. Calloway. "Nice big purple berries that look like a cross between blueberries and grapes. There's some up the hill behind our place."

"You wouldn't want to use them in a salad, though," said Mrs.

Dehart thoughtfully. "Bein' poison and all. Course, they might not kill you."

"We lost a cow to eating chokecherry leaves once," said Mrs. Fletcher. "It almost always kills a cow if you let one in a field with chokecherry. I never heard tell of a human getting hold of any, though. We got some growing in our woods, but it's outside the fence."

"That ain't nothin' to hemlock," sniffed Serena Walkenshaw. "Looks just like parsley, if you don't know any better. They're kin, of course. Wild carrot family, same as Queen Anne's lace. But that hemlock beats all you ever seen for being . . . *toxic*?"

Miriam nodded. "I don't suppose you find it much around here."

Serena Walkenshaw shrugged. "I believe I saw some in the marsh near that little creek on your place. Course, it might have been parsley. . . ."

Miriam felt a tug on her sleeve and looked up to see Kathryn peering at her intently. "Are you all right, Miriam? You're just staring at your salad."

Miriam smiled. "I was just thinking that I had to fix a salad for Andrew tonight, before I go off to the garden club."

Jayne laughed. "The *garden club*! What can you possibly get out of that?"

"Recipes," said Miriam softly.

A Predatory Woman

"She looks a proper murderess, doesn't she?" said Ernie Sleaford, tapping the photo of a bleached blonde. His face bore that derisive grin he reserved for the "puir doggies," his term for unattractive women.

With a self-conscious pat at her own more professionally lightened hair, Jackie Duncan nodded. Because she was twenty-nine and petite, she had never been the object of Ernie's derision. When he shouted at her, it was for more professional reasons—a missed photo opportunity or a bit of careless reporting. She picked up the unappealing photograph. "She looks quite tough. One wonders that children would have trusted her in the first place."

"What did they know, poor lambs? We never had a woman like our Erma before, had we?"

Jackie studied the picture, wondering if the face were truly evil, or if their knowledge of its possessor had colored the likeness. Whether or not it was a cruel face, it was certainly a plain one. Erma Bradley had dumpling features with gooseberry eyes, and that look of sullen defensiveness that plain women often have in anticipation of slights to come.

Ernie had marked the photo *Page One*. It was not the sort of female face that usually appeared in the pages of *Stellar*, a tabloid known for its daily photo of Princess Diana, and for its bosomy beauties on page three. A beefy woman with a thatch of

badly bleached hair had to earn her way into the tabloids, which
Erma Bradley certainly had. Convicted of four child murders in
1966, she was serving a life sentence in Holloway Prison in
north London.

Gone, but not forgotten. Because she was Britain's only female
serial killer, the tabloids kept her memory green with frequent stories about her, all accompanied by that menacing 1965 photo of
the scowling, just-arrested Erma. Most of the recent articles about
her didn't even attempt to be plausible: "Erma Bradley: Hitler's
Illegitimate Daughter," "Children's Ghosts Seen Outside Erma's
Cell," and, the October favorite, "Is Erma Bradley a Vampire?"
That last one was perhaps the most apt, because it acknowledged
the fact that the public hardly thought of her as a real person anymore; she was just another addition to the pantheon of monsters,
taking her place alongside Frankenstein, Dracula, and another
overrated criminal, Guy Fawkes. Thinking up new excuses to use
the old Erma picture was Ernie Sleaford's specialty. Erma's face
was always good for a sales boost.

Jackie Duncan had never done an Erma story. She had been
four years old at the time of the infamous trial, and later, with the
crimes solved and the killers locked away, the case had never particularly interested her. "I thought it was her boyfriend, Sean
Hardie, who actually did the killing," she said, frowning to
remember the details of the case.

Stellar's editor sneered at her question. "Hardie? I never
thought he had a patch on Erma for toughness. Look at him now.
He's completely mental, in a prison hospital, making no more
sense than a vegetable marrow. That's how you *ought* to be with
the lives of four kids on your conscience. But not our Erma! Got
her university degree by telly, didn't she? Learned to talk posh in
the cage? And now a bunch of bloody do-gooders have got her
out!"

Jackie, who had almost tuned out this tirade as she contemplated her new shade of nail varnish, stared at him with renewed interest. "I hadn't heard that, Sleaford! Are you sure it isn't another of your fairy tales?" She grinned. " 'Erma Bradley, Bride of Prince Edward'? That was my favorite."

Ernie had the grace to blush at the reminder of his last Erma headline, but he remained solemn. "S'truth, Jackie. I had it on the quiet from a screw in Holloway. She's getting out next week."

"Go on! It would have been on every news show in Britain by now! Banner headlines in *The Guardian*. Questions asked in the House."

"The prison officials are keeping it dark. They don't want Erma to be pestered by the likes of us upon her release. She wants to be let alone." He smirked. "I had to pay dear for this bit of information, I can tell you."

Jackie smiled. "Poor mean Ernie! Where do I come into it, then?"

"Can't you guess?"

"I think so. You want Erma's own story, no matter what."

"Well, we can write that ourselves in any case. I have Paul working on that already. What I really need is a new picture, Jackie. The old cow hasn't let herself be photographed in twenty years. Wants her privacy, does our Erma. I think *Stellar*'s readers would like to take a butcher's at what Erma Bradley looks like today, don't you?"

"So they don't hire her as the nanny." Jackie let him finish laughing before she turned the conversation round to money.

The cell was beginning to look the way it had when she first arrived. Newly swept and curtainless, it was a ten-by-six-foot rectangle containing a bed, a cupboard, a table and chair, a wooden washbasin, a plastic bowl and jug, and a bucket. Gone were the posters and the photos of home. Her books were stowed away in a Marks & Spencer shopping bag.

Ruthie, whose small, sharp features earned her the nickname Minx, was sitting on the edge of the bed, watching her pack. "Taking the lot, are you?" she asked cheerfully.

The thin dark woman stared at the array of items on the table. "I suppose not," she said, scowling. She held up a tin of green tooth powder. "Here. D'you want this, then?"

The Minx shrugged and reached for it. "Why not? After all, you're getting out, and I've a few years to go. Will you write to me when you're on the outside?"

"You know that isn't permitted."

The younger woman giggled. "As if that ever stopped you!" She reached for another of the items on the bed. "How about your Christmas soap? You can get more on the outside, you know."

She handed it over. "I shan't want freesia soap ever again."

"Taking your posters, love? Anyone would think you'd be sick of them by now."

"I am. I've promised them to Senga." She set the rolled-up posters on the bed beside Ruthie, and picked up a small framed photograph. "Do you want this, then, Minx?"

The little blonde's eyes widened at the sight of the grainy snapshot of a scowling man. "Christ! It's Sean, isn't it? Put it away. I'll be glad when you've taken that out of here."

Erma Bradley smiled and tucked the photograph in among her clothes. "I shall keep this."

Jackie Duncan seldom wore her best silk suit when she conducted interviews, but this time she felt that it would help to look both glamorous and prosperous. Her blond hair, shingled into a stylish bob, revealed shell-shaped earrings of real gold, and her calf leather handbag and shoes were an expensive matched set. It wasn't at all the way a working *Stellar* reporter usually dressed, but it lent Jackie an air of authority and professionalism that she needed to profit from this interview.

She looked around the shabby conference room, wondering if

Erma Bradley had ever been there, and, if so, where she had sat. In preparation for the new assignment, Jackie had read everything she could find on the Bradley case: the melodramatic book by the BBC journalist, the measured prose of the prosecuting attorney, and a host of articles from newspapers more reliable than *Stellar*. She had begun to be interested in Erma Bradley and her deadly lover, Sean Hardie: *the couple that slays together stays together?* The analyses of the case had made much of the evidence and horror at the thought of child murder, but they had been at a loss to provide motive, and they had been reticent about details of the killings themselves. There was a book in that, and it would earn a fortune for whoever could get the material to write it. Jackie intended to find out more than she had uncovered, but first she had to find Erma Bradley.

Her Sloane Ranger outfit had charmed the old cats in the prison office into letting her in to pursue the story in the first place. The story they thought she was after. Jackie glanced at herself in the mirror. Very useful for impressing old sahibs, this posh outfit. Besides, she thought, why not give the prison birds a bit of a fashion show?

The six inmates, dressed in shapeless outfits of polyester, sprawled in their chairs and stared at her with no apparent interest. One of them was reading a Barbara Cartland novel.

"Hello, girls!" said Jackie in her best nursing home voice. She was used to jollying up old ladies for feature stories, and she decided that this couldn't be much different. "Did they tell you what I'm here for?"

More blank stares, until a heavy-set redhead asked, "You ever do it with a woman?"

Jackie ignored her. "I'm here to do a story about what it's like in prison. Here's your chance to complain, if there are things you want changed."

Grudgingly then, they began to talk about the food, and the illogical, unbending rules that governed every part of their lives.

The tension eased as they talked, and she could tell that they were becoming more willing to confide in her. Jackie scribbled a few cursory notes to keep them talking. Finally one of them said that she missed her children: Jackie's cue.

As if on impulse, she put down her notepad. "Children!" she said breathlessly. "That reminds me! Wasn't Erma Bradley a prisoner here?"

They glanced at each other. "So?" said a dull-eyed woman with unwashed hair.

A ferrety blonde, who seemed more taken by Jackie's glamour than the older ones, answered eagerly, "I knew her! We were best friends!"

"To say the least, Minx," said the frowsy embezzler from Croyden.

Jackie didn't have to feign interest anymore. "Really?" she said to the one called Minx. "I'd be terrified! What was she like?"

They all began to talk about Erma now.

"A bit reserved," said one. "She never knew who she could trust, because of her rep, you know. A lot of us here have kids of our own, so there was feeling against her. In the kitchen, they used to spit in her food before they took it to her. And sometimes, new girls would go at her to prove they were tough."

"That must have taken nerve!" cried Jackie. "I've seen her pictures!"

"Oh, she didn't look like that anymore!" said Minx. "She'd let her hair go back to its natural dark color, and she was much smaller. Not bad, really. She must have lost fifty pounds since the trial days!"

"Do you have a snapshot of her?" asked Jackie, still doing her best impression of breathless and impressed.

The redhead laid a meaty hand on Minx's shoulder. "Just a minute. What are you really here for?"

Jackie took a deep breath. "I need to find Erma Bradley. Can you help me? I'll pay you."

A few minutes later, Jackie was bidding a simpering farewell to the warden, telling her that she'd have to come back in a few days for a follow-up. She had until then to come up with a way to smuggle in two bottles of Glenlivet: the price on Erma Bradley's head. Ernie would probably make her pay for the liquor out of her own pocket. It would serve him right if she got a book deal out of it on the side.

The flat could have used a coat of paint, and some better quality furniture, but that could wait. She was used to shabbiness. What she liked best about it was its high ceiling and the big casement window overlooking the moors. From that window you could see nothing but hills and heather and sky. No roads, no houses, no people. After twenty-five years in the beehive of a women's prison, the solitude was blissful. She spent hours each day just staring out that window, knowing that she could walk on the moors whenever she liked, without guards or passes or physical restraints.

Erma Bradley tried to remember if she had ever been alone before. She had lived in a tiny flat with her mother until she finished O-levels, and then when she'd taken the secretarial job at Hadlands, there had been Sean. She had gone into prison at the age of twenty-two, an end to even the right to privacy. She could remember no time when she could have had solitude, to get to know her own likes and dislikes. She had gone from Mum's shadow to Sean's. She kept his picture, and her mother's, not out of love, but as a reminder of the prisons she had endured before Holloway.

Now she was learning that she liked plants, and the music of Sibelius. She liked things to be clean, too. She wondered if she could paint the flat by herself. It would never look clean until she covered those dingy green walls.

She reminded herself that she could have had a house, *if.* If she had given up some of that solitude. Sell your story to a book publisher; sell the film rights to this movie company. Keith, her long-suffering attorney, dutifully passed along all the offers for her consideration. The world seemed willing to throw money at her, but all she wanted was for it to go away. The dowdy but slender Miss Emily Kay, newborn at forty-seven, would manage on her own, with tinned food and secondhand furniture, while the pack of journalists went baying after Erma Bradley, who didn't exist anymore. She wanted solitude. She never thought about those terrible months with Sean, the things they did together. For twenty-five years she had not let herself remember any of it.

Jackie Duncan looked up at the gracefully ornamented stone building, carved into apartments for working-class people. The builders in that gentler age had worked leaf designs into the stonework framing the windows, and they had set gargoyles at a corner of each roof. Jackie made a mental note of this useful detail: yet another monster has been added to the building.

In the worn but genteel hallway, Jackie checked the names on mailboxes to make sure that her information was correct. There it was: E. KAY. She hurried up the stairs with only a moment's thought to the change in herself these past few weeks. When Ernie first gave her the assignment, she might have been fearful of confronting a murderess, or she might have gone upstairs with the camera poised to take the shot just as Erma Bradley opened the door, and then she would have fled. But now she was as anxious to meet the woman as she would be to interview a famous film star. More so, because this celebrity was hers alone. She had not even told Ernie that she had found Erma. This was her show, not *Stellar*'s. Without another moment's thought about what she would say, Jackie knocked at the lair of the beast.

After a few moments, the door opened part way, and a small dark-haired woman peered nervously out at her. The woman was thin, and dressed in a simple green jumper and skirt. She was no longer the brassy blonde of the Sixties. But the eyes were the same. The face was still Erma Bradley's.

Jackie was brisk. "May I come in, Miss *Kay*? You wouldn't want me to pound on your door calling out your real name, would you?"

The woman fell back and let her enter. "I suppose it wouldn't help to tell you that you're mistaken?" No trace remained of her Midlands accent. She spoke in quiet, cultured tones.

"Not a hope. I swotted for weeks to find you, dear."

"Couldn't you just leave me alone?"

Jackie sat down on the threadbare brown sofa and smiled up at her hostess. "I suppose I could arrange it. I could, for instance, *not* tell the BBC, the tabloids, and the rest of the world what you look like, and where you are."

The woman looked down at her ringless hands. "I haven't any money," she said.

"Oh, but you're worth a packet all the same, aren't you? In all the years you've been locked up, you never said anything except *I didn't do it*, which is rubbish, because the world knows you did. You taped the Doyle boy's killing on a bloody tape recorder!"

The woman hung her head for a moment, turning away. "What do you want?" she said at last, sitting in the chair by the sofa.

Jackie Duncan touched the other woman's arm. "I want you to tell me about it."

"No. I can't. I've forgotten."

"No, you haven't. Nobody could. And that's the book the world wants to read. Not this mealymouthed rubbish the others have written about you. I want you to tell me every single detail, all the way through. That's the book I want to write." She took a deep breath, and forced a smile. "And in exchange, I'll keep your identity and whereabouts a secret, the way Ursula Bloom did when she interviewed Crippen's mistress in the Fifties."

Erma Bradley shrugged. "I don't read crime stories," she said.

The light had faded from the big window facing the moors. On the scarred pine table a tape recorder was running, and in the deepening shadows, Erma Bradley's voice rose and fell with weary resignation, punctuated by Jackie's eager questions.

"I don't know," she said again.

"Come on. Think about it. Have a biscuit while you think. Sean didn't have sex with the Allen girl, but did he make love to *you* afterwards? Do you think he got an erection while he was doing the strangling?"

A pause. "I didn't look."

"But you made love after he killed her?"

"Yes."

"On the same bed?"

"But later. A few hours later. After we had taken away the body. It was Sean's bedroom, you see. It's where we always slept."

"Did you picture the child's ghost watching you do it?"

"I was twenty-two. He said—he used to get me drunk—and I—"

"Oh, come on, Erma. There's no bloody jury here. Just tell me if it turned you on to watch Sean throttling kids. When he did it, were both of you naked, or just him?"

"Please, I— Please."

"All right, Erma. I can have the BBC here in time for the wake-up news."

"Just him."

An hour later. "Do stop sniveling, Erma. You lived through it once, didn't you? What's the harm in talking about it? They can't try you again. Now come on, dear, answer the question."

"Yes. The little boy—Brian Doyle—he was quite brave, really. Kept saying he had to take care of his mum, because she was divorced now, and asking us to let him go. He was only eight, and quite small. He even offered to fight us if we'd untie him. When Sean was getting the masking tape out of the cupboard, I went up to him, and I whispered to him to let the boy go, but he . . ."

"There you go again, Erma. Now I've got to shut the machine off again while you get hold of yourself."

She was alone now. At least, the reporter woman was gone. Just before eleven, she had scooped up her notes and her tape recorder, and the photos of the dead children she had brought from the photo archives, and she'd gone away, promising to return in a few days, to "put the finishing touches on the interview." The dates and places, and forensic details, she could get from other sources, she'd said.

The reporter had gone, and the room was empty, but Miss Emily Kay wasn't alone anymore. Now Erma Bradley had got in as well.

She knew, though, that no other journalists would come. This one, Jackie, would keep her secret well enough, but only to ensure the exclusivity of her own book. Other than that, Miss Emily Kay would be allowed to enjoy her freedom in the shabby little room overlooking the moors. But it wasn't a pleasant retreat any longer, now that she wasn't alone. Erma had brought the ghosts back with her.

Somehow the events of twenty-five years ago had become more real when she told them than when she lived them. It had been so confused back then. Sean drank a lot, and he liked her to keep him company in that. And it happened so quickly that first time, and then there was no turning back. But she never let herself think about it. It was Sean's doing, she would tell herself, and then that part of her mind would close right down, and she would turn her attention to something else. At the trial, she had thought about the hatred that she could almost touch, flaring at her from nearly everyone in the courtroom. She couldn't think then, for if she broke down, they would win. They never put her on the stand.

She answered no questions, except to say, when a microphone was thrust in her face, "I didn't do it." And then later in prison there were adjustments to make, and bad times with the other inmates to be faced. She didn't need a lot of sentiment dragging her down as well. *I didn't do it* came to have a truth for her: it meant, I am no longer the somebody who did that. I am small, and thin, and well-spoken. The ugly, ungainly monster is gone.

But now she had testified. Her own voice had conjured up the images of Sarah Allen calling out for her mother, and of Brian Doyle, offering to sell his bike to ransom himself, for his mum's sake. The hatchet-faced blonde, who had told them to shut up, who had held them down . . . she was here. And she was going to live here, too, with the sounds of weeping, and the screams. And every tread on the stair would be Sean, bringing home another little lad for a wee visit.

"I didn't do it," she whispered. And it had come to have another meaning. *I didn't do it.* Stop Sean Hardie from hurting them. Go to the police. Apologize to the parents during the years in prison. Kill myself from the shame of it. "I didn't do it," she whispered again. *But I should have.*

Ernie Sleaford was more deferential to her now. When he heard about the new book, and the size of her advance, he realized that she was a player, and he began to treat her with a new respect. He had even offered her a raise, in case she was thinking of quitting. But she wasn't going to quit. She quite enjoyed her work. Besides, it was so amusing now to see him stand up for her when she came into his grubby little office.

"We'll need a picture of you for the front page, love," he said in his most civil tones. "Would you mind if Denny took your picture, or is there one you'd rather use?"

Jackie shrugged. "Let him take one. I just had my hair done. So I make the front page as well?"

"Oh, yes. We're devoting the whole page to Erma Bradley's

suicide, and we want a sidebar of your piece: 'I Was the Last to See the Monster Alive.' It will make a nice contrast. Your picture beside pudding-faced Erma."

"I thought she looked all right for forty-seven. Didn't the picture I got turn out all right?"

Ernie looked shocked. "We're not using that one, Jackie. We want to remember her the way she *was*. A vicious ugly beastie in contrast to a pure young thing like yourself. Sort of a moral statement, like."

Happiness Is
a Dead Poet

➥

The first thing Rose Hanelon did at the Unicoi Writers' Conference was to commandeer the reservation clerk's typewriter and change her name tag from GUEST AUTHOR to NOBODY IN PARTICULAR.

It wouldn't work for long, of course. By the end of the welcoming reception, the conference organizers would have introduced her to enough novices for word to get around, and she would spend the rest of the conference listening to plot summaries of romance novels (surely superfluous, since romance novels *had* only one plot), dodging poets carrying yellow legal pads, and trying to look sympathetic while housewives explained why they were only on chapter one after four years.

You had to go, though, she told herself, as she took the green-tagged room key and trudged off in search of an elevator. Agents and editors often turned up at these conferences, apparently under the delusion that a weekend's confinement in a motel outside the state of New York constituted *travel*. These people could be useful. She always waited until two days into the conference to talk business with them, because by then they had been so steeped in novice-babble that she seemed brilliant by comparison.

Rose did not get the opportunity to feel brilliant as often as she thought she deserved, which was perhaps another reason to attend these regional conferences. Being hailed as a literary lion by

Writer's Market junkies compensated for the well-bred scorn she endured more or less regularly from the college English department, to which she did not belong. She and several of its faculty members sniped at each other with less than good-natured derision over their respective literary efforts.

The opinion in Bartleby Hall was that Rose was not worthy of serious consideration as a writer, because she wrote "accessible" fiction. That is, she used the past tense, quotation marks, and plots in her books, rather than venturing into their literary realm: experimental fiction of the sort published by the "little" magazines. These tiny subsidized (sometimes mimeographed) journals paid nothing, and were read chiefly by those planning to submit manuscripts, but they counted for much in prestige and tenure.

Rose didn't have to worry about tenure. She was the college director of public relations (the English gang pronounced her job title as if it were something she did with no clothes on). For her part, Rose professed not to want a job teaching semicolons to future stockbrokers, and she often said that the English department would give a job to a Melville scholar any day, but that they would never have hired Herman Melville. Still, the steady trickle of disdain ate away at her ego, and she often threatened to write a "serious and pretentious novel" just to prove that she could. So far, though, time had not permitted her such an indulgence. The time that she could steal away from her job, her dog, and her laundry was spent producing carefully plotted mystery novels featuring a female deputy sheriff. Her works had not made her a household name, but they covered her car payments and inspired an occasional fan letter, which was better than nothing. Certainly better than writing derivative drivel for years and then not getting tenure.

This weekend's conference was as much as she could manage in the way of career development. She could practice her lecturing style and sign a few books. Besides, the setting was wonderfully picturesque: a modern glass-and-redwood lodge on Whitethorn

Island in Lake Adair. The choice of site was an indication that the
conference organizers believed the myth about writers craving solitude. Apparently it had not occurred to them that the likes of
Emily Dickinson wouldn't be caught dead at a conference in the
first place. Rose often wished she were rich enough to be tempera-
mental, but since this was not the case, she had learned to cope
with the world. The place looked pleasant enough to her, and she
had quite enjoyed the boat ride over. All in all, Rose was feeling quite festive, until she remembered what writers' conferences
tended to be like.

It was a regional conference, devoted to all types of writers,
without regard to merit or credentials. All that these people had in
common was geography. Rose had decided she needed the practice
of attending such a small, unimportant conference. If it went well,
she could work up to an important event like an all-mystery convention. Being nice to people was not a thing that came naturally
to Rose Hanelon, despite her job title. Public Relations at the university simply meant generating puff press releases for anyone's
slightest achievement and minimizing the football scandals with
understatement and misdirection. Even a curmudgeon could do it.
Thus her need to practice charm. After a few minutes' observation
of her fellow attendees, Rose began to think that she had set herself too great a task for her annual venture in celebrity.

The other guests waiting for the elevator were smiling at her,
having noticed that the name tag of NOBODY IN PARTICULAR had
the gold star for PROGRAM GUEST. They glanced at each other,
trying to guess what this dumpy little lady with the bobbed hair
and rimless spectacles could be an expert in. She did not look
benevolent enough to be in Children's Books. Children's book
editors were popularly supposed to resemble Helen Hayes or
Goldie Hawn. Perhaps she was an agent. No one knew *what* an
agent would look like.

Rose in turn noticed that the gawkers' name tags were pale
pink, signifying aspiring romance novelists. Would-be mystery

writers had name tags edged in black, and western writers had a little red cowboy hat beside their names. Rose wondered what symbol would indicate the poets. Not that a mere notation on a name tag would be warning enough, she thought sardonically. Amateur poets ought to be belled and cowled like lepers, so that you could hear them coming and flee.

This thought made her smile so broadly that one of the pink tags actually ventured to speak to her. "I see you're one of our program guests," said the grandmotherly woman in lavender.

Rose nodded warily, edging her way into the elevator. The doors slid shut behind them, turning the elevator into an interrogation room until the third floor, at which stop Rose planned to bolt.

"Are you an editor?" the plump one asked breathlessly.

"No." Editors were like ghosts: all novices talked about them, but very few had actually seen one. "I'm a writer," she admitted, noting that her stock with them had dropped considerably.

The novices exchanged glances. "Not . . . Deidre Bellaire!"

"No. Rose Hanelon." *And you've never heard of me,* she wanted to add.

Their faces looked blank, but at least they did not begin to thumb through their programs in search of her biography. The elevator creaked to a stop and Rose hoisted her bag out into the hallway.

"A published writer!" the lavender lady called after her. "How wonderful! Well, we're here to take Deidre Bellaire's workshop in writing romance novels. Tell me, what's your advice for writing a romance novel?"

"Try sticking your finger down your throat!" said Rose, as the metal doors closed behind them.

Jess Scarberry eased through the front doors of the hotel, balancing a small canvas bag, containing his weekend wardrobe, and a large leather suitcase, containing sample copies of his

mimeographed poetry magazine *The Scarberry Scriptures* and 137
assorted copies of his own books—softcover, $5.95. Scarberry
liked to call each volume a limited edition, which indeed they
were, since he could only afford to print a few hundred copies at
a time, and these would take years to sell.

He looked the part of a poet, Walt Whitman variety, with his
short gray beard, well-worn Levi's, and chambray work shirt. *A
man who gets his inspiration from the land,* his appearance seemed
to suggest. But if Jess Scarberry heard America singing, the tune
was "How Great Thou Art," directed admiringly at himself, in a
chorus of feminine voices.

The fact that Scarberry neither had, nor wanted, any male
followers was evident from his books, which all had titles like
Shadows in the Mist or *Rivers of Memory,* and from the poems
they contained, which were all variations on the idea that the poet
was a lonely wanderer occasionally seeking refuge from the cruel
world in the arms of love. His photo on the back of each book
showed a pensive Scarberry, wearing a sheepskin jacket and
leaning over a saddle that had been placed atop a split-rail fence.
The biographical notes said that the Poet had been a working
cowboy, an ambulance driver, a tugboat captain, and that he
was an honorary medicine man of the Tuscarora Indian tribe.
His most recent occupation—literary con man and jackleg
publisher—was *not* mentioned.

Scarberry cast an appraising glance around the hotel lobby,
sizing up the livestock at what he liked to think of as a literary
rodeo. During the weekend he would bulldog a few heifers, rope
and brand some new Scarberry fans, and collect enough of a grub-
stake to keep himself in Budweiser and wheat germ until the next
conference.

As he approached the registration desk, he remembered to walk
a bit bowlegged, suggesting one who has left his horse in the
parking lot. He hoped the twittery ladies near the potted palm
had noticed him. When he finished registering, he would go over,

personally invite them to attend his workshop ("The Poetry of Experience"), and graciously allow them to buy him dinner.

"**M**ay I have a new name tag?" asked the tall young woman at the conference registration table. The fact that she had just torn the old one in half suggested that this was not a request.

Margie Collier's felt tip pen poised in midair while she checked the registration form. "We spelled it right," she declared. "Connie Maria Samari. S-a-m—"

The woman winced. "I only use one name," she said. "Just *Samari*." *Samari* . . . a lilting word that conjured up images of Omar Khayyám and jasmine-scented gardens, but prefaced by *Connie Maria*, the word sank back into an ordinary Italian surname, containing no romance at all. With all due respect to her Italian grandmother, Connie Maria felt that being called Samari would be a definite advantage to her career as a poet.

With only a small sigh (because she was used to humoring eccentrics), Margie Collier took out a new name tag and obligingly wrote SAMARI in large capital letters. "There you are," she said with a friendly smile. "I suppose you write Japanese haiku?"

Samari's response was a puzzled stare, until half a minute later, when enlightenment dawned. "That is *not* how my name is pronounced!"

Several ego-encounters later, Margie Collier looked up at a registrant, who had signaled her presence simply by the shadow she cast on Margie's paperwork. The awkward-looking young woman in an unflattering black plaid suit looked faintly ridiculous clutching a vase of red carnations. Margie found herself thinking of Ferdinand the Bull. "Those flowers will look nice in your room," Margie remarked, hoping that the woman wasn't planning to tote them around during the conference. She looked in the collection of Poet badges just in case, though.

"They're not for me!" said the young woman blushing. "They're for John Clay Hawkins. For his room, I mean. I'd like to pick up his name tag, too, if I may."

Margie frowned. "Are you his wife?"

"Certainly not! I am his graduate student. My name is Amy Dillow, and I also have a name tag. Dr. Hawkins will be arriving sometime this afternoon, and I wanted to make sure that his room is ready, and that the copies of his books arrived, and I'll need his name tag and a copy of the schedule."

When Margie Collier, still trying to make sense of this, did not reply, Amy sighed with impatience. "Dr. Hawkins," she explained, "is *required reading*."

By whom? thought Margie, but she only smiled, and began to search the desk for the requested items. Some people thought that being rude was the first step to becoming a writer. She found Hawkins's name tag—not surprisingly—filed in the Poet section. *Really,* she thought, *these male poets seem to attract groupies like maggots to a dead cat.* She couldn't see what all the fuss was about. Margie's husband, a football coach at the junior high, often said that writing—and reading, for that matter—was women's work, and secretly she agreed with him. Give her a middle-linebacker any old day, instead of these peevish, sensitive artistes that didn't know *spit* from *come here.* Her idea of a real writer was Deidre Bellaire, who was just as sweet as peach jam, and she outsold those poet types by ten thousand to one, so that ought to show them, with their literary airs!

The first scheduled event for the Unicoi Writers' Conference was a get-acquainted cocktail party, in which all the attendees met in the Nolichucky Room and either asked or endured the Writers' Conference Litany: *What name do you write under? Where do you get your ideas? Should I have heard of you?* Outside, a raging thunderstorm lent the appropriate literary atmosphere to the setting. Rose Hanelon decided that the next person who came up to her and said "It is a dark and stormy night" was going to get a cup of punch in the face.

Now she had retreated into a corner, clutching a plastic cup of lukewarm strawberry punch, with nothing but a glazed smile between her and a plot summary. She had long since lost the ability to nod, but the droning woman had yet to notice. Every so often she would pat her crimped brown curls. (*As if anything short of barbecue tongs could have moved them,* thought Rose). "And then," said the aspiring author, prattling happily, mistaking silence for interest, "the heroine gets on a train and goes to New Hampshire. Or do I mean Vermont? Which one is the one on the right? Well, anyway, meanwhile, the hero has decided to go mountain climbing on a glacier. Do they have glaciers in New Hampshire? Well, it doesn't matter. Nobody's ever been there. So he goes to a psychic to, you know, see if it's going to be okay—what with his wooden leg and all, and—"

"Excuse me," said Rose. "Could I ask you something? If I give you two eggs, can you tell me if the cake will be any good?"

The narrator blinked. "What? The cake? What cake?"

"Any cake," sighed Rose. "You can't judge a cake from two eggs, and you can't judge a book from a plot summary. A bad writer can ruin anything. Just write the book and shut up." She stalked off in the direction of the hors d'oeuvres, but her way was blocked by a bearded man in a fringed buckskin jacket.

"Hello, little lady," he beamed at her in a B-movie twang. "You wouldn't happen to be an editor, would you?"

"Why do you ask?" Her eyes were glittering, the way they always did when people said words like *shorty* or *pulp fiction*.

"Why, I just happen to have a new chapbook here that is Rod McKuen and Kahlil Gibran rolled into one. I'm Jess Scarberry." He paused, waiting for cries of recognition that were not forthcoming. "I'm going to be doing a reading from it at eleven tomorrow. Why don't you come?" He beamed at a serious young woman in horn-rimmed glasses who was standing near Rose. "And you, too, of course, ma'am."

"I'll keep it in mind," said Rose, edging past him as she reached for a cheese cube. Jess Scarberry wandered away in search of other victims.

When he was out of earshot, Amy Dillow snickered. "I can't believe he thinks anybody will come to his stupid reading," she sniffed. "John Clay Hawkins is lecturing that hour on the poetic tradition."

"Really?" Rose wondered what else was going on at that hour. Flea-dipping seemed preferable.

Amy nodded, eyes shining. "He's been published everywhere! Even the *Virginia Quarterly Review*. And John Ciardi once called his work *well-crafted.*"

"That silver-tongued devil," murmured Rose.

"I'm doing my dissertation on Dr. Hawkins," Amy confided. "I think Sylvia Plath and Philip Larkin are just too overdone, don't you?"

"Well, that's because people have heard of them," said Rose. "I suppose you'd have a better chance of getting a professorship as a Larkin scholar than as a Hawkins expert. Still, it must be useful to be able to discuss the symbolism of the poetry with its author."

Amy looked shocked. "Oh, I wouldn't do that! What would he know about that? He just writes them. It's up to us scholars to determine what they mean. But I do see quite a bit of Dr. Hawkins. I'm sort of working as his volunteer secretary, too. I just hate to see him wasting his time on anything but his Muse."

Rose grunted. "I wish somebody felt that way about mystery writers."

"That's him over there," whispered Amy, pointing at a silver-haired man with a shiny blue suit and a leathery tan. The substance in his glass did not look like fruit punch. He was surrounded by several other men—an unusual occurrence for a male poet at a writers' conference. Even Amy seemed to feel that the phenomenon warranted an explanation. "Those other men are also regional poets. That young one in the leather jacket is Carter Jute, and the gaunt, elderly one is Mr. Snowfield. And there's the guy in the cowboy outfit who just invited us to his poetry class. I don't know who he thinks he is."

Rose smiled in the direction of Jess Scarberry, talking shop and, no doubt, chapbooks with the academic gentry of his field. "That," she said solemnly, "is the *poet lariat.*"

Meanwhile, in the Poets' Corner, John Clay Hawkins was smiling genially as the discussion of poetry went on around him. He had already sized up Scarberry as a con man poet, but he wasn't particularly offended by him. After all, was an iambic pentameter sex life really so much worse than what poor old Snowfield did—using his lackluster lyrics to evade teaching freshmen, and as an excuse for pomposity with other members of his department. Young Jute, he decided, was going through a phase, probably on his way to becoming a William Faulkner clone. He had already acquired the drinking problem, and he seemed to revel in the inaccessibility of his work, as though being incoherent made him smarter than anybody else. Hawkins sometimes wanted to say to these people, "All babies are incoherent, but they grow up. That is the principal difference between an infant and a poet." But he never said anything so unkind. Other people's folly didn't really annoy John Clay Hawkins; they all seemed very remote.

Mostly he was tired. His career as a poet had begun while he was in graduate school, when he had written a slim volume of poems commemorating the marriage of his former roommate, Norman Grant, to a cheerleader named Lee Locklear. The poems were tastefully obscure, so as not to resemble the bawdy limericks usually offered by groomsmen on such occasions. He had meant them as a gift, since he couldn't afford so much as a shard of the expensive china pattern the couple had chosen, but the former roommate had been a literary type himself, and flattered by this poetic tribute, he had sent copies of *Grant and Lee's Union* to *The Carolina Quarterly* and to various other prestigious Southern publications. The editors of those august journals, not apprised of the coming nuptials, assumed that the verses were a retrospective of the Civil War, and the verses were published to considerable acclaim in several magazines. The LSU Press brought out the entire collection the following year, and it won an obscure prize thanks to the presence of an LSU man and a Civil War buff on the panel of judges. After that, John Clay Hawkins found that people took it for granted that he wanted to continue being a poet, and to his surprise he found that he was rather good at it, so he kept writing. Long after Mrs. Lee Locklear Grant had dumped Norman Grant for a Wachovia Bank vice president, Hawkins continued to receive writing fellowships, and to spend a good part of his non-teaching time lecturing at various universities. After twenty years of unfailingly patient workshops and well-performed readings that people actually understood, Hawkins found himself enshrined in academic hearts somewhere between Robert Frost and Yoda, the Jedi Master of *Star Wars*. He bore beatification with quiet dignity, and went on writing simple, beautifully phrased poems about rural life. Sometimes, though, hearing the same old questions for the hundredth time that day left him feeling unutterably weary.

He turned to smile at a twittery woman who was tugging at his elbow. "Tell me," she said, through Bambi eyelashes, "where do you get your ideas for a poem?"

An elegant woman also bent on speaking to him had overheard this remark. "Poets get ideas everywhere," she snapped. "That's what makes them poets!" Having thus frightened the church bulletin versifier out of the fold, the dark-eyed young woman offered her hand to John Clay Hawkins. "My name is Samari," she purred. "I also write verse."

"You must meet Carter Jute," Hawkins murmured, recognizing an example of his colleague's taste in women.

The woman ignored his ploy. "I especially wanted to speak to you. I have found the ranks of scholarly poetry to be rather a closed circle"—she glanced over at Jess Scarberry and shuddered delicately—"with good reason, perhaps. But I do think I have a special gift, and I'd like you to read my work and to suggest some places that I could send it."

As often as this trap had sprung shut on him, John Clay Hawkins had not yet devised a foolproof way to get out of it. He tried his first tactic: the Aw Shucks Maneuver. "Oh, I just buy *Poet's Market* every year, and send 'em on out to whoever seems to like my sort of work," he said modestly, studying the tops of his shoes.

"Yes, but you're a *name*," Samari persisted. "I'm not. It would really help if you'd recommend it. Then I could say that *you* told me to send it to them."

Hawkins studied the jut of Connie Maria Samari's jaw, and the sharklike glitter of her eyes, and he recognized the Type Three Poet, the Lady Praying Mantis. In relationships she eats her mate alive, and professionally, she is as singleminded as Attila the Hun. Struggling would only prolong and embitter the encounter. Worst of all, he actually had to look at her work. A simple "Send it to Bob at *Whistlepig Review*" would not satisfy her. She wanted a diagnosis based on a reading. "Well, bring it along later," he sighed. "I'll be in my room—406—after eleven. I'll look at it then."

As she moved away in search of other prey, Hawkins remembered that he had also promised to have drinks with Jute, Snowfield, and Scarberry after eleven, and he had promised interviews or consultations with two other novices. Fortunately, Hawkins was a night person, and his lecture wasn't until eleven the next morning. *Surely,* he thought, *there must be quicker forms of martyrdom.*

Rose Hanelon, who went to bed with the chickens (exclusively), had been sound asleep for several hours when the pounding on her door called her forth from slumber. Groping for her eye-glasses and then her terry cloth bathrobe, she stumbled toward the door, propelled only by the thought of dismembering whoever she found when she opened it.

"Miss Hanelon?" An anxious Margie Collier, looking as if she'd thrown her clothes on with a pitchfork, fidgeted in the doorway. The sight of a glaring gargoyle in a dressing gown did little to calm her. "Did I wake you?" she gasped. "I mean—I thought you writers worked late at night on your manuscripts."

"No," said Rose between her teeth. "I'm usually out robbing graves at this hour, but it's raining! Now what do you want?"

"I'm sorry to disturb you, but since you are a mystery writer, we thought— Oh, Miss Hanelon, there's been a murder!"

"How amusing for you." Rose started to close the door. "These little parlor games are of no interest to me, however."

"No! Not a murder game! A real murder. Someone has killed John Clay Hawkins!"

"That is too bad," said Rose, shaking her head sadly. "He wasn't my first choice at all."

Eventually Margie Collier's urgency persuaded Rose that the matter was indeed serious, and her next reaction was to ask why they had bothered to wake her about it, instead of calling the local police. "They aren't here yet. Besides, we thought they might need some help," said Margie. "The people at this writers' conference are hardly the criminal types they're used to."

"No, I suppose not. They're the criminal types *I'm* used to." She stifled a yawn. "All right. Give me ten minutes to get dressed. Oh, you might as well tell me about it while I do. Save time. What happened?"

Margie sat down on the bed, and modestly fixed her eyes at a point on the ceiling while she recited her narrative. "About mid-night, a woman named Samari went to Dr. Hawkins's room to show him her manuscript—"

"I've never heard it called that before—" Rose called from the bathroom.

"She's a poetess." Margie's tone was reproachful. "She knocked, and found the door ajar, and there he was, slumped in his chair at the writing table. Someone had hit him over the head with a bottle of Jack Daniel's."

"Was it empty?"

"I believe so. There wasn't any spilled on the body. Ms. Samari came and got me, not knowing what else to do."

"An empty whiskey bottle." Rose wriggled a black sweater over her head. "Dylan Thomas would probably approve of that finale," she remarked. "There. I'm ready. If you insist on doing this. I'll bet the police shut down this show the minute they get here."

"Maybe so," said Margie. "But that won't be until sometime tomorrow. The storm is too bad to take a boat across. And they won't risk a helicopter, either."

"What? We're stuck here? What if somebody becomes seriously ill?"

"I asked the hotel manager about that. He said there's a registered nurse on the staff. Actually, she's the dietician, but in an emergency—"

"Never mind. I guess I'm elected. Let's go investigate this thing."

Margie brightened. "It's just like a mystery story, isn't it?"

"Not one that my editor would buy."

Although Rose Hanelon wrote what she liked to call traditional mysteries, she was well-versed in police procedure, first of all because she read widely within the genre, and secondly because the townhouse adjoining hers belonged to a police detective who liked to talk shop at his backyard cookouts. He particularly enjoyed critiquing the police procedurals written by Rose's fellow authors. With no effort on her part, Rose had assimilated quite a good working knowledge of law enforcement. She wondered if it would serve her well in the current emergency. Probably not. People had to cooperate with police officers, but they were perfectly free to ignore an inquisitive mystery writer, no matter how knowledgeable she was about investigative procedure.

"Do you think you'll be able to solve the crime?" asked Margie, who was scurrying along after Rose like a terrier in the wake of a St. Bernard.

"I doubt it," said Rose. "The police have computers, and other useful tools for ferreting out the truth. Paraffin tests, ballistics experts. If Joe Villanova had to use his powers of deduction to solve cases, he'd be in big trouble. He's a police officer; lives next door to me. He'd probably arrest me for even trying to meddle in this case. Too bad he's not here."

"Oh, but you've written so many mysteries!" said Margie. "I'm sure you know quite a bit."

"I can tell you who I want to be guilty," Rose replied. "That's what I do in my books."

"Do you want to examine Mr. Hawkins's body?"

"No. I'm not a doctor, and I don't want to get hassled for tampering with evidence. Let's just go and badger some suspects, shall we?"

Margie nodded. "I asked the hotel manager to put the poets in the hospitality suite."

"I hope they didn't bring along any manuscripts," muttered Rose. "The very thought of being cooped up with a bunch of bards gives me hives."

"It seems strange, doesn't it, to think of poets as murder suspects. They are such gentle people."

Rose Hanelon raised her eyebrows. "Have you ever been in an English department?"

The door to the hospitality suite was open, and the sounds of bickering could be heard halfway down the hall. "I think we should just conduct a memorial service in Hawkins's scheduled hour tomorrow," Carter Jute was saying. "It would be a nice way to honor his memory. I wouldn't mind conducting the service."

Jess Scarberry, the poet lariat, sneered. "I'll bet you wouldn't mind, Sonny, but remember that I'm also scheduled to do a reading at that hour. You're not taking away my audience for some phony displays of grief."

Connie Samari, mothlike in a red-and-black polyester kimono, toyed with her crystal earrings. "I suppose we could all write commemorative poems in honor of John Clay Hawkins," she murmured. "Read them at the memorial service."

Snowfield held up a restraining hand. "Just a moment," he said. "I think that I am the obvious choice for regional poet laureate, now that Hawkins has shuffled off the mortal coil. In light of that, the hour ought to be spent introducing people to my own works, with perhaps a short farewell to Hawkins." He shrugged. "I don't care which of you does that."

The poets were so intent upon their territorial struggles that they did not notice the two self-appointed investigators watching them from the doorway. What, after all, was a trifle like murder compared to their artistic considerations?

Amy Dillow, Hawkins's graduate student, glared at the upstarts. Two spots of color appeared in her pale cheeks, and she drew herself up with as much dignity as one can muster when wearing a pink chenille bathrobe and bunny slippers. "I am appalled at your attitudes!" she announced. "John Clay Hawkins was a major poet, deserving of much greater recognition than he ever received. The idea of any of you assuming his mantle is laughable. I will conduct Dr. Hawkins's conference hour myself. I have just completed a paper on the symbolism in the works of Hawkins, and it seems logical to read that tomorrow as we pause to consider his achievements."

Rose Hanelon strode into the fray, rubbing her hands together in cheerful anticipation. "Well, this won't be hard!" she announced. "It sounds just like a faculty meeting in the English department."

The poets stopped quarreling and stared at her. "Who are you?" Snowfield demanded with a touch of apprehension. He didn't think any major women poets had been invited to this piddling conference. Anyway, she wasn't Nikki Giovanni, so she probably didn't matter.

"Relax," said Rose. "If anybody called me a poet, I'd sue them for slander. I'm not here to replace Caesar, but to bury him. He was murdered, you know."

Amy Dillow sighed theatrically. "Now he belongs to the ages."

Margie Collier, ever the peacemaker, said, "Why don't I get us some coffee while Miss Hanelon speaks to you about the murder. We thought it might be nice to get the preliminary questioning done while we wait for the police." She hurried away before anyone could raise any objections to this plan, leaving Rose Hanelon alone with a roomful of egotists and possibly one murderer.

The poets sat down in a semicircle and faced her with varying degrees of resentment. Some of them were sputtering about the indignity of being a suspect in a sordid murder case.

Rose sighed. "I always find this the boring part of murder mysteries," she confided to the assembly. "It seems to go on for pages and pages, while we listen to alibis, and tedious contradictory accounts of the deceased's relationships with all present. And in order to find out who's lying, I need access to outside documents detailing the life and loves of the victim. Obviously, I can't do that, since we're stormbound on this island."

"Perhaps we could tell the police that Hawkins committed suicide," said Carter Jute. "That would protect us all from notoriety, and it's very correct in literary circles. Hemingway, Sylvia Plath."

"We *could* blame it on Ted Hughes," said Rose sarcastically, "but that wouldn't be true, either. You'll find that the police are awfully wedded to facts, as opposed to hopeful interpretation. They will investigate the crime scene, get fingerprints off the bottle, and that'll be that."

"Surely the killer would wipe the fingerprints off the murder weapon?" said Snowfield. He reddened under the stares of everyone else present. "Well, I've read a few whodunits. After all, C. Day Lewis, the English poet laureate, wrote some under the name of Nicholas Blake."

"Never mind about the murder!" said Carter Jute. "What are we going to do about Hawkins's time slot tomorrow?"

"Yes," said Rose. "Why don't you discuss that among yourselves? And while you do, I'd like to read that paper on the life and works of John Clay Hawkins. Do you have it with you, Ms. Dillow?"

Amy Dillow stood up, and yawned. "It's in my room. I'll get it for you. But why do you want to read it now?"

"It helps to have a clear idea who the victim was," said Rose.

"Oh, all right." She shuffled off in her bunny slippers. "I haven't proofed it yet, though."

In the doorway she nearly collided with Margie Collier, who was returning with a pot of coffee and seven cups. She set the tray on the coffee table, and beamed at Rose Hanelon. "Have you solved it yet?"

"Not yet," said Rose. "It's easier on television, where one of the actors is paid to confess. Real life is less tidy. This lot haven't even decided what to do with Hawkins's hour yet."

"Well, you could read John Clay Hawkins's last poem," said Margie. "The one he was writing when he died."

"He was working?" said Rose.

"Yes. I looked at the paper under poor Mr. Hawkins's hand when we examined his body. Of course, we can't remove the actual paper from the room. I'm sure the police would object to that, but I did make a copy while I was waiting for the hotel manager to arrive. Would you like to see it?" She fished a sheet of hotel stationery out of the pocket of her robe and handed it to Rose.

"Read it aloud!" Snowfield called out. The others nodded assent.

"Oh, all right," grumbled the mystery writer. "I knew you would find some way to turn this into a poetry reading." Holding

the paper at arm's length, she squinted at the spidery writing, and
recited:

> *There's this guy.*
> *his name is Norman*
> *and he's sitting in a white room.*
> *he's sitting in a white room,*
> *but you might as well call it*
> *white death.*
> *Norman is holding death like*
> *a white peach to the window*
> *and turning,*
> *turning death*
> *like the dial of a timer*
> *in the white light of the sun.*
> *death begins to tick.*
> *Norman puts death down*
> *and stares with his white eyes*
> *at the white wall.*
> *his shadow is white and moves*
> *without him around the white room.*
>
> *then death goes off.*

She lowered the paper and blinked at the assortment of poets.
"That is the most stupid and pointless thing I have ever read. Do
any of you bards get any meaning out of that?"

Jess Scarberry shrugged. "Shucks, ma'am, these professor types
don't have to make sense. If you don't understand what they write,
they reckon it's your fault."

Snowfield scowled at him. "It seems clear enough to me.
Hawkins was obviously contemplating his own mortality. Perhaps he had a premonition. Keats did."

Rose Hanelon rolled her eyes. "Keats had medical training and symptoms of tuberculosis. I'd hardly call that a premonition. I should have thought that if Hawkins foresaw his own murder, he'd have gotten out of there, rather than sit down and write a poem about it. Still, with poets, you never know."

"Who's Norman?" asked Margie with a puzzled frown.

"A metaphor for Everyman," said Carter Jute.

Connie Samari snickered. "*Everyman.* How typical of the male poet's arrogance! And I think that poem stinks!"

"I expect it's over your head," said Snowfield.

Amy Dillow returned just then with a sheaf of dot matrix–printed papers. "Here's my thesis on Hawkins. It isn't finished, of course, but you may find it helpful."

"A polygraph machine would be helpful," said Rose. "Reading this is an act of desperation. But it will have to do. Pour me some of that coffee." She settled down on one of the sofas and began to read, while the bickering went on about her.

Carter Jute handed a cup of coffee to Amy Dillow. "It's such a shame about poor old Hawkins," he said. "By the way, Amy, do you have a copy of his current vita?"

"Why do you ask?"

Jute gave her a boyish smile. "Well, I was thinking what a void his passing will leave in literary circles. There were certain editorial positions he held, and workshops that he taught year after year—"

"And you thought you'd apply for them?" Amy Dillow looked shocked.

"He'd want someone to carry on his work," Jute assured her.

Connie Samari laughed. "And heaven forbid that his honors should go to someone outside the old-boy network, right?"

Margie Collier looked dismayed to be caught in such a maelstrom of ill will. She had always thought of poets as gentle people, wandering lonely as a cloud while they composed their little odes to nature. "Why don't we all try to write a poem in memory of poor Dr. Hawkins?" she suggested. "Does anyone do haiku?"

Rose Hanelon looked up from her reading. "You say here that Hawkins was married."

"He's divorced," said Amy.

"From whom?"

"A librarian named Dreama Belcher. They didn't have any children, though."

"Just as well," muttered Snowfield, shuddering. "Imagine what the progeny of someone named Dreama Belcher would look like!"

"What became of her?"

"I don't know," said Amy. "Nothing much, I expect. She didn't have the temperament to be married to a poet."

"She preferred monogamy, I expect," said Samari. "I've often thought that male poets were reincarnations of walruses. Can't you just picture them up there on a rock, surrounded by a herd of sunbathing cow-wives?"

Jess Scarberry reddened. "It's understandable," he said. "Poets need inspiration like a car needs a battery. If you're writing love poems, you need something to jump-start the creative process."

Rose Hanelon ignored him. "Walruses," she echoed. "That's interesting. So John Clay Hawkins was . . . er . . . Byronic. That could have been hazardous to his health. Especially if one of his girlfriends objected to his philandering. Are any of his conquests here?" She peered at Amy Dillow with a glint of malicious interest.

The young graduate student blushed and looked away. "Certainly not!" she murmured. "I was solely interested in his work."

"Don't look at me," said Connie Samari. "I met him for the first time tonight. And he definitely wasn't my type."

"Yes, but if you went to his room to discuss your poetry, and he made a pass at you, you might have killed him by accident, trying to fend him off."

"If I had, I would have called a press conference to announce it," said Samari. "I certainly wouldn't have fled the scene and denied it."

Jute and Snowfield, seated on either side of her, unobtrusively edged away. Jess Scarberry crossed his legs and whistled tunelessly. Rose Hanelon went back to reading the thesis.

"Would anybody like more coffee?" asked Margie nervously.

After a few moments of uneasy silence, the poets returned to the topic of Hawkins and the professional repercussions that would ensue.

"Wasn't he set to do a guest professorship in Virginia this summer?" asked Snowfield.

"Probably. I know he was slated to write the introduction to the Regional Poets Anthology," said Samari. "Had he written that?"

Amy Dillow shrugged. "Not that I know of."

"I was thinking of applying for his slot at Bread Loaf," mused Carter Jute.

"There'll never be another John Clay Hawkins," Amy Dillow assured them. "He was the greatest poet of our region."

"Oh, come now!" Snowfield protested. "You ladies always say that about a good-looking fellow who reads well."

"Oh, don't be such a dinosaur!" said the graduate student. "I loved Hawkins's work before I even knew what he looked like. He's one of the few original voices in contemporary poetry. The fact that he was a drunk and a lecher is neither here nor there."

Rose Hanelon was wondering if Detective Joe Villanova was awake at—what was it?—four A.M. Probably not. He wouldn't be much better at this than she would, though, with no forensic evidence to go on. "Oh, well," said Rose. "Even if I don't figure out who the murderer is, all of you will be too exhausted tomorrow to commit any more murders, no matter which of you is guilty."

Carter Jute consulted his watch. "Gosh, that's right! We all have to be on panels tomorrow. Or rather, today. And we still haven't decided what to do with Hawkins's hour."

The others stood up, yawned and stretched. "Long day," they murmured.

"Wait! I'm not finished!" Rose was still riffling through the clues. "Is anyone here named Norman?" she asked in tones of desperation. "Does anyone know Hawkins's ex-wife?"

They all shook their heads. "Sorry we can't help, little lady," drawled Scarberry.

"Wait!" said Connie Samari. "We never decided what to do with Hawkins's hour!"

"Ah! Hawkins's hour," said Rose Hanelon with a feral smile. "I will be taking that."

By skipping breakfast, Rose managed to get three hours of sleep before the conference sessions began, but she still looked like a catatonic bag lady. Five cups of coffee later, she had recovered the use of most of her brain cells, but she was still considerably lacking in presentability. When she ran into Joe Villanova, helping himself to doughnuts at the coffee break in the hall, he did a double take and said, "If you'll lie down, I'll draw chalk marks around you and ask the coroner to take a look at you."

His next-door neighbor managed a feeble snarl. "Buzz off, Villanova. I'm solving this case for you. Come to the next lecture in the Catawba Room, and you'll see."

"You don't mind if we continue doing the fingerprinting and the suspect interrogations in the meantime, do you?"

"Not at all. So glad you could finally manage to come."

"Hey, I'm not risking my neck in a helicopter for a guy who is already dead. Listen, when you do this lecture of yours, don't violate anybody's rights, okay? I have to get a conviction."

Rose looked up as a gaggle of silver-haired women walked by. They were wearing Poet name tags and they seemed to be earnestly discussing onomatopoeia. "I don't suppose you could arrest all of them, Joe," she said. "We have quite a surplus of poets."

The Catawba Room was packed. Some of those present were groupies of the distinguished and handsome poet, and they had not been informed of his death. Others had heard that a mystery writer was going to conduct the session, and attended in hopes of hearing a post mortem. All the poets were there in force in case Rose Hanelon didn't use the whole hour. Scarberry, whose session had consisted of three elderly ladies, adjourned his group and joined the crowd in the Catawba Room. Villanova, with a ridiculous smirk on his face, sprawled in the front row with his arms folded, waiting for Rose to make an idiot of herself.

Rose surveyed the sheeplike faces and wished she'd had time for another cup of coffee. "Good morning," she began. "I have come to bury John Clay Hawkins, not to praise him. As you know, our featured speaker was murdered last night with an empty bottle of Jack Daniel's."

"Those who live by the sword . . ." muttered Samari from the front row.

"Even now the police are measuring and photographing, and doing all that they can to collect the physical evidence to convict the killer. I used another approach—the examination of motives. Who would want to kill a poet?"

A suppressed whoop of laughter emanated from the romance writers' contingent in the back of the room.

"Precisely," said Rose. "Who *wouldn't* want to kill a poet? But why this particular poet, when there are so many more annoying and less-talented specimens around. Besides, in this case, the suspects were all poets themselves, or people well acquainted with John Clay Hawkins as a human being."

Hawkins's fellow bards glared up at her from their front-row seats.

"The main motive that occurred to me was professional competitiveness. Hawkins, as a well-known minor poet, had a number of workshop engagements, editorships, and other poetic plums that everyone else seemed to want very badly." Rose nodded in the direction of Jess Scarberry's waving hand, acknowledging his objection. "Yes. Except for Jess Scarberry. No one would give him any literary recognition, not even if he was the last poet on earth. But I doubt if he minds. He's in the game to pick up women and sell chapbooks, and he can do all of that without any academic recognition. If he killed Mr. Hawkins, it would have to be for more personal reasons. I didn't find any."

"That left Samari, Snowfield, and Carter Jute, whose personal attributes suggest that poems are made by barracudas. I didn't even have a favorite suspect among them. So I read Amy Dillow's thesis about John Clay Hawkins. And I read the last poem of Hawkins himself. Bear with me."

She read the poem in clear measured tones to the startled audience. "At least it's timely," she remarked. "I wondered why Hawkins was thinking of Norman, and if in fact he knew anyone by that name." Rose held up Amy Dillow's thesis. "It turns out that he did. His old college roommate Norman Grant, interviewed by Ms. Dillow here as a source for material about Hawkins's early years. I called Norman Grant, and read him the poem."

"Since you had no address, how'd you find him on a Saturday morning?" Villanova called out from the front row. He was obviously enjoying himself.

Rose smiled. "Professional connections. The PR director of his alma mater is a colleague of mine. She looked him up in the alumni directory. Anyway, I called Norman Grant, and read the poem to him."

There was a murmur of interest from the audience.

Rose shrugged. "He said it made no sense to him, either. But then he said Hawkins's poems never did make sense, as far as he could tell. People just read them and assigned them meanings. He said John Clay used to joke that once a critic found one of your works profound, then anything else you ever wrote would be

analyzed to death. Didn't matter what it was. He said John Clay
was getting pretty tired of all the pretension, and of the old-boy
network of you-blurb-my-chapbook-and-I'll-publish-your-poem-
in-my-literary-magazine. He said it was the Mafia with meter. He
said that Hawkins was talking about quitting the poetry business
and coming to work with him. Mr. Grant is a crop duster in north
Georgia."

"He's lying!" Amy Dillow called out. "He was always jealous of
Hawkins's success. Norman Grant flunked English!"

"He told me that, too," said Rose. "He said they used to laugh
about it, because John Clay Hawkins wrote his papers for him that
term. Now assuming Hawkins was planning to quit poetry, there
would be no need for the other poets to do him in, but that still
leaves one very clear motive." She pointed to Amy Dillow. "If
Hawkins renounced poetry, your graduate career would have been
ruined, wouldn't it? You couldn't very well make your literary
reputation on an ex-poet who was never widely recognized to
begin with. Besides, dead poets are so much more respected than
live ones. Look at Sylvia Plath: famous for being dead."

Amy Dillow jumped to her feet. "He had no ambition!" she
cried. "He wouldn't apply for the right fellowships, or curry favor
with the really important critics. I had to do something! His work
really had potential, but he was holding back his own reputation. I
did it for scholarly reasons! I had to kill him so that I could devote
myself to the legend!"

Rose's jaw dropped. "You did?" she exclaimed. "You mean *you*
did it?"

Amy Dillow nodded. "I thought you had figured it out."

"No," Rose blurted before she thought better of it. (It had been
a long night.) "I was just using that theory for dramatic effect,
building up for the big finish. You see, Norman Grant also told
me that Hawkins's first wife, Dreama Belcher, is still a librarian,
but now she writes romance novels as Deidre Bellaire. I assumed
she had done it."

A wizened figure in rhinestones and green chiffon stood up in the back of the room, waving her fan. "I killed the bastard off in eight Harlequins and three Silhouettes," she called out. "That was enough. Got it out of my system."

Joe Villanova's shouts of laughter drowned out the polite applause from the mystery fans. Rose Hanelon shrugged. "My editor will want me to change this ending."

Nine Lives to Live

~

It had seemed like a good idea at the time. Of course, Philip Danby had only been joking, but he had said it in a serious tone in order to humor those idiot New Age clients who actually seemed to believe in the stuff. "I want to come back as a cat," he'd said, smiling facetiously into the candlelight at the Eskeridge dinner table. He had to hold his breath to keep from laughing as the others babbled about reincarnation. The women wanted to come back blonder and thinner, and the men wanted be everything from Dallas Cowboys to oak trees. *Oak trees?* And he had to keep a straight face through it all, hoping these dodos would give the firm some business.

The things he had to put up with to humor clients. His partner, Giles Eskeridge, seemed to have no difficulties in that quarter, however. Giles often said that rich and crazy went together; therefore, architects who wanted a lucrative business had to be prepared to put up with eccentrics. They also had to put up with long hours, obstinate building contractors, and capricious zoning boards. Perhaps that was why Danby had plumped for life as a cat next time. As he had explained to his dinner companions that night, "Cats are independent. They don't have to kowtow to anybody; they sleep sixteen hours a day; and yet they get fed and sheltered and even loved—just for being their contrary little selves. It sounds like a good deal to me."

Julie Eskeridge tapped him playfully on the cheek. "You'd better take care to be a pretty, pedigreed kitty, Philip." She laughed. "Because life isn't so pleasant for an ugly old alley cat!"

"I'll keep that in mind," he told her. "In fifty years or so."

It had been more like fifty days. The fact that Giles had wanted to come back as a shark should have tipped him off. When they found out that they'd just built a three-million-dollar building on top of a toxic landfill, the contractor was happy to keep his mouth shut about it for a mere ten grand, and Giles was perfectly prepared to bury the evidence to protect the firm from lawsuits and EPA fines.

Looking back on it, Danby realized that he should not have insisted that they report the landfill to the authorities. In particular, he should not have insisted on it at six P.M. at the building site with no one present but himself and Giles. That was literally a fatal error. Before you could say "philosophical differences," Giles had picked up a shovel lying near the offending trench, and with one brisk swing, he had sent the matter to a higher court. As he pitched headlong into the reeking evidence, Danby's last thought was a flicker of cold anger at the injustice of it all.

His next thought was that he was watching a black-and-white movie, while his brain seemed intent upon sorting out a flood of olfactory sensations. *Furniture polish . . . stale coffee . . . sweaty socks . . . Prell shampoo . . . potting soil . . .* He shook his head, trying to clear his thoughts. Where was he? The apparent answer to that was: lying on a gray sofa inside the black-and-white movie, because everywhere he looked he saw the same colorless vista. A concussion, maybe? The memory of Giles Eskeridge swinging a shovel came back in a flash. Danby decided to call the police before Giles turned up to try again. He stood up, and promptly fell off the sofa.

Of course, he landed on his feet.

All four of them.

Idly, to keep from thinking anything more ominous for the moment, Danby wondered what *else* the New Age clients had been right about. Was Stonehenge a flying saucer landing pad? Did crystals lower cholesterol? He was in no position to doubt anything just now. He sat twitching his plume of a tail and wishing he hadn't been so flippant about the afterlife at the Eskeridge dinner party. He didn't even particularly like cats. He also wished that he could get his paws on Giles in retribution for the shovel incident. First he would bite Giles's neck, snapping his spine, and then he would let him escape for a few seconds. Then he'd sneak up behind him and pounce. Then bat him into a corner. Danby began to purr in happy contemplation.

The sight of a coffee table looming a foot above his head brought the problem into perspective. At present Danby weighed approximately fifteen furry pounds, and he was unsure of his exact whereabouts. Under those circumstances avenging his murder would be difficult. On the other hand, he didn't have any other pressing business, apart from an eight-hour nap which he felt in need of. First things first, though. Danby wanted to know what he looked like, and then he needed to find out where the kitchen was, and whether Sweaty Socks and Prell Shampoo had left anything edible on the countertops. There would be time enough for philosophical thoughts and revenge plans when he was cleaning his whiskers.

The living room was enough to make an architect shudder. Clunky Early American sofas and clutter. He was glad he couldn't see the color scheme.

There was a mirror above the sofa, though, and he hopped up on the cheap upholstery to take a look at his new self. The face that looked back at him was definitely feline, and so malevolent that Danby wondered how anyone could mistake cats for pets. The yellow (or possibly green) almond eyes glowered at him from a massive triangular face, tiger-striped, and surrounded by a ruff of gray-brown fur. Just visible beneath the ruff was a dark leather collar equipped with a little brass bell. That would explain the ringing in his ears. The rest of his body seemed massive, even allowing for the fur, and the great plumed tail swayed rhythmically as he watched. He resisted a silly urge to swat at the reflected movement. So he was a tortoiseshell, or tabby, or whatever they called those brown-striped cats, and his hair was long. And he was still male. He didn't need to check beneath his tail to confirm that. Besides, the reek of ammonia in the vicinity of the sofa suggested that he was not shy about proclaiming his masculinity in various corners of his domain.

No doubt it would have interested those New Age clowns to learn that he was not a kitten, but a fully grown cat. Apparently the arrival had been instantaneous as well. He had always been given to understand that the afterlife would provide some kind of preliminary orientation before assigning him a new identity. A deity resembling John Denver, in rimless glasses and a Sierra Club T-shirt, should have been on hand with some paperwork regarding his case, and in a nonthreatening conference they would decide what his karma entitled him to become. At least, that's what the New Agers had led him to believe. But it hadn't been like that at all. One minute he had been tumbling into a sewage pit, and the next, he had a craving for Meow Mix. Just like that. He wondered what sort of consciousness had been flickering inside that narrow skull prior to his arrival. Probably not much. A brain with the wattage of a lightning bug could control most of the items on the feline agenda: eat, sleep, snack, doze, dine, nap, and so on. Speaking of eating . . .

He made it to the floor in two moderate bounds, and jingled toward the kitchen, conveniently signposted by the smell of lemon-scented dishwashing soap and stale coffee. The floor could do with a good sweeping, too, he thought, noting with distaste the gritty feel of tracked-in dirt on his velvet paws.

The cat dish, tucked in a corner beside the sink cabinet, confirmed his worst fears about the inhabitants' instinct for tackiness.

Two plastic bowls were inserted into a plywood cat model, painted white, and decorated with a cartoonish cat face. If his food hadn't been at stake, Danby would have sprayed *that* as an indication of his professional judgment. As it was, he summoned a regal sneer and bent down to inspect the offering. The water wasn't fresh; there were bits of dry catfood floating in it. Did they expect him to drink *that*? Perhaps he ought to dump it out so that they'd take the hint. And the dry catfood hadn't been stored in an airtight container, either. He sniffed contemptuously: the cheap brand, mostly cereal. He supposed he'd have to go out and kill something just to keep his ribs from crashing together. Better check out the counters for other options. It took considerable force to launch his bulk from floor to countertop, and for a moment he teetered on the edge of the sink fighting to regain his balance, while his bell tolled ominously, but once he righted himself he strolled onto the counter with an expression of nonchalance suggesting that his dignity had never been imperiled. He found two breakfast plates stacked in the sink. The top one was a trove of congealing egg yolk and bits of buttered toast. He finished it off, licking off every scrap of egg with his rough tongue, and thinking what a favor he was doing the people by cleaning the plate for them.

While he was on the sink, he peeked out the kitchen window to see if he could figure out where he was. The lawn outside was thick and luxurious, and a spreading oak tree grew beside a low stone wall. Well, it wasn't Albuquerque. Probably not California, either, considering the healthy appearance of the grass. Maybe he was still in Maryland. It certainly looked like home. Perhaps the transmigration of souls has a limited geographic range, like AM radio stations.

After a few moments' consideration, while he washed an offending forepaw, it occurred to Danby to look at the wall phone above the counter. The numbers made sense to him, so apparently he hadn't lost the ability to read. Sure enough, the telephone area code was 301. He wasn't far from where he started. Theoretically, at least, Giles was within reach. He must mull that over, from the vantage point of the window sill, where the afternoon sun was marvelously warm, and soothing . . . zzzzz.

Danby awakened several hours later to a braying female voice calling out, "Tigger! Get down from there this minute! Are you glad Mommy's home, sweetie?"

Danby opened one eye, and regarded the woman with an insolent stare. *Tigger?* Was there no limit to the indignities he must bear? A fresh wave of Prell shampoo told him that the self-proclaimed *mommy* was chatelaine of this bourgeois bungalow. And didn't she look the part, too, with her polyester pants suit and her cascading chins! She set a grocery bag and a stack of letters on the countertop, and held out her arms to him. "And is my snookums ready for din-din?" she cooed.

He favored her with an extravagant yawn, followed by his most forbidding Mongol glare, but his hostility was wasted on the besotted Mrs.—he glanced down at the pile of letters—Sherrod. She continued to beam at him as if he had fawned at her feet. As it was, he was so busy studying the address on the Sherrod junk mail that he barely glanced at her. He hadn't left town! His tail twitched triumphantly. Morning Glory Lane was not familiar to him, but he'd be willing to bet that it was a street in Sussex Garden Estates, just off the bypass. That was a couple of miles from Giles Eskeridge's mock-Tudor monstrosity, but with a little luck and some common sense about traffic he could walk there in a couple of hours. If he cut through the fields, he might be able to score a mouse or two on the way.

Spurred on by the thought of a fresh, tasty dinner that would beg for its life, Danby/Tigger trotted to the back door and began to meow piteously, putting his forepaws as far up the screen door as he could reach.

"Now, Tigger!" said Mrs. Sherrod in her most arch tone. "You know perfectly well that there's a litter box in the bathroom. You just want to get outdoors so that you can tomcat around, don't you?" With that she began to put away groceries, humming tunelessly to herself.

Danby fixed a venomous stare at her retreating figure, and then turned his attention back to the problem at hand. Or rather, at paw. That was just the trouble: *Look, Ma, no hands!* Still, he thought, there ought to be a way. Because it was warm outside, the outer door was open, leaving only the metal storm door between himself and freedom. Its latch was the straight-handled kind that you pushed down to open the door. Danby considered the factors: door handle three feet above floor, latch opens on downward pressure, one fifteen-pound cat intent upon going out. With a vertical bound that Michael Jordan would have envied, Danby catapulted himself upward and caught onto the handle, which obligingly twisted downward, as the door swung open at the weight of the feline cannonball. By the time gravity took over and returned him to the ground, he was claw-deep in scratchy, sweet-smelling grass.

As he loped off toward the street, he could hear a plaintive voice wailing, "Ti-iii-gerrr!" It almost drowned out the jingling of that damned little bell around his neck.

Twenty minutes later Danby was sunning himself on a rock in an abandoned field, recovering from the exertion of moving faster than a stroll. In the distance he could hear the drone of cars from the interstate, as the smell of gasoline wafted in on a gentle breeze. As he had trotted through the neighborhood, he'd read street signs, so he had a better idea of his whereabouts now. Windsor Forest, that pretentious little suburb that Giles called home, was only a few miles away, and once he crossed the interstate, he could take a shortcut through the woods. He hoped that La Sherrod wouldn't put out an all-points bulletin for her missing kitty. He didn't want any SPCA interruptions once he reached his destination. He ought to ditch the collar as well, he thought. He couldn't very well pose as a stray with a little bell under his chin.

Fortunately, the collar was loose, probably because the ruff around his head made his neck look twice as large. Once he determined that, it took only a few minutes of concentrated effort to work the collar forward with his paws until it slipped over his ears. After that, a shake of the head—jingle! jingle!—rid him of Tigger's identity. He wondered how many pets who "just disappeared one day," had acquired new identities and gone off on more pressing business.

He managed to reach the bypass before five o'clock, thus avoiding the commuter traffic of rush hour. Since he understood automobiles, it was a relatively simple matter for Danby to cross the highway during a lull between cars. He didn't see what the possums found so difficult about road crossing. Sure enough, there was a ripe gray corpse on the white line, mute testimony to the dangers of indecision on highways. He took a perfunctory sniff, but the roadkill was too far gone to interest anything except the buzzards.

Once across the road, Danby stuck to the fields, making sure that he paralleled the road that led to Windsor Forest. His attention was occasionally diverted by a flock of birds overhead, or an enticing rustle in the grass that might have been a field mouse, but he kept going. If he didn't reach the Eskeridge house by nightfall, he would have to wait until morning to get himself noticed.

In order to get at Giles, Danby reasoned, he would first have to charm Julie Eskeridge. He wondered if she was susceptible to needy animals. He couldn't remember whether they had a cat or not. An unspayed female would be nice, he thought. A Siamese, perhaps, with big blue eyes and a sexy voice.

Danby reasoned that he wouldn't have too much trouble finding Giles's house. He had been there often enough as a guest. Besides, the firm had designed and built several of the overwrought mansions in the spacious subdivision. Danby had once suggested that they buy Palladian windows by the gross, since every nouveau riche home-builder insisted on having a brace of

them, no matter what style of house he had commissioned. Giles
had not been amused by Danby's observation. He seldom was.
What Giles lacked in humor, he also lacked in scruples and moral
restraint, but he compensated for these deficiencies with a highly
developed instinct for making and holding on to money. While
he'd lacked Danby's talent in design and execution, he had
a genius for turning up wealthy clients, and for persuading
these tasteless yobbos to spend a fortune on their showpiece
homes. Danby did draw the line at carving up antique Sheraton
sideboards to use as bathroom sink cabinets, though. When he
also drew the line at environmental crime, Giles had apparently
found his conscience an expensive luxury that the firm could
not afford. Hence, the shallow grave at the new construction site,
and Danby's new lease on life. It was really quite unfair of Giles,
Danby reflected. They'd been friends since college, and after
Danby's parents died, he had drawn up a will leaving his share of
the business to Giles. And how had Giles repaid this friendship?
With the blunt end of a shovel. Danby stopped to sharpen his
claws on the bark of a handy pine tree. Really, he thought, Giles
deserved no mercy whatsoever. Which was just as well, because,
catlike, Danby possessed none.

The sun was low behind the surrounding pines by the time
Danby arrived at the Eskeridge's mock-Tudor home. He had been
delayed en route by the scent of another cat, a neutered orange
male. (Even to his color-blind eyes, an orange cat was recogniz-
able. It might be the shade of gray, or the configuration of white at
the throat and chest.) He had hunted up this fellow feline, and
made considerable efforts to communicate, but as far as he could
tell, there was no higher intelligence flickering behind its blank
green eyes. There was no intelligence at all, as far as Danby was
concerned; he'd as soon try talking to a shrub. Finally tiring of the
eunuch's unblinking stare, he'd stalked off, forgoing more social
experiments in favor of his mission.

He sat for a long time under the forsythia hedge in Giles's front yard, studying the house for signs of life. He refused to be distracted by a cluster of sparrows cavorting on the birdbath, but he realized that unless a meal was coming soon, he would be reduced to foraging. The idea of hurling his bulk at a few ounces of twittering songbird made his scowl even more forbidding than usual. He licked a front paw and glowered at the silent house.

After twenty minutes or so, he heard the distant hum of a car engine, and smelled gasoline fumes. Danby peered out from the hedge in time to see Julie Eskeridge's Mercedes rounding the corner from Windsor Way. With a few hasty licks to smooth down his ruff, Danby sauntered toward the driveway just as the car pulled in. Now for the hard part: how do you impress Julie Eskeridge without a checkbook?

He had never noticed before how much Giles's wife resembled a giraffe. He blinked at the sight of her huge feet swinging out of the car perilously close to his nose. They were followed by two replicas of the Alaska pipeline, both encased in nylon. Better not jump up on her; one claw on the stockings, and he'd have an enemy for life. Julie was one of those people who air-kissed because she couldn't bear to spoil her makeup. Instead of trying to attract her attention at the car (where she could have skewered him with one spike heel), Danby loped to the steps of the side porch, and began meowing piteously. As Julie approached the steps, he looked up at her with wide-eyed supplication, waiting to be admired.

"Shoo, cat!" said Julie, nudging him aside with her foot.

As the door slammed in his face, Danby realized that he had badly miscalculated. He had also neglected to devise a backup plan. A fine mess he was in now. It wasn't enough that he was murdered and reassigned to cathood. Now he was also homeless.

He was still hanging around the steps twenty minutes later when Giles came home, mainly because he couldn't think of an alternate plan just yet. When he saw Giles's black sports car pull up behind Julie's Mercedes, Danby's first impulse was to run, but then he realized that, while Giles might see him, he certainly wouldn't recognize him as his old business partner. Besides, he was curious to see how an uncaught murderer looked. Would Giles be haggard with grief and remorse? Furtive, as he listened for police sirens in the distance?

Giles Eskeridge was whistling. He climbed out of his car, suntanned and smiling, with his lips pursed in a cheerfully tuneless whistle. Danby trotted forward to confront his murderer with his haughtiest scowl of indignation. The reaction was not quite what he expected.

Giles saw the huge, fluffy cat, and immediately knelt down, calling, "Here, kitty, kitty!"

Danby looked at him as if he had been propositioned.

"Aren't you a beauty!" said Giles, holding out his hand to the strange cat. "I'll bet you're a pedigreed animal, aren't you, fella? Are you lost, boy?"

Much as it pained him to associate with a remorseless killer, Danby sidled over to the outstretched hand, and allowed his ears to be scratched. He reasoned that Giles's interest in him was his one chance to gain entry to the house. It was obvious that Julie wasn't a cat fancier. Who would have taken heartless old Giles for an animal lover? Probably similarity of temperament, Danby decided.

He allowed himself to be picked up and carried into the house, while Giles stroked his back and told him what a pretty fellow he was. This was an indignity, but still an improvement over Giles's behavior toward him during their last encounter. Once inside Giles called out to Julie, "Look what I've got, honey!"

She came in from the kitchen, scowling. "That nasty cat!" she said. "Put him right back outside!"

At this point Danby concentrated all his energies toward making himself purr. It was something like snoring, he decided, but it had the desired effect on his intended victim, for at once Giles made for his den and plumped down in an armchair, arranging Danby in his lap, with more petting and praise. "He's a wonderful cat, Julie," Giles told his wife. "I'll bet he's a purebred Maine coon. Probably worth a couple of hundred bucks."

"So are my wool carpets," Mrs. Eskeridge replied. "So are my new sofas! And who's going to clean up his messes?"

That was Danby's cue. He had already thought out the pièce de résistance in his campaign of endearment. With a trill that meant "This way, folks!," Danby hopped off his ex-partner's lap and trotted to the downstairs bathroom. He had used it often enough at dinner parties, and he knew that the door was left ajar. He had been saving up for this moment. With Giles and his missus watching from the doorway, Danby hopped up on the toilet seat, twitched his elegant plumed tail, and proceeded to use the toilet in the correct manner.

He felt a strange tingling in his paws, and he longed to scratch at something and cover it up, but he ignored these urges, and basked instead in the effusive praise from his self-appointed champion. Why couldn't Giles have been that enthusiastic over his design for the Jenner building, Danby thought resentfully. Some people's sense of values was so warped. Meanwhile, though, he might as well savor the Eskeridges' transports of joy over his bowel control; there weren't too many ways for cats to demonstrate superior intelligence. He couldn't quote a little Shakespeare or identify the dinner wine. Fortunately, among felines toilet training passed for genius, and even Julie was impressed with his accomplishments. After that, there was no question of Giles turning him out into the cruel world. Instead, they carried him back to the kitchen and opened a can of tuna fish for his dining pleasure. He had to eat it in a bowl on the floor, but the bowl was Royal Doulton, which was some consolation. And while he ate, he could still hear

Giles in the background, raving about what a wonderful cat he was. He was in.

"No collar, Julie. Someone must have abandoned him on the highway. What shall we call him?"

"Varmint," his wife suggested. She was a hard sell.

Giles ignored her lack of enthusiasm for his newfound prodigy. "I think I'll call him Merlin. He's a wizard of a cat."

Merlin? Danby looked up with a mouthful of tuna. Oh well, he thought, Merlin and tuna were better than Tigger and cheap dry cat food. You couldn't have everything.

After that, he quickly became a full-fledged member of the household, with a newly purchased plastic feeding bowl, a catnip mouse toy, and another little collar with another damned bell. Danby felt the urge to bite Giles's thumb off while he was attaching this loathsome neckpiece over his ruff, but he restrained himself. By now he was accustomed to the accompaniment of a maniacal jingling with every step he took. What was it with human beings and bells?

Of course, that spoiled his plans for songbird hunting outdoors. He'd have to travel faster than the speed of sound to catch a sparrow now. Not that he got out much, anyhow. Giles seemed to think that he might wander off again, so he was generally careful to keep Danby housebound.

That was all right with Danby, though. It gave him an excellent opportunity to become familiar with the house, and with the routine of its inhabitants—all useful information for someone planning revenge. So far he (the old Danby, that is) had not been mentioned in the Eskeridge conversations. He wondered what story Giles was giving out about his disappearance. Apparently the body had not been found. It was up to him to punish the guilty, then.

Danby welcomed the days when both Giles and Julie left the house. Then he would forgo his morning, midmorning, and early afternoon naps in order to investigate each room of his domain, looking for lethal opportunities: medicine bottles or perhaps a small appliance that he could push into the bathtub.

So far, though, he had not attempted to stage any accidents, for fear that the wrong Eskeridge would fall victim to his snare. He didn't like Julie any more than she liked him, but he had no reason to kill her. The whole business needed careful study. He could afford to take his time analyzing the opportunities for revenge. The food was good, the job of house cat was undemanding, and he rather enjoyed the irony of being doted on by his intended victim. Giles was certainly better as an owner than he was as a partner.

An evening conversation between Giles and Julie convinced him that he must accelerate his efforts. They were sitting in the den, after a meal of baked chicken. They wouldn't give him the bones, though. Giles kept insisting that they'd splinter in his stomach and kill him. Danby was lying on the hearth rug, pretending to be asleep until they forgot about him, at which time he would sneak back into the kitchen and raid the garbage. He'd given up smoking, hadn't he? And although he'd lapped up a bit of Giles's scotch one night, he seemed to have lost the taste for it. How much prudence could he stand?

"If you're absolutely set on keeping this cat, Giles," said Julie Eskeridge, examining her newly polished talons, "I suppose I'll have to be the one to take him to the vet."

"The vet. I hadn't thought about it. Of course, he'll have to have shots, won't he?" murmured Giles, still studying the newspaper. "Rabies, and so on."

"And while we're at it, we might as well have him neutered," said Julie. "Otherwise, he'll start spraying the drapes and all."

Danby rocketed to full alert. To keep them from suspecting his comprehension, he centered his attention on the cleaning of a perfectly tidy front paw. It was time to step up the pace on his plans for revenge, or he'd be meowing in soprano. And forget the scruples about innocent bystanders: now it was a matter of self-defense.

T hat night he waited until the house was dark and quiet. Giles and Julie usually went to bed about eleven-thirty, turning off all the lights, which didn't faze him in the least. He rather enjoyed skulking about the silent house using his infrared vision, although he rather missed late night television. He had once considered turning the set on with his paw, but that seemed too precocious, even for a cat named Merlin. Danby didn't want to end up in somebody's behavior lab with wires coming out of his head.

He examined his collection of cat toys, stowed by Julie in his cat basket because she hated clutter. He had a mouse-shaped catnip toy, a rubber fish, and a little red ball. Giles had bought the ball under the ludicrous impression that Danby could be induced to play catch. When he'd rolled it across the floor, Danby lay down and gave him an insolent stare. He had enjoyed the next quarter of an hour, watching Giles on his hands and knees, batting the ball and trying to teach Danby to fetch. But finally Giles gave up, and the ball had been tucked in the cat basket ever since. Danby picked it up with his teeth, and carried it upstairs. Giles and Julie came down the right side of the staircase, didn't they? That's where the bannister was. He set the ball carefully on the third step, in the approximate place that a human foot would touch the stair. A trip wire would be more reliable, but Danby couldn't manage the technology involved.

What else could he devise for the Eskeridges' peril? He couldn't poison their food, and since they'd provided him with a flea collar, he couldn't even hope to get bubonic plague started in the household. Attacking them with tooth and claw seemed foolhardy, even if they were sleeping. The one he wasn't biting could always fight him off, and a fifteen-pound cat can be killed with relative ease by any human determined to do it. Even if they didn't kill him on the spot, they'd get rid of him immediately, and then he'd lose his chance forever. It was too risky.

It had to be stealth, then. Danby inspected the house, looking for lethal opportunities. There weren't any electrical appliances close to the bathtub, and besides, Giles took showers. In another life Danby might have been able to rewire the electric razor to shock its user, but such a feat was well beyond his present level of dexterity. No wonder human beings had taken over the earth; they were so damned hard to kill.

Even his efforts to enlist help in the task had proved fruitless. On one of his rare excursions out of the house (Giles had gone golfing, and Danby slipped out without Julie's noticing), Danby had roamed the neighborhood, looking for . . . well . . . pussy. Instead he'd found dimwitted tomcats, and a Doberman pinscher, who was definitely Somebody. Danby had kept conversation to a minimum, not quite liking the look of the beast's prominent fangs. Danby suspected that the Doberman had previously been an IRS agent. Of course, the dog had *said* that it had been a serial killer, but that was just to lull Danby into a false sense of security. Anyhow, much as the dog approved of Danby's plan to kill his humans, he wasn't interested in forming a conspiracy. Why should he go to the gas chamber to solve someone else's problem?

Danby himself had similar qualms about doing anything too drastic—such as setting fire to the house. He didn't want to stage an accident that would include himself among the victims. After puttering about the darkened house for a wearying few hours, he stretched out on the sofa in the den to take a quick nap before resuming his plotting. He'd be able to think better after he rested.

The next thing Danby felt was a ruthless grip on his collar, dragging him forward. He opened his eyes to find that it was morning, and that the hand at his throat belonged to Julie Eskeridge, who was trying to stuff him into a metal cat carrier. He tried to dig his claws into the sofa, but it was too late. Before he could blink, he had been hoisted along by his tail, and shoved into the box. He barely got his tail out of the way before the door slammed shut behind him. Danby crouched in the plastic carrier, peeking out the side slits, and trying to figure out what to do next. Obviously the rubber ball on the steps had been a dismal failure as a murder weapon. Why couldn't he have come back as a mountain lion?

Danby fumed about the slings and arrows of outrageous fortune all the way out to the car. It didn't help to remember where he was going, and what was scheduled to be done with him shortly thereafter. Julie Eskeridge set the cat carrier on the backseat and slammed the door. When she started the car, Danby howled in protest.

"Be quiet back there!" Julie called out. "There's nothing you can do about it."

We'll see about that, thought Danby, turning to peer out the door of his cage. The steel bars of the door were about an inch apart, and there was no mesh or other obstruction between them. He found that he could easily slide one paw sideways out of the cage. Now, if he could just get a look at the workings of the latch, there was a slight chance that he could extricate himself. He lay down on his side and squinted up at the metal catch. It seemed to be a glorified bolt. To lock the carrier, a metal bar was slid into a socket, and then rotated downward to latch. If he could push the bar back up and then slide it back . . .

It wasn't easy to maneuver with the car changing speed and turning corners. Danby felt himself getting quite dizzy with the effort of concentrating as the carrier gently rocked. But finally, when the car reached the interstate and sped along smoothly, he succeeded in positioning his paw at the right place on the bar, and easing it upward. Another three minutes of tense probing allowed him to slide the bar a fraction of an inch, and then another. The bolt was now clear of the latch. There was no getting out of the car, of course. Julie had rolled up the windows, and they were going sixty miles an hour. Danby spent a full minute pondering the implications of his dilemma. But no matter which way he looked at the problem, the alternative was always the same: do something desperate or go under the knife. It wasn't as if dying had been such a big deal, after all. There was always next time.

Quickly, before the fear could stop him, Danby hurled his furry bulk against the door of the cat carrier, landing in the floor of the backseat with a solid thump. He sprang back up on the seat, and launched himself into the air with a heartfelt snarl, landing precariously on Julie Eskeridge's right shoulder, and digging his claws in to keep from falling.

The last things he remembered were Julie's screams and the feel of the car swerving out of control.

When Danby opened his eyes, the world was still playing in black-and-white. He could hear muffled voices, and smell a jumble of scents: blood, gasoline, smoke. He struggled to get up, and found that he was still less than a foot off the ground. Still furry. Still the Eskeridges' cat. In the distance he could see the crumpled wreckage of Julie's car.

A familiar voice was droning on above him. "He must have been thrown free of the cat carrier during the wreck, officer. That's definitely Merlin, though. My poor wife was taking him to the vet."

A burly policeman was standing next to Giles, nodding sympathetically. "I guess it's true what they say about cats, sir. Having nine lives, I mean. I'm very sorry about your wife. She wasn't so lucky."

Giles hung his head. "No. It's been a great strain. First my business partner disappears, and now I lose my wife." He stooped and picked up Danby. "At least I have my beautiful kitty-cat for consolation. Come on, boy. Let's go home."

Danby's malevolent yellow stare did not waver. He allowed himself to be carried away to Giles's waiting car without protest. He could wait. Cats were good at waiting. And life with Giles wasn't so bad, now that Julie wouldn't be around to harass him. Danby would enjoy a spell of being doted on by an indulgent human, fed gourmet catfood, and given the run of the house. Meanwhile he could continue to leave the occasional ball on the stairs, and think of other ways to toy with Giles, while he waited to see if the police ever turned up to ask Giles about his missing partner. If not, Danby could work on more ways to kill humans. Sooner or later he would succeed. Cats are endlessly patient at stalking their prey.

"It's just you and me, now, fella," said Giles, placing his cat on the seat beside him.

And after he killed Giles, perhaps he could go in search of the building contractor that Giles bribed to keep his dirty secret. He certainly deserved to die. And that nasty woman Danby used to live next door to, who used to complain about his stereo and his crabgrass. And perhaps the surly headwaiter at Chantage. Stray cats can turn up anywhere.

Danby began to purr.

Gentle Reader

↵

367 Calabria Road
Passaic, New Jersey 07055

Dear Laurie Gunsel:

I hope you don't mind me writing to you via your publishers.
It says on the book jacket that you live in the Atlanta area, but
that's a big place, so I figured this was the best way to make sure
that you got my letter.

I have just finished reading your new book *Bullet Proof*, and I
had to write and tell you how much I enjoyed it. Since finding
that book, I have been looking for the rest of the Cass Cairncross
detective series. I located your first book (*Dead in the Water*) in a
used bookstore, and I hope to acquire first editions of all your
works. In hardcover yet, which is something I don't do for many
authors.

I especially liked the scene in *Bullet Proof* in which Cass's
preppy boyfriend Bradley turns out to be the killer, and, as he's
attacking our heroine, he falls out the window of the apartment
when he trips over Cass's cat Diesel. Nice touch!

Anyhow, Ms. Gunsel, you do good work. So I wanted to write
and tell you that you have a satisfied customer, and that I'm
looking forward to Cass's next adventure, which I'm sure you're

working on even as I write.

Here's wishing you the best of luck and continued success.

Sincerely,
Monty Vincent

Laurie Gunsel

Mr. Monty Vincent
367 Calabria Road
Passaic, New Jersey 07055

Dear Mr. Vincent:

Thank you very much for your kind letter about my books. It's always nice to hear from readers. It's nice to *have* readers.

I'm glad you liked *Bullet Proof.* It's one of my favorites, not only because it went book club, but also because I got some rage out of my system toward an old ... acquaintance, shall we say? I don't think libel comes into it, because unfortunately, he *didn't* trip over a cat and fall out a window. But I certainly enjoyed writing the scene and picturing him taking the plunge. Getting paid for it was just a bonus. Thanks again for writing!

Feloniously yours,
Laurie Gunsel

367 Calabria Road
Passaic, New Jersey 07055

Dear Laurie Gunsel:

I can't tell you what a kick it was to get your letter! Wow! A busy lady like yourself answering fan mail. I'm amazed.

Since I last wrote, I've finished the superb *Dead in the Water* and started *The Gang's All Here*, in which the intrepid Cass goes up against the Mafia on Martha's Vineyard. An interesting choice of locales, and, having never been there myself, I certainly enjoyed all the New England seaside ambiance with which you high-lighted your story. I'd never have thought to set a Mafia story on Martha's Vineyard. What creativity and contrast! A great read.

A question, though: in the scene in which Enzio Lombardi is pushed out of the lobster boat by Sewell, gets entangled in the lobster traps, and is left to drown and be eaten by lobsters, I thought I detected a note of satisfaction—dare I say *glee*?—in the narration, which would be the voice of you personally, I gather. So then I had to wonder. I went back and looked at the window scene in *Bullet Proof* again, and, to my unliterary eye, there seems to be a marked resemblance between the preppy boyfriend in that book and Enzio the mob guy in *The Gang's All Here*. They don't look alike, but I notice that they're both "pretentious" dressers and that they have prominent ears. An interesting coincidence, I say to myself. Either the talented Ms. Gunsel has a thing about ears, or else we are seeing the same guy meet his demise yet again. So I decided to presume upon your good nature and ask.

Congratulations on making the B. Dalton bestseller list. I noticed your name on the list on my last visit to the mall, and cheered you silently as I passed the mystery section.

Sincerely yours,
Monty Vincent

Laurie Gunsel

                                        Mr. Monty Vincent
                                        367 Calabria Road
                                        Passaic, New Jersey 07055

Dear Mr. Vincent:

Thanks for writing. I'm glad the Cass Cairncross series has kept you interested. I'm fond of her myself. After all, I suppose she makes my house payments. She's certainly fictional (I should be so sylphlike!) but at times, she seems quite real—like a roommate who has gone on vacation, but may be back any time now. Not that I've ever had a roommate—not another woman, that is. And judging from my one unfortunate experience with a live-in guy, maybe I'll just stick to cats. Diesel is quite agreeable, and never wants to watch pro football when *Murphy Brown* is on, so we get along fine. I wonder if Cass would be a good roommate. She's obsessively neat, and having a detective around the house would certainly diminish one's privacy.

You are quite a detective yourself, Mr. Vincent. Not even my editor Joni, who has known me for *years*, spotted the resemblance between Enzio in *The Gang's All Here* and Bradley, the preppy boyfriend in *Bullet Proof*. But then, she received the manuscripts several years apart, whereas you are speeding through the books at the rate I wish I could write them! Okay, Monty, you got me. I confess. Bradley and Enzio are the same guy. He's not in the earlier books, because I didn't know I hated him back then.

So how come he's real? There are many ways to create characters, and one is to take hostages from life, because people never recognize themselves. Of course you change most of the details about the person, but you leave the one little mannerism that drives you crazy, so that deep inside you (the author) know who the character is, and it makes the narrative so much more— sincere, I guess. (I am never more sincere than when I am plotting the demise of Bradley/Enzio in a novel.)

I used to worry that he might read my books and know which character was him, but apparently that hasn't happened. He probably doesn't even bother to buy my books—when did he ever care what I thought? And I assure you that a conceited lout like him wouldn't see himself as a gangster, or even as the preppy boyfriend. (That window scene was appropriate. He and Diesel cordially loathed each other. I think I kept the right one.) He probably *likes* his Windsor ears.

Sorry. I didn't mean to burble to you on the fine points of characterization. I'm so used to being interviewed that sometimes I go on automatic pilot. Anyhow, if you ever do a book review for a fanzine, please don't mention that Bradley/Enzio have roots in real life. That's something I *don't* tell interviewers. Besides, the last thing I need is for *him* to come after me with a subpoena.

As to setting the Mafia book on Martha's Vineyard—I'm not sure that was terribly creative of me, except in terms of tax management. You see, I took a vacation that year at the Cape, and if I set the book there, the whole thing was deductible. And I didn't see any guys there wearing white ties and answering to the name of Vinnie, so maybe the Mob doesn't vacation there after all, but it made a good setting, and I knew I could describe it accurately. Glad you approved.

So, tell me something about *you*, Mr. Vincent. Writers always wonder who we're talking to when we send a book out into the world. It's nice to know someone out there is listening.

With all best wishes,
Laurie Gunsel
and
Cass Cairncross

367 Calabria Road
Passaic, New Jersey 07055

Dear Ms. Gunsel:

What a great letter! Thank you so much for taking the time to answer my foolish questions. I was absolutely delighted with your explanations about the characters and the Martha's Vineyard setting. Knowing little facts like that adds a whole new dimension to the book when you learn the background. I reread both books, and enjoyed them all over again. Paperback, of course. My first editions are in plastic covers, stored safely away like the treasures they are.

So Enzio and the Preppy are based on a real guy. This explains what a ring of truth there is in your characterization. But how sad that such a gracious and talented lady like yourself should have to put up with a jerk like that. But you show admirable spunk in getting the rage out of your system, instead of weeping quietly into a lace hankie about how wronged you were. Cass must get her style from you.

Great line about Martha's Vineyard! I'm not surprised you didn't see any "Vinnies" in white ties. Those are strictly the legmen in the operation, and I think Martha's Vineyard is a little beyond them in taste, if not in price. They'd be happier in Atlantic City, I think. But your big shots in the Armani suits and the Italian silk ties—*them* you would find on Martha's Vineyard, but you'd never notice them, because they have money and they know how to fit in with the society types. When you have to hobnob with senators and company presidents, it doesn't pay to look like a cheap hood. Of course, in fiction we have to be able to spot the bad guys, so you very rightly gave your readers the gangsters they expected. What a storyteller!

I was also impressed with your knowledge of medical matters in *The Gang's All Here*. The scene of poor Enzio in the lobster trap still makes me shudder. One thing you might look into, though, is the bit about the Kevlar body armor. Remember when Cass gets shot in the back, and it doesn't even slow her down because she's wearing the Kevlar vest? Actually, she'd feel a little more discomfort than that. Depending on the distance and the caliber of the weapon, the impact would probably knock her down, and she'd have anything from a bad bruise to a cracked rib to show for the experience. Check with some of your Atlanta policemen on this. I'm sure they'd be honored to help you with your literary research.

You asked me to tell you a little about myself. There's not much to tell, I'm afraid. I'm a grandfather—got two beautiful little grandkids living in Rockaway, but, alas, I don't get to see them very often. I'm retired now, and maybe I miss the old business a little bit, but I have my garden to tend to, and my collection of books. It's terrific to finally have time to read anything I want, and not have to cram in a chapter here and there on a plane or waiting around for my next appointment. My copy of *Freelance Murder* just arrived in the mail from Murder By the Book, and that will be my evening's entertainment. So, Ms. Gunsel, I want to thank you for being the highlight of my "golden years." I'm enjoying my armchair adventures with the intrepid Cass Cairncross. Keep 'em coming!

> Sincerely yours,
> Monty Vincent

Laurie Gunsel

> Mr. Monty Vincent
> 367 Calabria Road
> Passaic, New Jersey 07055

Dear Mr. Vincent:

You've already got *Freelance Murder*? They haven't even sent me my author's copies yet! That was quick work on your part. At least I know it's out in stores now. Can the autographings be far behind? Which reminds me: since you're spending your hard-earned pension buying my books and keeping Diesel in catfood with my royalties, wouldn't you like to have your copies signed? I wouldn't mind at all, really. All you do is put the books in a mailer, and enclose another stamped mailer in with them, and I'll sign the books and ship them right back to you. Book collectors tell me they're more valuable if I just sign and date them, but if you want them personalized to you (or the grandchildren?), I'd be happy to.

Thanks for pointing out my mistake with the Kevlar vest. I

guess I took the term *bulletproof* a little too literally. Actually, I'm kind of shy about asking the local police to proof my work, because the ones I know were *his* buddies. You know how cops and lawyers stick together. (I hope I didn't just offend you. You sound knowledgeable enough to be a retired policeman. Just put me down as a victim of a legal shark attack.) I suppose I ought to find a new source somewhere like downtown Atlanta, especially since I need some technical advice for the new plot. I need to know how my professional hit man can smuggle his .44 Magnum onto an airplane. I would call the airport and ask, but it would probably make them nervous.

Since you're one of Cass's most faithful friends, I thought I'd let you know that she appears in a short story in this month's issue of *Criminal Minds*, which should be on newsstands about now. It's called "Better Never."

Thanks again for your encouragement!

> Sincerely,
> Laurie Gunsel
> P.O. Box 97184
> Peachtree City, GA 30269

> 367 Calabria Road
> Passaic, New Jersey 07055

Dear Ms. Gunsel:

Thank you for your kind offer to sign my collection of eight Cass Cairncross first editions. I am speechless with joy. Also, I am shamelessly taking you up on it. A package of books should arrive shortly, along with return postage and a self-addressed sticker for you to put on the box and mail back. Please inscribe them to *Monty*. In case you are busy with your latest masterpiece, I want you to know that there is no hurry in doing me this favor. I know the books are safe with you. I've already read them, so don't waste a minute of your writing time on this chore.

Thanks for the tip about the new Cass story in *Criminal Minds*. Most enjoyable. Such description! When Cass Cairncross breaks into Hepler's room to search for the documents, and finds that he has been shot in the head while sleeping, I was afraid that the shooter would come tippytoeing out of the bathroom and get her next. This can happen. But then I tell myself: Laurie Gunsel is in charge here, and she is not going to shoot the hand that feeds her, and, sure enough, all is well. Interesting that you said Hepler's cheek felt like warm leather to Cass's touch, when she checked to see if he was really dead. I've always thought that deceased personages felt like a package of plastic-wrapped meat like you get at the deli. But your description is more elegant. I suppose Cass was too delicate to mention the smell. She couldn't miss it. And I was a little surprised to hear that there was a spatter pattern of blood on the wall by the bed. Surely if the individual is lying down, you would put the barrel just above his ear and aim downward. Shooting your mark in the temple is messy, no question about that, but people have been known to recover. You want to take out as much of the braincase as possible with one slug so as to guarantee a clean kill. Of course, as I recall, the murderer was the blackmailed Unitarian minister, so maybe he didn't know from forensic medicine. He probably wouldn't know all that technical stuff. Anyway, it was a great yarn, and you fooled me completely. I especially liked the neat touch of the shooter's having put a roll of toilet paper under Hepler's chin and unrolling it to make a necktie—to show his opinion of the deceased. A nice bit of symbolism, which was not lost on yours truly.

Speaking of technical difficulties, your letter mentioned that you had a dilemma in your current project.—What's this one called? I'll put my name on the waiting list at the bookstore.— Can I be so bold as to make a suggestion about this gun and airplane problem? (I don't want your next book delayed because the FAA has you locked away as a suspected terrorist.) You did say that the individual in question was a pro this time, I believe. (I'll try to forget these details when I purchase the book. I want to figure it out fair and square with no advance warnings.) Probably the guy would pack his weapon in his checked luggage, dismantled and—it goes without saying—unloaded. This is a legal and therefore hassle-free mode of transport, but perhaps that lacks the necessary drama for the plot. Or maybe the guy doesn't trust the airline to get his bags and him to the same destination— a very wise concern in my experience. So he has to have the thing in carry-on or concealed about his person.

Let me recommend that you not make the weapon a .44 Magnum, since, with all due respect to the brilliant Mr. Eastwood, this is not what a gentleman in the sanction business would use professionally. There are some very nice firearms out now that are made of space-age polymers—the 9mm. Glock is very good—that can perform adequately in the field and still not be unduly ostentatious. This piece, dismantled in carry-on baggage, should make it through airport security, as the polymer parts of the pistol will not register on the metal detector, and the metal parts can be concealed in, say, a false-bottomed can of shaving cream. Not that I am trying to write your book. I'm happy to be just reading them. (Dare I hope that this mythical hit man will be dispatched to off a "pretentious dresser with prominent ears," who is maybe also a lawyer?)

Of course, by the time you receive this you will probably have figured out your own brilliant solution to the airport problem. I have great faith in your inventive abilities. Just don't try sneaking a rod on your next flight for research. They have no sense of humor, these bureaucrats.

I hope all is well with you in sunny Georgia. My garden is doing well despite the dry spell, as my water bill will no doubt show at the end of the month. I'm putting in chrysanthemums to try to keep summer around for a few more weeks. And if you should find yourself in need of zucchini, seek no further. I am begging people to take it.

Again, my deepest thanks for your generosity in autographing my favorite works of literature. It was a gracious gesture. I owe you one, Ms. Gunsel.

With gratitude and best wishes,
Monty

Laurie Gunsel

Mr. Monty Vincent
367 Calabria Road
Passaic, New Jersey 07055

Dear Monty,

Signing your books was no trouble at all. Really. I still get a kick out of seeing my name on the title page. Anyhow, they're all inscribed *To Monty*, as you requested, and they're on their way back to you in New Jersey. Incidentally, I insured the package for you. My treat. Actually, I didn't want to worry about the where-abouts of those books, considering their cumulative value. I trust the post office like you trust the airlines! I don't mean to brag, but just for your information as an investor, that first Cass Cairncross book, *Dead in the Water*, is worth (they tell me) seven hundred and fifty dollars. Maybe more if it's autographed. I don't keep track of such things, but I thought you might like to know. In case the grandkids ever want a pony.

Thanks for your advice about the gun-and-airport caper. I can tell you've read a lot of crime fiction. You're well-versed in the lit-erary gambits! Do I detect an Ed McBain fan, or maybe John D. MacDonald?

Don't worry. I wouldn't dream of trying to smuggle a gun onto an airplane for research. I know how grim airport officials are about weapons jokes. There's a crime writer of my acquaintance with a bizarre sense of humor, who always travels with a laptop computer, and when he went through airport security, they always make him turn on the machine to prove that it really is a working computer. So one day before he left the hotel—I'm not sure this fellow was entirely sober at the time—he programmed the computer with an automatic boot, which means that when you switch on the computer, a message automatically appears on the screen. At the airport screening gate, they made him turn on the computer as usual, and a sign on the screen said: READY . . . ARMING . . . NINETY SECONDS TO DETONATION. Needless to say he missed his flight, and if he wasn't so rich and famous, he'd probably be playing racquetball at a celebrity prison these days, but apparently he managed to talk his way out of trouble, because he's still turning up at conventions. (I wish I'd known how to do one of those auto-boots. My ex-the-attorney used to travel with a laptop, and I'd have enjoyed getting him sent to prison. I don't suppose I can use that computer story in a book, though, because my friend the prankster would probably see it and complain.)

I *had* thought of killing him again in this new book. (The Ex, I mean, not the Prankster.) This book is called *Buck in the Snow* (thank you for asking!), and the title comes from a poem by Edna St. Vincent Millay, a favorite poet of mine from my shady past as an English major, before I turned to crime. Buck is going to be the hit man. (I thought *Vito* might be too obvious. No white ties this time, either.) Or maybe I'll make Buck a serial killer. Serial killers are very popular with readers these days.

As you may have guessed, I'm still fine-tuning the plot. Actually, I'm finding it a little difficult to concentrate on a new book just now, because I have another court date coming up with the monster ex-husband. (Tennis courts, racquetball courts, magistrate's courts—it's all recreation to them.) He'll have fun, play golf while he's back in Georgia, and visit all his old buddies. I'm

losing sleep, and getting no writing done, worrying about
the whole thing. Why did I ever let him talk me into a mutual-
incompatibility no-fault divorce? I should have hired a private
detective and got the evidence on him and the law firm bimbo.
(Except I wasn't all that solvent back then. My first couple of
books went for peanuts. Anyhow, Malcolm convinced me that
my pride wouldn't let me stand up in court and admit what a
patsy I'd been. He's a great convincer, thanks to me. I put him
through law school! The student loans were in *both* our names,
and he insisted that I pay half—even after the divorce!) And
you wonder why I've been knocking him off from book to book.
At first it was cheaper than a therapist. Now I can't afford to
get well.

How embarrassing. This is what I get for using a typewriter. If I
were on the word processor, I'd have deleted that last paragraph.
Sorry to be such a bore, Monty. I'm depending on the kindness of
strangers, as a better writer once said. Unfortunately, there's a
thunderstorm here in Peachtree, and I'm afraid that if I use the
computer, lightning could zap my hard drive and take out what
little I've got on this damned new book. And I don't have time to
rewrite the letter, so I'm afraid you'll have to pardon my pathetic
ramblings. Maybe you can write out rage, but it must take more
words than I've already used.

I hope I didn't let too much daylight in on the magic for you,
Monty. Thanks for listening.

                                              Your friend,
                                              Laurie

P.S. You *really* have a lot of technical know-how, Monty. I hope
you're a retired cop, because if you're Elmore Leonard or Donald
Westlake writing me prank fan letters, I'll just fall apart. Are you
going to be at the Charlotte, North Carolina, mystery convention
Labor Day weekend? If so, introduce yourself. I'm on a panel, and
I'm giving a talk on characterization. L.G.

367 Calabria Road
Passaic, New Jersey 07055

Dear Ms. Gunsel:

The package of signed books arrived with impressive alacrity, and I thank you again for being so kind as to inscribe them. Also thank you for your thoughtfulness in warning me about the value of my investment, but, believe you me, I wouldn't take a million dollars for any of the Cass Cairncross novels, so the book dealers' valuations are not a major concern, except maybe that I will brag once in a while to my poker buddies about what good taste in books I have. They may have to become a codicil in my will.

Also, you needn't worry about your last letter "letting daylight in on the magic," as you so eloquently put it. And though I'm overwhelmed with the honor of being suspected of being Mr. Leonard or Mr. Westlake—would that I could write one sentence like either of them!—no, I'm an honest-to-God fan, Ms. Gunsel. While I am also not Father Andrew Greeley, let me add that, like him, keeping secrets was part of my business, and you may rest assured that not a word of your most sincere and anguished missive will I divulge to anyone, ever. You may trust my discretion absolutely. Allow me to state how very sorry I am for the emotional distress this bum, your former spouse, is causing you. I do not approve of attorneys who use their skills for sport and personal vendettas, just as I do not care for the so-called serial killers who impose their sickness on others at random. Indeed, one of my favorite things about the Cass Cairncross novels was the fact that good and evil are not watered down with all this psychological mumbo jumbo we get in those devil-made-me-do-it books. The world would be a better place without those sleazy types.

For my own selfish reasons as a reader, I hope that you can put all this domestic turmoil behind you and get back to your true mission in life: writing the adventures of Cass Cairncross. It grieves me to think of you, sleepless and upset, persecuted by this gorilla in a three-piece suit. So I would advise you to remain calm, as your heroine Cass always does, because anger only gets you in more trouble. And remember how many friends and faithful readers you have out here wishing you well—and hoping for the next installment!

Sincerely your friend,
Monty

P.S. I don't attend mystery conventions. I'm strictly a reader. But I know you'll do a great job on your talk. Knock 'em dead.

Laurie Gunsel

Mr. Monty Vincent
367 Calabria Road
Passaic, New Jersey 07055

Dear Monty,

Thank you for your concern in my personal disasters. It did cheer me up to know that, in addition to the other bounties she's given me, Cass Cairncross has made me some thoughtful and caring friends. I haven't made very many friends for her in return, have I? Her boyfriends keep turning out to be crooked, and her friends get murdered. Maybe this reflects my own jaundiced view of the world. I don't know. My outlook isn't any rosier at the moment.

The piranha-at-law must have been staying up nights thinking up new ways to torment me, and he has hit upon a dandy. Why didn't I see this coming when we were in college together? He seemed like such a nice fellow back then. I was a dewy English major who had dated one engineer too many, and I suppose I lost my head when I found myself dating someone who didn't think

Hawthorne was a point guard for the Knicks. (Who even knew that the word *Knicks* should conjure up visions of Washington Irving!) We went to Ingmar Bergman movies together, and listened to Kris Kristofferson—enchanted by the idea that a Rhodes scholar could be a country singer. (So we were already prepared for the Clinton era.) Then we got married and I put Malcolm through law school, teaching high school English five periods a day for what felt like forty-seven years. People ask me how I can think up such convincing bad guys. Ha! They should teach for a year.

When was the last time Ingmar Bergman made a movie? Now Kris Kristofferson makes movies. The world changed. We changed. And we went different ways. Malcolm went *out*. With the law firm bimbo, now the second Mrs. Dracula. This might have been her idea. I expect it takes a lot of money to keep her in spandex. (It takes a lot of spandex to keep her in spandex. Trust me.)

But I digress. You are probably wondering why I am in such high dudgeon. I'll tell you.

Malcolm wants in on the books. I mean, he wants to get paid a percentage of the earnings that I make from the Cass Cairncross novels. I thought they wouldn't be an issue, because they didn't come up in our fangs-bared no-fault divorce. Back then I wasn't making enough per book to matter. He used to say that if the company opened a nursery business and sold the trees instead of making paper out of them to print my books, they'd make more money. He couldn't be bothered with the chump change of my life's work.

Now, of course, it's different. Now they go book club, and movie producers buy them to hoard the rights for a year while they threaten to cast Goldie Hawn in the role of Cass, before the one-year option expires, but still they pay—as do the book clubs, foreign publishers, audio people, and so on. The money adds up. Now, suddenly my "little hobby" is a valuable commodity. I guess one of his friends bought a Cass novel. I had hoped that wouldn't happen, but it has. Malcolm scented money.

And not only does Malcolm the Merciless want part ownership of the early books, written when I was still Mrs. Bluebeard—*get this*—he also claims that he has an interest in all the books containing that character because he "provided financial, intellectual, and emotional assistance in the creation of the character and the series." I quote from his latest legal torpedo.

Monty, you've been a dear friend and a faithful reader, so I thought I'd better explain this to you, so that you'll understand. I can't let my work be used to provide Malcolm and the Bimbo with sports car and spandex money. It would be like turning Cass into a hooker. So I'm afraid that my work in progress will be the last Cass Cairncross novel. When I turn this book in, I'll be out of contract, and I'll tell them I'm through. I'd rather go back to teaching sophomores about semicolons than pay blackmail to Malcolm.

Thanks for being such a great audience, both for Cass and for me. I'm sorry it has to end this way, but it was me or Cass—and either way, *she'd* be gone, so I figured this was a compromise on self-destruction. I hope you find another gumshoe to love. Try Kinsey Millhone.

With all best wishes,
Laurie and Cass

367 Calabria Road
Passaic, New Jersey 07055

Dear Ms. Gunsel:

Forgive the delay in my response to your heartfelt letter of last month, but just after receiving it, I discovered that I had tasks to take care of in a distant city, and I could not spare even a moment for correspondence. Hence the delay. I was working on a job much reminiscent of my old profession, and while it felt good to be back in action, I must say I'm getting a little old and short of wind these days. Glad to be retired. But this was a labor of love.

So, now that I have returned, I am answering your letter as my first priority, even before I tend to the shocking condition of my unweeded and unwatered calla lilies and dusty miller plants, the erstwhile showpieces of my little garden. Nature waits for no man, Ms. Gunsel. But as distressing as I find my neglected botanical friends, the news of your plight upset me even more. Perhaps that is mere selfishness on my part, since I value Cass Cairncross far above calla lilies, and I would not want to lose the pleasure of her fictional company for such a shabby reason as the greed of that arrogant creep, your former spouse.

Let me just say that things tend to work out for the best, and I trust that you will see your way clear to continue your wonderful writing career. Sometimes people reap their just rewards, if you get my drift. Good people are allowed to keep doing good work, and bad people are stopped in their tracks. That's my philosophy, anyhow.

So, your letter notwithstanding, I will continue to wait for the next Cass Cairncross novel, and the next. . . .

Wishing you all the best,
M.V.

Laurie Gunsel

Mr. Monty Vincent
367 Calabria Road
Passaic, New Jersey 07055

Dear Monty,

Thanks for your letter. I have finished the Cass Cairncross novel that I was working on when I last wrote to you, and I'm about to take off for Spain to begin my research on the next one.

Yes, there is going to be a next one. I am in the process of signing a new contract with Meadows & Hall for two more Cass Cairncross books. They're very excited about the deal, and they promise TV advertising, a coast-to-coast tour, and a half-page ad in *The New York Times*! It's a wonderful break for me, and I'm glad that I could accept it.

Of course, the circumstances under which I'm able to accept are sobering. I think you summed it up best when you said that sometimes "bad people are stopped in their tracks." There is no longer a lawsuit pending about the Cass Cairncross novels, because—I can't think of any delicate way to put this—Malcolm and his new wife are dead. Apparently, it was an act of random urban violence, perhaps a robbery. At least the police have no suspects and no leads. According to the news reports, Malcolm and Kristi were in their room at the Atlanta Hyatt, when someone entered through the door (with a passkey?) and shot them as they slept. They were both shot above the left ear with a 9mm. Glock, killing them instantly. In Malcolm's case a roll of toilet paper was placed under his chin and unrolled to the level of his waist.

The police questioned me, of course, because of the lawsuit, but it happened over Labor Day weekend when I was in Charlotte at the mystery conference, so my alibi was the rest of the nine A.M. panel: Joan Hess, Sharyn McCrumb, and Carolyn Hart ("Southern Mysteries: Mayhem, Malice, and Mirth"). I told the investigators that I knew nothing whatsoever about the incident, and could not help them in any way. Of course, I issued a press release from my publishers' publicity department saying that I regretted violence of any sort against anyone, and that even though Malcolm and I had our differences, he was a respected member of the legal profession, and I was sure he would be missed.

So, rather unexpectedly, all the domestic hassles are over. Now I'm going to Spain (with an indignant Diesel in the cat carrier) to try to regain my composure and to wait for the furor to die down. Publicity is nice, but I don't want my personal life on *A Current Affair*. (Book sales *are* up, though.) There seems to be a lot of new interest in me. I even got a letter from a publisher asking if I'd consider ghostwriting the autobiography of hit man Vinnie Montuori, now in the federal witness protection program and living somewhere in obscurity under an assumed name. But I said I didn't do nonfiction, and anyway I'd be too busy writing the adventures of Cass Cairncross, and I hoped they'd understand.

So, anyway, Monty, you won't hear from me again anytime soon. But I'm taking a laptop with me to Spain so that I can work on the new novel. If all goes well, it should be out next summer. When the book comes out, I'll be sure to send you a signed copy, Monty. I owe you one.

Gratefully yours,
Laurie Gunsel

The Monster
of Glamis

$\sim$

HRH The Princess of Wales
Balmoral
August 1992

My dearest Wills,

Mummy has a longish letter to write you, although you won't get it for years and years, as I'm going to leave instructions with someone clever whom I *really* trust. *Not* Robert Fellowes! He may be your Auntie Jane's husband, but he is also "Brenda's" private secretary, and to me he is neither kith nor kind! (I realize that you will be reading this years from now, so you may not know that "Brenda" was the magazine *Private Eye*'s name for HM, your Granny. I think I shall continue to call her that in this letter. Much safer really.)

I thought I'd better put all this down so that you'll know what happened, in case there's something you can do when you become King. I do hope you will believe what I tell you in this letter, and investigate the matter very, very carefully yourself. Courtiers cannot be trusted to tell you the truth, Wills! It is most important.

This week at Balmoral seemed the best time to write an account of what happened. Heaven knows there's nothing else to do here in the wilds of Scotland! I can't think why

Queen Victoria ever wanted to buy it, but apparently the madness was hereditary, because her descendants adore the place. Every morning everyone goes out with their beastly guns, stopping at noon to gobble sandwiches, and coming back at teatime caked with mud. Once they actually asked if I wanted to go with you boys and act as a beater, frightening the little birds out of the hedges. I said I thought not. I can be quite stubborn when I choose, you know, Wills. Anyhow, it's damp and dreary outside, and even more dreary inside, with nothing to do but work on jigsaw puzzles and listen to that family go on about their horses' ailments. No one will miss me, because I never say anything anyway, so I came away to write to you.

Funny to think of you as a great grown man reading this. I simply cannot picture it, or picture *me* having to drop a curtsey to my own darlingest King Wills. So you must pardon me there in the future as you read this for addressing you as a nine-year-old boy, but that is what you are as I write this. You and Harry have gone pony-trekking with the Phillips children, so I shall be quite alone for hours to write. It will take hours, as I've never been much of a hand at composition, so do bear with me if I ramble. I'm not clever, you know. Not with books. I daresay I'm clever enough in other ways.

Your Auntie Fergie (the Duchess of York) was always said to be the clever one, but it was me that she came to two summers ago when she found the papers and wondered what it all meant. It was here at Balmoral that it happened, as a matter of fact. Things weren't so dreary here then, because she was such a lot of fun. Sarah and I had each other to talk to, and once we even took the family cars and raced each other round the back roads of the estate. We got a proper ticking off for it, too! It was a bit after that—I was in my rooms doing ballet exercises—when Sarah turned up, with that impish grin she always has. She was wearing a heavy green woolen jumper and fawn corduroy trousers—good colors to offset her red hair, but not flattering for her rather bulky figure. Inwardly I shuddered, but I was too glad of her company to risk offending her with well-meaning criticism. She was raw from having got too much of the other kind.

"Hullo-ullo," she said, waggling her fingers at me. "Stop trying to get a flatter tummy. You'll only make me look worse in the tabloids."

I made a face at her, and went on doing pliés. "You're welcome to join me," I said. "It wouldn't kill you, you know."

"No, but look, do stop for a bit. I've found something," said Sarah. "Something actually interesting. Come and see."

I thought it was a ploy to get me to stop practicing, but she seemed so earnest that I left off, and plopped beside her on the sofa. "What is it now? Did you come upon a stash of wine gums?"

Sarah shook her red curls, and her eyes glowed with that look that always means mischief. "I've been snooping!" she whispered, glancing about to make sure that no one was hovering.

"All clear," I told her. "We're off-duty at Balmoral, so there aren't so many servants underfoot. If you want guaranteed privacy for hours, though, try ordering a sandwich. Now, what have you been up to?"

"I've been poking around. You know how dreary it gets, waiting for teatime. And I happened to go into the box room that holds junk—old vases, spare fishing rods—and I came across a trunk labeled *Mary R*, and I thought I'd have a look inside, to see why they stashed it. I could guess, of course."

"I can guess, too," I said, stifling a yawn. "You mean Queen Mary, Her Majesty's grandmother, I take it, not the ancient Tudor one? Then it's hats. I've seen pictures of her wearing them. Dreadful! Was that it? A trunk full of ghastly hats?"

Sarah's eyes widened. "You mean you haven't heard about old Queen Mary? The old guard still whispers about it. Diana, she took things!"

"Oh, I knew that. It was common knowledge. Once in my grandfather's time she came to Althorp, and the servants had spent hours packing away every little objet d'art and knick-knack in the house. She didn't pocket them, though. She asked for them and wouldn't take no for an answer, so of course one always knew whether one's treasures had gone, but the gifts were not cheerfully given."

"And they dare to call me Freebie Fergie," Sarah said, scowling. "At least people give me things because they want to. Nice tax deductible dresses and trips. I don't go to people's houses and nick the bric-a-brac!"

"One mustn't be too hard on her, Sarah. She grew up terribly poor, in a grace-and-favor apartment at Kensington Palace with bill collectors forever trying to dun her father, Prince Francis, Duke of Teck. I suppose she became rather mercenary. Her little hobby does make life awkward for the rest of us, even though she's been dead for forty years. Has anyone asked you about the teapot yet?"

Sarah was rooting around in our fruit basket, hoping that you and Harry had overlooked a banana. You hadn't. "What teapot?"

"The one from Badminton House in Gloucestershire. Queen Mary spent the war there, and when she left, a few of the Duchess of Beaufort's possessions went with her. The Beauforts are always trying to corner one of us and ask us to have a look round for the family trinkets. They're particularly keen to get back a silver teakettle on silver gates that belonged to the Duchess, but I know you didn't find that in the trunk."

"No." Sarah had settled for an orange and was peeling it with a look of intense concentration.

"That particular teapot is on the Queen Mum's breakfast tray every morning. Hard luck to the Beauforts. What did you find in the trunk, then?"

"Oh, the usual array. Old silver brushes, and gloves, and yellowed handkerchiefs, but there were a few jade carvings that looked quite old, and one of those carved wooden puzzle boxes. I had one as a child."

"A jewelry box?"

"It could be," said Sarah. "There is a brass plate on the top that says DUNGAVEL HOUSE. The box is about eight inches long, made of different kinds of wood, inlaid in strips, and it opens to reveal a compartment that you can put things in. But the trick is that if you push a certain slot on the side, a hidden compartment opens up beneath the first one."

"And did you find any jewelry?" I asked. I wish Sarah wouldn't wear rubies. They clash dreadfully with her coloring.

She shook her head. "No. Just some papers."

"How tiresome for you." I yawned. "Did you bother to read them?"

"Of course I did. They were addressed to the Duke of Hamilton at Dungavel House."

"Oh, a Scottish peer. Surely you don't mean that he and Queen Mary—"

"Lord, no!" squealed Sarah. "They weren't love letters, Diana. They were an official communiqué to the Duke from the Third Reich, dated 1941."

I lost interest at once. I always found history quite stupendously boring. "I daresay Oxford might like to see them, or the British Museum for one of their moldy collections."

Sarah's eyes danced. "Oh no," she whispered. "Not these papers! I'd rank this lot as yet another unexploded bomb from the war. They contain an offer from Adolf Hitler, proposing to put Edward VIII on the throne of Russia."

Sarah insisted on explaining it all to me, as if I wouldn't

know that Edward VIII was Queen Mary's eldest son, the family's "Uncle David," the one who abdicated to marry that woman from Baltimore and sent the Crown into such a tizzy that the word *divorce* still gives them palpitations. It cost poor Margo her romance with Peter Townsend in the Fifties, and pretty well ruined her life. People were always muttering about Edward VIII whenever Charles and I had a row, so I should jolly well know who he was by now. He left off being King in 1936, and went to France, leaving his younger brother Bertie to take the throne of England. I couldn't see why Adolf Hitler would want to offer Uncle David another throne, though. Rather uncharacteristically thoughtful of him, I said. Still, nothing came of it, because the Russians kept their communist leaders for years and years, and Uncle David and Wallis Simpson kept on knocking about the world partying and staying in expensive hotels for decades until they both went gaga, so I couldn't see what Sarah was looking so fluffed up for.

"What difference does an old letter make?"

"Quite amazingly dim." Sarah sighed, tapping her head, and looking at me in a sorrowful way. The sort of look I got from Charles when I asked if one of his modern paintings was done by Pablo Casals.

"Rubbish," I said. "The letter was written fifty years ago by a now-defunct government. Uncle David's dead. The Soviet Union is a hodgepodge of little states. The Nazis are just a bunch of old war movies now. *The Great Escape. The Dirty Dozen.* So what?" Another thought occurred to me. "Why did they address the message to the Duke of Hamilton, anyhow? Why not to the King?"

Sarah looked pleased with herself. "What's the only thing you know about Dungavel House?" she prompted me.

"It's in Scotland, so it's cold and damp."

"No. It's been converted into a prison now, as a matter of

fact, but in 1941, Rudolf Hess bailed out of his plane on the grounds there. You *have* heard of him, haven't you, Diana?"

"Vaguely. Some sort of spy, wasn't he?" I shrugged. "Anyhow, don't tell me you knew all this off your own bat. You've been mugging it up in the library, haven't you?"

"One or two encyclopedias," Sarah said. "I knew it was important, and I wanted to get it all straight. Rudolf Hess was Hitler's deputy führer. In May 1941 he stole a plane, flew to Scotland, and asked to speak to the Duke of Hamilton. Apparently, they had met at the 1936 Olympics in Berlin."

"I thought we were at war with Germany in 1941," I said. I've always hated trying to remember dates.

"We were. Hess claimed that he was acting on his own initiative, and that all he wanted was to negotiate a peace between Britain and Germany."

"That sounds rather noble. I don't suppose anybody was grateful." I was pretty sure that I'd have heard of him if he'd won the Nobel Peace Prize.

"*Ungrateful* is understating the case," said Sarah. "This is where it all gets madly interesting. The Duke of Hamilton did go and talk to him, but after that, the government shut Hess up in the Tower of London for the duration of the war. He was the last prisoner ever kept in the Tower of London, in fact."

Sarah's frightfully good at crossword puzzles. You can see why. Four letters: *last prisoner wishes to trade Tower for Cassel,* that sort of thing. "Was the job offer to Edward VIII part of Mr. Hess's peace plan?" I still couldn't see why it mattered, but it was hours till teatime, so I humored her.

"No. It was never mentioned. No one would have dared." She could see I wasn't following her. "Look. The offer was that Edward should have the throne of Russia upon the following conditions: that Britain should ally with Germany, and that Britain should help Germany invade and defeat Russia."

"Offer refused, of course."

"Yes, of course, but here's the thing: the secret offer was made on May 11, 1941. Germany invaded Russia in late June. Britain did not warn the Russians of the coming invasion. According to these papers, Hess told our government about the invasion plans, but we did not pass along the information to the Russians, our allies. Well, not our allies yet, but not our enemy, either. They had declared themselves neutral. Yet we didn't warn them."

"Why didn't we warn them?" I tried to work it out for myself. "We didn't like the Russians frightfully, did we? They had a revolution during the First World War, and killed off the Czar and all the Royals, who were relatives of our lot."

"Close relatives. The Czar and George V were first cousins, and could have passed for twins. Their mothers were Danish princesses. So I don't suppose anyone in Britain actually liked Stalin and his government, but that isn't why they withheld the information about the Nazi invasion."

"Are you sure? It wouldn't be the first thing the family's done for spite. Remember how they refused to make Uncle David's wife a *royal* duchess, just because they loathed her?" I can't remember battles or dates, but titles and family trees do make a fair bit of sense to me. It's all people ever seem to talk about.

"I know exactly why we didn't warn the Russians about the invasion," said Sarah dramatically. "It's because we would have had to show the Russians the paper that Rudolf Hess was carrying—in order to prove how we knew. And we couldn't show them the paper, because it also proved that Edward VIII was a traitor."

I was very shocked indeed. And indignant. Imagine being

a collaborator with the Nazis and not having the tabloids crucify you! Sarah can't even wear polka dots without getting narky stories run, and they go on about my shopping until I could scream, but here's a Royal who actually did something frightful and—not a word! Unfair, I call it. Beastly.

"Do you really think the government would have protected Uncle David even at the risk of offending a wartime ally?" If so, I thought, things have certainly changed for us Royals.

Sarah frowned. I could tell that she was thinking about all the lectures she'd got from the palace watchdogs, and all the ticking off for the most trivial of reasons. "Well," she said at last, "he was the King."

"Not then he wasn't," I pointed out. "By 1941, he'd already abdicated, and was being a royal nuisance, ringing up the new king, and trying to tell him how to run the show. And the Queen Mum, who was Queen Consort then, hated him. She still practically spits his name, because she thinks his abdication shortened her husband's life—all the extra responsibility of being king. Edward hated her, too. He called her the Monster of Glamis, because she was so mean about his dear Wallis. I don't think the courtiers or the government would have lifted a finger to get him an extra ration coupon, much less risked national security to save him from his own silly blunders."

"It's true," said Sarah. "All of Edward's staff would have left royal service, because the new king would have wanted people whose loyalty he could trust. The new courtiers would have been in their jobs because they *opposed* Edward VIII. So, no. The government wouldn't have kept it a secret."

We looked at each other, realizing the truth of it at the same time. "But the family would!" Even if they loathed him, they'd have kept the secret to keep the rest of them from looking guilty by association.

I went back to my ballet exercises, and Sarah began to pace up and down, as we worked it out. "The government was never given these papers," Sarah announced. "They were never told about them. Hess landed in Scotland, said his piece to the Duke of Hamilton—"

"And Hamilton notified the family instead of the government!" Of course he would. He was a duke. *My* father would have done the same.

"Douglas-Hamilton was a Scottish duke," said Sarah. "All the more reason. The Queen was the daughter of a Scottish earl. Of course he'd warn their majesties about the family scandal."

"They wouldn't tell the government, would they? No. It would make the whole family suspect."

"People thought there was far too much German blood in the family as it was," said Sarah. "Remember that everyone had to change their surnames during the First World War. The Saxe-Coburgs became the house of Windsor; the Battenbergs became Mountbattens, and—I forget—who did the Cambridges used to be?"

"Teck, I think. That was Queen Mary's maiden name. Her father was a German prince, you know."

Sarah gave a low whistle. "They dared not let the secret out, did they? Britain might have dumped the monarchy then and there."

I nodded. "So they took the papers—but they turned Hess over to the government. Why didn't he tell what he knew to Churchill?"

"I don't know. Maybe he did, and he wasn't believed. But I doubt it. I wonder what became of him."

I shrugged. "Too bad the encyclopedias here are so out of

date. What are you going to do with the papers? Destroy them?"

"No," said Sarah. "I think I'll keep them. They might come in handy someday."

I shouldn't have let Sarah keep those papers, but I don't see how I could have prevented her. I was never any good at talking her out of mischief. I even helped her poke people with umbrellas at Ascot once. I thought people would never shut up about that. I did wonder what had become of Rudolf Hess, though. It was tricky thinking of people to ask. They might want to know why I was interested. Your grandfather, Prince Philip, would know, of course, but he's terribly touchy about the subject of Nazi Germany. His sisters were married to German soldiers, and they weren't even invited to his wedding in 1947, so I thought I'd better not broach the subject with him.

I waited until we got back to London and I was trotted out for a formal reception. I have to make small talk with diplomats and generals, and I thought that might be an intelligent thing to ask, instead of "Does your wife polish your medals for you?"

I picked a doddery old fellow, who looked old enough to remember Napoleon, and worked the conversation round to the war, and then I said, "By the way, General, do you happen to know what happened to Rudolf Hess?"

He got a funny look on his face, and for a moment I thought I was doomed, but then he harrumphed, and said, "Officially, you mean?"

That set me wondering. "After the war," I said. "I know he was in the Tower of London until then."

"Oh, that. We turned him over to the Americans and the Russians, and they put him in Spandau prison in Berlin."

I smiled prettily. "And when did they let him out?"

"Never did. He committed suicide in there a few years ago, at the age of ninety-something. Good riddance, Nazi bugger." The general peered at me curiously. "Are you thinking of resitting your O-levels, ma'am?"

I gave him the downcast, eyelash look that people take for shyness, and murmured, "Oh, no, General. It's just that I thought he went on to become a ballet dancer in the Sixties." That's the sort of remark people expect me to make, and I got away with it and drifted on to the next guest. I had hoped to find out what he meant by *officially*, but I'm not allowed to dawdle with any one guest. Besides, it might have made him suspicious.

When the party was over, I barricaded myself in the bathroom, and rang up Sarah. "Found out what happened to Rudolf!" I told her, reciting the general's account of Hess's life imprisonment.

"Life?" said Sarah in disbelieving tones. "That seems a bit stiff for someone who sat out most of the war in London. And on a peace mission, too. And he lived to ninety, and they didn't let him out?"

"It's an unforgiving world," I said. "When did Wallis Simpson see the inside of Buckingham Palace? Not until her husband's funeral."

"That was family spite," said Sarah. "Government memories are shorter. I still say it doesn't make sense."

"Well, the general did say something else. When I first asked him what had happened to Hess, he said, *'Officially?'* Now what do you suppose he meant by that?"

"It suggests a secret. Perhaps we should ask a few more generals."

"No," I said. "I don't want anyone to notice. I'll ask my hairdresser. He always knows everything."

ALTHORP
DECEMBER 1992

Bear with me, Wills. I know this is a longish letter about ancient, ancient history, but Mummy does have a reason. And it took ever so much longer for me to find it all out than it will take you to read. Besides, I should think by now that you'll be doing the government boxes, so you should be used to reading longish wrangles about government intrigue. But this is special. This is family.

It's Christmastime now, but I couldn't bear to spend another holiday at Sandringham, pretending we're all happy families, now that the separation is official, so I came home to spend the season with your Uncle Charles, Earl Spencer. I miss your Auntie Sarah more than ever, but I dare not talk about her to anyone. This has been the worst year of all of our lives, with Sarah and Andrew splitting up, and the problems between your father and me coming to light and ending in separation, and now the year ending with the fire at Windsor. If I've learnt anything these past twelve months, it's that I must never let anyone see this paper. Nothing I do is safe. Not even a telephone call. Poor Sarah. For all her cleverness, she trusted the System far too much. I only hope that when You are the System, Wills, you can fix things.

I was right about my hairdresser. He knows absolutely all the dirt, and he *never* tells tales to the press. I just adore him. I must admit, he was surprised when I asked him about Rudolf Hess.

"Rudolf Nureyev, Your Royal Highness?" he murmured, tucking a curl into place.

"No. It isn't a ballet question," I told him. "I mean the Nazi fellow who crashed in Scotland on a peace mission during the war. I heard that there was some sort of rumor about his case."

He thought for a moment, while he combed. "Seems like there was a bit of talk when he died, back in the Eighties, ma'am. While this side bit sets, let me nip over to the other booth and ask Nigel. Loves war movies, does Nigel." A few minutes later he was back, combing again. "Nigel says you must be referring to the theory that it wasn't Hess at all in the prison."

"Who was it?" I asked, turning my head at just the wrong time, and getting a hair-pull. "Ouch!"

"Beg your pardon, Your Royal Highness. Nigel says that it's been rumored for years that the fellow in prison didn't look like Rudolf Hess, and didn't seem to remember people and details from his life before the war. Apparently there are all sorts of bits of proof that the fellow in the German prison wasn't the chap who landed in Scotland in 1941. Nigel says he could find you an article on the Hess mystery if you liked."

"No, thank you," I said quickly. "It was only something I heard at a party. I'm not really interested." I didn't want any rumors to surface about my inquiry. I had a feeling that Mr. Hess was a very dangerous topic.

I told Sarah so when I visited her at Sunninghill Park later that week. Andrew was off at sea in those days, and Eugenie was still an adorable little baby, so I looked in on her when I could spare the time. She was terribly lonely. That day I made her come out for a walk in the garden so that we wouldn't be overheard. Sarah received my news of the substitute Rudolf Hess with satisfaction, but no surprise.

"That explains why Hess didn't tell the government that the ex-King was a traitor," she said. "After the real Hess told the Duke of Hamilton about the offer, his papers were confiscated, and someone else was brought in to impersonate Hess. The government never saw the real Hess at all."

"Why not just kill him and present the authorities with a corpse?" I asked.

"Because a Scottish farmer had captured Hess when he parachuted. He was taken alive, you see. If he subsequently died, it might have been suspicious. Instead, he was hustled to London and put in the Tower for four years. Or *somebody* was!"

"Who would agree to go to prison as a Nazi?" I asked, but Sarah gave me one of those meaningful looks, and said very firmly, "Her Majesty's Bobo. Queen Victoria's Mr. Brown. Princess Anne's bodyguard."

I knew what she meant. The Royal Family has always had a few adoring, utterly faithful servants who would do anything for their favorite Royal. They spend their entire lives in royal service, and become the closest of confidants. I supposed that in Queen Mary's day there may have been even more servants who would have felt it their duty to sacrifice their very lives for the good of the Firm.

"I don't suppose the servant realized that it would be forever," Sarah said thoughtfully. "Probably he assumed that it would be just until the war was over. He'd have been assured of a royal pardon, but of course the government wasn't told about any of it, and they handed him over to the other Allies, and then there was no saving him. He had to play out his role to the death."

"A royal servant impersonating a German?" I said.

"Use your loaf, Diana! Half the family *was* German. I'm sure they had servants from the old country. There was always a German governess in tow. There were probably other retainers from Germany as well."

"Wouldn't someone miss a royal servant?"

"Not if he had a relatively minor position. Footman or—"

"Gardener!" I suddenly realized that we were talking about

Scotland. "A servant at Balmoral. It's so remote, no one would know what went on there. Is it far from Dungavel House?"

Sarah considered it. "A hundred miles perhaps. They could have done it in a few hours, I think. One telephone call to Balmoral from the Duke of Hamilton, and it could all have been arranged by morning."

I began to pull leaves off a branch of rowan. The wind felt suddenly cold. "But what did they do with the real Rudolf Hess, Sarah? Surely you can't think that he agreed to become a gardener at Balmoral?"

"No. But I don't think they'd kill him. It's not the family style. We tend to shut people up when they're inconvenient, at least at first. Richard III and the two little princes. Brenda the First imprisoning Mary Queen of Scots."

I giggled at "Brenda the First." Sarah is awfully jolly, but I'm always afraid she'll slip and say something like that in public or to the press. Then heads would roll!

"I wonder if there's any way of finding out what they did with the real Rudolf Hess," said Sarah.

I shivered. "Are you sure you want to know?"

I don't know exactly where Sarah got the information about the family secret, but I do know *when* she got it. It was in January of 1991, just before she left for a trip to the Everglades Club in Palm Beach, Florida. I know that she had been looking into old records books on Balmoral, and researching family history, and she did publish that nonfiction book about the royal ancestors, but I think that book was just an excuse to cover up her real inquiries. I wasn't seeing much of her by then, because she had become rather too impulsive for safety, and besides I had more than enough troubles of my own, but just before she left for the United

States, she sent me a coded package to my secret postal address in Knightsbridge. (There is no privacy at the palace, with all those prying eyes!)

Even then, Sarah was unusually careful. There was no message from her, and no explanation. All the package contained was a souvenir guidebook of Glamis Castle. That was the Queen Mum's girlhood home in Scotland, so at first I thought it was another of Sarah's jokes, so I paged through it to see if she had put any funny little drawings in the illustrations, or perhaps written crude remarks in the margins, but she hadn't. The book was perfectly ordinary, I couldn't see what she meant by sending me such a thing, so I put it away in my desk at Kensington.

Later, of course, I must have read it twenty times. After I realized that the woman who came back from Florida, the one who got drunk on the plane and threw sugar packets, was not Sarah Ferguson, Duchess of York. The family knew about the substitution, of course, but the resemblance was nearly perfect, and by then Sarah's public appearances had been curtailed, so that she didn't go out much. No one ever gets very chummy with a Royal, anyhow. "How do you do, ma'am?" is about the sum total of anyone's acquaintance with us. Except for the servants and courtiers, but I've warned you already that one cannot trust *them*. Believe it.

I stayed away from the imposter Fergie after that. I didn't want anyone to think that I suspected. I knew too much, you see, and it would be dangerous to let them find out that I knew. I think poor Andrew minded very much about losing his wife and having to put up with that imposter, but the family's word is law, so he had to go along, and pretend that the stranger was Sarah. He didn't have to pretend for long. A few months later the "Duchess of York" took a holiday on the Riviera with a silly-looking Texan, and a photographer conveniently snapped some scandalous photographs

that finished the Yorks' marriage. After that, "Sarah" left
Sunninghill Park, left the family, and left public life. I think
the family hopes people will forget about her. I wonder
where the imposter will go when the furor dies down. Back
where she came from?

Not that it matters. What really concerns me is the whereabouts of poor Sarah, who knew too much. She must have
tried to use her knowledge of the family secret as leverage in
some battle with the family. Sarah was just impulsive enough
to have done such a foolhardy thing. But I know where she is,
just as she knew where the real Rudolf Hess ended *his* days.

I don't know what she did with the Hess papers, though. I
suspect that the family never found them. When the fire
broke out at Windsor Castle, and Andrew was the only
family member present, I did rather wonder, but I'm not
sure I even want to know where those papers are. They've
done enough damage as it is. And at least I know what has
become of poor Sarah.

Glamis Castle is in Scotland, a few hours north of the
Duke of Hamilton's estate. In the guidebook I finally found
the message Sarah was trying to send me. It is on page six:

> The secret chamber, about which are woven many leg-
> ends, is thought to be located deep in the thickness of the
> crypt walls on the left as you face the two small windows
> at the end. In this room it is said that one of the Lords of
> Glamis and the "Tiger" Earl of Crawford played cards
> with the Devil himself on the Sabbath. So great were the
> resulting disturbances that eventually the room was built
> up and permanently sealed. . . .

I've done quite a bit of reading on Glamis Castle, birth-
place of the Queen Mother—and home of Macbeth. There
is a secret room behind walls that are three feet thick. From

the left side of the castle one can see the narrow windows
high up the wall of rosy stone. They say there is no way into
that room, but there must be. Someone took food in to
Rudolf Hess for however long he lived there, before he took
his secret to the grave. I'm sure the family sees that its pris-
oners are well-treated. They are not cruel people, only singleminded.

If you are reading this, Wills, you are now the King, and
you must make them do as you say. Take people that you
trust and go to Glamis Castle. Your cousin Simon will be the
nineteenth Earl of Strathmore and Kinghorne by now. I
wonder if he will know the family secret. Anyhow, you must
find that secret room, and if your Auntie Sarah is still alive,
you must get her out.

Mummy is counting on you.

With lots of love to my own dear King,
HRH Diana, The Princess of Wales

The Matchmaker

"**Y**ou don't look like the head of a dating service," said Carl, nervously licking his lips.

The large woman behind the desk smiled and fingered a lock of greasy brown hair that dangled over her glasses. "You were expecting someone more like a game-show hostess, Mr., er . . ." She consulted the manila folder in front of her. "Mr. Wallin."

Just as she said this, the woman looked up from Carl's file, and Carl had to pretend that he hadn't been wiping his sweaty palms on his slacks. "Did I expect glamour?" He shrugged. "I guess so. I've never been to one of these dating places before."

"Naturally not, Mr. Wallin," said the director blandly. Her expression suggested that all the clients said that, and that nothing could interest her less. "Please sit down. I am Ms. Erinyes."

Carl blinked. "Is that Spanish?" His dating preferences tended more toward northern European ancestry.

"It is Greek. Ancient Greek, as a matter of fact." Her jowls creased into a smile. "Now let's talk about you."

"I thought you people matched couples up by computer," said Carl, frowning.

Another smile. "And so we do, Mr. Wallin, which is why I don't look like a centerfold. I started this company with personality-matching software of my own design. So, you see, my specialty is not romance or even the social niceties. I am a psychologist and an expert in computer technology."

Carl nodded his understanding. That made sense. Now that he thought about it, this Ms. Erinyes reminded him of a couple of people in his night class: the intellectual nerds. The ones whose whole lives revolved around computers. Even their friends were electronic pen pals. Of course Carl didn't have any friends, either, but he still felt himself superior to the hackers. The one difference between Ms. Erinyes and his ungainly classmates was that she was female. There were no women in the class. Too bad; then he might not have needed a dating service. But, after all, the community college course was in electronics. Carl thought it was fitting that there were no women taking it.

With a condescending smile at the lard-assed misfit behind the desk, Carl flopped down in the chair and leaned back. "So how come you wanted to see me? I filled out the opscan form, just like the girl out there told me to, but I thought some of the questions were pretty off-the-wall. Like asking me to draw a woman. What was the point of that? Does it matter that I can't draw?"

Ms. Erinyes had her nose back in the manila folder again. She was looking at Carl's drawing: a stick figure with scrawled curls and a triangle for a skirt. The penciled woman had fingerless hands like catchers' mitts, and no mouth. Her eyes were closed.

"The questions? Consider it quality control, Mr. Wallin," she said without looking up. "Computers aren't perfect, you know. Sometimes we like to check our results against good old human know-how. After all, love isn't entirely logical, is it?"

Carl wanted to say, "No, but sex is," but he thought this remark might count against him somehow, so he simply shrugged.

"Now, let's see. . . . Your medical form came back satisfactory, including the blood test. Good. Good. Can't be too careful these days. I know you appreciate that."

Carl nodded. The medical certification was one of the reasons he'd decided to come to Matchmakers.

"I see you had a head injury a few years ago. All well now, I hope?"

Carl nodded. "Fell off my motorcycle. Lucky I had a helmet on, or I'd have got worse than a bad concussion."

"I expect you would have," murmured Ms. Erinyes, dismissing motorcycles from the conversation. "Now, let's see. . . . You are five feet nine," Ms. Erinyes was saying. "You weigh one hundred and fifty-eight pounds. You are twenty-eight years old, nominally Protestant, never married. You have brown hair and green eyes. Regular features. I'd say average-looking, would you?"

"I guess," said Carl. It didn't sound very complimentary.

"And do you have any pets?"

"No. I like things to be clean and neat. I never could see what the big deal was about animals." He smiled, remembering. "My grandmother had a tomcat, though. We didn't get along."

Something in his voice made Ms. Erinyes look up, but all she said was, "I see that you were raised by your grandmother from the age of two."

"What does it matter?" Carl Wallin was annoyed. "I thought women would be more interested in what kind of car I drive."

"A 1977 AMC Concord?" Ms. Erinyes laughed merrily. "Well, some of them will be willing to overlook this, perhaps."

Carl's lips tightened. "Look, I don't make a lot of money, okay? I work as a file clerk in an insurance office. But I'm going to night school to learn about these stinking computers, which is what you have to do to get a job anymore. I figure I'll be doing a lot better someday. Besides, I don't want a lousy gold digger."

"Nobody does. Or they think they don't. We have to wonder, though, when sixty-year-old gentlemen come in again and again asking for ninety-eight-pound blondes younger than twenty-eight." She grinned. "We tell them to skip the question about hobbies and substitute a list of their assets."

"I don't need a movie star."

"Well, that brings us to the big question. Just what kind of companion are you looking for?"

"Like it says on the form. A nice girl. She doesn't have to be Miss America, but I don't want anyone who—" He groped for a polite phrase, eyeing Ms. Erinyes with alarm.

"No, you don't want somebody like me," said Ms. Erinyes smoothly, as if there had been no offense taken. "I assure you that I don't play this game, Mr. Wallin. I just watch. You want someone slender."

"Yeah, but I don't want one of those arty types either. You know, the kind with dyed black hair and claws for fingernails. The foreign-film-and-white-wine type. They make me puke."

"We are not shocked to hear it," said Ms. Erinyes solemnly.

Carl suspected that she was teasing him, but he saw no trace of a smile. "She should be clean and neat, and, you know, feminine. Not too much makeup. Not flashy. And not one of those career types, either. It's okay if she works. Who doesn't, these days? But I don't want her thinking she's more important than me. I hate that."

For the first time, Ms. Erinyes looked completely solemn. "I think we can find the woman you are looking for," she said. "There's a rather special girl. We haven't succeeded in matching her before, but this time . . . Yes, I think you've told me enough. One last question: have you always lived in this city?"

Carl looked puzzled. "Yes, I have. Why?"

"You didn't go off to college—no, I see here that you didn't attend college. No stint in the armed forces?"

"Nope. Straight out of high school into the rat race," said Carl. "But why do you ask? Does it matter?"

"Not to the young lady, perhaps," said Ms. Erinyes carefully. "But I like to have a clear picture of our clients before proceeding. Well, I think I have everything. It will take a day or two to process the information, and after that we'll send you a card in the mail with the young lady's name and phone number. It will be up to you to take it from there."

Carl reached for his wallet, but the director shook her head. "You pay on your way out, Mr. Wallin. It's our policy."

He stared at the numbers on the apartment door, trying to swallow his rage. Being nervous always made him angry for some reason. But what was there to be anxious about? His shirt was clean; his shoes were shined; he had cash. He looked fine. A proper little gentleman, as Granny used to say when she slicked his hair down for church. But he didn't want to think about Granny just now.

Who did this woman think she was, this Patricia Bissel, making him dress up for her inspection, and dangling rejection over his head? That's all dating was. It was like some kind of lousy job interview: getting all dressed up and going to meet a total stranger who *judges* you without knowing you at all. He clenched his teeth at the thought of Patricia Bissel, who was probably sneering at him right now from behind her nice safe apartment door with the little peephole. His palms were sweating.

Carl leaned against the wall and took a few steadying breaths. *Take it easy,* he told himself. He had never even seen Patricia Bissel. She was just a name on a card from the dating service. He had thought that they were supposed to send you a couple of choices, maybe some background information about the person, but all that was on the card was just the name: Patricia Bissel.

It had taken him two days to get up the nerve to call her, and then her line had been busy. *Playing hard to get,* he thought. *Damned little tease.* Women liked making you sweat. When he had finally got through, he'd talked for less than a minute. Just long enough to tell her that the dating service had sent him, and to let her hem and haw and then suggest a meeting on Friday night at eight. Her place. It had taken her three tries to give the directions correctly.

She hadn't asked anything about him, and he couldn't think of anything about her that he wanted to know. Nothing that she could tell him anyway. He'd decide for himself when he saw her.

He was one minute early. He liked to be precise. That way she would have no excuse for keeping him waiting when he rang the bell, because they had agreed on eight o'clock. She couldn't pretend not to be ready and keep him hanging around in the hall like a kid waiting to be let out of the closet. Like a poor, shaking kid waiting for his granny to let him out of the closet, and trying so hard not to cry, because if she heard him, she'd make him stay in there another half hour, and he had to go to the bathroom so bad. . . . She had to let him out—in.

The door opened. He saw his fist still upraised, and he wondered how long he had pounded on it, or if she had just happened to open it in time. He tried to smile, mostly out of relief that the waiting was over. The woman smiled back.

She wasn't exactly pretty, this Patricia Bissel, but she was slender. To the dating service people, that probably counted for a lot; real beauties did not need to use such desperate means to meet someone. Neither did successful guys. Maybe she was a bargain, considering. She was several inches shorter than he, with dull brown hair, worn indifferently long, and mild brown eyes behind rimless granny glasses. She offered a fleeting smile and a movement of her lips that might have been hello, and he edged past her into the shabby apartment, muttering his name, in case she hadn't guessed who he was. Women could be really dense.

Carl glanced around at the battered sofa beneath the unframed kitten poster and the drooping plants on the metal bookcase. He didn't see any dust, though. He sat down in the vinyl armchair, nodding to himself. He didn't take off his coat and gloves because she hadn't offered to hang them up for him. She probably just threw things anywhere, the slut.

Patricia Bissel hunched down in the center of the sofa, twisting her hands. "You're not the first," she said in a small voice.

Carl looked as if he hadn't heard.

"Not the first one the dating service has sent over, I mean. I just thought I'd try it, but I'm not sure it'll do any good. I don't meet many people where I work. I'm a bookkeeper, and the only other people in my office are two other women—both grandmothers."

Carl tried to look interested. "Did your co-workers suggest the dating service to you?"

She blushed. "No. I didn't tell them. I didn't tell anybody. Did you?"

"No." What a stupid question, he thought. As if a man would admit to anybody that he had to have help in finding a woman. Why, if a man let people know a thing like that, they'd think he was some kind of spineless bed-wetting wimp who ought to be locked in a dark closet somewhere, and . . .

She kept lacing her fingers and twisting them, and she would only glance at him, never meeting his eyes. She was so tiny and quiet, it was hard to tell how old she was.

"You live here with your folks?" he asked.

"No. Daddy died, and Mama got married again. I don't see her much. But it's okay. We weren't ever what you call close. And I don't mind being by myself. I know I could have a nicer place if I had a roommate to chip in, but this is all right for me. I don't mind that it isn't fancy. A kitten would be nice, though." She sighed. "They don't allow pets."

"No," said Carl. He thought animals were filthy, disease-ridden vermin. They were sly and hateful, too. His granny's cat scratched him once and drew blood, just because he tried to pet it, but he had evened that score.

Patricia was still talking in her mousy little whine. "Would you like to see my postcards? I have three albums of postcards, mostly animals. Some of them are kind of old. I get postcards at yard sales sometimes . . ." The whine went on and on.

Carl shrugged. At least she wasn't going to give him the third degree about himself, asking if he'd gone to college or what kind of job he had. As if it were any of her business. And she couldn't very well sneer at his car, considering the dump she lived in. And so what if his clothes were Kmart polyester? She was no prize herself, with her skinny bird legs and those stupid old-lady glasses. Those granny glasses. What made her think she was so special, going on about her stupid hobbies and never asking one word about him? What made her think she was better than him?

"I have one album of old Christmas cards and valentines," she was saying. "Would you like to see that one? I keep it here in the coat closet."

She edged past him as she got up to get the postcard album. Her wool skirt brushed against him like the mangy fur of a cat, and he shuddered. Her whining voice went on and on, like the meowing of an old lady's cat, and the closet door creaked when she pulled it open. Carl smelled the mothballs. He felt a wave of dizziness as he stood up.

She was standing on tiptoe, trying to reach the closet shelf when Carl's hands closed around her throat. It was such a scrawny little neck that his hands overlapped, and he laced his fingers as he choked her. He left her there in the dark closet, propped up against the back wall, behind a drab brown winter coat.

Before he left the apartment, he wiped a paper towel over everything he had touched, and he found the dating service card with his name on it propped up on the bookcase, and he took that with him. His palms weren't sweating now. He felt hungry.

Carl was not so nervous this time. It had been several days since his "date," and there had been no repercussions. He had slept well for the first time in months. The old stifling tension had eased up now, and he smiled happily at Ms. Erinyes. He had been here before. He tilted the straight-backed chair, his mouth still creased into a semblance of a smile.

Ms. Erinyes did not smile back. She was concentrating on the open folder. "I see you are applying for another match from our dating service, Mr. Wallin. Didn't the first one satisfy you?"

Carl wondered whether he ought to say he hadn't found the woman to his liking, or whether he was expected to know that she was dead. The newspaper item on her death had been a small paragraph, tucked away on an inside page. Police apparently had no clues in the case. He smiled again, wondering if they'd ever show photos of the crime scene anywhere. He'd like to have one to keep, to look at sometimes when the nightmares came. He thought of mentioning it, but perhaps Ms. Erinyes had not seen the death notice.

Carl realized that there was complete silence in the room. He had been asked a question. What was it? Oh, yes, had he liked the previous match arranged for him? Finally, he said, "No, I suppose it didn't work out. That's why I'm back."

The director set down the folder and stared across the desk with raised eyebrows and an unpleasant smile. "Didn't work out. Oh, Mr. Wallin, you're too modest. We think it did work out. Very well, indeed."

Carl kept his face carefully blank, wondering if it would look suspicious if he just got up and walked out. Slowly, of course, as if he couldn't be bothered with such an inefficient business.

Ms. Erinyes went on talking in her steady, slightly ironic voice. "Perhaps it's time we revealed a little more about Matchmakers to you, Mr. Wallin. Most of the time, you see, we are just what we say we are: a dating service, matching up poor lonely souls who are too afraid of AIDS or con artists to pick up strangers on their own. People don't want to risk their lives or their life savings in the search for love. So we provide a safe referral. Ninety-nine percent of the time that is all we do; ninety-nine percent of the time, that is quite sufficient. But sometimes it is *not* enough. Sometimes, Mr. Wallin, we get a wolf asking to be let loose among the sheep."

"Con men?"

"Occasionally. We can usually spot them by their psychological profiles. And of course we do a criminal record check. I don't believe I mentioned that to you."

"So what? I've never been arrested."

"Quite true. You are a different kind of danger to our little flock." Carl shook his head, but Ms. Erinyes tapped his folder emphatically. "Oh, yes, you are, Mr. Wallin. Our questionnaires are carefully designed to screen out abnormal personalities, and we are very seldom mistaken."

"There's nothing wrong with me," said Carl. He wanted to walk out, but something about the fat lady's stare transfixed him. She was a tough old bird. Like his grandmother.

"There's quite a bit wrong with you, I'm afraid. Not that we're blaming you, necessarily, but on this particular scavenger hunt, you come up with every single item: abuse in childhood, alcoholism in the family, lower-middle-class background, illegitimacy, cruelty to animals. Oh dear, even a head injury. And the answers you gave on our test questions were chilling. I'm afraid that you are a psychopath with a dangerous hatred for women. There's no cure for that, you know. It's very sad indeed."

"What are you talking about?" said Carl. "I never—"

"Just so," said Ms. Erinyes, nodding. "You never had. We know that. We checked your criminal record quite thoroughly. But the tendency is there, and apparently it is only a matter of time before the rage in you builds up past all containment, and then—you strike. An unfortunate, untreatable compulsion on your part, perhaps, but all the same, some poor innocent girl pays the price of your maladjustment. Usually quite a few innocent girls. Ted Bundy killed more than thirty before he was stopped. But how could we stop you? The deadly potential was there, but, as you pointed out, you had done nothing."

Carl glanced at the closed door that led to the receptionist's office. Was anyone listening behind that door, waiting for him to make a fatal confession? He had to stay calm. He hadn't been accused of anything yet. Besides, what could they prove with all this crap about psychology? There were no witnesses, no fingerprints. He had made sure of that. The girl had no friends. It had taken two days to find her body, and the police had no clue. Carl's palms were sweating.

The director had taken a piece of paper out of the manila folder labeled WALLIN, C. It was Carl's drawing of the stick figure woman with no mouth. "Not a very attractive opinion of women, is it, Mr. Wallin? I'm afraid there's no way to alter your mind-set, though. We could not cure you, but we had to stop you. That's the dilemma: how do we prevent you from slaughtering a dozen trusting young women in your rage? That is always the difficult part—making the sacrifice, for the good of the majority. We don't like doing it, but in cases like yours, there's really no alternative. So, we found a match for you."

Carl sneered. "Her? Miss Mousy? I'm supposed to be a dangerous guy, and you pick her as my ideal woman?"

"Precisely. It was not a love match, you understand. Far from it. Although, I suppose it was 'till death do us part,' wasn't it?"

Carl did not smile at this witticism. He thought of lunging across the desk, but Ms. Erinyes simply nodded toward the corner of the office, and he saw a video camera mounted near the ceiling. He had not noticed it before. Still, they had no evidence. Let the stupid woman talk.

"It was definitely a match," Ms. Erinyes was saying. "Just as we get the occasional killer for a client, we also get from time to time his natural mate: the victim. Patricia Bissel was, as you say, a mouse. Shy, indifferent in looks and intelligence—and, most important, she was suicidal. Her childhood was quite sad, too. It is unfortunate that you could not have comforted each other, but I'm afraid you were both past that by the time you met. Patricia Bissel wanted to die, perhaps without even being aware of it herself. Did she mention any of her accidents to you?"

Carl shook his head.

"She fell down the stairs once and broke her ankle. She ran her mother's car into a tree, when she was sober, in daylight on a dry, well-paved road. Twice she has been treated for an overdose of medication, because—she said—she had forgotten how much she'd taken."

"She *wanted* to die?" said Carl.

"She was quite determined, I'm afraid, and through her own fatal blunders, she would have managed it, or—worse—she would have found someone else to do it for her. If not a psychotic blind date picked up in a bar, then an abusive husband or a drunken boyfriend. Since the accidents had failed, but the suicidal impulses were still strong, we concluded that cringing, whining little Patricia was going to make someone a murderer. Why not you?"

"Maybe she needed a doctor," said Carl.

"She'd had them. Years of therapy, all financed by her long-suffering mother. Medicine can't cure everybody, Mr. Wallin. Nice of you to care, though."

Her sarcasm was evident now. Carl's eyes narrowed. He was beginning to feel himself losing control of the interview. The tension was seeping back into his muscles, knotting his stomach, and making him sweat more profusely. "You can't prove a thing, lady!"

Ms. Erinyes's sigh seemed to convey her pity for anyone who could be so obtuse. "Did our brochure not assure you that we had years of experience, Mr. Wallin? Years." She withdrew a half-letter-size envelope from his folder, and took out a stack of photographs. "We are not a shoestring operation, Mr. Wallin. You have been observed by a number of Matchmaker employees, who took care that you should not see them. Here is a nice telephoto shot of you entering Patricia Bissel's apartment building. A concealed camera snapped this one of you knocking on the door of her apartment. Didn't the number come out clearly? And there are the two of you in the doorway, together for the first and last time."

Carl stuck out his hand, as if to make a grab for the pictures.

"Why, Mr. Wallin, how rude of me. Would you like this set of prints? The negatives and several other copies are, of course, elsewhere. You do look nice in this one. No? All right, then. Where was I? Oh, yes, the police. So far they have no leads in the Bissel case, but I think that if pointed in the right direction—*your* direction, that is—they could find some evidence to connect you to the murder."

Carl had the closet feeling again. He knew that he must be a good boy and sit quietly, or else the feeling would never go away. "What are you going to do?" he asked in his most polite voice.

Ms. Erinyes put the pictures back in the envelope and slid it into Carl's folder. "Ah, Mr. Wallin, there's the question. What shall we do? We've spent the past week looking into your background, and there is no doubt that you have had a rough life. Your grandmother—well, let's just say that some of your rage is entirely understandable. And it's true that Patricia was self-programmed to die. So for now, we will do nothing."

Carl exhaled in a long sigh of relief. He could feel his muscles relaxing.

The director shook her head. "It's not that simple, Mr. Wallin. You understand, of course, that this cannot continue. You have no right to take the lives of people who don't want to die. So we will keep the evidence, and we will watch you. If you ever strike again, I assure you that you will be caught immediately."

Carl returned her stern gaze with an expressionless stare. The director seemed to understand. "Oh, no, Mr. Wallin, you won't try to harm any of us here at the dating service. For you, it has to be passive, powerless women."

She stood up to indicate that the interview was over. "Well, I think that's all. You won't be coming here again, but we will keep in touch. You were one of our greatest successes, Mr. Wallin."

Carl blinked. "What do you mean?"

"You were going to be a serial killer, but we have stopped you. Oh—one last thing. We will keep your description in the active file of our computer. If anyone should come in with your particular problem—the urge to kill—and you happen to fit his or her victim profile . . ." She shrugged. "Who knows? You may find yourself matched up again."

Old Rattler

~

She was a city woman, and she looked too old to want to get pregnant, so I reckoned she had hate in her heart.

That's mostly the only reasons I ever see city folks: babies and meanness. Country people come to me right along, though, for poultices and tonics for the rheumatism, to go dowsing for well water on their land, or to help them find what's lost, and such like, but them city folks from Knoxville, and Johnson City, and from Asheville, over in North Carolina—the skinny ones with their fancy colorless cars, talking all educated, slick as goose grease— they don't hold with home remedies or the Sight. Superstition, they call it. Unless you label your potions "macrobiotic," or "holistic," and package them up fancy for the customers in earth-tone clay jars, or call your visions "channeling."

Shoot, I know what city folks are like. I coulda been rich if I'd had the stomach for it. But I didn't care to cater to their notions, or to have to listen to their self-centered whining, when a city doctor could see to their needs by charging more and taking longer. I say, let him. They don't need me so bad nohow. They'd rather pay a hundred dollars to some fool boy doctor who's likely guessing about what ails them. Of course, they got insurance to cover it, which country people mostly don't—them as makes do with me, anyhow.

"That old Rattler," city people say. "Holed up in that filthy old shanty up a dirt road. Wearing those ragged overalls. Living on Pepsis and Twinkies. What does he know about doctoring?"

And I smile and let 'em think that, because when they are desperate enough, and they have nowhere else to turn, they'll be along to see me, same as the country people. Meanwhile, I go right on helping the halt and the blind who have no one else to turn to. *For I will restore health unto thee, and I will heal thee of thy wounds, saith the Lord.* Jeremiah 30. What do I know? A lot. I can tell more from looking at a person's fingernails, smelling their breath, and looking at the whites of their eyes than the doctoring tribe in Knoxville can tell with their high-priced X rays and such. And sometimes I can pray the sickness out of them and sometimes I can't. If I can't, I don't charge for it—you show me a city doctor that will make you that promise.

The first thing I do is, I look at the patient, before I even listen to a word. I look at the way they walk, the set of the jaw, whether they look straight ahead or down at the ground, like they was waiting to crawl into it. I could tell right much from looking at the city woman—what she had wrong with her wasn't no praying matter.

She parked her colorless cracker box of a car on the gravel patch by the spring, and she stood squinting up through the sunshine at my corrugated tin shanty (*I* know it's a shanty, but it's paid for. Think on that awhile). She looked doubtful at first—that was her common sense trying to talk her out of taking her troubles to some backwoods witch doctor. But then her eyes narrowed, and her jaw set, and her lips tightened into a long, thin line, and I could tell that she was thinking on whatever it was that hurt her so bad that she was willing to resort to me. I got out a new milk jug of my comfrey and chamomile tea and two Dixie cups, and went out on the porch to meet her.

"Come on up!" I called out to her, smiling and waving most friendly-like. A lot of people say that rural mountain folks don't take kindly to strangers, but that's mainly if they don't know what you've come about, and it makes them anxious, not knowing if you're a welfare snoop or a paint-your-house-with-whitewash con man, or the law. I knew what this stranger had come about, though, so I didn't mind her at all. She was as harmless as a buckshot doe, and hurting just as bad, I reckoned. Only she didn't know she was hurting. She thought she was just angry.

If she could have kept her eyes young and her neck smooth, she would have looked thirty-two, even close-up, but as it was, she looked like a prosperous, well-maintained forty-four-year-old, who could use less coffee and more sleep. She was slender, with natural-like brownish hair—though I knew better—wearing a khaki skirt and a navy top and a silver necklace with a crystal pendant, which she might have believed was a talisman. There's no telling what city people will believe. But she smiled at me, a little nervous, and asked if I had time to talk to her. That pleased me. When people are taken up with their own troubles, they seldom worry about anybody else's convenience.

"Sit down," I said, smiling to put her at ease. "Time runs slow on the mountain. Why don't you have a swig of my herb tea, and rest a spell. That's a rough road if you're not used to it."

She looked back at the dusty trail winding its way down the mountain. "It certainly is," she said. "Somebody told me how to get here, but I was positive I'd got lost."

I handed her the Dixie cup of herb tea, and made a point of sipping mine, so she'd know I wasn't attempting to drug her into white slavery. They get fanciful, these college types. Must be all that reading they do. "If you're looking for old Rattler, you found him," I told her.

"I thought you must be." She nodded. "Is your name really Rattler?"

"Not on my birth certificate, assuming I had one, but it's done me for a raft of years now. It's what I answer to. How about yourself?"

"My name is Evelyn Johnson." She stumbled a little bit before she said *Johnson*. Just once I wish somebody would come here claiming to be a *Robinson* or an *Evans*. Those names are every bit as common as Jones, Johnson, and Smith, but nobody ever resorts to them. I guess they think I don't know any better. But I didn't bring it up, because she looked troubled enough, without me trying to find out who she really was, and why she was lying about it. Mostly people lie because they feel foolish coming to me at all, and they don't want word to get back to town about it. I let it pass.

"This tea is good," she said, looking surprised. "You made this?"

I smiled. "Cherokee recipe. I'd give it to you, but you couldn't get the ingredients in town—not even at the health-food store."

"Somebody told me that you were something of a miracle worker." Her hands fluttered in her lap, because she was sounding silly to herself, but I didn't look surprised, because I wasn't. People have said that for a long time, and it's nothing for me to get puffed up about, because it's not my doing. It's a gift.

"I can do things other folks can't explain," I told her. "That might be a few logs short of a miracle. But I can find water with a forked stick, and charm bees, and locate lost objects. There's some sicknesses I can minister to. Not yours, though."

Her eyes saucered, and she said, "I'm perfectly well, thank you."

I just sat there looking at her, deadpan. I waited. She waited. Silence.

Finally, she turned a little pinker, and ducked her head. "All right," she whispered, like it hurt. "I'm not perfectly well. I'm a nervous wreck. I guess I have to tell you about it."

"That would be best, Evelyn," I said.

"My daughter has been missing since July." She opened her purse and took out a picture of a pretty young girl, soft brown hair like her mother's, and young, happy eyes. "Her name is Amy. She was a freshman at East Tennessee State, and she went rafting with three of her friends on the Nolichucky. They all got separated by the current. When the other three met up farther downstream, they got out and went looking for Amy, but there was no trace of her. She hasn't been seen since."

"They dragged the river, I reckon." Rock-studded mountain rivers are bad for keeping bodies snagged down where you can't find them.

"They dragged that stretch of the Nolichucky for three days. They even sent down divers. They said even if she'd got wedged under a rock, we'd have something by now." It cost her something to say that.

"Well, she's a grown girl," I said, to turn the flow of words. "Sometimes they get an urge to kick over the traces."

"Not Amy. She wasn't the party type. And even supposing she felt like that—because I know people don't believe a mother's assessment of character—would she run away in her bathing suit? All her clothes were back in her dorm, and her boyfriend was walking up and down the riverbank with the other two students, calling out to her. I don't think she went anywhere on her own."

"Likely not," I said. "But it would have been a comfort to think so, wouldn't it?"

Her eyes went wet. "I kept checking her bank account for withdrawals, and I looked at her last phone bill to see if any calls were made after July sixth. But there's no indication that she was alive past that date. We put posters up all over Johnson City, asking for information about her. There's been no response."

"Of course, the police are doing what they can," I said.

"It's the Wake County sheriff's department, actually," she said. "But the Tennessee Bureau of Investigation is helping them. They don't have much to go on. They've questioned people who were at the river. One fellow claims to have seen a red pickup leaving the scene with a girl in it, but they haven't been able to trace it. The investigators have questioned all her college friends and her professors, but they're running out of leads. It's been three months. Pretty soon they'll quit trying altogether." Her voice shook. "You see, Mr.—Rattler—they all think she's dead."

"So you came to me?"

She nodded. "I didn't know what else to do. Amy's father is no help. He says to let the police handle it. We're divorced, and he's remarried and has a two-year-old son. But Amy is all I've got. I can't let her go!" She set down the paper cup, and covered her face with her hands.

"Could I see that picture of Amy, Mrs.—Johnson?"

"It's Albright," she said softly, handing me the photograph. "Our real last name is Albright. I just felt foolish before, so I didn't tell you my real name."

"It happens," I said, but I wasn't really listening to her apology. I had closed my eyes, and I was trying to make the edges of the snapshot curl around me, so that I would be standing next to the smiling girl, and get some sense of how she was. But the photograph stayed cold and flat in my hand, and no matter how hard I tried to think my way into it, the picture shut me out. There was nothing.

I opened my eyes, and she was looking at me, scared, but waiting, too, for what I could tell her. I handed back the picture. "I could be wrong," I said. "I told you I'm no miracle worker."

"She's dead, isn't she?"

"Oh, yes. Since the first day, I do believe."

She straightened up, and those slanting lines deepened around her mouth. "I've felt it, too," she said. "I'd reach out to her with my thoughts, and I'd feel nothing. Even when she was away at school, I could always sense her somehow. Sometimes I'd call, and she'd say, 'Mom, I was just thinking about you.' But now I reach out to her and I feel empty. She's just—gone."

"Finding mortal remains is a sorrowful business," I said. "And I don't know that I'll be able to help you."

Evelyn Albright shook her head. "I didn't come here about finding Amy's body, Rattler," she said. "I came to find her killer."

I spent three more Dixie cups of herb tea trying to bring back her faith in the Tennessee legal system. Now, I never was much bothered with the process of the law, but, like I told her, in this case I did know that pulling a live coal from an iron potbellied stove was a mighty puny miracle compared to finding the one guilty sinner with the mark of Cain in all this world, when there are so many evildoers to choose from. It seemed to me that for all their frailty, the law had the manpower and the system to sort through a thousand possible killers, and to find the one fingerprint or the exact bloodstain that would lay the matter of Amy Albright to rest.

"But you knew she was dead when you touched her picture!" she said. "Can't you tell from that who did it? Can't you see where she is?"

I shook my head. "My grandma might could have done it, rest her soul. She had a wonderful gift of prophecy, but I wasn't trained to it the way she was. *Her* grandmother was a Cherokee medicine woman, and she could read the signs like yesterday's newspaper. I only have the little flicker of Sight I was born with. Some things I know, but I can't see it happening like she could have done."

"What did you see?"

"Nothing. I just felt that the person I was trying to reach in that photograph was gone. And I think the lawmen are the ones you should be trusting to hunt down the killer."

Evelyn didn't see it that way. "They aren't getting anywhere," she kept telling me. "They've questioned all of Amy's friends, and asked the public to call in for information, and now they're at a standstill."

"I hear tell they're sly, these hunters of humans. He could be miles away by now," I said, but she was shaking her head no.

"The sheriff's department thinks it was someone who knew the area. First of all, because that section of the river isn't a tourist spot, and secondly, because he apparently knew where to take Amy so that he wouldn't be seen by anyone with her in the car, and he has managed to keep her from being found. Besides"—she looked away, and her eyes were wet again—"they won't say much about this, but apparently Amy isn't the first. There was a high school girl who disappeared around here two years ago. Some hunters found her body in an abandoned well. I heard one of the sheriff's deputies say that he thought the same person might be responsible for both crimes."

"Then he's like a dog killing sheep. He's doing it for the fun of it, and he must be stopped, because a sheep killer never stops of his own accord."

"People told me you could do marvelous things—find water with a forked stick; heal the sick. I was hoping that you would be able to tell me something about what happened to Amy. I thought you might be able to see who killed her. Because I want him to suffer."

I shook my head. "A dishonest man would string you along," I told her. "A well-meaning one might tell you what you want to hear just to make you feel better. But all I can offer you is the truth: when I touched that photograph, I felt her death, but I saw nothing."

"I had hoped for more." She twisted the rings on her hands. "Do you think you could find her body?"

"I have done something like that, once. When I was twelve, an old man wandered away from his home in December. He was my best friend's grandfather, and they lived on the next farm, so I knew him, you see. I went out with the searchers on that cold, dark afternoon, with the wind baying like a hound through the hollers. As I walked along by myself, I looked up at the clouds, and I had a sudden vision of that old man sitting down next to a broken rail fence. He looked like he was asleep, but I reckoned I knew better. Anyhow, I thought on it as I walked, and I reckoned that the nearest rail fence to his farm was at an abandoned homestead at the back of our land. It was in one of our pastures. I hollered for the others to follow me, and I led them out there to the back pasture."

"Was he there?"

"He was there. He'd wandered off—his mind was going—and when he got lost, he sat down to rest a spell, and he'd dozed off where he sat. Another couple of hours would have finished him, but we got him home to a hot bath and scalding coffee, and he lived till spring."

"He was alive, though."

"Well, that's it. The life in him might have been a beacon. It might not work when the life is gone."

"I'd like you to try, though. If we can find Amy, there might be some clue that will help us find the man who did this."

"I tell you what: you send the sheriff to see me, and I'll have a talk with him. If it suits him, I'll do my level best to find her. But I have to speak to him first."

"Why?"

"Professional courtesy," I said, which was partly true, but, also, because I wanted to be sure she was who she claimed to be. City people usually do give me a fake name out of embarrassment, but I didn't want to chance her being a reporter on the Amy Albright case, or, worse, someone on the killer's side. Besides, I wanted to stay on good terms with Sheriff Spencer Arrowood. We go back a long way. He used to ride out this way on his bike when he was a kid, and he'd sit and listen to tales about the Indian times—stories I'd heard from my grandma—or I'd take him fishing at the trout pool in Broom Creek. One year, his older brother Cal talked me into taking the two of them out owling, since they were too young to hunt. I walked them across every ridge over the holler, and taught them to look for the sweep of wings above the tall grass in the field, and to listen for the sound of the waking owl, ready to track his prey by the slightest sound, the shade of movement. I taught them how to make owl calls, to where we couldn't tell if it was an owl calling out from the woods or one of us. Look out, I told them. When the owl calls your name, it means death.

Later on, they became owls, I reckon. Cal Arrowood went to Vietnam, and died in a dark jungle full of screeching birds. I felt him go. And Spencer grew up to be sheriff, so I reckon he hunts prey of his own by the slightest sound, and by one false move. A lot of people had heard him call their name.

I hadn't seen much of Spencer since he grew up, but I hoped we were still buddies. Now that he was sheriff, I knew he could make trouble for me if he wanted to, and so far he never has. I wanted to keep things cordial.

"All right," said Evelyn. "I can't promise they'll come out here, but I will tell them what you said. Will you call and tell me what you're going to do?"

"No phone," I said, jerking my thumb back toward the shack. "Send the sheriff out here. He'll let you know."

She must have gone to the sheriff's office straightaway after leaving my place. I thought she would. I wasn't surprised at that, because I could see that she wasn't doing much else right now besides brood about her loss. She needed an ending so that she could go on. I had tried to make her take a milk jug of herb tea, because I never saw anybody so much in need of a night's sleep, but she wouldn't have it. "Just find my girl for me," she'd said. "Help us find the man who did it, and put him away. Then I'll sleep."

When the brown sheriff's car rolled up my dirt road about noon the next day, I was expecting it. I was sitting in my cane chair on the porch whittling a face onto a hickory broom handle when I saw the flash of the gold star on the side of the car door, and the sheriff himself got out. I waved, and he touched his hat, like they used to do in cowboy movies. I reckon little boys who grow up to be sheriff watch a lot of cowboy movies in their day. I didn't mind Spencer Arrowood, though. He hadn't changed all that much from when I knew him. There were gray flecks in his fair hair, but they didn't show much, and he never did make it to six feet, but he'd managed to keep his weight down, so he looked all right. He was kin to the Pigeon Roost Arrowoods, and like them he was smart and honest without being a glad-hander. He seemed a little young to be the high sheriff to an old-timer like me, but that's never a permanent problem for anybody, is it? Anyhow, I trusted him, and that's worth a lot in these sorry times.

I made him sit down in the other cane chair, because I hate people hovering over me while I whittle. He asked did I remember him.

"Spencer," I said, "I'd have to be drinking something a lot stronger than chamomile tea to forget you."

He grinned, but then he seemed to remember what sad errand had brought him out here, and the faint lines came back around his eyes. "I guess you've heard about this case I'm on."

"I was told. It sounds to me like we've got a human sheep killer in the fold. I hate to hear that. Killing for pleasure is an unclean act. I said I'd help the law any way I could to dispose of the killer, if it was all right with you."

"That's what I heard," the sheriff said. "For what it's worth, the TBI agrees with you about the sort of person we're after, although they didn't liken it to *sheep killing*. They meant the same thing, though."

"So Mrs. Albright did come to see you?" I asked him, keeping my eyes fixed on the curl of the beard of that hickory face.

"Sure did, Rattler," said the sheriff. "She tells me that you've agreed to try to locate Amy's body."

"It can't do no harm to try," I said. "Unless you mind too awful much. I don't reckon you believe in such like."

He smiled. "It doesn't matter what I believe if it works, does it, Rattler? You're welcome to try. But, actually, I've thought of another way that you might be useful in this case."

"What's that?"

"You heard about the other murdered girl, didn't you? They found her body in an abandoned well up on Locust Ridge."

"Whose land?"

"National forest now. The homestead has been in ruins for at least a century. But that's a remote area of the county. It's a couple of miles from the Appalachian Trail, and just as far from the river, so I wouldn't expect an outsider to know about it. The only way up there is on an old county road. The TBI psychologist thinks the killer has dumped Amy Albright's body somewhere in the vicinity of the other burial. He says they do that. Serial killers, I mean. They establish territories."

"Painters do that," I said, and the sheriff remembered his roots well enough to know that I meant a mountain lion, not a fellow with an easel. We called them painters in the old days, when there were more of them in the mountains than just a scream and a shadow every couple of years. City people think I'm crazy to live on the mountain where the wild creatures are, and then they shut themselves up in cities with the most pitiless killers ever put on this earth—each other. I marvel at the logic.

"Since you reckon he's leaving his victims in one area, why haven't you searched it?"

"Oh, we have," said the sheriff, looking weary. "I've had volunteers combing that mountain, and they haven't turned up a thing. There's a lot of square miles of forest to cover up there. Besides, I think our man has been more careful about concealment this time. What we need is more help. Not more searchers, but a more precise location."

"Where do I come in? You said you wanted me to do more than just find the body. Not that I can even promise to do that."

"I want to get your permission to try something that may help us catch this individual," Spencer Arrowood was saying.

"What's that?"

"I want you to give some newspaper interviews. Local TV, even, if we can talk them into it. I want to publicize the fact that you are gong to search for Amy Albright on Locust Ridge. Give them your background as a psychic and healer. I want a lot of coverage on this."

I shuddered. You didn't have to be psychic to foresee the outcome of that. A stream of city people in colorless cars, wanting babies and diet tonics.

"When were you planning to search for the body, Rattler?"

"I was waiting on you. Any day will suit me, as long as it isn't raining. Rain distracts me."

"Okay, let's announce that you're conducting the psychic search on Locust Ridge next Tuesday. I'll send some reporters out here to interview you. Give them the full treatment."

"How does all this harassment help you catch the killer, Spencer?"

"This is not for publication, Rattler, but I think we can smoke him out," said the sheriff. "We announce in all the media that you're going to be dowsing for bones on Tuesday. We insist that you can work wonders, and that we're confident you'll find Amy. If the killer is a local man, he'll see the notices, and get nervous. I'm betting that he'll go up there Monday night, just to make sure the body is still well-hidden. There's only one road into that area. If we can keep the killer from spotting us, I think he'll lead us to Amy's body."

"That's fine, Sheriff, but how are you going to track this fellow in the dark?"

Spencer Arrowood smiled. "Why, Rattler," he said, "I've got the Sight."

You have to do what you can to keep a sheep killer out of your fold, even if it means talking to a bunch of reporters who don't know ass from aardvark. I put up with all their fool questions, and dispensed about a dozen jugs of comfrey and chamomile tea, and I even told that blond lady on Channel Seven that she didn't need any herbs for getting pregnant, because she already was, which surprised her so much that she almost dropped her microphone, but I reckon my hospitality worked to Spencer Arrowood's satisfaction, because he came along Monday afternoon to show me a stack of newspapers with my picture looking out of the page, and he thanked me for being helpful.

"Don't thank me," I said. "Just let me go with you tonight. You'll need all the watchers you can get to cover that ridge."

He saw the sense of that, and agreed without too much argument. I wanted to see what he meant about having the Sight, because I'd known him since he was knee-high to a grasshopper, and he didn't have so much as a flicker of the power. None of the Arrowoods did. But he was smart enough in regular ways, and I knew he had some kind of ace up his sleeve.

An hour past sunset that night I was standing in a clearing on Locust Ridge, surrounded by law enforcement people from three counties. There were nine of us. We were so far from town that there seemed to be twice as many stars, so dark was that October sky without the haze of streetlights to bleed out the fainter ones. The sheriff was talking one notch above a whisper, in case the suspect had come early. He opened a big cardboard box, and started passing out yellow-and-black binoculars.

"These are called ITT Night Mariners," he told us. "I borrowed ten pair from a dealer at Watauga Lake, so take care of them. They run about $2500 apiece."

"Are they infrared?" somebody asked him.

"No. But they collect available light and magnify it up to 20,000 times, so they will allow you excellent night vision. The full moon will give us all the light we need. You'll be able to walk around without a flashlight, and you'll be able to see obstacles, terrain features, and anything that's out there moving around."

"The military developed this technology in Desert Storm," said Deputy LeDonne.

"Well, let's hope it works for us tonight," said the sheriff. "Try looking through them."

I held them up to my eyes. They didn't weigh much—about the same as two apples, I reckoned. Around me, everybody was muttering surprise, tickled pink over this new gadget. I looked through mine, and I could see the dark shapes of trees up on the hill—not in a clump, the way they look at night, but one by one, with spaces between them. The sheriff walked away from us, and I could see him go, but when I took the Night Mariners down from my eyes, he was gone. I put them back on, and there he was again.

"I reckon you do have the *Sight*, Sheriff," I told him. "Your man won't know we're watching him with these babies."

"I wonder if they're legal for hunting," said a Unicoi County man. "This sure beats spotlighting deer."

"They're illegal for deer," Spencer told him. "But they're perfect for catching sheep killers." He smiled over at me. "Now that we've tested the equipment, y'all split up. I've given you your patrol areas. Don't use your walkie-talkies unless it's absolutely necessary. Rattler, you just go where you please, but try not to let the suspect catch you at it. Are you going to do your stuff?"

"I'm going to try to let it happen," I said. It's a gift. I don't control it. I just receive.

We went our separate ways. I walked awhile, enjoying the new magic of seeing the night woods same as a possum would, but when I tried to clear my mind and summon up that other kind of seeing, I found I couldn't do it. So, instead of helping, the Night Mariners were blinding me. I slipped the fancy goggles into the pocket of my jacket, and stood there under an oak tree for a minute or two, trying to open my heart for guidance. I whispered a verse from Psalm 27: *Teach me thy way, O Lord, and lead me in a plain path, because of mine enemies.* Then I looked up at the stars and tried to think of nothing. After a while I started walking, trying to keep my mind clear and go where I was led.

Maybe five minutes later, maybe an hour, I was walking across an abandoned field overgrown with scrub cedars. The moonlight glowed in the long grass, and the cold air made my ears and fingers tingle. When I touched a post of the broken split-rail fence, it happened. I saw the field in daylight. I saw brown grass, drying up in the summer heat, and flies making lazy circles around my head. When I looked down at the fence rail at my feet, I saw her. She was wearing a watermelon-colored T-shirt and jean shorts. Her brown hair spilled across her shoulders and twined with the chicory weeds. Her eyes were closed. I could see a smear of blood at one corner of her mouth, and I knew. I looked up at the moon, and when I looked back, the grass was dead, and the darkness had closed in again. I crouched behind a cedar tree before I heard the footsteps.

They weren't footsteps, really. Just the swish sound of boots and trouser legs brushing against tall, dry grass. I could see his shape in the moonlight, and he wasn't one of the searchers. He was here to keep his secrets. He stepped over the fence rail, and walked toward the one big tree in the clearing—a twisted old maple, big around as two men. He knelt down beside that tree, and I saw him moving his hands on the ground, picking up a dead branch, and brushing leaves away. He looked, rocked back on his heels, leaned forward, and started pushing the leaves back again.

They hadn't given me a walkie-talkie, and I didn't hold with guns, though I knew he might have one. I wasn't really part of the posse. Old Rattler with his Twinkies and his root tea and his prophecies. I was just bait. But I couldn't risk letting the sheep killer slip away. Finding the grave might catch him; might not. None of my visions would help Spencer in a court of law, which is why I mostly stick to dispensing tonics and leave evil alone.

I cupped my hands to my mouth and gave an owl cry, loud as I could. Just one. The dark shape jumped up, took a couple of steps up and back, moving its head from side to side.

Far off in the woods, I heard an owl reply. I pulled out the Night Mariners then, and started scanning the hillsides around that meadow, and in less than a minute I could make out the sheriff, with that badge pinned to his coat, standing at the edge of the trees with his field glasses on, scanning the clearing. I started waving and pointing.

The sheep killer was hurrying away now, but he was headed in my direction, and I thought, *Risk it. What called your name, Rattler, wasn't an owl.* So just as he's about to pass by, I stepped out at him, and said, "Hush now. You'll scare the deer."

He was startled into screaming, and he swung out at me with something that flashed silver in the moonlight. As I went down, he broke into a run, crashing through weeds, noisy enough to scare the deer across the state line—but the moonlight wasn't bright enough for him to get far. He covered maybe twenty yards before his foot caught on a fieldstone, and he went down. I saw the sheriff closing distance, and I went to help, but I felt light-headed all of a sudden, and my shirt was wet. I was glad it wasn't light enough to see colors in that field. Red was never my favorite.

I opened my eyes and shut them again, because the flashing orange light of the rescue squad van was too bright for the ache in my head. When I looked away, I saw cold and dark, and knew I was still on Locust Ridge. "Where's Spencer Arrowood?" I asked a blue jacket bending near me.

"Sheriff! He's coming around."

Spencer Arrowood was bending over me then, with that worried look he used to have when a big one hit his fishing line. "We got him," he said. "You've got a puncture in your lung that will need more than herbal tea to fix, but you're going to be all right, Rattler."

"Since when did you get the Sight?" I asked him. But he was right. I needed to get off that mountain and get well, because the last thing I saw before I went down was the same scene that came to me when I first saw her get out of her car and walk toward my cabin. I saw what Evelyn Albright was going to do at the trial, with that flash of silver half hidden in her hand, and I didn't want it to end that way.

Among My Souvenirs

~

The face was a little blurry, but she was used to seeing it that way. She must have looked at it a thousand times in old magazines—grainy black-and-white shots, snapped by a magazine photographer at a nightclub; amateurish candid photos on the back of record albums; misty publicity stills that erased even the pores of his skin. She knew that face. A poster-sized version of it had stared down at her from beneath the high school banner on her bedroom wall, twenty-odd years ago. God, had it been that long? Now the face was blurry with booze, fatigue, and the sagging of a jawline that was no longer boyish. But it was still him, sitting in the bar, big as life.

Maggie used to wonder what she would do if she met him in the flesh. In the tenth grade she and Kathy Ryan used to philosophize about such things at slumber parties: "Why don't you fix your hair like Connie Stevens's?" "Which Man from U.N.C.L.E. do you like best?" "What would you do if you met Devlin Robey?" Then they'd collapse in giggles, unable even to fantasize meeting a real, live rock 'n' roll singer. He lived a glamorous life of limousines and penthouse suites while they suffered through gym class, and algebra with Mrs. Cady. Growing up seemed a hundred years away.

When Maggie was a senior, she did get to see Devlin Robey. When you live on Long Island, sooner or later your prince will come. Everybody comes to the Big Apple. But the encounter was as distant and unreal as the airbrushed poster on her closet door. Devlin Robey was a shining blur glimpsed on a distant stage, and Maggie was a tiny speck in a sea of screaming adolescents. She and Kathy squealed and cried and threw paper roses at the stage, but it didn't really feel like *seeing* him. He was a lot clearer on the television screen when she watched *American Bandstand*. After the concert, they had fought their way through a horde of fans to reach the stage door, only to be driven off by three thugs in overcoats—Mr. Robey's *handlers*—while Devlin himself plowed his way through the throng to a waiting limousine, oblivious to the screams of protest in his wake.

They cried all the way home.

Maggie was so disillusioned by her idol's callous behavior that she wrote him a letter, in care of his record company, complaining about how he let his fans be treated. She enclosed her ticket stub from the concert, and one of her wallet-size class pictures. A few weeks later, she received an autographed eight-by-ten of Devlin Robey, a copy of his latest album, and a handwritten apology on Epic Records notepaper. He said he was sorry to rush past them like that, but that he'd had to hurry back to the hotel to call his mother, who had been ill that night. He hoped that Maggie would forgive him for his thoughtlessness, and he promised to visit with his fans after concerts whenever he possibly could.

That letter was enough magic to keep Maggie going for weeks, and she played the album until it was scarred from wear. But eventually the wonder of it faded, and the memory, like the albums and the fan magazines, was packed away in tissue paper in the closet of her youth, while Maggie got on with her life.

She took business courses, and made mostly B's. She thought she'd probably end up as a secretary somewhere after high school. It was no use thinking about college. Her parents didn't have that kind of money, and if they had, they wouldn't have spent it sending her off to get more educated. Since she'd just end up

getting married anyway, her father reasoned, wasting her time and
their savings on fancy schooling made no sense. Maggie wished
she could have taken shop or auto mechanics like the guys did, but
the guidance counselor had smiled and vetoed the suggestion.
Home economics and typing—that's what girls took. He was sure
that Maggie would be happier in one of those courses, where she
belonged. Now, sometimes, when the plumbing needed fixing or
the toaster wouldn't work, Maggie wished she had insisted on
being allowed to take practical courses, so that she wouldn't have
to use the grocery money to pay repair bills. But it was no use
looking back, she figured. What's done is done.

The summer after high school, Maggie married Leon Holtz,
who wasn't as handsome as Devlin Robey, but he was real. He said
he loved her, and he rented a sky blue tux and bought her a white
gardenia corsage when he took her to the senior prom. There
wasn't any reason *not* to get married, that Maggie could see. Leon
had a construction job in his uncle's business, and she was a clerk
at the Ford dealership, which meant nearly six hundred a month
in take-home pay. They could afford a small apartment, and some
furniture from Sofa City, so why wait? If Maggie had any flashes
of pre-wedding jitters about happily-ever-after with Leon, or any
lingering regrets at relinquishing dreams of some other existence,
where one could actually know people like Devlin Robey—if she
had misgivings about any of it, she gave no sign.

Richie was born fourteen months later. The marriage lasted
until he was two. He was a round-faced, solemn child with his
mother's brown eyes, but he had scoliosis—which is doctor talk
for crookback—so there were medical bills on top of everything
else, and finally Leon, fed up with the confinement of wedded
poverty, took off. Maggie moved to Manhattan, because she figured the pay would be better, especially if she forgot about being a
clerk. She was just twenty-one then, and her looks were still okay.

After a couple of false starts, she got a job as a cocktail waitress
in the Red Lion Lounge. She didn't like the red velvet uniform

that came to the top of her thighs, or the black net stockings she had to wear with it, but the tips were good, and Maggie supposed that the outfit had a lot to do with that. She was twenty-seven now. Sometimes, when her feet throbbed from spending six hours in spike heels and her face ached from smiling at jerks who like to put the make on waitresses, she'd think about the high school shop classes, wondering what life would have been like if she'd learned how to fix cars.

"You want to bring me a drink?" He smiled up at her lazily. The ladies' man who is sure of his magnetism. *You want to bring me a drink?* Like he was conferring a privilege on her. Well, maybe he was. Maggie looked down at Devlin Robey's blurring middle-aged features and thought with surprise that once she would have been honored to serve this man. Would have fought for the chance to do it. But that was half a lifetime ago. Now she was just tired, trying to get through the shift with enough money to pay the phone bill. She'd been up most of the night before with one of Richie's backaches, and now she felt as if she were sleepwalking. She stared at the graying curls of chest hair at the top of his purple shirt, the pouches under his eyes that were darker than his fading tan, and the plastic smile. What the hell. "Sure," she said with no more than her customary brightness. "A drink. What do you want?"

When she brought back the Dewar's-rocks, he was reading the racing news, but as she approached, he set the page aside and smiled up at her. "Thanks," he said, and then after a beat: "You know who I am?"

It struck her as kind of sad the way he asked it. Hesitant, like he had heard no too many times lately, as if each denial of his fame cut the lines deeper into his face. She felt sorry for him. Wished it were twenty years ago. But it wasn't. "Yeah," said Maggie, smoothing out the napkin as she set down his drink. "Yeah, I remember. You're Devlin Robey. I seen you sing once."

The lines smoothed out and his eyes widened: you could just

see the teen idol somewhere in there. "No kiddin'!" he said, with a laugh that sounded like sheer relief. "Well, here . . ." *That ought to be good for a twenty,* Maggie was thinking, but as she watched, Devlin Robey pulled the cocktail napkin out from under his drink and signed his name with a flourish.

"Thanks," said Maggie, slipping the napkin into her pocket with the tips. Maybe the twenty would come later. At least it would be something to tell Kathy Ryan if she ever saw her again. She started to move away to another table, but he touched her arm. "Don't leave yet. So, you heard me sing, huh? At Paradise Alley?"

She told him where the concert had been, and for a moment she thought of mentioning her letter to him, but the two suits at table nine were waving like their tongues might shrivel up, so she eased out of his grasp. "I'll check on you in a few," she promised, summoning her smile for the thirsting suits.

For the rest of her shift, Maggie alternated between real customers and the wistful face of Devlin Robey, who ordered drinks just for the small talk that came with them. "Which one of my songs did you like best?"

" 'I'm Afraid to Go Home,' " said Maggie instantly. When he looked puzzled, she reminded him, "It was the B side to 'Tiger Lily.' "

"Yeah! Yeah! I almost got an award for that one." His eyes crinkled with pleasure.

Another round he wanted to know if she'd seen him in the beach movie he made for Buena Vista. She remembered the movie and didn't say that she couldn't place him in it. It had been a bit part, leading nowhere. After that he went back to singing, mostly in Vegas. Now in Atlantic City. "They love me in the casinos," he told her. "The folks from the 'burbs go wild over me—makes 'em remember the good times, they tell me."

Maggie tried to remember some good times, but all she found was stills of her and Kathy Ryan listening to records and talking about the future. She was going to be a fashion model and live in Paris. Kathy would be a vet in an African wildlife preserve. They would spend holidays together in the Bahamas. "You want some peanuts to go with that drink?" Maggie asked.

At two o'clock the Red Lion was closing, but Devlin Robey had not budged. He kept nursing a Dewar's that was more water than scotch, hunched down like a stray dog who didn't want to be thrown out in the street. Maggie wondered what was wrong with the guy. He was rich and famous, right?

"Are you about finished with that drink? Boss says it's quittin' time."

"Yeah, yeah. I'm a night owl, I guess. All those years of doing casino shows at eleven. Seems like the shank of the evening to me." He glanced at his watch, and then at her: the red velvet tunic, the black fishnet stockings, the cleavage. "You're getting off work now?"

The smile never wavered, but inside she groaned. Tonight had seemed about two days long, and all that kept her going was the thought of a hot bubble bath to soak her feet and the softness of clean sheets to sink into before she passed out from sheer weariness. So now—ten years too late to be an answer to prayer—Devlin Robey wants to take her out. Where was he when it would have mattered?

"I'm sorry," she said. "Thanks anyway, but not tonight." *Maybe ten years ago, but not tonight.*

The one answer she wouldn't have made back when she was Devlin Robey's vestal virgin turned out to be the only one that worked the charm. Suddenly his half-hearted invitation became urgent. "I'll be straight with you," he said, with eyes like stained glass. "I'm feeling kind of down tonight, and I thought it might help to spend some time with an old friend."

Is that what we were? Maggie thought. *I was twenty-five rows back at the concert; I was on the other side of the speakers when WABC's Cousin Brucie played your records, and while you were air-*

brushed and glossy, I was wearing Clearasil and holding the fan magazine. We were friends? She didn't say it, though. If Maggie had learned anything in seven years as a cocktail waitress, it was not to reply to outrageous statements. She shrugged. "I'm sorry," she said, thinking that would be the end of it. Wondering if she'd even bother to tell anybody about it. It wouldn't be any fun to talk about if you had to explain to the other waitresses, bunch of kids, who Devlin Robey was.

"At least give me your phone number—uh—Maggie." Her name was signed with a flourish on his check: *Thank you! Maggie.* "I get to the city every so often. Maybe I could call you, give you more notice. We could set something up. You're all right. You ever think about the business?"

No. Show business offered the same hours as nightclub wait-ressing, and besides she couldn't sing or dance. But Lana Turner had been discovered in a drug store, so maybe . . . After all, who was Maggie Holtz to slap the hand of fate? She tore off the busi-ness expense tab from the Red Lion check and scribbled her name and phone number across it. "Sure. Why not," she said. "Call me sometime."

She patted the autographed cocktail napkin folded in the pocket with her tips, wondering if Richie would like to have it for his scrapbook. Or maybe she should put it in his baby book: *the guy I was pretending to make it with the night you were conceived.* Two scraps of paper; one for each of them to toss. She figured that would be the end of it.

It wasn't, though. Four nights later—four A.M.—the Advil had finally kicked in, allowing her to plunge into sleep, when the phone screamed, dragging her back. She'd forgotten to turn on the damned answering machine. She grabbed for the receiver, only to reinstate the silence, but his voice came through to her, a little swacked, crooning "I'm Afraid to Go Home," and she knew it was him.

"Devlin Robey," she said, wondering why wishes got granted only when you no longer wanted them.

"Maggie doll." He slurred her name. "I just wanted a friendly voice. I got the blues so bad."

"Hangover?"

"No. That'll be after I wake up—if I ever get to sleep, that is. Thought I might get sleepy talking about old times, you know?"

"Old times."

"I lost big tonight at the tables. I played seventeen in roulette a dozen times and it wouldn't come up for me. Seventeen—my number!"

She caught herself nodding forward, and forced the number seventeen to roll around in her memories. Oh, yeah. " 'Seventeen, My Heaven Teen,' " she murmured. "That was your big hit, wasn't it?"

"I got a Cashbox Award for that one. S'in the den at my place in Vegas. Maybe I'll show it to you sometime."

"Wouldn't your wife object?"

She heard him sigh. "Jeez. Trina. What a cow. She was a show-girl when I married her. Ninety-five pounds of blonde. Now she acts like giving me a blow job is a major act of charity, and she's in the tanning salon so much she looks like a leather Barbie doll. Not that I'm home much. I'm on the road a lot."

"Yeah. It's a tough life." She pictured him in a suite the size of her apartment. Maybe one of those sunken tubs in a black marble bathroom.

"It's not like I'm too keen to go home, you know? I have a daughter, Claudia, but jeez it breaks my heart to see her. She was born premature. Probably 'cause Trina was always trying to barf up her dinner to stay skinny. She's never been right, Claudia hasn't. Brain damage at birth. But she always smiles so big when she sees me, and throws her little arms out."

"How old is she?"

"Twelve, I guess. I always picture her when she was little. She was beautiful when she was three all over. Now she's just three inside. Her birthday is the seventeenth of June. My lucky number. Seventeen."

"Not tonight, though, huh?"

"No. Tonight it cost me plenty. I shouldn't bet when I'm loaded. Loaded drunk, I mean; the other kind is never an issue. I like to be with people, though. I'd like to be with you. You don't have an ax to grind. You're not like these glitter tarts here, running around in feathers, can't remember past 1975. You're good people, Maggie. Look, can I come over sometime?"

"I bet you get lotsa offers," said Maggie, hoping somebody else would take the heat.

"I like you," he said. "You're real. Like my kid. Not just some hard-ass in the chorus line with a Pepsodent smile and an angle. I've had a bellyful of them."

She shouldn't have let him tell her about his kid. It made her think of Richie, and made her think that maybe Devlin Robey hadn't had it all his way like she'd figured. All of a sudden, he wasn't just some glossy poster that she could toss when she tired of it. He was a regular guy with feelings. And maybe she owed him. After all, she had used him as her fantasy all those years ago. Maybe it was time to pay up.

"Okay, like Tuesday? That's when I'm off." She could send Richie to her folks in Rockaway. They kept talking until his voice slurred into unconsciousness.

"Your monogamous john is here," said Cap the bartender, nodding toward table seven.

"Yeah," said Maggie. She'd already seen Devlin Robey come in, trying to look casual. He came three days a month now, whenever he could get away from his casino gig. Sometimes it was her night off, and if it wasn't he'd sit at number seven until closing time, nursing a Dewar's-water, and trying to keep a conversation going as Maggie edged her way past to wait on the paying customers.

On her nights off they'd eat Italian, which meant mostly vino for Devlin Robey, and then go back to her place for sex. Robey was only good for once a night, so he liked to prolong it with kinky stuff, strip shows, and listening to Maggie talk dirty, which she found she could do while her mind focused on planning her grocery list for the coming week, and thinking what she needed to take to the cleaners. She felt sorry for Robey, because he had been famous once, and the coddling he'd received as a star had crippled him for life. He couldn't get used to people not being kind anymore; to being ignored by all the regular folks who used to envy him. Whereas she'd had a lifetime of getting used to the world's indifference. But he had been her idol, and he had once stooped down to be kind to her, a nobody, with a beautiful, sincere handwritten letter. So now he needed somebody, so it was Payback. And Payback is a mother. She thought about how famous he was while he grunted and strained on top of her. She pictured that airbrushed poster on her wall.

"Maybe you should charge him," said Cap, as she was about to walk away.

"I ain't on the game," said Maggie.

"Didn't say you were. But you're providing a service. Shrinks charge, don't they? And they got more money than you, Maggie dearest."

She shrugged. "Some things aren't about money."

"Well, if money is no object with you, you can leave early tonight. You might as well. It's dead in here."

He said it too loud. Devlin Robey heard him, and she saw his face light up. No use telling him she was stuck here now. Thanks a heap, Cap. At least Richie was gone—sleeping over at Kevin's tonight. Devlin Robey was already putting his coat on by the time she reached his table. "Boy, am I glad we can get outta here! I'm afraid I might have company tonight."

His face was even more like a fish belly than usual, and his eyes sagged into dark pouches. "What do you mean, company?" asked Maggie, glancing toward the door.

"Tell you later."

They went to a different Italian restaurant, but it had the same oilcloth table covers, and the same vino, which he drank in equal quantities to the usual stuff, and she had the angel-hair pasta, less rubbery than that of the old place. He wouldn't talk about *company*, while they were eating, but he kept looking around, and he whispered, even when he was just talking to her. She had to get him back to her place—in a cab, because he was scared to walk—and get two cups of black decaf down him, before he'd open up.

"Tell me," she said, and she wasn't being Fantasy Girl this time.

"It's okay." He took a thick brown envelope out of the breast pocket of his suit, and laid it on top of the stacks of *Redbook* and *Enquirer*. "I got it covered, see? Most of it anyhow. I think it's enough to call the dogs off."

"You've been gambling again," she said.

"Hey, sooner or later *seventeen* will sing for me again, right?"

"So you owe some pretty heavy people, I guess."

He shrugged, palms up. "It's Atlantic City. They're not Boy Scouts. I was supposed to meet them tonight with the cash, but I was a little short. Had to come up here, hock some things. Borrow what I could from a homeboy, and hope I got it together before they came looking for me. Now I'm okay. I can take the meeting. It's not all there, but it's enough to keep me going. I wrote a note with it, promising more next week. I got record royalties coming."

Maggie's eyes narrowed. "Why'd you want to see me?"

"Not for money!" He laughed a little. "Maggie, this is way out of your league, doll. You just keep your stash in that cookie jar of yours, and let me worry about these gentlemen. I just came to see you 'cause I love you."

He probably does, Maggie thought sadly as she led him to the bedroom. He can see the reflection of the record album poster in my eyes.

It was past two when she got up to take a leak. Robey had been asleep for hours, sated with sweat and swearwords. She saw the envelope lying on the coffee table, and scooped it up as she passed. Might as well see how deep he's in, she thought. Was saving a fallen idol part of the deal? Maybe she could talk him into getting counseling. Gamblers Anonymous, or something. She wondered why dead and famous were the only two choices some people seemed to want.

She didn't go back to bed. When Robey woke up at nine, she gave him aspirin and Bloody Mary mix for his hangover, and a plastic cup of decaf for the road, but no kiss. He was headed back to Atlantic City, still too sleepy and hungover for pleasantries.

Devlin Robey was not a morning person. Neither was Maggie Holtz, but this morning she was wide awake. She sat in front of the television, listening to the game shows, but watching the phone. It rang at five past noon. The answering machine kicked in, and after it said its piece, she heard Devlin Robey's famous, not-so-velvet voice, now shrill in the speaker. "Maggie! Are you there? Pick up! It's me. Listen, you know that envelope I told you about? The one with the cash in it. Listen, I must have left it at your place. There are some gentlemen here who need to know I had it. Could you just pick up, Maggie? Could you tell them about the cash in the envelope, please? It's important."

She heard another voice say, "Real important."

Maggie picked up the phone. "I never saw any envelope, Devlin," she said. "Can't you just stall those guys like you said you would? Till you get some money?"

She heard him cry out as she was replacing the receiver. She set the brown envelope back on the table. There were a lot of hundreds inside it, but that wasn't the point. Some things aren't about money. It was the letter that mattered, the one he wrote to the gamblers asking for more time to pay in full. That wasn't anything like the handwriting she'd seen on his other letter, the one she'd received so long ago containing an apology from *Devlin Robey*. So she really didn't owe him anything. She owed herself a lot of years. She wondered how much it would cost to go to trade school, and if the bills in the brown envelope would cover it. Maggie wanted to learn to fix things.

Typewriter Man

BY SHARYN MCCRUMB WITH
SPENCER AND LAURA MCCRUMB

Working at Northfield Nursing Home isn't nearly as boring as you think, even if it is a building full of old people. It's not like I'm a volunteer or anything, all right? I mean, they pay me. Less than I'm worth, I admit, but it's enough to keep me in video games and halfway decent sneakers.

Ever since my dad died of cancer last year, money has been a little tight at home. My mom went back to work full-time. She's a registered nurse, and now she works as the nursing supervisor at Northfield, and when she told me that the home was short on orderlies, and suggested that they might be able to use a responsible twelve-year-old for a few hours a week, I jumped at the chance. It made me feel good to know that I was helping out with expenses, even if they were mostly *my* expenses. Now I work part-time, late afternoons and weekends, with time off during soccer season. We almost made it to the play-offs last year.

Working at Northfield isn't exactly taxing labor. I load the dishwashers, and I go down to the basement laundry and gather up the clean sheets and towels and deliver them to the four residential floors for the housekeeping staff. Everybody told me that there was a ghost in the basement, because the morgue is right next to the laundry, but I always turn all the lights on when I go down there, and I don't waste any time, so frankly I've never seen anything weird down there. But Kenny Jeffreys swears he once saw

the top half of a guy in a Confederate uniform. Just the *top* half.
Too strange for me, man. The live ones around here are bizarre
enough.

I see them every evening when I push the meal trolley around
the halls, delivering dinner. It doesn't take you long to get the residents scoped out: there's senile ones, who barely notice you; feeble
but chatty ones that treat me like a grandson, which is nice; and
then there are a few space cadets scattered about. Mrs. Graham in
room 239 always has to have *two* dinner trays taken to her. One
for her and one for her husband Lincoln. That's her late husband
Lincoln, you understand. Mr. Graham left the planet in '85, but
he still gets a dinner tray. And, no, he doesn't eat it. I go back at
seven to pick up the trays, and his is never touched. And Mrs.
Whitbread in 202 has an evil twin. Yeah, in the mirror. She's
always scolding the mirror twin, telling her what a hag she is, and
how she ought to behave herself. I swear I'm not making this up.
You can ask Kenny Jeffreys, the orderly who works the same hours
I do. He's in his second year at the community college, majoring
in health care, so he's working for tuition and car insurance
money. Plus, of course, the experience he can get in the health care
field, which does not seem to excite him too much most of the
time. He talks about changing his career to TV anchorman, but as
far as I know he's still in health care.

Northfield has its share of oddities, from ghosts to dotty old
folks, but the patient that really got to me was the white-haired
guy in 226. He was weirder than all the others put together.
Kenny calls him Typewriter Man. The name on his door is *Mr.
Pierce*, and you never see him out of his room, or wearing anything
except a robe and pajamas. Every time I go into his room with the
meal tray, Mr. Pierce is sitting in front of his nonelectric typewriter, tapping away like mad. He must be doing fifty words a
minute. Never stops. Never looks up when you set his food down.
Just keeps typing, like it's some urgent report he's got to finish.

Only there's no paper in the typewriter. Ever.

And he just keeps typing away.

"What do you think Mr. Pierce is writing that's so important?" I asked Kenny one evening, when I had delivered the supper tray through another burst of paperless typing in 226.

Kenny shrugged. "Beats me," he said. "Why don't you ask him?"

"He never looks up. He never stops typing, or even notices that I'm there."

"Guess you'll never know then, kid," said Kenny, wheeling the laundry cart toward the elevator.

But I wasn't willing to give up. And I had just come up with an idea that might work.

The next afternoon when I showed up for work, I dropped by my mom's office and took about twenty sheets of typing paper from the bottom drawer of her desk. She wasn't there at the time, and I knew she'd never miss it. Then I went upstairs to room 226, and tapped on the door before I let myself in. Mr. Pierce was asleep in front of his television, snoring gently, which didn't surprise me, because not even weird people can type twenty-four hours a day. I tiptoed up to his desk, and stuck a sheet of paper in the empty typewriter.

"Pleasant dreams, Mr. Pierce," I whispered as I crept away. "I'll be back to check on you at mealtime."

Two hours later, I was pushing the dinner trolley from room to room, tingling with excitement. I told the grandmotherly types about my history project, and I asked Mrs. Graham how her invisible husband was doing, but all the time my mind was on Mr. Pierce and his typewriter.

Finally, I reached room 226. I heard the familiar tapping sounds through the door, and I knocked once, and let myself in, calling out, "Suppertime, Mr. Pierce!" just like I always did, despite the fact that Mr. Pierce never, ever answered back.

I set the tray on the empty desk space beside the typewriter, moving as slowly as I could, so that I could see what he was typing. The paper was still in place, and it was covered with words. I didn't have to take the paper, because I could memorize the whole thing in thirty seconds. It was the same line over and over: *Alva, please come back. I'm sorry. Please come back.*

I looked over at Mr. Pierce, but he was hunched over his plate, shoveling in food and ignoring me, the way he always did. I wished him a good evening, and went to find Kenny.

"He just keeps typing the same sentence," I told him. "He's telling someone named Alva to please come back, and he says he's sorry."

"Maybe it's his wife," said Kenny. "I wonder if she knows where he is."

"Somebody had to sign him in here," I pointed out.

"Maybe it wasn't her, though. Maybe they got divorced, and his kids put him here. Maybe she misses him now. A list of his relatives would probably be entered on his records folder." Kenny reads a lot of paperback mysteries while he's doing the laundry in the basement. He says it keeps his mind off the ghosts. He looked at me slyly. "Of course, I couldn't look in those folders, but since they're in your mom's office . . ."

"I'll see what I can do," I muttered. I felt sorry for Mr. Pierce, typing that same sad sentence day after day with no hope of getting an answer. Maybe there was hope, though.

The next evening I pushed my meal cart up close to Kenny's trolley full of towels. "So much for your theories, Sherlock," I told him. "I read Mr. Pierce's folder while Mom was at the photocopy machine. She almost caught me, too! Anyhow, his wife's name was Rosalie, and she died the year he was admitted to Northfield. They didn't have any children, which is probably why he is here. There was no mention of anyone named Alva in his folder."

"Has he always lived around here?"

"I think so. Why?"

"You could ask one of the local old ladies if she knew Mr. Pierce before he came here, and if there was ever anyone named Alva in his life. It's not a very common name. Sounds old-fashioned to me."

I couldn't think of any better idea, and Mr. Pierce certainly wasn't talking, so the next evening when I delivered the meals I got into a conversation with all the residents who weren't gaga. I asked if they'd always lived around here, and then asked about Mr. Pierce. It was Mrs. Graham who knew him from the old days.

"Francis Pierce!" she said, smiling. "Yes, we've known him forever, haven't we, dear?" That last remark was addressed to the invisible (deceased) Mr. Graham, and I am happy to say that he did not reply.

"Well, do you know of anyone called Alva that he once knew?"

"Alva Pierce. I hadn't thought about her in years. It was front-page news at the time, though."

She knew! I almost dropped the tray, which wouldn't have mattered, because it was Mr. Graham's and he still hadn't come back from the Hereafter for spaghetti and Jell-O, but still it would have been a mess to clean up, and suddenly I felt I needed every minute of extra time I could manage. "Was Alva his wife, then?" I asked, trying to sound polite and casual about it.

"No, dear, his sister. Such a sad thing. People did wonder if it was murder—" She looked up at me then (or maybe Mr. Graham tipped her off) and she realized that she was about to talk scandal to a twelve-year-old kid. She smiled at me and said, "Well, never mind, dear. It was a long time ago, and I expect you have a good many meals to deliver."

I could see that I wasn't going to be able to talk her into finishing the story, so I went back to delivering dinners, but my mind was going ninety miles an hour, trying to figure out another way to find out about Alva.

"You seem preoccupied tonight, young man." It was Mr. Lagerveld, who was a really nice guy, even if he didn't care too much for the food. I could tell he was in no hurry to get to his spaghetti. He had been a college professor years ago, and I liked to talk to him anyhow. I was thinking: *if I can just word the question right, maybe Mr. L. can help me.*

"I have to do some research," I told him, as I set his tray down on the table, and rustled up his silverware. "It's for school. It's about something that happened around here about sixty years ago, and I don't know how to go about finding the information."

"Sixty years ago? The Great Depression?"

I shook my head. "A local thing—like a person got kidnapped, or something." I was guessing about the time and the event, but I thought I had the general idea anyhow.

"Have you tried looking in the newspapers?"

"How would I find a sixty-year-old newspaper? They'd fall apart, wouldn't they?"

He sighed. "No wonder my students couldn't do research. What do they teach you these days? How to feed your hamster?"

"We use encyclopedias to look up stuff, but there wouldn't be anything local in the *Britannica*."

"That is correct. So you need newspapers. So you go to a library, and you ask the nice librarian for the microfilm. You see, they put old newspapers on microfilm, so they won't fall apart when grubby-handed kids use them to do history reports." He sounded gruff, but he was grinning at me, and I think he suspected that what I wanted to find wasn't an assignment for school.

"Microfilm. The public library will have papers from sixty years ago?"

"I hope so. Our tax dollars at work, young man. Good luck with your investigation. And if you ever have a question about geology—that I can help with."

I had to wait until Sunday afternoon to see if Mr. Lagerveld was right about the microfilm. Since I didn't have a date to go by, I knew I was going to have to scroll through about ten years' worth of newspapers to see what happened to Alva. I just hoped Mrs. Graham was right about the story being front-page news.

Mom was delighted to take me to the library for a change, instead of to the video store, which is my usual Sunday afternoon destination. I told her I'd be a couple of hours getting material for my report, and she gave me a dollar's worth of change for the photocopy machine and went off to the grocery store, happy in the knowledge that her kid had suddenly become so studious. I hated to disappoint her. I'd try to score a few A's on the old report card to bolster her faith in the new me. Meanwhile, I had to find someone named Alva.

While I was waiting for Sunday to roll around so that I could check the microfilm newspapers, I had tried to figure out a way to narrow down the search time to the smallest possible number of years. I looked up Mr. Pierce's age in his record file. He was seventy-five. That meant that he was born in 1920. But Mrs. Graham remembered the case, and she was only seventy-one. I figured that she had to have been at least seven years old to remember a local tragedy—which meant that 1931 was the first year I planned to search. Mr. Pierce would have been eleven years old. I didn't know if Alva was his younger sister or an older one.

The librarian was very helpful. She showed me how to use the microfilm machines, and she showed me where the reels were kept, all carefully labeled by month and year. I started with January 1931 and flipped through day by day, reading the headlines of each front-page story. An hour and a half later I was in June of 1932, and there it was: LOCAL GIRL MISSING: BELIEVED LOST IN WOODS. There was a drawing of a pretty girl who looked about eight years old. The story said that Alva Pierce had followed her big brother Francis into the woods, where he was playing with two

other boys. They ran off and left the little girl, telling her to go
back home. When they came out of the woods at suppertime, they
discovered that little Alva had not returned home. The boys, their
parents, and the whole neighborhood searched the woods, calling
for the little girl, but she was not found. I kept checking the newspapers, day after day, to see what happened to Alva Pierce. One
day they brought in dogs. Another day they questioned everybody
who had used the nearby road that day. After a week, the stories
got smaller and smaller, and they were no longer on the front
page. Finally the stories stopped altogether. Alva Pierce had never
been found.

"Well, now you know," said Kenny Jeffreys, when I showed
him the articles I photocopied from the microfilm newspapers.
"Mr. Pierce was responsible for his sister getting lost in the woods,
and he still feels guilty about it after all these years."

"It's because they never found her," I said. "I'll bet he still wonders what happened to her."

"Poor old guy," said Kenny, loading the last of the towels on his
trolley. "Well, gotta go now. Too bad we can't help Mr. Pierce."

"I'm not ready to give up," I said. "I looked up the patch of
woods that Alva got lost in back in 1932."

"Dream on, kid," said Kenny. "If no one has found that little
girl after sixty-something years, I don't think your chances are all
that good."

"I'm not giving up yet. I got a topographical map of the
woods—the librarian suggested it. And I have one more person
that might be able to help."

That evening I took Mr. Lagerveld his Salisbury steak, and
before he could ask if it was Roy Rogers's horse, like he always did,
I said, "Remember how you said I could come to you if I ever had
a geology question?"

"I don't do term papers," he warned me.

I pulled out my newspaper articles and my photocopied map of the woods. "Look at this, Mr. L. This was my library project. A little girl got lost in these woods sixty years ago, and they never found her. If you were going to look for her, where would you start?"

He put on his reading glasses and studied the map, and the fine print at the bottom that told where it was, and he muttered to himself some. Finally he said, "Strictly speaking, this is geography, but I think I can help you out. People looked a couple of days in these woods and didn't find her?"

I nodded.

"Did they try the caves?"

"What caves?" I looked at the article. I didn't remember anything about caves.

"Look at this analysis of the land. Limestone. Creek nearby. Of course there are caves. But the opening might be too small for an adult to notice. Low to the ground, maybe. A little girl would find it easily enough." He took off his glasses and glared at me. "Please note that I am not advising you to go caving alone. Remember what happened to that little girl."

"No problem," I said. "I know just the person to take with me."

Saturday morning was sort of cold and drizzly, but Kenny would have been complaining anyhow, because he hated to get up early on Saturday, and he was missing a trip to the movies with his friends, and about a dozen other gripes, but he agreed that I ought not to go alone, and he was curious about the little girl's disappearance. So, with a lot of grumbling, he picked me up at my house at seven A.M. and told my mother we were going hiking, which was almost true.

The house that had belonged to the Pierce family was in ruins now, but it was still there, so we parked the car in the yard, and set

off on foot from its backyard. That's the way Francis and Alva
would have gone. We had knapsacks with food, rope, and flash-
lights, and Kenny had brought a shovel in case we needed it, but
he said I had to take turns with him carrying it.

The woods hadn't changed much in sixty years. It was still a
rural part of the county, thick with underbrush, and easy to get
lost in. I stayed close to Kenny, and tried not to think about
snakes.

We followed the creek, examining boulders, ridges, and any
kind of land formation that might hide an opening to a cave. Since
it was early March, I thought we might have a better chance of
finding a cave than the searchers would have had in June, when
summer plants had covered everything with vines and grasses. We
walked around for hours, getting our boots muddy, and snagging
our trousers on brambles and old bits of barbed wire.

Finally, I sat down to rest near the stream, wishing I'd packed
two more sandwiches in my knapsack. As I leaned back, putting
one arm behind me for balance, I slipped and fell flat on my back.
My arm had sunk into the ground.

"Kenny! Bring the shovel!" I yelled. "I think I found it!"

After all these years, mud had filled up most of the entrance,
but Kenny and I took turns digging like mad, and soon we had an
opening big enough for me to fit into.

"I don't like the idea of you going in alone," he told me.

"At least you know where I am," I said. "If I get in trouble, you
can go for help."

I tied the rope around my waist, took the flashlight, and wriggled through the muddy opening, and into the darkness. "It's
okay!" I yelled back to Kenny.

The cave was too low to stand up in, so I inched my way along,
keeping the beam of the flashlight trained at my feet, so that
I wouldn't tumble into a pit. I hadn't gone more than about ten
feet before the light showed a flash of white on the ground in
front of me. I crept forward, shivering as a trickle of water ran

down the neck of my shirt, and I reached out my hand and touched—a bone. I dug a little in the soft mud, and found more bones and a few scraps of cloth. There was a large boulder near the bones, and I think it must have fallen, either killing the person, or pinning them down so that they could not escape. This was Alva. She had found the cave and had been trapped there, without anyone knowing where to look for her.

I made my way back out as quickly as I could. I hadn't thought about cave-ins until I saw the boulder beside those tiny white bones. "She's there," I told Kenny, as I gasped for fresh air. "Now we have to tell the police, I guess."

A couple of days later, I was back at work, and Mom had finished yelling at me for being a daredevil. As I took the meal tray in to room 226, I saw that Mr. Pierce was asleep, so I stopped at the desk, and set a newspaper down on top of the empty typewriter. It was open to the front page story about Alva Pierce being found after all these years. The search and rescue team had recovered the body, and she was buried now in the little church cemetery next to her parents. I thought Mr. Pierce would be glad to know that his sister had been found.

I did wonder, though, when I got to Mrs. Graham's room to deliver her two dinners. She took her dinner, and set the other one down in front of her late husband's empty chair. Then she said, "Young man, I thought children were not allowed in Northfield except at visiting hours."

"Yes, ma'am," I said, "but I work here. Remember?"

"Not you!" she snapped. "Mr. Graham tells me that he distinctly saw a little blond girl going into room 226 just now. Didn't you, dear?"

Whatever he said, I didn't hear it.

How We Wrote "Typewriter Man"
Sharyn McCrumb
Spencer and Laura McCrumb

Laura, who is six years old, came up with the idea for the story by listening to her big sister's boyfriend talking about his job at a nursing home. Spencer, age seven, figured out how to find out what the man would be typing by putting paper into the typewriter, and Laura decided that the mystery would be that the man's sister had gone missing as a little girl. Spencer worked out what happened to the little girl, and how to go about finding her after all these years. Sharyn McCrumb, Spencer and Laura's mom, did most of the wording. She would read drafts of it to Spencer and Laura, and they would suggest changes, and make sure that not too many big words were used. Finally, they came up with a story that everyone was happy with. Laura is especially pleased with the ending.

Gerda's Sense of Snow

[INSPIRED BY HANS CHRISTIAN ANDERSEN'S
"THE SNOW QUEEN"]

꙳

"Gerda! Kay's gone!"

"Kay has been gone a long time, Niels," I said wearily. "And you're dripping snow on my rug."

Niels Lausten stood there blocking my fireplace with his shivering body, while his parka rained on my caribou-skin rug. I could tell that he wasn't going away, despite my apparent lack of interest in his news. I took a sip of my tea and read a few more lines of my book, but the sense of them never quite reached my brain, so I gave it up. I would have to hear him out, and I knew it was going to hurt, because it always did, no matter how many times I told myself that the Kay I once knew, my childhood best friend, was gone forever. I wrote him off every time one of the old gang showed up to tell me the latest about poor Kay—shameful stories about a life going down the drain in a haze of vodka, in a swirl of drunken brawls and petty acts of vandalism that seemed to gain him neither profit nor comfort. It had never made sense to me. I had tried to see him a couple of times, early on, to see if he'd accept my help, but the bleary-eyed lout who leered back at me bore no resemblance to the quiet, handsome boy next door, whose hobby had been growing roses in the window box. In the winter we used to heat copper pennies on our stoves and hold the hot pennies to the glass to melt the ice so that we could look through the peepholes and wave to each other. I thought we'd always be

279

together, our lives as intertwined as our rose trees, but a thicker
sheet of ice had grown up between us as we grew older, and
nothing seemed capable of melting it. The old Kay that I'd loved
was gone. I knew it. I whispered it over and over to myself like a
litany. Why couldn't I believe it? Why couldn't Niels leave me
alone to mourn?

"He's gone, Gerda. Really." Niels had peeled off his gloves, and
now he was blowing on his fingers to warm them. He was still
shaking, though, and his white face went beyond a winter pallor.

It wasn't that cold outside. About average for a Danish winter. I
wondered what else had been going on in town while I was
escaping the winter at my fireside, engrossed in a book. Now that
I looked at him, Niels seemed more frightened than cold. He
was always a follower, always the first one to run when trouble
appeared. I wondered what trouble had appeared this time.

"All right." I sighed. "Tell me about it."

"We were just horsing around, Gerda. We'd had a few drinks,
and somebody said, 'Wouldn't it be fun to swipe some of the kids'
sleds and hitch them to the horse-drawn sleighs?' That would be a
real fast ride—and you wouldn't have to keep climbing a hill in
between rides. So a couple of the lads tried it, but the sleds
skidded, and they fell off in a minute or so. Then we saw a different sleigh. We'd never seen it before. It was painted white, so
that it blended into the snowdrifts, and the driver was wrapped in
rough white fur, with a white fur hood covering the head and
hiding the face. The rest of us hung back, because the sleigh was so
big and fast-looking, and we couldn't tell who was driving it. But
Kay laughed at us, and said that he wasn't afraid of a fast ride.
Before we could stop him, he'd tied his sled to the runners of the
white sleigh, and the thing took off like a thunderbolt. The sled
was sliding all over the road behind that sleigh, but he managed to
hold on. We yelled for him to roll off. He almost got run over by
the horse of an oncoming sleigh. He wouldn't turn loose. Then
the white sleigh got clear of traffic and Kay was gone! We

followed the tracks outside town a mile or so beyond the river, until the snow started up again, and then we lost the trail, so we came on back. . . ." He shrugged. "So—he's gone. I figured you'd want to know, Gerda."

"Yeah, thanks," I said. "Maybe I'll ask around."

"He's probably dead," said Niels.

"Yeah. He's probably dead." I went back to my book.

I tried to put him out of my mind, and I nearly succeeded for the rest of the winter. I kept thinking that Niels or Hans would turn up with some new story about Kay—that he was back after robbing the rich owner of the sleigh, and wilder, drunker than ever. But the town was silent under the deepening snow. I waited out the silence.

In the spring the thaws came, and the sun coaxed people back out into the streets to pass the time of day with their neighbors. They started asking each other what had become of that wild young man, Kay. Nobody had seen him since midwinter. His friends told their story about the sleigh ride, and how he never came back. "Oh, well, he must have been killed," people said. When the ice floes broke up on the river outside town, people said that Kay's body would come floating to the surface any day now. Surely he had drowned while crossing the river ice, trying to make his way back to town after his reckless sleigh ride. A few days later they found the wooden sled buried in a snowbank farther still from town. Kay's hat was in a clump of melting snow nearby, but there was no sign of his body. But maybe the wolves had got him. They wouldn't have left anything, not even a bone.

"He's dead," I said to the old street singer, who appears on the corner even before the birds come back.

"I don't believe it," he said, and went on with a warbling tune about sunshine.

"I'll ask around," I said. And this time I meant it.

I didn't go to the town constable. If Kay had died in an accident, the constable would have discovered it already. If something
more sinister had happened to him, the constable would be the
last to know. I didn't waste my time with official inquiries.

I went to the river. My grandmother used to tell me that the
river would answer your question if you threw in one of your possessions as a sacrifice. I was tempted to try it, but before I could
work myself up to that stage of desperation—or belief—I saw the
old man I had come looking for. He lived in a shack downstream
from the brewery, and I always wondered how he made it through
the winter, dressed in his layers of reeking rags, with skin as
translucent as ice under his matted hair. He grinned at me with
stumps of teeth that looked like the pilings of the dock. I used to
dream about him. I thought he was Kay in thirty years' time.
Maybe dead would be better. But I had to ask.

"You remember Kay? Young blond fellow. Drinking buddy of
yours. He's been gone since midwinter."

The bloodshot eyes rolled, and the old man gave a grunt that
was more smell than sound. I took it to be a yes.

"He hitched a child's sled onto the back of a white sleigh, and it
sped away with him. The word around town is that he drowned—
only his body hasn't turned up. Or maybe the wolves got him." I
could taste salt on my tongue. "Not that it matters," I whispered.

The old derelict wet his lips, and warmed up his throat with a
rheumy cough. I fished a coin out of my pocket and handed it to
him. "Get something for that cough," I muttered, knowing what
he would prescribe.

"I know the white sleigh," he rasped. "I wish it had been me."

"You know it?"

"Ar—they call her the Snow Queen." He flashed a gap-toothed
smile. "She brings the white powder to town. Ar. Kay would like
that. White powder lasts longer than this stuff." He dug in his
overcoat pocket for the nearly empty bottle, and waved it at me.

"And it's the only thing that would take the hurt away. You know about the crack, do you?"

I shook my head. "I knew Kay was in trouble. I never cared what kind of trouble. If I couldn't help him, what did it matter?"

"The crack. That wasn't the Snow Queen's doing. They do say it's mirror glass from heaven. Trolls built a magic mirror that made everything ugly. Took it up into the clouds so that they could distort the whole world at once. Got to laughing so hard they dropped the mirror. Shattered to earth in a million tiny pieces. Crack of the mirror. They do say."

"Sounds like my grandmother's tales," I said. It was a lot prettier than the truth.

"They say if the mirror crack gets into your eye, then you see everything as ugly and misshapen. Worse if it gets into your heart. Then your heart freezes, and you don't feel anything ever at all. From the look of him, I'd say that Kay has got a piece in his eye and his heart. And nothing would make the coldness pass, except what the Snow Queen has—that perfect white powder that makes you dream when you're awake. He won't be leaving her, not while there's snow from her to ease his pain."

I hadn't realized that it was this bad. But maybe, I told myself, he's just sick, and then maybe he can be cured. Maybe I can get him past the craving for the white powder. I knew that I was going to try. "Where do I find the Snow Queen?" I asked the old man.

He pointed to a boat tied up at the dock. "Follow the river," he said. "She could be anywhere that people need dreams or a way to get out of the cold. Give her my love."

"You're better off without her," I told him. "You're better off than Kay."

There wasn't much to keep me in town. I had needed an excuse to get out of there for a long time. Too many memories. Too many people who thought they knew me. It took less than a day to tidy things up so that I could leave, and there wasn't any-body I wanted to say goodbye to. So I left. Looking for Kay was as good a reason as any.

I spent most of the summer working as a gardener on an estate in the country. The old lady who owned the place was a dear, and she'd wanted me to stay on, but the roses kept reminding me of Kay, and finally one day I told her I had to move on. I had enough money by then to get to the big city, where movies are made. That's where they sell dreams, I figured. That's where the Snow Queen would feel at home.

I got into the city in the early autumn, and since I didn't know anybody and had no place in particular to go, I just started walking around, looking at all the big houses, and all the flowers on the well-tended lawns. A gardener could always get a job here, I thought. It was always summer. I stopped to talk to one guy in shabby work clothes who was busy weeding a rose bed near the sidewalk.

"New in town, huh?" He was dark, and he didn't speak the lan-guage very well, but we managed to communicate, part smiles and gestures, and what words we knew in each other's tongue.

"I'm looking for a man," I said.

He grinned. "That—or a job. Aren't they all?"

I shook my head. "Not any man. One in particular, from back home. I think he's in trouble. I think he has a problem with . . . um . . . with snow. Know what I mean?"

"A lot of that in this town," said the gardener. By now I was helping him weed the rose bed, so he was more inclined to be chatty. "He hooked on snow—why you bothering?"

I shrugged. "We go back a-ways, I guess. And he's—well, he was an okay guy once. Tall, blond hair, good features, and a smile that could melt a glacier. Once upon a time."

The gardener narrowed his eyes and looked up at nothing, the way people do when they're thinking. After a moment he said, "This guy—does he talk like you?"

"I guess so. We're Danish. From the same town, even."

He looked at me closely. "Danish . . ." Then he snapped his fingers and grinned. "Girl, I know that fellow you're looking for! But I got some bad news for you—you ain't gonna get him back."

I wiped rose dirt on my jeans. "I just want to know that he's all right," I mumbled.

"Oh, he's better than all right. He's in high cotton. He's on the road to rich and famous. See, there's a movie princess in this town, getting ready to shoot the biggest-budget picture anybody's seen around here in a month of Sundays, and she was looking for a leading man. Not just anybody, mind you. She had to have a fellow who talked as good as he looked. Well, that's not something easy to find in anybody, male or female. But they had auditions. For *days*, girl. Every beach bum and pool shark in this town showed up at the gate, ready to take a shot at the part. Most of them talked pretty big to the newspapers. Pretty big to the interviewers. But as soon as they stood beside Miss Movie Princess, and the cameras were rolling, they started sounding like scarecrows. She was about ready to give up, when all of a sudden this guy talks his way past the guards, without even so much as a handwritten résumé. 'It must be boring to wait in line,' he told the receptionist, and he smiled at her, and she forgot to call Security. I got a lady friend, works for the Movie Princess, so I get all the news firsthand, you know what I'm saying?"

I nodded. "Most of it," I said. "Listen—this guy—was he tall and blond? Regular features?"

"Oh, he was a hunk, all right. And he talked just like you do."

"It's Kay!" I said. "I know it is. Look, I have to see him."

"Well, the thing is, he got more than just the part in the movie. He got the girl, too. So now he's living up in the mansion with Miss Movie Princess, and my lady friend says it looks like it's going to be permanent."

"I have to know if it's him," I said. "Please—he's like—he's like my brother."

The gardener believed that—more than I did. "All right," he said. "Let me talk to my lady friend, see what I can do. They'd never let you in the gate, dressed like that, and with no official business to bring you there. But we might be able to get you up the back stairway to see him. I got a key to the servants' entrance."

He took me back to the gardener's office, and fixed me something to eat. Then I helped him with the bedding plants while we waited for dusk. That evening we went up to the mansion in the hills, in through the back garden, and through the unlocked kitchen door. *I just want to see that he's all right,* I kept telling myself. *Maybe he's happy now. Maybe he's settled down, stopped the drinking. Maybe he's got his smile back, like in the old days, before it became a sneer. If I see that he's all right, I can go home,* I thought.

At least, I'd know for sure.

I didn't notice much about the house. It was big, and the grounds around it were kept as perfectly as a window box, but it didn't make me feel anything. I wondered if living in a land without seasons would be as boring as a long dream. *I don't have to stay,* I told myself.

"In there." My new friend had stopped and shined his flashlight at a white-and-gold door. The bedroom. "You're on your own from here on out, girl," he whispered, handing me the light. Soundlessly, he faded back into the darkness of the hallway.

I waited until his footsteps died away, and then I twisted the doorknob, slowly, as soundlessly as I could. Another minute passed before I eased inside. I could hear the regular breathing of the sleepers in the room. In the moonlight from the open window I could see two large pillars in the center of the room, and on either side of the pillars were white-and-gold water beds in the shape of lilies. I crept closer to one of the beds. Long blond hair streamed across the pillar, but the bare back and shoulders were muscular. Surely it was Kay. I switched on the flashlight, and let the light play over the features of the sleeping man.

"What the hell!" He sat up, shouting in alarm.

It wasn't him.

The Movie Princess was screaming, too, now, and she had set off the alarm that would bring her security guards into the room. Suddenly everything was noise and lights, like a very bad dream.

I lost it.

I sat down on the bed and began to cry, for the hopelessness of it all, and because I was so tired of noise and lights and a world without seasons. The Movie Princess, seeing that I wasn't a crazed admirer, told her guards to wait outside in the hall, and she and the man asked me what I was looking for. When I heard the blond man speak, I realized that he was from Minnesota. "Close but no fjord, my gardener friend," I thought. I guess we all sound alike to outsiders.

I told them about Kay's disappearance, and about my need to find the Snow Queen, which appalled them, because they were not into that sort of lifestyle, but they agreed that my purpose was noble, since I was trying to save a friend from the clutches of the powder dreams. They gave me money and jewelry to help me on my trip, and the Movie Lady insisted that I put on one of her dresses, and take her *wheels*, as she called them, to speed me on my way. They didn't have any advice for me about where to look, but they told me to stay cool. A funny wish, I thought, from people who choose to live where it is always hotter than copper pennies on a woodstove.

I sped away through the night, not really knowing where I was going, and wondering who to ask about the Snow Queen. I found myself going down streets that were darker and narrower, until I no longer knew which way I was going and which way I had come. I came to a stop to think about what to do next—and then the decision was no longer mine to make.

A shouting, screaming mob of people surrounded me, and hauled me out of the vehicle.

"She's wearing gold!" one of them shouted.

A dozen hands pawed at my throat and my wrists. I struggled to throw a punch, to kick at my attackers, but I was powerless in the grip of the mob. They pinned my arms behind my back and stuffed a dirty handkerchief in my mouth. I watched them dismantle the wheels of the Movie Princess until it was an unrecognizable hulk in the dark alley. The crowd began fighting among themselves for my money and for the jewelry the Princess had given me. I figured I wasn't going to live much longer, but nobody would come looking for me.

A large woman ambled over to me and peered into my face. "She like a little fat lamb," the woman said. I stared at the stubble beneath her chin, hoping to distract myself from her dead eyes. "She look good enough to eat—don'tcha, baby?" She pulled a hunting knife from the folds of her skirt and began running her finger along the blade.

I struggled harder to break free from my captors but it was no use. All I managed to do was spit out the gag. I swore in Danish: *"Pis og lort!"*

"Iddn't she cute? She just say *'Peace, O Lord!'*—Never had anybody pray before."

I didn't give her a Danish lesson. Let her think I was praying. Maybe it would help. She edged closer to me, the knife wavering at my throat. I had closed my eyes, wondering if I should have chosen prayer, when suddenly the fat woman drew back and screamed.

I opened my eyes and saw that a small brown girl had jumped on the woman's back and was biting her ear. The woman began to swing around, waving the knife, and swearing. "Get down, you devil of a child! What you want to do that for?"

"Give her to me!" said the girl. "I want her. She can give me her fancy clothes and her rings, and she can sleep with me in my bed!"

The men began to laugh and nudge each other. The fat woman shook her head, but her daughter bit her ear again, and she screamed, and everyone laughed even harder. "She's playing with her cub!" somebody said.

The small brown girl got her way. They bundled us into her set of wheels, and we took off through a maze of streets, all neon and no stars. The girl was about my height, but stronger, with nut-brown skin, big dark eyes, and white wolf teeth. "She won't kill you as long as I want you!" she told me. "Are you a movie princess?"

"No. I'm looking for somebody."

The dark girl cocked her head. "You lookin' for somebody? Down here? At this time of night? Girl, you were lookin' for Trouble, and you sure enough found him. You ain't goin' no-where, but at least you're safe with me. I won't let nobody hurt you. And if I get mad at you, why I'll just kill you myself. So you don't have to worry about none of the rest of them. You want a drink?"

We stopped at the curb in front of a ruined building. Some of the windows were boarded up, and some had the glass smashed from the frames, and birds flew in and out of the dark rooms. A sign on the double front doors said CONDEMNED, which was true enough, I thought. This was the place the gang called home. As they marched me into the building, lean snarling dogs clustered around us, but they did not bark. One looked up at me and growled in his throat.

"You will sleep with me and my little pets tonight," said the brown girl, patting the snarling dog. We went inside the derelict building. The gang had built a campfire on the marble floor of the entrance hall, and they were cooking their evening meal. I was given something greasy on a sort of pancake, and when I had eaten as much of it as I could, I was led upstairs and through a dark hall to the girl's room. There was no furniture in the room, only a sleeping bag on the floor, and some straw. Holes had been punched in the walls of the room, and the windows were empty squares looking down on the lights of the city. Pigeons milled around on the floor, occasionally rising to sail out the glassless window, then drifting back in on the next puff of breeze.

"These all belong to me," said the girl. She reached out and grabbed a waddling pigeon from the floor, and thrust it into my face. "Kiss it."

I pulled away, and worked on the rope binding my hands.

"The pigeons live in the hole in the wall," she said, smoothing the bird's feathers. "They come back at night. But I got to keep old Rudy tied up, or he'd run off for sure, wouldn't you, Rudy?" She opened the connecting door to another empty room. A frightened boy shied away from her as she approached him, but he couldn't go far because he was chained to the floor by a copper ring encircling his neck. His face and ragged clothes were caked with dirt. The dark girl drew her knife. "Rudy's a special pet. I'm saving him. Every night I got to tickle him a little with my blade just to remind him what would happen if he tried to run." She passed the knife gently across the boy's throat. He struggled and kicked at her, but she laughed and turned away.

"Are you going to sleep with that knife?" I asked her as she climbed into the sleeping bag.

"I always sleep with the knife," she said. "You never know what's going to happen—do you, sunshine? Now why don't you tell me a bedtime story? Tell me what you were doing out here all by yourself with no more protection than a pigeon got?"

"If I tell you, will you untie me then?"

She shook her head. "Make it good, and maybe I'll untie you tomorrow."

I started telling her about Kay, and how he had hitched his sled to the sleigh of the Snow Queen. The dark girl laughed, and said in a sleepy voice, "Boy strung out on the powder. Sure is. I heard about buying a one-way ticket on an airline made of snow. Old song. Never heard it called hitching a ride onto a sleigh before. Guess that's what they mean by cul-tu-ral di-ver-si-ty." Her voice trailed off into a slur of sounds. Soon her breathing became slow and even, and I knew she was asleep.

"I've seen her," said a soft voice in the darkness.

It was the boy. I heard the rattle of his chain as he edged closer.

"You can talk," I said. Somehow I had thought he wasn't quite right in the head, I guess. But he sounded okay—just scared to be talking with his tormentor so near.

"Yeah, I can talk. I been around. After I ran away from home, I lived on the street for a while—until *they* got me and brought me here—I used to see her—the one you call the Snow Queen. She'd ride by every now and again, and there was always a good supply of that white powder on the street after she'd been around. Oh, yeah, the Snow Queen. I know her, for sure."

"But do you know where to find her?"

"She got a place up in the hills. Couple of hours from here, where it's so high up it stays cold. She likes the cold. Big white showplace in the mountains, all by itself. I never been there, but I heard talk. I could find it."

"I wish I could let you try." I eased out of the sleeping bag and leaned back against the wall, listening to the pigeons cooing in the darkness, but I didn't sleep. I thought about Kay.

The next morning the dark girl crawled out of the sleeping bag. "I dreamed about that guy you talked about," she said. "Dreamed he was sitting on ice somewhere, trying to spell some big word with a bunch of crooked pieces of glass. Kept trying and trying to spell that word, and he couldn't do it. You believe in message dreams? I do. He's in a bad way, all right. Yes, he surely is that."

I nodded. "Rudy says he knows where to find him."

"What? Chain-boy? He don't know nothing." She reached for her knife and scowled at her prisoner, but this time he did not cringe.

"I do know," he said. "I seen a lot. Seen her on the street. I can find her, too."

"Maybe that's what your dream meant," I told her. "Maybe you're supposed to send us after the Snow Queen."

The dark girl looked afraid. "Even us don't mess with her."

"She won't know you're involved. It'll just be Rudy and me. We'll go after her." I stared at her until she looked away. "You've been told to let us go," I said. "Your dream."

"Yeah, okay. What do I need you two for? It's not like you were any fun or anything. Go chase the Snow Queen. Get yourself killed in a cold minute."

The boy and I waited in silence while she made up her mind. At last she said, "Okay. The men are all out for the day, but Mamacita is downstairs, and she won't like it if I let you go. So you have to wait a little until she goes to sleep, and then I'll lead you down the fire escape so she won't see you."

The boy and I exchanged smiles of relief.

The dark girl pulled on Rudy's chain. "I'm gonna miss tickling you with my knife, boy," she said. "You look so cute when you're afraid, but never mind. I'm gonna let you go, and I want you to take this lady to the house of the Snow Queen, and you help her get him out of there. And if you run out on her, I'm going to come and find you myself. You got that?"

He nodded. "I'll take her there."

"Okay. I'll get you some food." She moved behind me with her dagger, and cut the rope that bound my wrists. Then she handed me the key to the boy's copper neck ring, and nodded for me to unchain him. "Okay," she hissed at us. "Get over to the fire escape. I'll come back with the food when it's safe for you to go. After that—anybody asks, I ain't seen you."

Rudy took me back to the part of town where he had been before the dark girl's gang had captured him. "There's an old lady here who might help," he said. "She's been on the street so long she knows everything."

He led me down an alley to an old packing crate propped up against the side of a Dumpster. The sides of the crate were decorated with faded bumper stickers, and an earthenware pot of geraniums stood by the opening, which was covered with a ragged quilt. "This is her office. Well, it's her home, too. We have to knock."

We got down on our hands and knees to enter the tiny hovel that was home to Rudy's friend. When my eyes adjusted to the dim light, I saw a grizzled old woman cooking fish in a pan on a camping stove. She wore a grimy Hermés scarf wrapped around her head, several layers of cast-off designer clothing, and a pair of men's Nike running shoes.

Rudy gave the old woman a hug and immediately began to tell her the long tale about his troubles, which he apparently considered much more important than mine. At last, though, he had run out of complaints, and the woman's sympathetic clucks were becoming more perfunctory. Then Rudy said, "And this is my friend Gerda. She got me away from the gang, but she's looking for a guy named Kay who went off with the Snow Queen. You know what I'm saying?"

"Poor child!" said the old woman, nodding. "You still have a long way to go! You have a hundred miles to run before you reach the hill country. The Snow Queen lives up there now, and she burns blue lights every night. I will write some words for you on a paper bag, and you can take it to Finnish Mary. She never could get the hang of city life here, so she lit out for the mountains. She lives up there in an old mining ghost town now. She will advise you better than I can."

She gave us a little of her fish, and some produce from the grocery store Dumpster, and then she scribbled some words on the paper bag, gave Rudy directions to the mining town, and sent us off to the hill country, wishing us luck in our quest.

We walked out to the big highway, and started thumbing for rides. We were able to hitchhike most of the way into the hill country, so we made it by nightfall. The evening light was soft and silvery as we walked the last couple of miles from the highway into the ruins of the old mining town. We found Finnish Mary's shack by following the trail of wood smoke back to a crumbling hovel that was built over the basement of a demolished house. We crept into the hot dark room. Finnish Mary was huddled next to her stove. She wore an old cotton caftan over a layer of dirt. On a clothesline close to the ceiling hung bunches of dried herbs and crystals suspended from bits of fishing line. Finnish Mary was obviously into New Age arts and holistic medicine.

Rudy explained who had sent us, and handed her the paper bag bearing the message from the packing crate lady in the city. With her lips moving, Finnish Mary read the words on the paper bag three times until she knew the message by heart, and then she opened the door of the woodstove and tossed the bag into the flames. "Paper is fuel," she grunted. "Never waste anything."

We nodded politely.

"Talk," she said.

Rudy told her his story first, and then mine, and Finnish Mary smiled a little but she didn't interrupt or ask a single question. When Rudy had finished explaining, he said, "This is a dangerous job. Is there some kind of herbal medicine or maybe a crystal that you could give Gerda to help her? Maybe something to make her stronger in case she has to fight her way into the Snow Queen's estate? I figure she needs to be about as strong as twelve men to get her friend out of there."

Finnish Mary smiled up at him. "The strength of twelve men. That would not be of much use!" She took a parchment scroll down from a dusty shelf near the door, and read it silently, while beads of sweat ran down her forehead. We edged away from the woodstove, but it wasn't much cooler anywhere else in the shack. We waited.

Finally she said, "The Snow Queen isn't home right now. She's gone south to make another delivery of the white powder. Probably took most of her guards with her. So you won't have much trouble getting up there, but getting what you want is something else again. Kay is going to stay with the Snow Queen because he's hooked. He's got that mirror crack inside him, and as long as he's into that, then he will never feel like a human being again, and the Snow Queen will always have him in her power."

"Right. That's clear enough. What I'm saying to you is, can you give the girl something so that she can cut him loose from the habit? Some kind of potion that will break the spell, you know—"

Finnish Mary shrugged. "I can't give her any power greater than what she already has. It takes love to break a spell like the Snow Queen's. And sometimes even that won't do it. Gerda has to get into that house, and then try to get Kay to see what he's doing to himself. If that doesn't work, there's nothing else that you or I can do to help her. Here's what you do, boy: walk Gerda down the road until you come to the iron fence. That's the garden of the Snow Queen's estate. Leave her by the bush with the red berries on it. You going in with her?"

"Me? No!" Rudy's voice trembled, and for the first time I could see how afraid he was. It had taken all his courage to get me this far. "The Snow Queen may be gone, but who knows how they've booby-trapped that compound! I already lost one fight with a gang like hers. I'm playing it safe for the immediate future."

"You don't have to go with me," I told him. "I'm in this alone."

"Then leave her at that berry bush, and get back here fast, before anybody sees you. I'll come outside with you and show you the way."

It was nearly dark by the time we started on the dirt road that led up into the hills. I could see blue lights up ahead of us, and I knew that we were going in the right direction. I was a bit afraid of the Snow Queen and the guards that she might have around her estate, but I had come so far that I was eager now to reach journey's end, and to find Kay at last. I didn't know if I could save him, but I wasn't going back without trying.

Rudy walked with me as far as the berry bush beside the wrought iron fence. He kissed me on the cheek, but before I could thank him, he turned and began to run back down the hill toward Finnish Mary's ghost town. I was alone.

As I slipped between the bars of the iron fence and began to creep toward a thicket of shrubs, I noticed that it had begun to snow—a welcome change to me from the hot dusty city down on the plains. Maybe the snow helped me get past the Snow Queen's guards, too. As the wind picked up, it became darker and colder, not a night to be out patrolling a peaceful compound. I decided that they didn't get too many visitors in this remote mountain outpost. Or maybe there weren't any guards. Maybe they all went with her, for I sensed from the silent, dimly lit grounds that Finnish Mary had been telling the truth. The Snow Queen was not at home.

Within a few minutes I was within sight of the house. It looked like a palace made of drifted snow—very white, probably stucco, or adobe, or whatever it is they use to build in these unforested mountains. Spires and turrets spun out of the main building like icicles, and through the glass patio doors I could see soft blue lights illuminating the interior. I still didn't see any guards around, so I ran from one thicket to another until I reached the side of the house. I edged close to the glass doors and looked inside.

The great room beyond the doors was vast, empty, and icily white. In the center of the room stood a blue-lit ornamental pool that was frozen—the Snow Queen's *signature*, I supposed. But I had little time to notice any more of the details of that vast cold room, because by then I had caught sight of Kay, paper thin and blue with cold. He was sitting in shadow at the edge of the frozen pool, hunched on the floor, concentrating intently on some small pieces of ice. He was moving the broken shapes into one position and then another, as if he were trying to put together a pictureless puzzle. He was so absorbed in the complexity of his task that he did not even look up when I slid open the glass door and eased into the room.

As I came closer, I could hear Kay muttering, "I have to spell *eternity*. She said she'd give me whatever I wanted if I could spell it out with ice." His hand was shaking as he pushed more ice shards together. I could not make out any shapes at all in the design, but he seemed to think he was making a sensible pattern. *This is what the Snow Queen's powder has done to his mind,* I thought, and suddenly I felt so tired, and so sad that it had to end this way, that I began to cry. I thought that nothing could make this shell of a man recover his health and spirits.

I knelt down and put my arms around him. "I've found you, Kay!" I said, holding my wet cheek against his cold face. He felt like a sack of bones wrapped in parchment when I hugged him. "It's going to be all right. I've come to take you home."

He looked up at me then, and at first his stare was cold and emotionless, as if he had trouble remembering who I was, but I got him up and made him walk around, and gradually his eyes cleared a little, and he began to mumble responses to my questions, and before long we were both crying. "Gerda," he whispered. "Where have you been all this time? And—where have *I* been?"

He was like somebody waking up from a long nightmare. At one point he looked around the room, and said, "This place is cold and empty. Let's get out of here!"

"The sooner the better." The Snow Queen could come back any time now, and, since I wasn't armed, I wanted to be gone before she returned.

We had a long way to go to get back home, and Kay had an even longer way to go to get the craving for the Snow Queen's powder out of his system, but we took it slowly. First, out the garden and down the mountain, where Rudy met us and helped us back to the highway. Then back to the city, and finally the long journey home to Denmark, where Kay could get long-term medical care for his condition.

It is spring again now. More than a year has passed since Kay took off on the wild ride with the Snow Queen, but he is almost his old self again. He grows stronger every day, and he's talking about getting out of therapy soon, and looking for work. Maybe he'll become a gardener in the country. He's growing roses again.

I looked at him, tanned and fit in the warm sunshine, with roses in his cheeks as pink as the ones on the tree, and I whispered, "Peace, O Lord." This time I wasn't swearing.

An Autumn Migration

$\backsim$

The ghost of my father-in-law arrived today, smiling vaguely as he always does—or did, taking no notice of me. He acted for all the world as if I were the ghost instead of he. Not even a nod of greeting or a funny remark about the weather, which was about all the conversation we'd ever managed when he was alive. I'm not very good at conversing with people. Stephen says that I have no small talk. I listened a lot, though.

With my father-in-law, I became an audience of one to his endless supply of anecdotes, and I think he enjoyed having someone pay attention to him. He used to tell funny stories about his days in the Big One, by which he meant World War II, and he could always find a way to laugh at a rained-out ball game or a broken washing machine. This did not seem to endear him to his energetic wife and son, especially since his inability to hold a job made ball games and washing machines hard to come by, but his affability had made him a comforting in-law for the nervous and awkward bride that I had been. We were never really close, but we enjoyed each other's company.

Later I sometimes shared Stephen's exasperation with the smiling, tipsy ne'er-do-well who could never seem to hold on to a paycheck or a driver's license, but in truth I would have forgiven him a great deal more than poverty and drunkenness for giving me a few moments of ease in those early days when I had felt on trial before Stephen and his exacting mother, for whom nothing was ever clean enough.

I didn't hear the front door open and close—or perhaps it didn't.

When he arrived, I was alone, of course, in that long emptiness of the suburban afternoon. I told myself that I was waiting for Stephen to come home, but I was careful not to ask myself why. Certainly I was not expecting any visitors that day—or any other day—and my father-in-law was as far from my thoughts as he had ever been in life.

I had been dusting the coffee table, a favorite pastime of mine, because you can make your hand do lazy arcs across a smooth wooden surface while thinking of absolutely nothing, and if you happen to be holding a damp polishing rag in your hand at the time, it counts as actual work. When I looked up from my shining circles, I saw my father-in-law clumping soundlessly up the stairs in his baggy brown suit and his old scuffed wingtips. He was probably wearing a worn silk tie loosened at his throat. He looked just as I remembered him: a portly old gentleman with sparse gray hair and a ruddy face. I even fancied that I caught the scent of Jack Daniel's and stale tobacco as he sailed past. He was carrying the battered leather suitcase that used to sit in the hall closet at his house. I wondered where he was going, and why he needed luggage to get there.

He did not even glance around to see if anyone was watching him before he went upstairs. Perhaps he was looking for Stephen, but Stephen is never home at this hour of the day. For most of the year I scarcely see him in daylight. He works very hard, unlike his dad—or perhaps because of him—and he doesn't talk to me much these days. He is impatient with my depression, although he always asks if I am taking my medicine, and he is careful to remind me of doctors' appointments. But I know that secretly he thinks that I could snap out of it if I wanted to. An aerobics class or a new hairdo would do wonders for me, he suggests now and then, trying to sound casual about it. He thinks that depression is a luxury reserved for housewives whose husbands have adequate incomes.

Perhaps he is right. Perhaps those who are forced to go out and face the world with such a mental shroud about them throw themselves in front of trains or run their cars into trees rather than endure the tedium of another dark day. I have thought of such things myself, but it would take too much effort to leave the house.

I always promise to *cheer up*, as Stephen puts it, and that ends the discussion. Then when he leaves for the office, I crawl back into bed and sleep as long as I can. Sometimes I play endless games of solitaire on Stephen's home computer, watching the electronic cards flash by, and scarcely caring if the suits fit together or not. I do not watch much television. Seeing those noisy strangers on the screen making such a fuss over a new car or a better detergent always makes me feel sadder and even more out of step with the world. I would rather sleep.

I am tired all the time. I manage to get the washing done every day or so, and by four o'clock I can usually muster enough energy to cook a pork chop or perhaps some spaghetti, so that Stephen won't get annoyed with me, and ask me what it is I do all day. I push the emptiness around the polished surfaces of the coffee table with a polishing rag. It takes up most of my time. There is so much emptiness. I force myself to eat the dinner, so that he won't lecture me about the importance of nutrition to emotional health. Stephen is an architect, but he thinks that being my husband entitles him to express medical opinions about the state of my mind and body. It is practically the only interest he takes in either anymore.

He is not so observant about the state of the house. He never looks under the beds, or notices how long the cleaning supplies last. With only the two of us, there isn't much housekeeping to do. He has offered to hire a maid, but I cannot bear the thought of having someone around all the time. I do enough housework to get by and to stave off the dreaded cleaning woman, and he does not complain. I am so tired.

My father-in-law was still upstairs. At least, he hadn't reappeared. I could not be bothered to go and look for him. I sat down in Stephen's leather chair, running the polishing rag through my fingers like a silk scarf.

"Stephen isn't home!" I called out, in case that made any difference to my visitor. Apparently it didn't. Shouldn't a ghost know who is home and who isn't without having to make a room-to-room search? Surely—ten months dead—he was sober?

I wondered if I ought to call my mother-in-law in Wisconsin to tell her that he was here. He died last November. She'd be glad to know where he is. She had wanted to go to Florida for the coming winter, but she said she didn't like to go and have a good time, with her poor husband alone in his urn. They had been married fifty years to the month when he passed away, and they had never been apart in all that time. He had always talked about taking her somewhere for their fiftieth anniversary, but by then he was too ill and too broke to manage. They spent their anniversary in his hospital room, drinking apple juice out of paper cups. Now his widow talks wistfully of Florida, and Stephen has offered to pay for the trip, but she says that she hates to travel alone after all those years of togetherness. Why shouldn't she, though? He is.

I wonder why he has decided to call on us. It seems like a very unlikely choice on his part. I can imagine him haunting Wrigley Field, or a Dublin pub, or perhaps some tropical island in the South Pacific, or a Norwegian fishing village. We gave him a subscription to *National Geographic* every year for Christmas so that he could dream about all those far-off lands that he always claimed he wanted to visit, if his health would stand it. You'd think he would make good use of his afterlife to make up for lost time. But, no— after all those years of carefully paging through glorious photographs of exotic places, he turns up here, two states from home, uninvited. Surely if he could make it to Iowa, he could reach Peru.

What does he want here? His pre-mortem communication with us consisted of a few cheery monologues on the extension phone when Stephen's mother phoned for her monthly chat. Why the interest in us now? He cannot be haunting us out of malevolence. In life, he never seemed to mind about anything—no empty bottle or under-achieving racehorse could darken his mood for long. Not the sort of person you'd expect to stay bound to the earth, when presumably he could be in some heavenly Hialeah, watching Secretariat race against Man o' War and Whirlaway in the fifth—*with* a fifth. How could he pass up such a hereafter to haunt a brick colonial tract house in Woodland Hills, Iowa? He never came to visit us. Stephen said the old man wouldn't be caught dead here. Apparently he was wrong about that.

He can't be angry at us. We went to the funeral; we took a wreath to the crematorium. I even wrote the thank-you notes, so that Stephen's mother could concentrate on her bereavement. Stephen packed his clothes in cardboard boxes, and took them to Goodwill, and he took the whiskey bottles in the top of the closet to the recycling place. We ordered the deluxe bronze urn to put his ashes in, and we even paid extra to have his name engraved on a little plaque on the front. And now here he is, swooping down on us like a migrating heron, dropping in for an unannounced rest stop on his way south—or wherever it is that he is going.

If I called my mother-in-law and asked her if the brown leather suitcase was there in her hall closet, I wonder what she would say. Perhaps it is a ghost, too. After all, it is leather.

In the end I sat in the recliner in the living room, and took a nap. *We can resolve this when Stephen gets home,* I thought. *It is, after all,* his *father.*

Stephen finally arrived home at eight tonight, moaning about the heat of Indian summer, and the tempers of his co-workers. With a feeling approaching clinical interest, I watched him go upstairs.

What will he say when he meets his father on the landing? Should I have warned him? I could have told him that a relative dropped in for an unexpected visit. He would scowl, of course, but then he might have said, "Who?" and I could have said, "Someone from your side of the family," and thus we could have eased into the subject of his late father, and I could have broken the news to him gently. But I was too tired to plan conversational gambits, and Stephen's attention span for discussions with me is many minutes shorter than such a talk would have required, so I merely smiled and gave him a little wave, as he pulled his tie away from his collar and hurried upstairs.

Then I waited—I'm not sure what for. A shout perhaps, or even a scream of terror or astonishment. Certainly I expected Stephen to reappear very quickly, and to descend the stairs much faster than he went up. But several minutes passed in silence, and when I crept close to the bannister, I could hear drawers opening and closing in the bedroom. Stephen changing his clothes, as he did first thing every evening. I made myself climb the stairs to see if the apparition was gone. *If so, I won't mention it to Stephen,* I thought. *He would only think that my seeing ghosts is another symptom of my disorder.* Not *seeing the ghost may be a symptom of his.*

I stood in the doorway, smiling vaguely, as if I had come upstairs to ask him something, but had forgotten what. Stephen was sitting in the lounge chair beside the window, putting on his running shoes. He looked up at me, and when I didn't say anything, he shrugged and went back to tying the laces. His father was sitting on the edge of the bed, watching this performance with interest.

"Stephen, look at the bed," I said.

He frowned a little, and glanced at the bed, probably wondering what sort of response I was expecting. Was I propositioning him? Did I want new furniture? Was there a mouse on the pillow? He gave the question careful consideration. "The bed looks fine," he said at last. "I'm glad you made the bed, dear. It makes the room look tidy. Thank you."

Stephen was looking straight at his father. He could not miss him, and yet all he saw was a blue-flowered bedspread and four matching throw pillows.

My father-in-law looked at me and shrugged, as if to say that Stephen's lack of perception was not *his* fault. He was certainly visible, plain as day, and if Stephen could not or would not detect his presence, there wasn't much that either of us could do about it. I could have said, "Stephen, your dead father is sitting on the bed," but that would have gotten us nowhere. In fact, saying that would have been worse than ignoring the matter, because Stephen would have insisted on analyzing my medication to see if I was taking anything that might cause delusions, and this would distract me from considering the real problem at hand: what is my father-in-law doing here—and what does he want me to do about it?

Upon reflection I was not surprised that Stephen failed to see this apparition. Stephen never saw rainbows when I pointed them out through the car windshield as he was driving. Finally I stopped pointing them out, and then one day I stopped seeing them, too. He is completely unable to tell whether people are happy or sad by looking at them. And he insists that he never has dreams, nightmares or otherwise. Of course he would not notice anything so unconventional as a ghost. It is beneath the threshold of his rationality. As he is not likely to take my word for it, I have abandoned the idea of telling him about his father's visit. Some people do not qualify to be haunted.

We ate a hastily prepared meal of soup and salad. (In the excitement I had forgotten to cook dinner.) I asked Stephen a question about a project at work, and he answered so volubly that I knew he was talking to himself and had forgotten I was there. It was a very restful dinner. No awkward silences while one of us tried to think of something to say.

When we went upstairs afterward, my father-in-law was no-where to be seen. I wandered from room to room, on the pretext of shutting windows and making sure that the lights were off. I peeked into closets and behind doors, but he was not in evidence. I did not think that this absence was permanent, however. I sus-pected that he was on some astral plane biding his time until Stephen had left the house again. Perhaps even ghosts find it awk-ward to communicate with Stephen.

I had thought about the problem all through dinner, which I barely touched, and I puzzled over it later in bed. While Stephen read *Architectural Record*, I scanned the room beyond the pool of light from the reading lamp to see if one of the shadows was grin-ning back at me, but no one was there. Later, when Stephen's breathing evened out into the monotone of sleep, I lay awake won-dering about the visit. *He must be here for a reason,* I thought. *Since I am the only one who has noticed him, I suppose it is my problem.*

He has been here for five days now. He does not speak to me. Perhaps he can't. I see him here and there around the house, and sometimes we exchange looks or smiles, so I know he is aware of my presence, but he makes no sound. He does not seem distressed, as if he were anxious to communicate some urgent information to me about a lost bank account, or a cache of gold coins buried in the backyard. He does not seem to want any messages of love or regret taken to his wife or conveyed to Stephen. (I think if my father-in-law ever had any gold coins he would have cashed them in for Jack Daniel's long ago. I have more money in my savings account from my grandmother's legacy than he probably left to his family after a lifetime of desultory jobs. Messages for his loved ones? My father-in-law was a gentle and pleasant man, but I do not think his love for wife or son was the sort that would extend beyond the grave. They have certainly recovered from the loss of him, and I have no reason to suspect that the feeling is not mutual.) He is just . . . here.

I am no longer shy about his presence in the house. He is a courteous ghost. He never materializes in the bathroom, or sneaks up behind me when I am dusting. I find, though, that I am less inclined to sleep late, and I spend less time polishing the furniture. Even with uninvited guests there is the obligation to play hostess, I suppose. I tried turning the television on to the news channel, because I thought that he might be interested in what is going in in the world—an idle curiosity about familiar things, the way one might subscribe to a hometown newspaper after one has moved away—but he only glanced at the screen and drifted away again, so I gave it up. Perhaps the news is no longer interesting when nothing is a matter of life or death to the viewer. I didn't find it very interesting myself, though. I wonder what that means.

Today when Stephen came home I had fixed beef Stroganoff, and he grudgingly said that I seemed to be snapping out of it. I wish I could say the same for him. He is as monotonous as ever. I find myself thinking that I have more to say to the ghost than I do to my husband.

I wonder where he keeps the piano. In the attic? The broom closet under the stairs? Sometimes when I am downstairs with the polishing cloth, I can hear sounds floating down the stairs, the tinkly lilt of a barroom piano: Scott Joplin tunes. I polish to the rhythm of a ragtime piano, and I wonder what he is trying to tell me. It has been a week now, and I find myself talking aloud to the ghost as I work. I still call him the ghost. He had a first name in life, of course, but I never used it. I called him *Ummm*, the way one does with in-laws. I still think of him as Ummm, and I make an occasional remark to him while I vacuum the dust bunnies under the bed and dust the tops of the bookshelves, because who knows where a ghost goes when he's not in sight. It took a couple of days to get the house back into decent order, and then I began to wonder what else I could do. He was still there; he must be in need of something. Or perhaps he couldn't think of anywhere else to go.

The next time I cleaned the living room, I considered turning to ESPN, on the off chance that a horse race might be broadcast. He always did love a good horse race. But I decided that I have to watch enough sports as it is during football season with Stephen around. I certainly wasn't going to defer to the wishes of a dead man. Something else, then.

I switched to the Discovery Channel, and we watched a nice program about castles in the Alps. He seemed to enjoy the travel documentary much more than he had the news channel. He floated just behind the sofa and watched the screen intently. After a few minutes I put down my dust cloth and joined him, and we marveled at the splendors of Neunschwanstein and Linderhof for nearly a quarter of an hour, until at the end of a long commercial I looked over and found that I was alone. Overdecorated castles can fascinate one for just so long, I decided, but I had thoroughly enjoyed the tour, thinking how horrified Stephen would be by the glorification of nineteenth-century crimes against architecture. Still, his father had seemed to enjoy it. I felt I was on the right track.

After that I kept the television tuned to travel documentaries for as much of the day as I could. I noticed that my father-in-law's ghost had no particular fascination with Europe, and only a fleeting interest in Africa and the Middle East. I was about to give up the project and try the Shopping Network when the programmers turned their attention to Polynesia. For the ghostly viewer, the Pacific Islands were another matter altogether.

A program on Hawaii brought him closer to the television than he had ventured before, and he actually sat through two commercials before fading away. A few days later, when Samoa was featured, he hovered just above the sofa cushions and gazed enraptured at the palm trees and outriggers with a smile that no longer looked vague. Easter Island was the clincher. Not only did he watch the program in its entirety, he even stayed through the credits, apparently reading the names of the crew and filmmakers as they rolled up the screen.

I had watched all these programs as well, and quite enjoyed the imaginary holidays they provided. Still, after hours of looking at the shining sands and turquoise sea of the South Pacific, my own living room looked dingy and worn. This did not inspire me to further cleaning efforts, however. My reaction was more along the lines of, "What's the use?" No matter what I did to our sensible tweed sofa and the fashionable cherry colonial reproduction tables, it would still be dankest, brownest, latest autumn within these walls, and I was beginning to long for summer.

"It's a pity that we are dead and stuck here," I remarked aloud to the visitor. Something in his smile made me realize what I'd said. "I mean that *you're* dead," I amended.

On Monday, the daily documentary featured the irrigation system of the Netherlands, but neither my father-in-law nor I was ready to come back from the tropical paradises of the South Pacific. We sat there in gloomy silence for a few minutes, politely studying placid canals and bobbing fields of tulips, but neither of us could muster any enthusiasm for the subject. I clicked off the set just as he was beginning to fade out. "I'll go to the library," I said to the dimming apparition. "Perhaps I can borrow a video of the Pacific Islands—or at least a travel guide."

Stephen occasionally sent me to the library to research something for him, but I had never actually checked anything out for my own use. I suppose Mrs. Nagata, the librarian, was a bit surprised to see me walk past Architecture and into the Travel section. Or perhaps she was surprised to see me in jeans with my hair in a ponytail. In my haste I had not bothered to change into the costume I thought of as Suburban Respectable. Half an hour later, I had managed to find two coffee-table books on the Pacific Islands, a video documentary about Tahiti, and the old Disney film of *Treasure Island* that I remembered from childhood. As an afterthought I picked up a guidebook to Polynesia as well.

When I entered the house again I could hear the strains of "Bali H'ai" being played on a honky-tonk piano. I wondered if that was a hint. Surely Bali H'ai would be featured in one of the books I had selected. Where was it, anyhow? And had my father-in-law been there before? I tried to remember his stories about World War II, but exotic islands did not play a part in any tale that I recalled. "He's simply getting into the spirit of the thing," I said. Realizing my pun I laughed out loud.

"What's so funny?"

Stephen was home. I nearly dropped the books. He was lounging on the sofa watching the sports network. "The air conditioning was broken at the office, so I came home," he told me without taking his eyes off the flickering screen. "I was surprised to find you gone. I thought you moped around here all day."

"I went to the library," I mumbled.

"Oh?" He raised his eyebrows in that maddening way of his. "Whatever for? I didn't send you."

I felt like a child caught playing hooky. "I just went," I said.

I edged closer to the screen, careful not to block his view, and held out my armload of books and videos. "I just thought I'd do some reading."

A commercial came on just then, and he turned his attention to me, or rather to the materials from the library. He flipped through the stack of books, inspected the videos, and set them down on the sofa beside him. "The south Pacific," he said, sounding amused.

"Yes," I said. "Isn't it beautiful?"

"If you like heat and insects."

"I thought we might go there some day."

Stephen turned back to the television. "Paul Gauguin went to Tahiti. He was a painter."

"Yes."

"Went to Tahiti, got leprosy there, and died," said Stephen, with evident satisfaction that Gauguin's lapse of judgment had been so amply rewarded. Before I could reply, the commercial ended, and Stephen went back to the game, dismissing the subject of Polynesia from his thoughts entirely.

I left the room, unnoticed by Stephen, who was absorbed in the television and completely oblivious to my existence. Before I left, though, I took the pile of books, which he had discarded on the sofa beside him.

I was sitting on the bed, leafing through color pictures of beaches at sunset and lush island waterfalls, when my father-in-law materialized beside me and began peering at the pages with a look similar to Stephen's television face. Once when I turned a page too quickly, he reached for the book, and then drew back, as if he suddenly remembered that he could no longer hold objects for himself.

"It's beautiful, isn't it?" I sighed. "I wish I could see it for real."

The ghost nodded sadly. He tried to touch the page, but his fingers became transparent and passed through the photo.

"Just go!" I said. "Do it! I'm tied here. Stephen refuses to go anywhere. I'm too depressed to go to the mall, much less to another country. But you! *You're* not a prisoner. I wish *I* were a ghost. If I were, I certainly wouldn't be haunting a tract house in Iowa. I'd do whatever I wanted. I'd be free! I'd go to Tahiti—or Easter Island—or wherever I wanted!"

The ghost shook his head, and immediately I felt sorry for my outburst. Apparently there were rules to the afterlife, and I had no idea what his limitations were. I shouldn't have reproached him for things I don't understand, I thought.

"I'm sorry," I said. "I just wish we weren't trapped here." My eyes filled with tears. One of them plopped onto the waterfall picture and slid down the rocks, as if to join the cascading image.

I looked up to see my father-in-law's ghost smiling and shaking his head. He looked very much like Stephen for just that instant: his expression was the one Stephen always has when I've said something foolish. I thought over what I had said. *I wish we weren't trapped here.*

Why was I trapped here?

I had grandmother's legacy in the savings account. It had grown to nearly twelve thousand dollars, because in my depression I couldn't be bothered to go out and actually buy anything. I had a suitcase, and enough summer clothes to see me through a few months in the tropics. And—most important—I had no emotional ties to keep me in Woodland Hills. I felt that I had already been haunting Stephen for the last few years of our married life. It was time I left. And when I went, his memory would never haunt me.

I opened the closet and reached for the canvas suitcase on the top shelf. As I was pulling it down, I heard a thump at the back of the closet, and I stood on tiptoe to see what had been knocked over. It was a large bronze vase. I had to stand on a chair to reach it. When I pulled it out of a tangle of coat hangers, I saw the brass plate on the front bearing a name and two dates. My father-in-law!

I left the suitcase on the floor, and ran downstairs. "Stephen!" I said. "Did you know that your father's ashes are in the bedroom closet?"

"Shhh! They're kicking the extra point."

I waited an eternity for a commercial and asked again, keeping my voice casual.

"Dad? Sure. I took them after the funeral. I thought it would upset Mother too much to leave them on the mantel where she'd have to see them all the time. I figured I'd wait for the anniversary of his death—next month, isn't it?—and then scatter him under the rose bushes out back. Bone meal. Great compost, huh?"

"Great," I murmured.

As I fled back upstairs I heard him call out, "Thanks for reminding me!"

It took me twenty minutes to clean out the fireplace in the den, and another half hour to pack. Ten minutes to locate my passport and the passbook to my savings account. Five minutes to transfer the contents of the urn to a plastic cosmetics bag in my suitcase and replace them with the fireplace ashes. I didn't think I'd need my coat, but I put it on anyway, as a gesture of finality. My father-in-law was wearing his.

We stood for a moment in the foyer, staring at the back of Stephen's head, haloed in the light of the television. I picked up my suitcase, and flung open the door. "I'm going out!" I called.

"Yeah—okay," said Stephen.

"I may be some time."

Foggy Mountain
Breakdown

~

That afternoon the Haskell girls came by collecting money for a funeral wreath. Davy gave them a nickel and ten pennies from the baking powder can in the pantry. Mama would probably have given them a quarter, since Dad was working a couple of days a week at the railroad shop now, but she was visiting over at the Kesslers, talking about the accident. All the mothers in the community would be talking about the tragedy, with their eyes red from crying, because, as the preacher said, death is always a pang of sorrow no matter who is taken, but sooner or later, every one of them would say, "It might have been my boy." It wasn't one of their boys, though; it was Junior Mullins. Fifteen cents was enough for Junior Mullins, Davy thought.

The money collected from the twenty-three families living back in the hollow of Foggy Mountain would be enough for a decent bunch of store-bought flowers from the shop in Erwin. One of the Haskell girls would write every family's name on the card to be given to Junior's parents. There would probably be bigger, fancier wreaths from Mr. Mullins's fellow managers at the railroad, maybe even one from the president of the railroad himself, considering the circumstances, but the neighbors would want to send one anyway, to show that their thoughts and prayers were with the family in this time of sorrow.

Davy was still in mourning for his bicycle. Nobody was collecting flowers for it. Two dollars it had cost. Two dollars earned in solitary misery with sweat and briar-pricks, picking blackberries in the abandoned fields, and selling them door to door at ten cents a gallon. It takes a lot of blackberries to make a gallon. Getting two dollars' worth of dimes had cost Davy two precious weeks of summer—two weeks of working most of the day dragging a gallon bucket through the briars, sidestepping snakes and poison oak, while everybody else went swimming or played ball at the old gravel pit. Two weeks without candy, soda pop, or Saturday matinees.

Saturday afternoons were the hardest. Davy would be alone in a field of brambles, so hot that the air was wavy when you looked into the distance, with the mountains shutting him in like the green walls of an open air prison. Somewhere on the other side of that ridge, his friends were having fun. Hour after hour he stooped over blackberry thickets, and to keep his mind off his sore back and his stuck fingers he'd try to imagine what was playing at the picture show. The cowboys, like Buck Jones or Tom Mix and his horse Tony, were his favorite, but he went every Saturday he could afford, no matter what was playing. When you're eleven years old and home seems duller than ditch water, anything on the screen is better than real life. You had to want something real bad to miss the movies on account of it. Right now the movie house was showing *Hills of Peril*: Buck Jones helps a young woman save her gold mine from outlaws. The pictures were silent, but the dialogue was printed on cards that were projected onto the screen. Davy reckoned most of the boys in the county had learned more about reading at the picture show than they had in the schoolhouse. At Saturday matinees, with all those boys reading the lines out loud as they flashed on the screen, the theater hummed with a steady drone that sounded like the Johnsons' beehives at swarm time.

Davy'd missed most of the Phantom serial. He'd had to make

do with a summary of the story from Johnny Suttle, who forgot bits of the story and kept repeating the parts he liked. But Davy didn't care. There'd be other movies, and his reward for missing this one was his very own bicycle. He had done it.

His hard-earned two dollars bought one bicycle frame with no accessories: no tires, no brakes, no pedals. He had made tires for the wheels himself, with a little help from Old Lady Turner's yard. She had never missed that twelve feet of red rubber garden hose, and the tires he made from them were the perfect width and strength for the homemade bike. He'd caught hell, though, for cutting Mama's clothesline and taking the galvanized wire to run through the four lengths of garden hose so that he could fasten them around the wheel rims. The beating he got for taking the clothesline had been worth it, though. Now he was riding.

Davy's two-dollar bike had cast-off railroad spikes for pedals, and the Morris coaster brakes didn't work, but that didn't matter. He was riding. Dad had brought home an almost-empty can of blue paint from one of the railroad shops, and Davy had painted his bike so that from a distance it looked almost store-bought.

Up and down the gravel pit he wheeled and turned, dipping into the chug-holes and jumping out on the far side high enough to clear an upright Quaker Oats box set there as an obstacle. If he needed to stop the bike, he pressed his foot on the front wheel. That worked fairly well for solitary riding, but when he wanted to get into the bicycle polo games in Wells's pasture, he needed something more reliable.

Bicycle polo was played with an old softball and croquet mallets that one of the boys had scrounged from somebody's trash pile. They would divide up into teams and race up and down the pasture on their bikes, swatting at the softball. You needed brakes, though, to keep from crashing into your teammates, or so that you could change directions suddenly when the ball was intercepted by the other team and swatted off in the other direction. After a few hours of tinkering, he had repaired the Morris coaster brakes with a brake drum fashioned from a Coca-Cola bottle cap. After two or three hours of hard riding, the cap would grind up, leaving him brakeless again, but by then the polo game would be over, and he could go home and make repairs for the next match.

He had been able to hold his own just fine on his jerry-rigged bike—that is, until Junior Mullins showed up for the game, riding piggyback on Charlie Bestor's motorcycle. Davy thought Junior and Charlie were two of a kind: big arrogant bully, little arrogant bully. Charlie was a high school senior who had been going to ROTC Camp at Fort Oglethorpe, Georgia, every summer. On the last trip he had brought home the motorcycle, and now he roared up and down the paved roads, promising his toadies rides on his motorcycle, and lording it over every other boy around.

Junior Mullins was the kind of big, loud kid that other boys hate but nobody stands up to. His father was a manager down at the railroad, working steady, so Junior had clothes that weren't hand-me-downs, and meat sandwiches and an apple or an orange in his lunch box, while everybody else had corn bread and a cold potato. Junior Mullins had a store-bought bike, a shiny red one, brand-new, that his dad had bought in Johnson City for his birthday. Junior thought that he was better than the other boys in the neighborhood because his father was the boss of everybody else's father, because the Mullins family lived in a brick house, and because Junior got a toy truck and a model airplane for Christmas, instead of just an orange, a stick of rock candy, and a new pair of shoes. Junior enforced his superiority with the ruthless cruelty of a ten-year-old tyrant. His weapons were scorn, derision, taunting, and, as a last resort, his fists. Davy tried to stay out of his way, and most of the time he succeeded, but nobody could escape Junior Mullins's notice forever.

Davy's turn came in Wells's pasture, when Junior Mullins showed up just as the boys were starting a game of polo. Charlie Bestor stopped the motorcycle a few yards away from the group, and Junior climbed down, his red face curled into its usual sneer.

He was wearing a pair of blue dungarees without a single patch on them and a leather jacket. "You babies still riding bikes?" he said. "We've got a real set of wheels." He jerked his thumb toward the motorcycle.

Charlie Bestor patted his motorcycle and called out, "You fellows want to race?"

Johnny Suttle scuffed the toe of his shoe in the dirt. "We were just fixing to play polo," he mumbled.

Junior Mullins hooted. "Hear that, Charlie? They were fixing to play polo! You sissies don't know how to play polo," he announced, swaggering over to the gaggle of bikers. "I reckon I'll just have to teach you."

"You can't play without a bike," Dewey Givens pointed out. As soon as the words were out of his mouth, he wished he hadn't said them, because Junior's face lit up with spiteful glee, and he stepped back to survey the taut faces of his victims. He was showing off for his big-shot friend now, which would make him more vicious than ever. He let the boys squirm in silence while he pretended to consider the matter.

"I believe you're right about that, Dewey," Junior said at last. "Yep. I got to agree with you. I sure can't play polo without no bike, now can I? I reckon I'll just have to borrow me one." He surveyed the knot of squirming boys, each one carefully looking anywhere except in Junior Mullins's face.

When he couldn't stand the suspense anymore, Davy spoke up. "You could go home and get yours," he said.

Even Charlie Bestor laughed at that. Everybody knew that Junior Mullins wouldn't risk scratching up his brand-new bike in a rough-and-tumble game like polo, where crashing your bike into the other players' mounts was inevitable. All the other boys had beat-up second-hand bikes, or scrounged homemade ones. His was store-bought, too good for the likes of them. Junior grinned at Davy. "No. I think I'll just borrow one," he said. He eyed the polished blue bike at Davy's side. "Yours is new, isn't it? You make it yourself?"

Davy nodded, proud of himself, despite the threat of Junior Mullins, looming within punching distance and sneering at him like he was a night crawler in a fishing bucket. Junior made a great show of examining Davy's bike, inspecting the garden-hose tires, the flawless paint job, the Coca-Cola cap brakes. *Maybe he'll see how much pride I took in it, and he'll leave it be,* Davy thought, hoping that respect would win him what mercy could not.

"Nice job," drawled Junior, fingering the railroad-spike pedals. He glanced back to make sure that Charlie Bestor was watching. "For a homemade bike, that is. It looks sturdy enough. I guess I'll try it out for you so we can see what kind of job you did."

Davy gripped the handlebars tighter. "You're too big for it, Junior," he said. "You'd break it."

Junior's face turned a deeper shade of red. He was a stocky boy, verging on fat, and he didn't like comments about his size, however innocuously intended. He jerked the bike out of Davy's hands. "We'll just have to risk it, won't we. I've got a polo match to play." He snatched up a croquet mallet, hoisted his bulk onto the smaller boy's bicycle, and teetered off into the center of the pasture. "Let's get this show on the road!" he yelled to the other boys.

One by one they wheeled their bikes onto the playing field. Some of them gave Davy a look of apology or commiseration as they went past, but Davy didn't care what the other boys thought of Junior or how sorry they were that he had been singled out as victim. He wanted his bike, and nobody was going to help him get it back. If he tried to fight Junior on his own, he would end up with a bloody nose and a torn shirt, and Junior would destroy the bike.

He stood on the sidelines with clenched fists, watching as the teams pedaled up and down the pasture, swatting the softball back and forth. Above the thwack of the wooden mallets hitting the ball, and the shouts of the players, Davy thought he could hear the creaking of his overloaded bike. Junior Mullins was playing with a vengeance, going out of his way to collide with the other boys, whether they were close to the ball or not. He seemed to have no interest in scoring goals or in affecting the outcome of the game. For Junior the polo match was an excuse to hit something. Davy winced at every crash, thinking of the dents Junior was putting in the bike, and the scratches scoring the new paint job. A few yards away Charlie Bestor leaned his motorcycle against a tree and watched the game with the wry amusement of a superior being, sometimes shouting encouragement to Junior, and egging him on to more reckless playing.

After nearly an hour Junior tired of the game. He threw Davy's bike down in the weeds at the far end of the pasture, and loped back to Charlie Bestor's motorcycle. "Let's get out of here!" he said. "It's no fun playing with this bunch of babies."

As Junior climbed into the saddle behind the grinning Charlie Bestor, he called out to Davy, "Nice bike! Maybe I'll try it again sometime."

It was more than a threat. It was a promise.

Davy waited until the motorcycle roared out of sight, over the railroad track, and around the first curve, and then he hurried across the field to inspect the damage to his bike. The other boys hung back. One by one they drifted away from the pasture, and Davy was alone.

He reached into the briar-laced grass and pulled on the handlebars to his bike. After a few tugs, he was able to jerk it free. He set it down in the dirt, and ran his fingers along the shredded length of garden hose that had been the front tire. The frame was scratched and dented, and the handlebars were twisted out of alignment where the collisions and Junior's weight had combined to overstress the metal. Long gashes scarred the bike's paintwork, and the battered brakes needed much more than a bottle cap to repair them. Davy wheeled his wrecked creation home, across the empty pasture, half carrying it across the rocky creek, picking his way along the rougher parts of the path. Davy's face was pinched, and his jaw was set tighter than a bulldog's, but his eyes had a far-away look as if he was somewhere other than the road to Foggy Mountain. He never once cried.

No one saw Davy from that Saturday until the next. Nobody stopped by to see how he was doing, because they knew how he was doing, and there wasn't anything anybody could say. Best to let him be for a while. He'd come back when he was over it, and things would go on as before.

Davy stayed in the smokehouse in the backyard, working as long as it was light. He scrounged, and tinkered, and sanded, and hammered, and painted, and tinkered some more, until the bike looked almost the way it had before. It would never be as good, of course. He couldn't get the handlebars completely straight, and the deeper scars showed through the new paint job, but the bike was fixed. It had brakes again. He could ride it.

When Mama asked him what happened to his bike, Davy told her that he'd tried to take it down too steep a hill, and that he'd wrecked on a hidden tree root. She had looked at him for a long minute, as if she was fixing to say more, but finally she shrugged and went back into the house. There wasn't any point in telling his folks about Junior Mullins, whose dad was a boss down at the railroad shop. No point at all.

He practiced riding the bike on Friday night, up and down the road in front of the house until the fireflies lit up the yard and Mama called him in. He found that he could maneuver pretty well. With a few minor adjustments the bike would be ready to go.

On Saturday morning he set off early, before Dad could catch him with a list of chores or Mama could set him to work weeding the corn. His sneakers were still damp from dew when he heard shouting from up the dirt road past the quarry. He found the gang at the usual congregating place, Wells's pasture. This time, though, no game was in progress. Five boys had pulled their bikes into a circle, and now they were arguing about what to do on a long Saturday morning. Davy looked at them: Johnny Suttle, Dewey Givens, Jack Howell, Bob Miller, and Junior Mullins. Davy walked his bike across the expanse of field, and slid silently into place between Johnny and Bob.

"Polo is a sissy game!" Junior was saying.

This declaration was followed by a doubtful silence. The younger boys looked at one another. Finally Bob Miller said, "How 'bout we jump potholes in the quarry?"

"How 'bout we jump potholes in the quarry?" said Junior, changing his voice to a mocking whine.

More silence.

"Anybody want to play pony express?" said Junior. "Or are you boys too yellow?"

Johnny Suttle whistled. "Chase a freight train on our bikes? My mama would skin me alive if she found out I was doing that."

Several of the others grunted in agreement.

"How's she going to find out?" said Junior.

"When I come home with my bike all tore up," said Johnny.

Junior shrugged. "Not if you do it right. The only tricky part is when you grab onto the ladder of the boxcar and kick the bike away. But if we find a place where there's a grassy slope alongside the track, it shouldn't hurt the bike too much when it falls down the embankment.

"It's dangerous," said Davy softly.

"I've done it before," said Junior. "It's a great ride. When the freight train slows down to take the curve, you catch up to it, swing up on the ladder, and ride the rails until you find a nice soft jumping-off place. Don't tell me you sissies have never tried it?"

Junior looked at each one in turn, daring somebody to admit he was scared. The five Foggy Mountain boys stared back, wide-eyed, and redder than their sunburns, but nobody objected and nobody looked away.

"It's settled then," said Junior. "I know just the place."

The five boys followed him out to the dirt road, riding slowly along in single file up the hill until they reached the place where the railroad tracks crossed the road. Junior led the way on his store-bought red beauty, sitting tall in the saddle and signaling with an outstretched forearm, as if he were a cavalry officer in the matinee.

"We'll follow the tracks to the right!" he shouted to his troops.

They turned on command and dismounted, wheeling their bikes along the gravel shoulder of the railroad tracks, while Junior inspected the terrain. "We need a long straightaway where we can build up speed, but it has to be just after a curve, so that the train will be slow enough for us to catch up with it."

Nobody bothered to answer him. He was thinking out loud.

Johnny Suttle, following close behind Davy, was bringing up the rear. "He's not looking at the embankment like he said he would. He's not looking for a grassy place. There's rocks all the way down this slope."

"He doesn't care," said Davy.

They both knew why.

The solemn procession followed the tracks up the steep grade that would send the train up and over the mountain in a series of spirals. The fields below glistened green in the July sunshine, and the Nolichucky River sparkled as brightly as the railroad tracks that ran alongside it for the length of the valley. Here the gravel berm was two feet wide, and just beyond it the ground fell away into a steep slope of clay and loose rocks.

Johnny Suttle touched Davy's arm. "We could turn back," he said.

Davy shook his head. You couldn't chicken out on a dare. That was part of the code. If you showed that you were afraid, you were out of the group, and Junior Mullins would hunt you like a rabbit from there on out.

They trudged on, past two more curves that Junior judged unsuitable for their purpose, and then they rounded the sharpest curve, midway up the mountain, and saw that there was nearly a hundred yards of straightaway before the tracks started up another incline. Junior turned and nodded, pointing to the ground. "Here!"

It was a good place. There was a thicket of tall laurels on the edge of the embankment that would hide them from the view of the engineer. Once the locomotive hurtled past their hiding place, they could give chase, and they had a hundred yards to build up speed and grab for the boxcar ladder.

Junior motioned the pack under the laurels. "Should be a freight train along any minute now," he said, squinting up at the sun. He had sweated so much that his shirt stuck to his back, making the bulges show even more. He wiped his brow with a sweaty forearm, and surveyed the track. "This will do," he said. "There's just one more thing." He set his red bicycle carefully against the trunk of the laurel, and stared at the gaggle of boys. He was grinning.

Everybody looked away except Davy.

"I'll need to borrow a bike."

"I just fixed mine," said Davy quietly. He wasn't pleading or whining about it, just stating a fact that ought to be taken into consideration.

"That's real good," said Junior. "I'm glad you got it working again. I wouldn't want to borrow no *sorry* bike." He gripped the newly repaired bike with one hand, and shoved Davy out of the way with the other. "You can watch, kid," he said.

Davy shrugged. It wouldn't do any good to argue with Junior Mullins. Things went his way or not at all. Everybody knew that. Complaining about the unfairness of his action would only get Davy labeled a crybaby.

Johnny Suttle looked at the railroad track, and then at his own battered bicycle. "Here, Junior. Why don't you take mine?"

"That beat-up old thing? Naw. I want a nice blue one. I'm kinda used to Davy's anyhow."

Davy knelt down in the shade of the laurels next to Junior's bike. "Okay," he said.

Junior stepped forward, ready with another taunt, but a faint sound in the distance made him stop. They listened for the low whine, echoing down the valley, a long way off.

Train whistle.

"Okay," said Junior, turning away as if Davy were no longer there. "Mount up, boys. I lead off. You wait till the coal car has gone past us, and then you count to five, and you start riding. Got that? When you get up alongside the boxcar, grab the ladder with both hands, and pull yourself up off the saddle. Then kick the bike away with both feet. Got it?"

They nodded. Another blast of the train whistle made them shudder.

"Won't be long now," said Junior.

It seemed like an eternity to Davy before the rails shook and the air thickened with the clatter of metal wheels against track, and finally the black steam locomotive thundered into view. They hunkered down under the laurels, close enough to see the engineer's face, and to feel the gush of wind as the train swept past.

"Now!" screamed Junior above the roar. He took a running start out of the hiding place, and leaped onto Davy's bike in mid-stride, pedaling furiously in an effort to stay even with the train. The other boys climbed onto their own mounts and sped off after him, whooping like the marauding Indians who attacked trains in the Buck Jones westerns down in the movie house.

Davy watched them go.

Junior kept the lead, leaning almost flat across the handlebar in a burst of speed that kept pace with the rumbling freight train.

Fifty yards across the straightaway, he was nearly even with the ladder on the third boxcar.

What happened next seemed to take place in slow motion. The homemade bike seemed to pull up short, and wobble back and forth for one endless, frozen moment. Then, before Junior could scream or anyone else could blink, the bike crumpled and pitched to the left. It, and Junior, vanished beneath the wheels of the train. To Davy, despite the thunderous clatter of the boxcars, it all seemed to happen in perfect silence.

The oldest Haskell girl lingered in the doorway. She fingered the collection can with the words JUNIOR MULLINS printed in black capitals around the side. The funeral was tomorrow. Closed casket, they said. "You were there when it happened, weren't you?" she said.

Davy nodded.

She leaned in so close to him that he could see her pores and smell the mint on her breath. "What was it like?" she whispered.

"He just fell."

"I hear you couldn't even tell who he was—after."

"No." The bike was unrecognizable, too. Just a tangle of metal caught underneath the boxcar and dragged another fifty yards down the track. Dad had told him how the workmen cut the bits of it away from the underside of the train. Out of consideration for the Mullins family, they hosed it down before they threw it in the scrap heap.

"You won't be getting it back," his father said. "Seems a shame, you losing your friend and your bike, too. It was a good bike. I know you worked a long time on it."

Davy nodded. He had worked a long time. He had built it twice, almost from scratch, and he had been proud of it. On the night before the pony express game, the last thing he had done was to file through one link of the bicycle chain, so that when any stress was put on it, the chain would break, throwing the bike off balance.

"It's all right, Dad," said Davy. "It's all right."